SECRETS FROM THE GRAVE

B.L. BRUNNEMER

❀ Created with Vellum

To everyone who helped me pull this book together, thank you! You ladies are always amazing. And incredibly patient with my ramblings and three in the morning texts.

Also, to Robert. Thank you for being the amazing man you are.

CHAPTER 1

JULY 10TH, TUESDAY EVENING

I pulled into a spot in the already full parking lot of Shore Park. It was movie night in the park and Miles had thought it would be fun. I unhooked my seatbelt and climbed out of my Blazer, Hades followed closely, his tail already wagging. After pulling out the folded blanket, I closed the door just as Miles pulled up beside me in his used blue Nissan Altima. Hades barked once as Miles got out.

His high cheek bones and angled jaw made him cute but it was that smile that got me every time. His emerald eyes found me from behind his rimless glasses.

I grinned as he bent down to scratch Hades' ears with his now bare left hand. "So, he took the cast off."

He straightened and then flexed his hand. "Yes, he wants me to go to physical therapy in a week or so."

"Did he say you can start swimming again?" I asked with a grin. Miles was the state champion in his swimming division and he trained year-round. He usually swam a couple of miles a day. Since breaking his arm, he'd been stuck on land.

"Yes, he did." We started walking through the parking lot. "Though I'm limited to one mile a day for a week or so."

"Ah, darn," I said in my 'aw shucks' voice.

1

He chuckled. "I know, I have time to get back in shape-"

I started laughing. Out of shape for Miles was still ripped and drool worthy.

"What? I was up to four miles a day when we were hit by that truck." His ears started turning pink.

"Oh, it's just the idea of you being out of shape." I shook my head and tried to stop smiling.

"Out of swimming shape." He scratched behind his ear, the long scar on his forearm drawing my eyes. He noticed where I was looking, stopped walking and held his forearm out. "It's not bad. You have worse."

I reached out and ran my fingertips over the scar. He was right; my leg had claw marks from the demon that had possessed Isaac. So did my side, but he didn't know about those. Those didn't bother me; they were on me, not him.

"How was work?" he asked, sliding his arm back so he could take my hand.

"I did a lot of set up and take down today." We started walking again. "I didn't screw up this time and Don, the grumpy artist, actually grunted in approval. I think."

"That's good." He slowly let go of my hand as we headed toward the park.

Asher's red truck pulled up and parked just as we reached an empty spot. His ocean eyes spotted us through the windshield as we stopped. The light blue, dark blue and white flecks of his eyes found mine. My heart gave a painful beat as his gaze darted away to Miles. Asher shut off the truck and got out. He was your all-American boy, high cheekbones and a sharp chin made him look as if he had stepped out of a magazine. His sandy blonde hair was neat and short. He must have cut it recently; I wouldn't know, I haven't talked to him a lot in the last few weeks. Not since our kiss…

"I brought some food." Asher closed the truck door before reaching into the back.

Miles moved forward to take the blanket Asher brought. Asher pulled out two thermal tote bags as Miles made his way back toward me. "You didn't have to do that, we could have had dinner after."

"I had some time," Asher muttered.

"What'd you end up making?" I asked as Miles started toward the main park.

"Some sesame pasta salad and chicken satay with a peanut sauce." Asher glanced at me for half a heartbeat before looking somewhere else. "Also, some carrot and apple coleslaw."

"Sounds great," I said, trying to be patient. Asher and I hadn't talked on the phone or even been alone together since our kiss weeks ago. Now, he wasn't even looking at me. It was going to take time to get back to normal. I got that. But this was starting to irritate the hell out of me.

Miles led us out of the parking lot and onto the grass. The lawn was huge. Trees kept the fading summer sun at bay, leaving most of the lawn in the shade. It was still a little early, so the crowd hadn't gotten huge, though I did recognize a few faces here and there. I waved at Ryan and Riley who were sitting on their own blanket. They both smiled and waved back. I missed her; we hadn't spent much time together since she started dating Ryan. I made a mental note to call her this week and get together.

Miles found a great spot next to a log in the back of the crowd, we started to spread the two blankets out on the grass.

"I'm not even fucking talking to you right now." Ethan's boiling mad voice had me turning around. The twins were moving through the crowd toward us.

Ethan was a good six inches taller than me with wide shoulders and a muscled body that made it hard not to enjoy the view as he walked through the crowd. Ethan's jaw length straight black hair was back in a pony tail to beat the heat. Five silver loop earrings ran up his right earlobe. His square jaw, slightly pouty lips and straight nose made him striking rather than handsome. Although, today Ethan was limping a little.

Since they were identical twins, they were alike at least in looks. Though Isaac had vibrant blue hair with streaks of light and dark blue throughout the longer hair on top of his head. They both had the same velvety chocolate eyes but somehow Isaac's always had a light in them that turned them amber. It was there now, only he was also clenching his square jaw tight.

"You're an ass," Isaac bit out as he walked through the crowd. A woman shot him a look and covered her young daughter's ears. I rolled my eyes.

Ethan reached me first, his own eyes storming. "Hey, Beautiful." His smooth smoky voice rolled through my ear forcing me to consciously stop myself from curling my toes. He leaned down and kissed my cheek making my heart skip a beat.

"Why are you guys fighting this time?" I sighed. It had been like this for the last three weeks. It was always something stupid, but they kept going after each other.

"Him being an idiot," Ethan muttered as he passed me to go to sit on top of the log.

Isaac walked up to me and met my eyes. "Hey, Red." He leaned down and kissed the corner of my lips. My breath caught in my chest. When he pulled back, his eyes were warm as the anger faded.

"What's going on?" I asked.

The anger was back as he shook his head. "He's being a dick." He walked past me as if that was enough of an explanation.

I shook my head, turned and took a spot on the blanket so I could rest my back against the log. Ethan sat on the log to my right, petting Hades as he sat between his knees. While Isaac sat on the ground to my left.

"So, what's playing tonight?" I asked as I tried to ignore the twins shooting glares at each other over my head.

"Monsters Inc," Isaac supplied.

A familiar deep, loud rumble echoed from the parking lot.

"Zeke's here." I announced. The others chuckled a little. Zeke had started riding his motorcycle again after the big heat wave at the beginning of the summer.

"That thing is loud as hell," Isaac muttered.

"You okay over there, snowflake?" Ethan taunted.

Isaac shot a look at him. "Look who's talking."

I sighed and leaned my head back on the log to look up at the leaves. This was ridiculous. I lifted my head and looked at them both in turn. "Will you two please remove the sticks up your asses? This is supposed to be fun, and you're acting like toddlers fighting over what color the sky is."

The twins shut up and continued to glare at each other.

A large figure wearing only black moved through the crowd toward us. Zeke was a huge mountain of muscle. It was just a fact. Add in that he was fourteen inches taller than me and it was hard to ignore him. His wide cheekbones and wide, strong jaw gave him intimidating looks. But the guy was a big softie... well, he could be... okay, with me, he was a big softie. Unless I did something dangerous then he turned into a growling, grumpy giant. His sky-blue eyes met mine as a strand of his black hair fell into his face. He reached us, dropped down to the blanket and stretched out on his back near my feet then growled.

"Bad day?" I asked in a cheerful voice.

He covered his eyes with his forearm. "I'm taking a vacation. The fucking shop can run without me for a couple of weeks."

"How late did you work last night?" Miles asked.

Hades left Ethan and went to Zeke. The big dog laid down beside him and rested his head on Zeke's stomach.

"Midnight or so. Fucking Dennis quit yesterday leaving everyone in the lurch," he bit out as he started scratching Hades's ears.

I scooted forward and ran my fingers through his hair. He moved his arm only enough to see that it was me before covering his eyes again. "You do need a vacation. How many days do you have saved up?"

"About a month straight," he muttered.

"Damn, Zeke." I shook my head. That was a lot of hours.

"Work is work." He dropped his arm and sat up. Hades only moved enough to put his head on his knee for more scratches. I moved back to my spot between the twins as Asher and Miles started handing out plastic containers with dinner inside.

5

"Thanks for cooking, Asher," I said before digging in. The others thanked him too.

"You're welcome," Asher answered.

The food was delicious, as usual. The guys talked about their days and what their plans were for the rest of the week. During dinner I stayed quiet. Asher still didn't look at me. My temper smoldered, making me tap my leg.

After it got dark, the movie started. I settled back against the log with Ethan's leg against my shoulder. Isaac moved a little closer, his side touching mine. My body thrummed as the scent of limes and spice mixed. Keep it together, Lexie.

We were only ten minutes in when the back of Isaac's fingers brushed my thigh. I went still as chills ran through me. His fingers traced the line of scarring from one of the claw marks on my thigh. He traced it up, slowly so as not to draw attention, to the hem of my mid-thigh shorts. Then slowly back down again. Tingles ran up my leg, making me want to shift on the blanket. Instead, I tried to focus on the movie.

Ethan's fingers moved to my back then trailed to my shoulder nearest Isaac and started a massage.

Isaac stiffened. "Get your hand outta my face."

"Screw you," Ethan countered.

"Now, why are you two arguing?" Miles asked as he pushed his glasses up his nose.

"He's annoying the fuck out of me," Isaac muttered, his fingers stilling against my skin.

"He's being a jackass," Ethan spat.

"What about this time?" Miles asked in a weary sigh.

"Nothing," they both said in unison.

That's it. Between the twins touching me and their bickering, I couldn't take it anymore. I scooted out from between them and got to my feet. The guys turned to me.

I picked up Hades's leash and stepped away from everyone. "I'm going to take Hades for a walk." I left before anyone could even protest.

Away from the guys, I started to cool down. I didn't know what the hell was wrong with the twins. I'd never seen them like this. I was going to have to talk to Miles, see if he knew what was going on-

"Lexie!"

I turned and found Jake sitting on a blanket with Brooklyn.

"Where ya been, hon?" His short styled blonde hair was streaked with fresh lighter blonde highlights. His green eyes were bright as he smiled up at me.

I shrugged. "Around. It's been busy."

Brooklyn shook her head. "We need a girls night here soon." She pointed at Jake's long nails. "He's growing shivs."

I chuckled as I sat down. "We should, my polish came off my toes a week ago." Hades sat beside me then rolled his head into my lap. "So, what have you two been up to?"

"Well, Jake has been talking to a certain black and purple haired guy at night lately." Brooklyn grinned at him.

Jake's face turned pink as he played innocent.

"Derrick?" I asked, my own smile stretching across my face. Nothing would make me happier than Derrick and Jake getting back together.

"Maybe." He looked everywhere but at me.

"Spill, bitch," I ordered.

They chuckled.

Jake sighed. "Yeah, we're talking again."

"How'd that happen?" I asked, excited for him.

"He wrote him letters," Brooklyn supplied. "As in, pen to paper letters."

I turned back to Jake, my eyes wide. "Really? That's romantic as hell."

Jake's face grew red, he dropped onto his back with his hands covering his face. "Yes, okay, yes. I wrote him."

I turned to Brooklyn. "Did he keep copies?"

She chuckled. "No, I already tried."

Jake sat back up and flipped us both off. We snickered.

"It's private. All you need to know is that we are talking again. I'm working on not being a jealous ass and it's going well." He then eyed Brooklyn. "Now, if we could hook Brooklyn up..."

Brooklyn sputtered. "Yeah, good luck."

"Why?" I elbowed her. "There're a lot of cuties out there."

Brooklyn rolled her eyes. "Yeah, and a lot of straight girls with big mouths out there."

"I know someone." Jake sat up and wrapped his arm around her shoulders. "Just trust me."

Some woman behind us shushed us.

I muttered under my breath as Hades got to his feet and whined. "I gotta take the dog for a walk." I got to my feet. "Talk to you guys later."

They said goodbye as I walked with Hades toward the walking path into the trees. The sun was almost gone, throwing the pathway into shadows. Crickets chirped from their hiding spots in the grass. Hades still hadn't found a spot he liked so I walked further in.

The night was quiet as Hades finally stopped after a while and lifted his leg. The sun sank further down behind the mountains, the shadows grew deeper. My pulse picked up. How far did we walk down the path? A hundred yards? Two hundred? I couldn't remember. I took a deep breath and focused. Hades was here, he wasn't alerting me, hell, he was still peeing. Deep breath, I'm fine. I'm safe. I can keep myself safe. I started counting my breaths. At ten, Hades put down his leg and perked up his ears. He moved in front of me into guard position. I took a step back.

A figure walked around the corner and came up short. Eric tucked something into his back pocket. His shaggy brown hair had been cut several inches since I saw him last. His pointed chin and angled jaw gave him a nice open face. Not to mention his cute dimple. Too bad his personality didn't match up with his face.

"Uh, hey, Lexie," Eric said. "What are you doing?"

I gestured to Hades. "Hades needed to go. I thought it'd be polite to do it away from everyone."

He chuckled as he looked down at my massive dog. "Yeah, especially if he needed to take a dump."

I laughed. He had a point. Hades just watched him with a tilted head.

"What are you doing back here?" I asked, my gaze going behind him. "Did I just interrupt something?"

He raised an eyebrow. Understanding lit in his eyes before he chuckled. "Oh, no." He reached into his back pocket and held up a red pack of cigarettes. "Bad habit." He tapped the pack against his hand. "Do you want one?"

"Nah, I like my lungs, ya know, pink and functional," I countered.

He grinned. "Yeah, my dad's been smoking for years. So, I guess it was inevitable I'd get hooked too." He pulled a cigarette out. "You might want to get your healthy lungs away."

I shook my head. "Have a good one."

Hades and I left him to his cigarette and headed back down the path. When I turned the last corner, I found the grumpy giant striding down the path toward me.

"What's going on?" I asked as we reached him.

"You were taking a while," he grumbled.

"Yeah, he couldn't find a tree he liked." I gestured at Hades as we headed back. "Are the twins still bickering?"

"Yeah."

"Great," I sighed.

"Miles got them both to promise to knock it off. At least for the rest of the movie," he said.

"Good. I've been wanting to smack them both upside the head," I muttered.

His lips twitched. "Miles did that. At least verbally."

I snorted.

We went back to the others. This time, when I sat between the twins, Isaac didn't touch me. He was too busy stewing in whatever anger he had at Ethan. And Ethan was doing the same. I thought about moving to sit next to Miles, but that would mean sitting near Asher and frankly, I wouldn't be able to without opening my mouth. I stayed put until the end of the movie.

Afterwards, everyone headed back toward the parking lot. The twins held out as long as they could.

"You're still an asshole," Isaac muttered to Ethan as they started toward their car.

"I'm going to knock you...." Ethan's voice turned into a series of expletives as they walked out of earshot.

"Night, guys," I called over my shoulder as I walked with Hades to the Blazer. Hades jumped up onto my seat and moved to the other.

"Ally."

My heart jumped as I took a breath. I turned around and looked up to meet Asher's gaze. "Yeah?"

He handed me the blanket I had brought.

"Oh. Thanks," I said, trying not to let my disappointment show as he walked away. I began to mutter under my breath. "Hey, Ally. How are you? Not bad, how about you?"

"What?" Asher called.

Oh, shit. I turned back to Asher who was at least ten feet from me in the almost empty parking lot, frowning. Fuck it. "You can't even say a word to me?"

"It's not that easy." He began rubbing the back of his neck.

"No, it isn't," I bit out, my temper sparking. "But I fucking try. And you just ignore me."

He looked away from me, again. "I've been thinking," he sighed, turned back to me and dropped his hand to his side. "I think I should step back for a while."

"Step back?" What did that even mean?

He nodded. "Maybe I shouldn't be hanging out with everyone so much."

It was as if someone had punched me in the chest. I shook my head, not even needing to think about it. "No. Maybe I should." It had been in the back of my mind for the last couple of weeks. They had been friends since they were little kids. If anyone should back off...

"Ally, no," he said, taking a step closer. "You shouldn't have to-"

"And you should?"

"It's my fault." He shrugged. "I shouldn't have said anything."

"No. If anyone should phase out, it should be me." I took a step back, climbed into the Blazer and started it. I wasn't going to start separating the guys.

Asher was striding toward my door when I threw it into reverse and peeled out of the parking spot. I managed to hold off my tears until I was down the street. Ten points to me.

CHAPTER 2

JULY 11TH, WEDNESDAY BEFORE DAWN

Something woke me up. I grumbled and rolled over into Hades. The big lug didn't budge a millimeter. There was a small plink of something hitting glass. There it was again. I opened my eyes and listened. It was coming from my window.

Still half asleep, I crawled out of my bed and went to it. I jerked the blinds open and glared down at the lawn. Claire stood there waving her arms at me. It took me almost a full minute to realize what I was seeing. Then I bolted down the stairs and hurried out the front door on to the grass.

Claire was beaming, with her hair in copper braids, and wearing her usual Care Bears shirt and jeans. "Lexie!"

"Where the fuck have you been? You scared the shit outta me," I snapped at her.

She rolled her eyes and ignored my question. "I've got news."

"You do understand there are psycho ghosts out there, right?" I demanded. Claire had been gone for months without telling me where she went! Yeah. I was still pissed about that.

"I did it."

Her words stopped me cold. "Did what?" Don't tell me something went wrong...

She smiled that glowing smile again. "I found another Necromancer."

My jaw dropped.

"And he wants to meet you."

It took some time for me to grasp what she was saying. "Where?" My voice was barely above a whisper.

She smirked. "New Orleans."

I stood motionless for several heartbeats. "New Orleans? There's a Necro in New Orleans?" I asked, making sure to be very clear.

She nodded. "And he wants to meet you."

Holy…shit. If I could have, I would have hugged Claire tight. "You are the best!" I turned and ran for the door.

"Um, Lexie?"

I skidded to a stop in the foyer and turned back to her.

"Why can't I get in the house? And what's with the paint? And the lights?" she asked, stopping at the doorway.

"Long story, I'll explain on the drive," I promised as the sunlight began to crawl across the yard. I didn't waste any more time. I ran upstairs and dove into my closet, tearing clothes off hangers and stuffing them into my book bag. I'd only need a couple of pairs of jeans, shirts, some bras and underwear. Fuck clothes, I needed to get to Louisiana now! Someone finally had answers! I tore off my pajamas and pulled on jeans and a shirt.

"Screw it. That's enough." I jerked open my middle drawer and rummaged through my stash of books to find the book I kept my savings in. Jamming the money in my back pocket, I practically stumbled all the way to the bottom of the stairs.

"Lexie? What the hell are you doing?" Rory demanded from between the living room and the dining area. His copper hair was everywhere, his brown eyes still half asleep.

I turned with my hand on the door. Leaving without telling Rory or the guys, would not go well for me. I'd live but I'd be barbecue.

"I got a lead," I admitted, trying to calm down and think. "A ghost I've known for years told me that there's a Necromancer in New Orleans."

He blinked at me then seemed to grasp what I was saying. "Get your ass over here and explain." His voice told me not to argue.

I took a deep breath as I headed toward the dining table, dropping my backpack onto the couch as I passed. He went into the kitchen and turned on the coffee pot. I started bouncing my knee as I waited for him to come back and sit down.

"Now, what is going on?" Rory asked in a patient voice.

"A ghost I trust told me they found a Necromancer in New Orleans," I said carefully, trying not to give Claire away. "I have to go down there; I might finally be able to get some answers."

Rory took a deep breath and let it out slowly as the aroma of blessed coffee drifted from the kitchen. "Okay. I understand that." He met my eyes. "Now, why were you leaving without asking me?"

I chewed on the corner of my bottom lip. "Um, I didn't think about it?"

He closed his eyes, took a breath then let it out slowly. "You need to start thinking about it."

I nodded, he had a point...

"How the hell were you going to pay for a hotel down there? Or even the gas to get there?" he asked. "Did you even think about meals?"

I cringed. "I grabbed my savings but it's not much..." I only had a couple of hundred saved. That wouldn't be nearly enough. "But I have to go."

He sighed. "And you will."

My heart leaped in my chest. He said yes!

"But not alone and not without money." He got to his feet and went to the coffee maker. He grabbed a mug and pulled out the carafe as I waited impatiently.

He took a drink as he turned back to me and leaned against the counter. "I'll give you a credit card, and we'll see if one of the guys can go with you."

I went to pull out my phone and couldn't find it. Did I leave it in my room? I was about to leave without my phone. That more than anything calmed me down. But Rory wasn't done.

"If no one can go, then you'll have to wait a couple of days so I can find someone to cover my shifts and we'll go."

I shifted in my seat, maybe Tara could… Wait, Tara in New Orleans. With me. Oh, hell no. We may be on speaking terms, but we still were nowhere near good enough to be around one another that long.

"I'll call the guys." I got to my feet and made a point to calmly walk upstairs past a glaring Hades and Claire, who was still waiting outside watching through the open door. Shit. I was about to leave Hades too. Wow. I really had been freaking out.

I found my room a disaster area. Clothes thrown everywhere. The closet and the containers under my bed were open and empty. Holy shit. It was like a tornado had ran through here. I started searching among the debris for my phone. Finally finding it in the container under my bed that stored my underwear. Sitting on the pulled-out futon, I called Miles. He'd probably-

"Lexie? Are you alright?" Miles asked as soon as he answered his phone.

"Yeah, I'm okay," I said, trying to keep myself calm. "Were you in the middle of your laps?"

"No, I just finished," he said, his quiet timbre becoming silky smooth. I relaxed instantly at the sound of that voice. I just couldn't help it. "You never call this early, are you sure you're alright?"

I took a breath, stay calm. "Any chance you're free for a few days?"

"I don't have anything planned that can't be rescheduled," he said in a careful voice.

"I need to go to New Orleans." I explained that Claire was back and found a Necro down there and it was the chance of a lifetime. He listened patiently, asking questions as I told him everything.

"Of course, I'll go," he stated. I relaxed.

"Thank you, Miles." I sighed in relief.

"But we're not going alone," he told me as something slid open then shut again through the phone.

My heart filled with dread. "What? You mean… everyone?" Zeke in a big unfamiliar city, with all of us. That was not going to be fun.

Then again, Asher. I chewed on the corner of my lower lip. He probably won't even agree to go, not after last night.

"Yes, everyone," Miles said, his voice becoming muffled. "They'll all want to go. Plus, we can fly down in the jet. It'll be faster and it'll be easier to bring Hades."

"What are you doing?" I asked.

"I'm just... uh...." He swallowed hard enough that the phone picked it up. "I was changing."

My jaw dropped as I remembered Miles in a speedo. Damn...

"Oh." Was all I managed as I tried to control my breathing.

"I'll, um, I'll call the guys and tell them to pack for a week or so. It might take them a couple of hours." He hesitated to hang up. "I'm sorry about that."

His apology jarred me back to reality. "Oh, no, it's fine. I just didn't expect that answer," I rushed to explain. "I thought you were still out by the pool." My face burned. And dressed, and not... not dressed...

"Um, I'll, uh, see you in a little while." He hung up while I was still staring at the wall, that image back in my mind.

When I came back downstairs, Rory was pulling out stuff to make breakfast. I quickly took over.

I was scrambling the eggs in a mixing bowl when I broke the silence. "Miles wants to go, and he's calling the others. He said they'll be here in a couple of hours."

"Good. Then you should probably get packed," he pointed out. I looked over my shoulder to the backpack that was on the couch. It was half open, a bra spilling out the top. Yeah... I'd need more clothes than that.

I was just dishing up my own food when my phone chimed. I set my plate down on the table and checked my phone.

Cookie Monster: Didn't we just go to sleep?

I grinned. Isaac had needed to talk last night. Though, not about his fight with his brother. Since he'd been possessed by a demon, his nightmares had been pretty bad. We had hung up around three this morning. I sat down and sipped my coffee before answering.

Alexis: Yeah, I'm planning a plane nap.

Cookie Monster: I'll join ya.

Alexis: You're staying in your own seat.

Cookie Monster: But... cuddles...

I bit back a smile, put my phone down and started eating.

Rory came out of his bedroom, dressed and rolling a large suitcase. "You can use my suitcase, it's a bit dusty though."

"Thanks." I got to my feet and took my dishes into the sink. "That's a lot easier than book bags."

"I'm going to head out and get a prepaid credit card for you. Don't forget to call your boss and make sure you can get time off," he told me as he headed to the door.

"It should be fine, I'll call from the plane."

"I'll be back in a bit." The door closed behind him as I picked up the suitcase and headed for the stairs, picking my backpack up on my way to my room. My bedroom was still a mess, clothes were everywhere. I was a mess. I started cleaning up my clothes and began packing.

I was halfway done picking up when someone knocked on the front door. I grinned. Miles was still the only one who knocked. Careful not to fall, I hurried downstairs and opened the door for Miles. His chestnut hair was still wet and curling from the pool. He was subtly watching Claire out of the corner of his eye.

"Didn't he have thicker glasses last time?" Claire asked, eyeing him right back.

"They were broken," Miles supplied. "These are my back up pair."

Claire gaped at him.

"Oh, yeah," I said. "The guys have the Sight now."

Claire smiled and all but jumped up and down. "More people to talk to! You have no idea how boring dead people can be!"

We both chuckled as I got out of the way so Miles could come in.

"Want some coffee?" I asked as I closed the door.

Miles ears were pink as he turned to me. "Oh, yes. Thank you." He looked around the great room. "Where's Rory?"

"He ran to pick up a prepaid card for me to take." I headed for the kitchen.

He nodded. "The plane should be ready by the time the guys get here."

"We don't need to take your plane," I said over my shoulder.

"It's faster," he said. "We can make our own schedule and taking Hades will be a lot easier."

I pulled down a mug and started pouring coffee. "Okay, but still..."

"Lexie, I was going to get that," he said as he hurried into the kitchen as soon as he realized what I was doing.

I turned and handed him his coffee already made the way he liked. "Too late."

His ears tinged red as he took the mug from me. "Thank you."

"I'll be down in a bit. I've got to finish packing." I started up the stairs.

I searched through my almost fixed room and made a point to pack the research Miles had managed to find for me. I was on my way back from the bathroom with my toiletry bag when Tara's bedroom door opened. My cousin had a sweet face, long blonde hair and nice blue eyes. She always looked sweet, too bad she usually wasn't.

Still half asleep, she scowled at me. "Why are you up?"

I hesitated. "I'm going away for a few days." I hurried back into my room hoping she'd leave. No such luck. The front door opened and closed. Rory's voice drifted up the stairs.

Tara stepped into my doorway and watched as I packed. "Where are you going?"

"Um, I'm leaving town for a bit," I hedged.

"Where?" she asked again.

I sighed. "New Orleans."

"What?" she screeched.

"I'm going to New Orleans with the guys," I said. "There's someone down there that can do what I do. And they're willing to talk to me."

She growled then turned and stomped down the stairs. I went back to packing.

When she started shouting I cringed at the shrill sound. Poor Miles, he was stuck in the middle down there. I stopped packing and went to the top of the stairs. "Miles? Can you give me a hand?"

"He's outside," Rory answered before going back to talking to Tara. I went back to packing.

I had just packed another pair of shorts when heavy steps sounded on the stairs. I looked up just as Zeke leaned against the doorjamb. His ice blue eyes watched me pack.

"You almost packed?" he asked in his deep gravelly voice.

"Yeah." I finished closing the main zipper on the suitcase. "Are you having to use your vacation time for this?"

He shrugged. "I doubt we'll use all of it."

I focused on packing.

"You okay?" he asked quietly.

I nodded. "I just want to get down there and meet this Necro."

"Nothing is going to happen to you," he said.

I turned back to look up at him. "I wasn't worried about that. I was just…" I took a breath. "I'm excited. For the first time in my life, we can get some real answers."

His eyes ran over me then met mine. "Good."

"So, since we might be in New Orleans for your birthday, what do you want to do?" I asked. Zeke's eighteenth birthday was in a few days. His present was already in my suitcase.

He shrugged. "Doesn't really matter."

I shot him a look and went back to packing. "We're still celebrating."

He grumbled wordlessly. I smiled.

"Is Tara still having a fit?" I asked as I finished with the suitcase's last zipper.

Zeke stepped into the room and picked it up off my futon as if it weighed nothing. "No, she's been quiet since I walked in." He walked out into the hallway.

"I was going to get that," I told him.

"I don't want you falling on the stairs," he countered.

It was sweet but… he'd been super over protective of everyone the last few weeks and it was starting to get on my nerves. Miles said he was working on it with his shrink and to be patient but… I missed the Zeke who would let me carry my own suitcase, and wouldn't break into a safety lecture whenever one of us went outside.

By the time I reached the first floor, Zeke was out the door and the twins were just coming in.

Ethan came in first, still in the mesh shorts he usually wore to bed and a dark red tank. His chocolate eyes were half asleep as he passed me. "Tell me there's coffee."

"Of course," I said. He flashed me a half-hearted grin before heading for the kitchen. Isaac stepped into the house and shuffled toward me in his lime green monster pajama bottoms and slippers. A white tank undershirt sadly covered the muscles of his chest.

"Morning." I grinned up at him.

Instead of saying anything he pulled me close. My heart skipped a beat as I hugged him back. The scent of limes was everywhere.

"Why am I up?" he mumbled into my throat.

I chuckled. "Because there is a Necro in New Orleans and I need to go meet them."

He grumbled as he squeezed me tight, kissed a spot on my neck that sent sparks down my nerves then shuffled off to the kitchen.

"Tell me you two got permission this time?" Rory demanded as he refilled his coffee mug.

The twins nodded in unison. Tara sat at the table silently, her mouth pressed in a thin line.

"Ma thinks Miles has a family thing to go to and we're tagging along," Ethan explained before he took a sip.

Miles came through the front door, Asher wasn't too far behind. My heart ached as his eyes met mine. What was he doing... he was coming? What?

"Hey," he said in his rich baritone.

"Hey," I answered, confused. Silence stretched. Say something! Anything! Fix this! But I didn't know if there was anything that could fix it now.

"Do we have everything?" Miles asked before I could come up with something to say.

"Um, I think so." I dropped my eyes from Asher's and ran through a list in my head.

Rory left the kitchen to come to us. "Here." He handed me a credit card. "There should be enough there for food, a hotel and to get you around the city."

Tara made a small irritated noise but otherwise stayed silent.

"Thanks, Rory," I said as the twins left the kitchen to join us at the door. Zeke leaned on the door jamb and waited for us.

"Now, I know you are probably planning to take Hades. But I think that would be a mistake," Rory said.

My hand tightened on the leash. "Why?"

"New Orleans is humid. As in, almost a hundred percent." He gestured toward Hades. "And you'll be in the city. That's a lot of cement on his paws."

I sighed. He was probably right. Plus, the guys would be there, so I should be okay. I knelt down and hugged Hades tight. "I'm sorry, baby."

Hades whined.

"I'll spoil him." Rory promised. "Tonight's steak night." Hades started wagging his tail. He didn't seem too put out.

I got to my feet and turned back to Rory. He hugged me carefully. We hadn't really hugged much since I came to live here, it was awkward.

"Take care of yourself, kid. Alright?" He gave me a squeeze.

"Yeah, I will." I squeezed him back then stepped away.

Rory turned to the guys. "Be careful, pay attention around you. And stick together."

There was a chorus of 'we will' and 'yeah, we know'. Then we headed out.

The guys had loaded up my Blazer with my luggage. Isaac, Ethan, and Claire ended up with me. While Zeke, Miles, and Asher drove themselves. Before I got in I reminded them I needed to stop at the cemetery and that we'd meet them at the airport. No one argued.

When we reached the veteran's section of the cemetery, I parked and shut off the car.

"The crowd is thinning out," Isaac said as he unbuckled his seat belt.

I looked over the crowd of ghosts waiting for me. The size had gotten smaller but... I hadn't crossed *that* many.

"I'll wait here," Ethan stated as he played a game on his phone. Claire started watching over his shoulder. Ethan didn't like ghosts, he said they creeped him out. Especially the rotting ones. Though he didn't seem to mind Claire looking over his shoulder. In fact, he turned his phone a bit so she could see better.

I smiled to myself as I climbed out and walked around the Blazer.

I met the ghost who wore a long flowy skirt and cardigan set. What was her name...? The outfit screamed fifties librarian. But in life she had been a school teacher. A strict teacher who probably ran her class room like a drill sergeant, but a teacher none the less. She was extremely organized and liked lists. It was one of the things she missed the most about living, her lists. Prudence! That was it. I had barely reached her when she announced. "We're missing people."

"What?" That didn't make any sense. "They just might not have shown up today. People get tired of showing up when they're not crossing."

"Joy is one of them," she stated.

My stomach knotted. Joy had wandered here from Texas. She'd been waiting patiently for two weeks for her turn, which was today. She wouldn't just not show up. "Did anyone check where she was staying?"

Prudence nodded. "I sent one of the others to search the abandoned barn and she's just gone."

"Could she have crossed over?" Isaac asked.

I shook my head. "I don't think so; the walls are still really foggy in the Veil."

"What happens if they get too rotted out and don't cross?" Isaac asked.

I shrugged. "I don't know, but she wasn't that far along."

"She had some rotting on her hands but that's all," Prudence supplied. "She still had full capacity."

22

"And she's not the only one?" I asked, hoping I heard wrong.

She shook her head. Fuck.

"Okay, I'll have to look into it after I get back." I shrugged. "Let's get as many done as we can."

CHAPTER 3

JULY 11TH, WEDNESDAY AFTERNOON

A hand shook my shoulder gently.

"No," I groaned and curled up even more.

There was a soft chuckle. "Beautiful, you need to wake up. We're landing in a couple of minutes."

I grumbled as I opened an eye and glared at Ethan. He grinned down at me from his chair. Giving up, I uncurled myself and set my chair back to its upright position. He elbowed me carefully then pointed at Zeke. The giant was across the aisle, Zeke's knuckles were turning white from the death grip he had on the arm rests. I bit back a grin as the plane landed. We had learned on the way back from Boulder that Zeke hated flying. I hadn't noticed it on the way out but on the way home he paced, cursed and ran his hand through his hair so much I was amazed he had any left. The poor guy.

Once the plane had landed and we got the all clear to deboard, I stepped out on the ladder. The air was thick and heavy. Almost like walking through nacho cheese. I instantly wanted a shower as I broke out into a sweat. Quickly, I pulled my hair into a pony tail and hoped it wouldn't frizz too much in the humidity.

It wasn't too long before we were off the plane, had our bags and were leaving in a black SUV Miles had called ahead to rent.

"Okay, so what's the plan?" I asked as I settled between Ethan and Claire in the middle seat of the SUV.

"I want my rematch!" Claire declared. "Isaac cheated at checkers. I know he did."

The guys chuckled.

"Okay, but first we might want to go meet that Necromancer," I reminded her.

"Oh yeah," she grumbled, clearly disappointed.

"We'll play later tonight," Isaac promised with a grin.

She raised an eyebrow. "I'll hold you to that."

Everyone chuckled.

"I've reserved us a suite at a hotel in the French Quarter," Miles announced as he drove onto a freeway.

"You didn't have to do that," I said as Ethan moved his arm over the back of the backseat.

Miles shrugged. "This way we're all in the same place and we're in the same rooms."

"Good idea," Zeke muttered as he looked out the window.

Ethan's thumb started slowly stroking the exposed skin of my shoulder.

"Claire, how are we going to find this Necro?" I asked, trying to distract myself from the chills running over my skin.

"Oh, I memorized his, what do you call it? His email," Claire said cheerfully. "He's also at Tulane a lot."

I pulled out my phone.

Asher pulled the directions to Tulane up on his phone for Miles.

"He?" Isaac asked. "This Necro is a guy?"

"Yep," Claire chirped as she looked out the window at the beautiful garden-like setting of New Orleans.

"Can we grab some food on the way? I'm starving." Ethan announced.

"There should be a few restaurants near the university." Miles told us as he turned down another street.

"You'll have some time, I don't know where he is in his class schedule right now," Claire said. Isaac shifted in his seat.

"Then we can ask him to meet us at a café or restaurant," Miles decided.

"Jackson Square?" Asher suggested as he looked up from his phone. "There's a nice restaurant called Café Pontalba. It'll help ease Zeke into the crowds."

"Great," Zeke muttered.

We chuckled.

I pulled my phone out and typed in the email address that Claire gave me. I gave a vague message about meeting at Café Pontalba in Jackson Square. I hesitated. I was emailing another Necromancer. My stomach knotted as anxiety threatened to drown me. Oh, come on! I hit send.

A phone rang. Zeke picked Miles' cell up off the console and held it up for him to see. Miles glanced at it then went back to driving. "Voicemail."

"Happy to," Zeke growled as he swiped and set it back down.

I clutched my phone to me as I waited for a response. What if he changed his mind? I would have dragged everyone down here for no reason. And I'd still have no answers. Ethan pulled it out of my clutches. I turned and met his warm chocolate eyes.

"It's going to be okay, Beautiful," he said softly, his arm wrapping around my shoulders.

I gave him a tense smile. "It's just the what ifs."

His eyes grew softer. "I know but going through them doesn't help."

I sighed. He was right, I was just going to drive myself crazy. I needed a distraction.

Miles pulled to the curb near the gate to Jackson square. "I'll let you guys out here and go check in at the hotel."

"Aren't you having lunch with us?" I asked as Ethan opened up his door and got out. The others did the same, leaving me alone with Miles.

Miles looked over his shoulder to me. "Of course, I'm just going to check in and have the bell hops take our luggage up. I'll be back in forty-five minutes at most." His fingers began tapping on the wheel.

"Are you okay?" I asked, sure something was wrong.

He gave me a small smile. "Yes, I'm alright. I just don't want you to miss this Necromancer because we're checking in."

Okay... I still didn't believe him but if he didn't want to talk about it... I'd just have to drag it out of him later. One thing Isaac's demon possession taught me was to pay attention to the little stuff. "Alright. See you soon?"

He gave me that secret smile and nodded. My pulse picked up.

"I'll be back in a bit," he promised. I got out of the SUV, closing the door behind me. While the others were looking around, I was watching as Miles pulled out into traffic.

That chill ran down my neck. Shit. A ghost.

"Anyone else seeing this?" Asher's question had me turning.

I cursed. The dead were everywhere. The crowd was thick with them. Why didn't I think of this? Of course the city was going to be filled with dead. First, it's a large city. Second, there was no one here who could cross them. Third, it's New Orleans. Shit.

I looked up at the guys. Ethan was slightly cringing, Isaac looked curious, while Asher and Zeke looked around at all the souls. And they were rowdy as hell; several even ran through the crowd. Some hung from the street lights, others, believe it or not, were making out like drunken college students. What the hell was going on?

Several souls turned toward me in unison. Shit. I searched the crowd and tried to find a space for a quick ghost talk but I found nothing. The ghosts came toward me. I stepped in front of the boys and turned to face them. "Okay, this is happening in a crowd. So, you guys know the drill. Let's face each other and pretend I'm talking to you guys." They moved back to me, creating the illusion that we were normal.

"Can't we just ignore them?" Ethan asked, his shoulder bumping into mine.

"You can and get away with it, I can't," I said. "I look like a light to the dead and they're persistent."

The soul of a man with a large dark beard and scars on his face chose that moment to look over Zeke's shoulder. My gaze met his.

The bearded man's face was stunned. "You can see me."

Zeke turned his head to find the soul too close for his liking. "Get the fuck away from me."

A woman behind the soul turned, she saw Zeke. Her face turned pale as she grabbed her kid's hand and hurried away.

The soul stepped away before turning back to me. "Why can you see us?"

I kept my gaze on Zeke's chest. "I'm a Necromancer." I glanced at him then went back to looking at Asher's shoulder. "I can cross souls over. And I will. Where's the closest cemetery?"

"St Louis Cemetery Number One," the ghost supplied.

I nodded. "I'll be there at ten in the morning every day I'm here. As long as I'm left alone for the rest of the time."

"They'll leave you alone or deal with me," Claire added as she stepped out of the crowd. I bit back a grin.

"I'll spread the word. Thank you," the ghost said before he walked back through the living. I let out a deep breath.

"Think he'll keep them away?" Isaac asked.

"It's possible." I rubbed my temple. "Let's get to the restaurant. My neck is killing me." The circle broke apart as Asher led the way.

"Come on, we don't want to lose you in the crowd." Ethan took my hand and gave me a small tug.

I followed, still stunned by the amount of souls here. In Spring Mountain, I kept crossing the dead so they weren't everywhere. Then again... What Prudence said popped back into my mind. Souls were missing. Rotting souls mostly and some only starting to, but it's not like they just dissolved and disappeared. Right? I hadn't gone back to the bowling alley since I was jumped in December just in case the soul of that serial killer was still there. There was too much I didn't know. Which was the whole reason I was here, to meet this Necro and get some answers.

Jackson Square had a green lawn, a stunning church and many stores and restaurants. The whole place was buzzing with activity. I slowed to a stop as I spotted the artists selling their work around the gate to the square.

Ethan stopped me from going to get a closer look. "After food and meeting that Necro, Beautiful."

"But... art." I grinned up at him over my shoulder. Just because I was here on business didn't mean I couldn't enjoy myself.

He chuckled and pulled me in the direction where the others were waiting for us to catch up. "I promise we won't leave until you get to see everything you want to."

"Oh, that's a dangerous promise," I teased as we caught up with the others.

"What is?" Asher asked as everyone headed to the café.

"Beautiful saw the paintings and artwork they're selling. I had to reel her in," Ethan explained as we reached the café.

"Table for seven, please. Our eighth should be here soon and well, we might have a ninth coming, we're not sure yet," Asher said to the hostess. She eyed our group. I bit back a smile. Asher had counted Claire.

I stepped forward. "He means six and we might have a seventh coming."

She relaxed, picked up seven menus and led us to our tables. The boys helped her put two smaller tables together in front of the window.

I sat down on the end. Zeke sat beside me as Asher sat across from him. Claire sat a few chairs down on the other side of Zeke, across from Isaac at the end. Isaac pulled out his small magnetic traveling checkers game and set them up another game. As long as Isaac moved Claire's pieces for her, it shouldn't look too out of the ordinary. Ethan sat between Zeke and Claire.

I fanned myself and sighed. This was man's single greatest invention. Not the wheel, not penicillin, but air conditioning. Even in just shorts and a tank top I was sweating. And I wasn't the only one. Everyone living was wiping sweat off their foreheads.

"This humidity sucks balls," Isaac announced. Everyone agreed as we opened the menus.

"Are we waiting for Miles?" I asked them.

"We could," Asher said.

"I'm starving," Ethan reminded us.

"Well, we could get appetizers to hold us over until he can get back." I tucked a stray curl behind my ear.

The guys agreed then started arguing over what to get. I stayed quiet and smiled to myself. It was strange but I loved hearing them argue over little things. The blend of their voices as they argued made my heart warm. It was comforting.

Eventually, Zeke looked down at me. "Are you going to weigh in on this?"

"Nope," I chirped. "I'll eat whatever."

"Don't say that, Red. They've got alligator on the menu," Isaac warned.

I grinned my shit eating grin. "I'll try it."

That started the conversation all over again. By the time they figured out what they wanted, our drinks were half empty and Ethan was all but threatening murder. We finally ordered the appetizers and started talking about what we wanted to do in the city.

I was watching Isaac and Claire play a fierce game of checkers when my phone beeped. It was my email. The Necro, whose name was Louis, was going to be a couple of hours. He had two classes left for the day. I emailed him back that we'll most likely be in Jackson Square, still probably looking at artwork.

I set my phone down and found Zeke watching me. "The guy has some classes. It'll be a couple of hours."

His gaze moved over my face before meeting mine again. "Well, you'll have plenty of time to look at all the art you want."

I snorted. "Two hours or less? You have no idea how long I can wander around a museum."

His lips twitched as the waitress brought appetizers and pointed out which was the alligator. Everyone started nibbling as we waited for Miles. I met Isaac's smug eyes. He grinned and shook his head. He didn't think I'd eat it.

"Zeke, can you pass me a piece of the alligator, please?" I asked.

The corner of Zeke's lips lifted as he grabbed the entire plate and held it out to me. I grabbed a piece, met Isaac's eyes and popped it into my mouth. Zeke set the plate back down in the middle of the table. The meat was actually good. A little catfishy but still good.

I finished my bite and smirked at Isaac. He cursed and grumbled as he reached out and picked up a tiny piece.

"A piece of equal size or you'll have to do it again," Asher warned.

Isaac cursed again before popping a bigger piece into his mouth. He was two chews in when his face scrunched up and his eyes closed. When he finished he chugged his glass of water. "Gah! How can you eat that, Red?"

I just grinned. "Anyone else want to try?"

"No." Most of them answered in unison.

Asher reached over, plucked a piece from the platter and ate it. His eyes unfocused as he chewed. "Hmm. It's a mix of chicken and catfish, but not bad."

"Are you really going to eat that?" Ethan asked me.

I shrugged. "More for me."

Ethan and Zeke started talking about a video game that had just come out. I turned to Asher.

"So, how are things?" I asked, trying to break the ice. "Is Jessica getting any more speeding tickets?"

Ethan choked on the soda he was drinking, he set his glass down and continued to cough. Zeke reached around him and smacked him on the back. When Ethan stopped coughing he eyed me.

Asher started rubbing the back of his neck. "Uh, no. She's eased up a bit."

"Good," I said. "If she kept it up she would have lost her license."

He nodded and looked everywhere he could but at me. His gaze moved over my head and waved. "Over here."

I looked down to hide my disappointment.

"Sorry that took so long." Miles walked around the table. I gave him a smile as he took the chair on the other side of Asher.

His eyes were dark as he picked up his menu. "Traffic was a nightmare."

"Everything okay at the hotel?" I asked, wondering where those shadows came from.

"What?" he asked, his voice slightly strained.

"You were checking all of us in." Isn't that what he was doing?

"Oh, yes. Everything is fine just a misunderstanding with the reservation that needed to be cleared up." He looked past me down the table. "Did I miss lunch?"

"We got appetizers while we waited for you," Asher explained.

Miles winced. "Sorry."

Every one opened their menus again and talked about what looked good. Trying to put Miles's odd behavior out of my mind for now, I looked down at the menu. The words were blurry. I blinked hard and tried again. They were still blurry. I pulled the menu back until the writing was clear.

"Beautiful?"

"Yeah?" I found something that sounded good and closed my menu before I turned to him.

He was watching me, his eyebrow raised. "Can you see al-"

"Are we ready to order?" The waitress popped up at the end of the table with a big smile.

When the waitress was out of earshot I turned to look down the table at my aunt. "Claire, what can you tell me about this Louis guy?"

Claire walked around the table and took the empty seat across from me. "Well, he's pretty nice. He knows his stuff. His father was a Necromancer, so he was raised with it. Plus, he's lived this long."

"How old is he?" Isaac asked.

Claire grinned. "He's in his late forties."

My jaw dropped. Late forties? And he's still alive? Without a ward tattoo? "Holy shit."

Claire nodded. "Yeah, I was impressed too."

"My question is," Miles lowered his voice as a waitress walked by. "Are you going to give him the ward design that Evelyn made for you?"

Thinking, I stirred my drink with my straw. "I could ask her. But I can't give it out. She designed mine specifically for me. It might not even work for him."

"He might not even want it," Claire pointed out. "He's been doing great all his life and has a better understanding than we ever did."

"We'll have to play it by ear," I said. "So, what do you guys want to see while we're here?" That simple question started a debate among the guys

"There's a Butterfly Garden and Insectarium," Miles suggested.

I smiled while the others groaned.

"Bayou tour," Zeke stated.

"Oh, let's do a kayak one." Isaac grinned. "We could run into an alligator."

Zeke scowled at him. "As if I'd ever let one of you do that."

Isaac snickered. I shook my head as I listened to them. My heart grew warm as I relaxed.

"There's several culinary tours," Asher added, turning to the others. I just sat there and listened with a smile.

We were still at the restaurant when I felt it. A strange crawling sensation down my spine and over my skin. My hand went to the back of my neck as I searched the restaurant looking for its source. The only ghost inside was Claire but this was different. This... this I had never felt before.

"Ally?"

"I'm feeling something..." I muttered as I eyed everyone in the dining room. It was getting stronger, like fingertips moving over my skin. And not in an unpleasant way. "What the hell? Does anyone else feel that?"

"No." Isaac started looking around too.

"Not a thing." Miles turned in his chair and started looking around. That's when I spotted him. His golden-brown skin contrasted with his white linen short sleeve button down. Khaki shorts and a pair of chucks completed the outfit. His black hair was cut close to his head, with white at the temples. He had a strong jaw and sharp clear eyes.

"That's him." I knew it just as I knew my own name. He was a Necromancer.

Claire waved and got out of the chair across from me. Velvety black eyes met mine as he moved through the tables and his step slowed.

As he reached our table, his gaze moved to Claire. "Miss Claire, I was starting to worry if you ever made it back." His voice rolled off his lips like molasses. Sweet and deep.

"It was a long trek back," Claire admitted. She gestured to me. "This is my niece."

"I'm Lexie." I held my hand out to shake.

He didn't take it; his eyes ran over me before they met mine again. "Considering the strange feeling running over my skin, I think it best that we don't touch."

I dropped my hand. "Yeah, what the hell is that?"

"I'm not sure but I'll do some research and see if there's any mention of it." He eyed me again.

"Sounds fair." I clenched my fist as the sensation continued. It was starting to get distracting.

"I'm Louis." He looked down the table at the guys. "They are?"

"My friends. They've been saving my ass for months. They're also a bit protective." I started bouncing my knee.

"With the way the big one is glaring, I'd say so," he mused.

I turned. Zeke was indeed glaring. I smacked his shoulder. "Zeke, knock it off."

He grumbled under his breath as Louis took the seat Claire vacated.

"Don't mind him, he has resting glare face," I offered.

The guys chuckled and Zeke tried not to look murderous.

Louis's gaze ran over me again, measuring. "Look, I don't have long with that many souls outside. How old are you?"

"Seventeen, turning eighteen in August," I answered as I noticed the strands of beads going into the neckline of his shirt. Onyx, if I had to guess.

He shook his head. "How have you made it this long?"

"Luck. Salt, beads, and herbs," I answered quickly. I wasn't about to tell him about my tattoo until I knew him a bit more. "How about you?"

"I was lucky, my father was alive to raise me. The family also kept records." He pulled an envelope out of a cargo pocket of his shorts. He set it in front of me. "Here, this should get you started. It's basic but it's all I had time to put together. You can email me any questions you have." His eyes met mine. "Now, leave town tonight."

Leave town? I couldn't fucking believe this.

"That's not what we talked about!" Claire shouted, water glasses rattled on the table.

"I'm not fucking going anywhere," I bit out in a hushed voice. "You're the only Necro alive that I've ever met, you've already lived past anyone in my family. Did you really think I'm just going to walk away from this chance?"

He sighed and ran his hand down his face then met my eyes. "Honestly, I wish you had come a few weeks ago."

I raised an eyebrow. "Why?"

"Have you ever heard of the Witch's Council?" he asked, his voice tired.

I sat up straighter. "Yeah, they're supposed be policing magic users but there are some loop holes so you don't have to listen to them."

He nodded as the waitress came to the table. He ordered a large café au lait to go before turning back to us. "Well, some of their representatives are in town trying to 'recruit' the magic users here."

"Recruit?" Asher leaned forward.

"They're trying to force us to join them and be under their thumb," Louis explained. "No one here wants that and has told them so. They haven't taken it well."

"What did they do?" Miles asked as he leaned forward on his arms.

"To sum up, you've walked into a tense situation," he announced. The waitress arrived with his coffee. He paid her and told her to keep the change. When she was gone he turned back to us and rested his arms on the table. "The council witches are getting frustrated that the supernaturals in the area aren't jumping on board."

"You're expecting the situation to deteriorate?" Miles asked before I could.

"Unfortunately, yes," he said before taking a sip of his coffee then meeting my gaze. "But that's not the only problem in the city."

"The dead," I stated.

He nodded. "Something is wrong. The dead can't move on and there's energy everywhere. Ghosts are picking it up as I'm sure you've noticed."

I nodded. "Yeah, they're picking it up and using it to leave their haunting grounds."

"Exactly, it's rotting them out." He looked down the table to look out the large window. "The ghosts in New Orleans have been wreaking havoc around the city. It's at the point it's getting dangerous for anyone sensitive to the dead. So, watch yourself."

"Hold on, what's going on with the council?" Zeke demanded.

Louis eyed him before answering. "Right now, nothing. They're still trying to convince us to join them. But considering that Necros and other supernatural species don't do well when they are in charge, we're continuing to say no."

"Shit," I bit out as I began to rub my temples.

Zeke started cursing under his breath.

"What do you mean 'supernaturals don't do well with the council?'" I asked.

"I mean they're never heard from again," he said, turning back to me. "Now, you should be safe. You're seventeen and you don't live here. If you are insisting on staying, and are approached, tell them that. Then tell them you're here to learn how to control your abilities. But offer them no other information."

"If you can't guarantee that..." Zeke turned to Miles. "We're going home now."

I tried to remember to be patient. "Zeke..."

"No," he growled as he turned back to me.

"Ezekiel," Miles said in a quiet voice as he met Zeke's gaze. They seemed to have some silent communication that I couldn't understand before Zeke turned away, his jaw clenching and unclenching.

"All of you *should* be safe. Going after normals is against the laws," Louis announced. "As is going after minors."

Zeke muttered curses under his breath.

"They have the Sight," I corrected. "And Miles is eighteen and Zeke's about to be."

His gaze shot to them. "All of you?"

The guys nodded.

"It's a long story," Miles hedged.

Louis shook his head. "Then I don't have time now to hear it." He pulled out his phone. "Give me your information, I'll text you an address to meet tomorrow around noon. We'll go over some things then." I gave him my number.

He added it to his contacts, got to his feet then turned to me again. "Since you're insisting on staying, just stay aware. Stay together and you should be fine." He hurried out of the restaurant and through the crowd.

I let out a deep breath. Zeke was tense next to me.

I turned to look up at him and smiled a big smile. "Who wants dessert?"

~

Zeke

AFTER A HALF AN HOUR of Miles and Lexie reasoning with me, I finally calmed down. It took everyone agreeing to stay in pairs, but I calmed down. Mostly.

I stepped out of the restaurant and instantly started sweating again. Fuck. What was with this fucking humidity? It was like walking through a wet blanket all the time.

Lexie headed for an artist's display on the fence surrounding Jackson Square.

"Lexie…" This wasn't a good idea. A big crowd, fucking council witches in town…

Lexie turned and continued walking backward. "You guys promised."

Claire moved up beside Miles.

I growled wordlessly as we followed her to the first set up. I kept looking around, trying to keep an eye out for anything strange. Well, besides the dead. Ghosts were fucking everywhere, and sometimes they were hard to pick out from the living. Yeah, some were in dated clothes you could just see and know but others... Lexie always somehow knew which were which but the rest of us were catching on, though Miles was still struggling. The rest of us could figure it out after a minute or so.

Lexie made a small squeal, I turned back to find her showing Ethan a small print in plastic. Her face was glowing, she even had her big happy smile on. Something inside me settled. She hadn't gotten this excited since she got the wards and that wasn't really excited, that was more like deep relief.

As Lexie talked with the artist, she began gesturing wildly. I tore my eyes off her and checked on the others. Ethan was looking through more prints while Isaac, Miles and Asher stood near me. All of us were watching her enjoy herself. I turned back to watch as she pointed at a section of a painting and asked how the artist got that particular color.

"Do you still want to leave?" Miles asked without really asking. As if he already knew my answer. Hell, he probably did.

"No. She's..." I shook my head. She had never been able to leave the house without having to worry about the dead. She's never had a carefree day in her life. Neither one of us have but... she can now. And I wanted that for her. "Let's keep an eye on the crowd."

"We will," Miles assured me.

We followed her from artist to artist. I kept trying to pay attention to what was going on around us but her voice was distracting. Trying to stop listening so I could focus, I kept track of all of them and the crowd.

"Miles! Check this out!" Lexie all but shouted. I gave up trying not to watch her. She was standing in front of an oil painting of a squid. It was pretty cool to be honest. Miles reached her and looked at it. She said something about Nemo. The fish? What? Miles chuckled. She shrugged then moved on.

Everyone followed her except Miles, he hung back. I grumbled under my breath. He was probably going to buy her the damn painting. I checked to see her looking through the prints before heading back. I found him talking to the artist of the squid painting

"Thank you," Miles said as he tucked a piece of paper into his wallet.

"Miles." It was all I had to say.

His ears turned pink as he tucked his wallet into his back pocket. "Don't say a word."

"She's not going to like that you bought it for her," I warned him as we moved to catch up to the others.

"Her birthday is next month and it's small enough to fit on the wall with her other prints," Miles countered, his voice growing cold. He wanted me off the topic. "Besides, I got the print not the painting."

"Good call." Yeah, that she'd be okay with. We walked to catch up with the others.

We slowly made our way around the square as Lexie geeked out over the art. It was cute. God, I hate that word but the damn word fit. She continued to glow and enjoy herself until we reached where we started again.

Three hours later, she turned around, her face red and cringing. "I did it again, didn't I?"

The others chuckled.

"Don't worry about it, Beautiful," Ethan said. "You were having too much fun showing your art nerd side."

She smiled and shrugged, not bothering to deny it.

"Come on, let's go get settled in at the hotel," I announced. No one argued as Miles led the way. Lexie ended up behind me; her fingers slipped into my belt loop. I reached back, took her hand and stepped to the side so she could pass me. "Stay between me and Isaac." I wanted her where I could see her and everyone else.

"Worry-wort." She grinned up at me making my heart slam. Why was she so... She passed me, her fingers slipped from mine. I clenched my fist as my fingers tingled. Being around her like this, without touching her, without holding her... it was getting to me. We needed to have that talk on this trip, it was time. My decision made, I refocused on watching the crowd around us.

Lexie

THE HOTEL WAS BEAUTIFUL, obviously a five-star hotel. The marble floor of the lobby alone told me that this definitely wasn't the kind of hotel Rory could afford. I chewed on the corner of my bottom lip while Miles opened the door to the large penthouse suite. I followed Isaac in and had to stop my jaw from dropping. It was beautiful. The old brick was exposed here and there on the walls. The furniture was comfy but modern. We walked into the living room and kitchenette combo. Everything looked brand new and perfect.

"Hey, we have our own balcony!" Ethan said as he stepped through the white glass French doors and out onto the wrought iron balcony. We followed him out. He was right. The balcony stretched from one side of the building around the corner and to the other side. Flowers and ferns hung from the rails as we looked down at the bustling Bourbon Street.

"Alright, we have four bedrooms and two bathrooms." Miles's voice had me turning to lean against the railing of the balcony. He continued as he stepped out onto the balcony. "Two of them have two beds. One of the bedrooms has its own bathroom. So, I thought, if there are no objections, that Lexie can take that room."

The guys agreed immediately.

"Are you guys sure?" I asked.

"Yeah, there's no way you're sharing a bathroom with us," Zeke growled before taking a key card that Miles handed to him.

"Yeah, guys stink." Ethan grinned.

"Zeke, your room is supposed to be an office. So, it'll be small but it'll be yours. The sofa in there is a pull out and should already be made up."

"Thanks," Zeke muttered as he tucked his key card into his wallet.

Miles handed me my key card. I tucked it into my wallet. "Let's get our rooms sorted."

Everyone started back into the suite.

Miles pointed down a hallway past the kitchenette. "The other bedrooms are down that hall. Zeke, you're on the left. Everyone else is on the right."

Zeke grabbed his duffle bag while Asher grabbed his suitcase and followed Zeke down the hall.

Ethan paused in picking up his suitcase. "Where's Beautiful sleeping?"

Miles gestured at the closed double doors on the living room's east wall. "She's in this one."

Isaac picked up Ethan's suitcase and started down the hall.

"I didn't ask for your help," Ethan snapped.

Isaac all but threw the suitcase down as he turned toward us. "Fine, fuck up your back even more. What do I fucking care? Just don't expect me to fucking take care of you!"

Ethan stepped toward his brother. Miles stopped him.

"Isaac, I can use a hand," I said before I could stop myself.

Isaac glared at his brother as he passed him, grabbed my suitcase and opened my bedroom door. I shared a look with Miles.

He nodded slightly.

I had Isaac, he'd try to talk to Ethan. I followed Isaac into my bedroom. The room was stunning. Exposed brick on the wall with my own white narrow French doors. A large white carved wood headboard, white linens with a teal bed scarf on the end. A matching teal armchair near the window. My own tv was on the wall to the living room with a big dresser underneath. If the bathroom was anything like my room, I was going to be in heaven. Isaac set my suitcase on the bed scarf. I closed the door so the others couldn't hear us.

"What was that about?" I asked as I moved to his side.

"Nothing," he muttered as he turned to sit down on the bed. He looked up at me with amber eyes. "He's been like that since a couple of days after we got back from Boulder."

I moved to sit next to him on the bed. "He's just been... like that?"

He nodded, his eyes on the carpet. "I think he's pissed about something I said."

"First, that wasn't *you*. That was a demon," I told him firmly. "Second, what did it say?"

He shrugged. "I don't know, I've been too chicken shit to ask anyone."

My chest ached. "You haven't talked to anyone about it?"

His shadowed amber eyes met mine. "Just you."

"Cookie Monster," I sighed. "I think you need to ask. And not just him. I think you should ask Zeke, Asher, and Miles too."

He braced his elbows on his knees and hid his face in his hands. "I thought I didn't talk to them."

"*You* didn't, the *demon* spoke to Zeke. But it couldn't hurt to ask the others about the things it said. This way, you'd know," I said carefully.

His face was pained. "What if I did or said something-"

"It wasn't *you*," I said again. "You would never have said anything like that to us."

His eyes met mine again. "How can you forgive me, Lexie? The shit I said... Hearing what I said to you was bad enough-"

"It. Wasn't. You." My voice told him to stop arguing. "You didn't do it, you didn't say it. So, all this guilt isn't yours to carry. That belongs to a demon that was burned to death."

"I know. It just doesn't feel that way," he muttered.

I leaned into his side and propped my chin on his shoulder. "I know. But it's not the truth. Just-"

"Trust you," he finished for me before turning to look down at me. "I do trust you. It's me that I don't trust."

Heart aching, I moved my hand up his back to the back of his neck and traced the runes surrounding the symbol that kept all of them safe from demons. "You'll trust yourself again, Cookie Monster. It's just going to take time."

His hand came up to my face, his thumb traced my cheekbone. My heart raced as he leaned down and kissed me softly. My body thrummed with heat as he took his time, his lips lingering. The scent of limes filled my lungs as he pulled back slowly.

I opened my eyes. "Isaac..."

"I couldn't help it," he admitted with a smile. "You make me feel better."

I sighed and pulled back until I was just sitting next to him again. I needed to stop kissing him, it was only a matter of time before we got caught. But I really didn't want to stop... Not knowing what else to do, I got to my feet and grinned at him over my shoulder. "Come on, let's play Hot or Cold."

HOT OR COLD was a game I'd invented to play with the guys when we people watched. I sat in the patio chair, my feet on the bottom rung of the balcony railing while I sipped ice water with lemon. The sun had set and the night was starting to cool off.

I pointed at a person on the street below. He was bald, wearing Mardi Gras beads and well, even dead he looked sweaty. "Hot or cold?"

Ethan and Miles leaned forward in their chairs so they could see who I was pointing at.

"Hot," Miles answered.

"Nope. Cold," I chimed.

Miles sighed. "How could you tell?"

I grinned. "Well, if you look closely, he's in his tighty whities and no one's noticing." He was also doing a marvelous impression of a windmill.

Everyone chuckled.

Isaac and Zeke came out onto the balcony.

"What are you three doing?" Zeke asked.

I tilted my head back so I was looking up at him upside down. "Playing Hot or Cold."

Isaac shook his head. "Still? It's been a couple of hours."

"Miles is getting better, you just got the hang of it first." I brought my head back up and looked out over the crowd again. "There. Hot or cold?" I pointed at a woman in vintage clothes who was standing out of the crowd next to a pillar.

Ethan leaned forward. "Hot."

I raised an eyebrow. "Why?"

"She's leaning on the pillar," he pointed out.

"One point to Ethan," I announced.

Miles's eyes narrowed on the crowd, searching for more of the dead.

I smiled. He was determined to get better at it. It was cute.

"Hey, there're more musicians out on the street now. Let's go check it out," Isaac said from the doorway.

"Oh, that sounds like fun." I set my glass down.

The others and I got to our feet then headed inside. Claire was sitting on the coffee table watching cartoons with Asher.

"Claire, do you want to go check out the musicians?" I asked as I slipped my sandals back on.

"Nah," she turned around on the table. "Can I watch cartoons though? It really freaks out the living when I change the channels to cartoons so I haven't watched them in years."

The guys chuckled.

"No problem," Asher assured her before getting to his feet.

Before we could leave Zeke stopped everyone at the door.

"Does everyone have their keys?" he asked.

"Yes." We answered in unison.

"Stick together, don't go off alone. If you get in a situation, call for Asher," Zeke lectured.

"Yeah, yeah, we know," Isaac grumbled as he grabbed the door knob and opened the door. Zeke moved to the side and let the others through. When I started through the door, he took my arm and pulled me to the side. Asher shook his head as he left the suite.

"Do you have your pepper spray?" he demanded.

I took a breath and let it out, trying to be patient. You and Isaac almost died, he freaked and he's trying to deal. "Yes, and my Kubotan." I pulled my keys out to show him the striking tool next to my pepper spray.

He nodded. "Stay close to someone, if those witches show-"

"Zeke," I stopped him. "They don't even know I'm here or who I am. I think we'll be okay."

He clenched and unclenched his jaw.

I smiled up at him, patted his chest then followed the others out into the hall where the guys were holding the elevator for us.

We stepped out into the cooling air outside the hotel, though it didn't seem the humidity was going anywhere. I moved up next to Miles and wrapped my arm around his. "So, what kind of music are we looking for?"

"I figured we were going from street musicians to street musicians," Miles admitted, his ears turning pink.

"Sounds good to me." I looked ahead of us and smiled. "Besides, it looks like Isaac is taking off on his own."

Zeke cursed and moved his large frame through the crowd after Isaac. Miles and I both chuckled as the two disappeared from view.

"He's going to give Zeke a coronary one day," I said.

"Let's hope it's not soon," Miles answered with a grin that sent my heart racing. "Did he tell you what was going on between him and Ethan?"

Asher and Ethan moved further into the crowd, we followed when they started to get too far ahead.

I sighed as we came to a stop near a small band playing. "He thinks it's something the demon said to Ethan. He hasn't talked to anyone about it."

He looked down at me with his thinking face, the one that made the small wrinkle between his eyebrows. "I know for a fact he hasn't asked Zeke."

"He might now," I countered. "We had our talk a few days after we got home."

"Good," he muttered, his eyes unfocused. "Maybe I should-" His cellphone rang. Miles pulled out his phone, his posture grew rigid as he sent it to voicemail.

"Nemo?" I squeezed his arm. He looked down at me again. "Who do you keep sending to voicemail?"

He looked away. "It's nothing."

"Last time someone told me something was nothing, they ended up possessed by a demon." His hunter green eyes met mine. "What's going on?"

He gestured to a spot where we could get out of the crush of the crowd. We started making our way there, Miles' hand moved to my lower back as he tried to keep people from bumping into me. Warm chills ran up my spine.

When we were out of the crush he turned to me. His eyes were shadowed. "It's my father."

CHAPTER 4

JULY 11TH, WEDNESDAY EVENING

"*Your* dad?" I didn't even know his dad talked to him.

He nodded, his face blank. "When I made the hotel reservation, the manager called my father."

I raised an eyebrow. "What? How? Why?"

His gaze dropped to the ground. "We own the hotel."

"Wait, I thought your dad had a shipping business?" I asked.

Miles lifted his head, his gaze going over my shoulder. His fingers began tapping on his leg. "He diversified years ago. The company has a hotel in just about every major city around the world."

"What does he want?" I asked carefully.

His gaze finally met mine. "I honestly have no idea. Traveling isn't really anything new for me." He shook his head as he looked away.

"I didn't even know you still talked to him," I said, my voice quiet.

"I don't. Mostly he talks and I start running through equations. For the last year, I've just been hanging up." His gaze met mine again. "When I went to check in, the manager had been given instructions not to give us the rooms if I didn't call."

"Seriously?" Hell, he sounded like a piece of work.

His tapping grew faster. "Yes, it took a while to work out without calling him."

"And he's still calling?" I asked gently.

"I refuse to answer. There is nothing I need to hear from him and nothing I need to say." His voice grew colder, practically making me shiver.

Not knowing what to say, I stepped closer and wrapped my arms around his waist. He moved his arms around me and held me close. Wintergreen tickled my senses as I relaxed into him. "I'm sorry, Nemo. I didn't know coming down here would cause you problems."

He rested his cheek against my hair. "It's alright, Angel."

I smiled against his shirt. His voice always softened when he called me Angel. I loved it. Guilt hit me hard. What the hell was I doing? I pulled away and gave him a tense smile. Miles's eyes narrowed on me but I turned away to look at the crowd. I needed to stop touching the guys so much. I tucked my hands into my pockets, searched the crowd for the others and found Zeke practically dragging Isaac back by the back of his shirt.

Miles followed my gaze. "Did he tell you he quit MMA?"

My head snapped around to him. "What?"

Miles gaze went back to Zeke and Isaac as they moved through the crowd. "I talked to Dave, his trainer, he's backed out of the season."

I cursed. That wasn't good. MMA was Isaac's passion, he lived it, breathed it. If he backed out… "He doesn't trust himself."

Miles turned back to me. "With what?"

"I think with everything right now," I said, my heart aching. "He's scared to talk to you guys about what happened. He doesn't trust his own judgement…" Okay, yeah, Isaac quitting wasn't out of the blue.

A crowd of people came down the sidewalk, Miles' hand moved to my lower back again as we moved back into the crowd. "I think there's something we can do."

"I hope so."

We joined the others. I took Zeke, while Miles walked with Isaac. Asher stuck with Ethan. We strolled around the Quarter, listening to brass bands on the street. Trying food from here and there. We laughed, we had fun. We kept playing Hot or Cold. Miles was really hopeless at it. I just kept laughing.

48

Isaac

MY HEART POUNDED as Miles and I followed the others through the crowd. Lexie teased Zeke as they walked further ahead. The giant just muttered under his breath, making her laugh again.

I sighed, she was right. I needed to ask Miles what I had said to him. I took several deep breaths before I managed to say a word. "What did I say to you?"

"When?" Miles asked, slowing his stride.

I sighed, my stomach in knots. "In Boulder."

Miles didn't even twitch as we made our way through the crowd. "You didn't say anything. You weren't there."

I stopped in the crowd. "I was there in the ring."

Miles turned back to me. "Not entirely." He gestured for me to follow.

We walked out of the crowd and into a small coffee shop. We found a small corner table and sat down.

Before Miles could say anything, the waitress came to the table. "Evening, what can I get you two?"

"An iced coffee, please?" Miles asked.

She gave him a thousand-megawatt smile. "Sure, cutie." She turned to me with the same smile. "How about you, sexy?"

"A lemonade, please?" I ignored the sexy part. Her smile dimmed as she turned to head back to the counter.

"Isaac," Miles said, his voice calm. "That wasn't you in that fight. You don't fight that way."

I wished he was right but... "I beat the shit out of Joshua a couple of days before that." I waited for him to react. He didn't, he just met my eyes and waited.

"Here are your drinks." The waitress returned and set down our glasses. "If you need anything else, please just let me know." I kept Miles's gaze as she stood there for a couple of heartbeats before walking away.

"Lexie mentioned your knuckles were scraped," he finally said. "What do you remember about it?"

"We were at some party at a friend's house," I muttered, taking the paper off my straw. "I was drunk, pissed off because Lexie blew me off that day to go to her grandfather's-"

"She hadn't planned that," he reminded me. "And it was important for her to go-"

"I know." I stopped him there. I didn't need the lecture. "I know that now, but then... that thing was in my head and twisting me around."

"Do you remember what started it?"

I nodded. "He came outside and said I was pussy whipped."

Miles eyed me. "Is that all?"

"No." I met his gaze again. "He called Red a bitch. That's when I started hitting him."

Miles's eyes flashed cold before he looked down at the table. He used his straw to stir his coffee. "I would have done the same."

"Yeah," I mumbled. "I beat the shit out of him and left him on the grass."

"You were angry," he said. "Did you check on him?."

"No, I fucking didn't." I shook my head. "I kicked my friend's ass and walked away without even checking on him."

Miles sighed and leaned forwarded. "Isaac. Why do you judge yourself so harshly?"

"What?" I didn't understand.

"Do you think no one else has a temper? That no one has a dark part of themselves that they keep hidden?" he asked, watching me.

"I'm not Zeke," I bit out.

He sighed. "I'm not talking about Zeke. Besides, he doesn't try to hide it," he said. "You know I have a darker side. You've seen it over the years."

"Yeah, beating the shit out of Jason in seventh grade was great," I admitted. "So was slamming Dylan onto the car hood."

"That's not the point." His ears burned red. "The point is, that everyone has a part of themselves they don't want to come to light. Everyone has a dark side. You are just like everyone else."

I started to shake my head and argue but he cut me off.

"For years you've tried to hide it, hide who you were. Then you started to show it more after Sophie passed," he sighed. "And after that, you tried to hide yourself behind making people laugh."

Looking down at the table I clenched my jaw. I didn't want to talk about this but... maybe I needed to. "What are you getting at?"

"Maybe you're just tired of hiding who you are," he said, his voice low and smooth. "You're not always the jokester. You're not always the angry one. But you are Isaac. And you are human."

I looked out the window and watched people walking by. "I don't really know who that is anymore."

"Yes, you do. You're Isaac." His certainty had me turning back to him. "You're the guy who held his dying sister in his arms and made her laugh. You're the guy who was possessed by a demon and barely survived. You're a person who is loved by his family and friends. You're the guy who created an explosion with cesium in chemistry. You like jokes, poking at Zeke's serious nature, and you are a bit of an adrenaline junkie." He sighed. "You are still that person. Only for once, you're not hiding. And I think, that means even from yourself."

I started to turn my plastic cup. "What do I do?"

"You take a good hard truthful look at who you are," Miles answered without hesitation. "If you need to work on something, own it. But if you're expecting to be perfect... I'll tell you what I tell Asher. No one is perfect. And to expect yourself to be is setting you up for a lifetime of disappointment."

What he said made sense. He usually did. I always hated that. "You're an asshole."

He grinned. "I know."

I sighed. "But you're a right asshole."

His grin turned into an understanding smile. "I'm aware." He picked up his ice coffee. "We should probably head back."

We grabbed our drinks and headed up to the cash register. Before I could pull out my wallet, Miles paid.

"Thanks for the drink," I said.

"You're welcome." He put his wallet away and met my gaze. "Thanks for talking to me."

"You two make such a cute couple." The waitress announced. We both turned to her.

Miles's face was annoyed. "We're not."

She looked at us doubtfully, then down at her cleavage then back to us. "Well, I'm sure you both will find Mr. Right."

Miles opened his mouth to correct her.

"Come on, darling," I said in a more effeminate voice while I put my arm around his shoulders. "We need to get the poodles back from the dog sitter in an hour."

He sighed as we walked toward the door. "Why does every girl think I'm gay just because I'm not ogling her?"

I shrugged. "I have no idea."

Lexie

IT WAS LATE. I was lying in bed in my room and I couldn't sleep. Zeke was being a grumpy butt and Asher... My heart ached. Asher was here. After what he said last night, I figured he'd stay behind. I got up, went to my balcony doors and looked out. My mind kept running around in circles, bringing up the same questions over and over.

A door opened and closed. I got up and looked out my window. Asher sat down in one of the chairs at the table. He was in his usual summer pjs, a pair of mesh shorts and a tank under shirt. He sat at the table, his elbows braced, his face buried in his hands. He looked exhausted. I opened my door and slipped out.

His head snapped up, his eyes ran over me before he looked away over the balcony railing. "I didn't mean to wake you up."

"You didn't. I was already awake." I stood behind the chair next to him. "Can't sleep?"

He dropped his hands and shook his head. "It's too loud. I'll have to pick up some noise cancelling head phones tomorrow."

A heavy silence fell. We both made a point of looking anywhere else but at each other. Noise from the street was the only sound on the balcony. Asher shifted in his seat. I couldn't take this.

"What are you doing here, Ash?" My quiet voice was loud on the balcony. "Last night you said… You could have stayed home. I was sure you weren't coming."

His eyes were like rough seas when he lifted his head and met my gaze. "I miss you, Ally. I miss talking to you, cooking with you, hearing your voice on the phone. I miss you."

My heart leaped and tried to fly out of my chest. "I keep reaching for my phone to call you and… then I remember."

"I know I can't be with you." His eyes held mine. "But I still want to be here *for* you."

I swallowed hard. "Ash…" I wanted to say that he could be with me. I wanted to say that I loved him, that I hated this. But I couldn't. I could only stand here and hurt.

He took a deep breath. "So, let me try this just being your friend thing again."

I sat down in the chair then brought my knees to my chest and wrapped my arms around them. "What have you been doing the last couple of weeks?"

"I've been pulling double shifts at work, taking on more clients. And I hung out with Miles and the twins," Asher said.

"You're avoiding Zeke," I guessed.

He nodded as he met my gaze. "It didn't start that way. I just got busy, then I made sure I stayed busy."

"Ash, you can't let that happen." My voice was soft and quiet. Those warm ocean eyes met mine, the noise from the street fading away. "You guys have been friends for almost your entire lives. I can't ruin that."

"I know." His own voice was rich and soft.

"What the fuck do I do?" I whispered. Unable to look him in the eye, I stared at my knees. I hadn't been joking when I said it last night, and I wasn't joking now. It was only a matter of time before one of the guys talked to one of the others or caught me with Isaac, since I couldn't seem to stop kissing him. It was only a matter of time. The original plan had been to not tell anyone, but bit by bit that plan fell apart. Then there was the plan to not date anyone. My symptoms had gotten worse and I was dying, so that wasn't too hard to keep to. Only I kissed Asher. And Isaac. But now that I'm going to live… I was in the middle of a situation that had the potential to go nuclear. And it was all of my own making. I had dug my own grave, and I'll just have to lie in it.

He leaned forward, his warm calloused fingertips going to my calves. "We act like friends again."

I met his eyes. "Don't let me destroy everything."

He narrowed his eyes on me. "What are you going to destroy?"

Realizing what I said, I shook my head and blinked away the tears that burned in my eyes. "Nothing, never mind."

"Ally." His soft rich voice had me turning back to him. "Talk to me."

I swallowed hard.

Asher blinked and pulled back until he was sitting back in his chair again. I was about to ask what was wrong when Ethan stepped through the open balcony doors with a limp.

"What's going on?" Asher asked, his voice back to his rich baritone.

Ethan shook his head. "Is Lexie still-" He looked up and smiled in relief. "Beautiful, can I borrow your hands?"

I gave him a small smile and got out of my chair. "Come on, Snoopy." I led him across the balcony and opened the French doors to my room. As Ethan walked in ahead of me, I looked back to find Asher watching me. Our eyes met, my heart raced. It was a look full of warmth and confusion. Ethan's groan brought me back to the present. I went back into my room and closed the doors. Ethan was lying in the middle of my bed, stretched out in his dark red mesh shorts, his upper body bare. I bit my lip at the sight of all those nice lines.

"Kill me, Lexie," he groaned. "Just do it. Put me out of my misery."

I smiled to myself as I picked up my lotion and climbed onto the bed. "You'll survive." I got to my knees beside him and put a portion of the lotion into my palms. "What happened? I thought you were doing okay today."

He sighed. "I was. Just a little stiffness from the flight. Then I was stupid."

I rubbed my hands together to warm up the lotion. "You picked up your suitcase."

"Yeah," he growled.

I ran my hands in long broad strokes to get his back to start loosening up. "Why didn't you let Isaac take it in?"

Out of the corner of my eye, I noticed him twirling his rings. "Because I didn't ask him to."

I started to work on the knots in his back. "Ethan, he was trying to help."

"Yeah, well, he can start by being my brother again," he muttered.

My hands stilled. "What do you mean?"

He sighed and buried his face in the comforter. "Beautiful, I've got your hands on me, massaging my back. I don't want to think about my brother."

I snorted as I went back to running my hands over the muscular lines of his back. "You're going to have to stop fighting and talk to him at some point."

He groaned deeply. "So good..."

"Why did you have that limp yesterday?" I asked, my voice low.

"I stubbed my toe," he said in a dry voice.

"It's getting worse, isn't it?" I moved on to another knot.

"Yeah," he sighed.

"Anything I can do?"

"You're doing it, Beautiful," he murmured.

I started working on his back again. It took a while but eventually the last knot let go.

"You're a miracle," he groaned deeply.

I grinned as I laid beside him. "I know."

He turned his head. "Thanks, Beautiful. How are your hands?"

I flexed them a bit to see how they felt. "They feel okay." I got comfy on my bed and met his eyes. "Are you okay?"

He closed his eyes. "Yeah. I'm just trying not to take my pain meds."

"The stronger ones?"

He nodded. "I'll sleep for, like, twelve hours."

I reached out and ran my fingers down the back of his neck. "I wish I could make it better."

His hand moved over the blanket to find mine. "You do, Beautiful." He opened his eyes. "Can I crash in here with you?"

I grinned. "Always."

THERE WAS A NOISE. I shifted under the covers and the heavy weight around my waist. A rattle, a muffled curse had me opening my eyes. Light from the street lamps outside came through the glass French doors giving me enough light to recognize Zeke's hulking frame.

"Zeke?" I muttered, still more than half asleep.

Ethan muttered and moved his arm off of me.

Zeke locked the bolt at the top of the door then turned back to me. "Go back to sleep."

I blinked at him. "What ya doin'?" I started to rub the sleep from my eyes.

"I needed to check the locks on your balcony doors," he whispered as he ran his hand through his hair. He was still in his clothes from today. What was he doing? He needed something... huh?

I started to get out of bed to help with whatever he needed. His big calloused hand wrapped around my bare arm, stopping me. "No, no, no." The weight of his hand alone had me lying back down. He squatted next to the bed and pulled my blankets back over me. "Go back to sleep, it's not time to get up yet." His fingers stroked my cheek.

I took a deep breath of leather, engine grease and spicy cologne. It relaxed me. I reached up and wrapped my fingers around his thick wrist and smiled as I slipped back under.

"I'll keep everyone safe, Baby."

CHAPTER 5

JULY 12TH, THURSDAY MORNING

*M*y alarm went off, shrill and shrieking. Spicy cologne tickled my nose from the warm weight against my side. I blindly reached out and fumbled to turn off the alarm on my phone. It took entirely too long before it stopped. Ugh, why did I choose that alarm?

The air conditioner switched on, blowing cold air over my skin. Oh, that was nice... I snuggled my pillow and started to drift off again.

Ethan's hand squeezed me. That's when I noticed his hand was on my ass over my cotton shorts. He was on his back beside me, his hand holding my butt cheek closest to him. Warmth washed through me, my body throbbed waking me up completely. I took his hand off me and tried to slip out of bed.

His arm snagged me around the waist and pulled me back under the blankets. I chuckled as he wrapped around me. His face buried in my hair, his arms around me holding me to him. His hips pressed against my ass, his morning wood rather obvious.

"Stay," he mumbled, his nose rubbing against the back of my neck.

I smiled, secretly loving it. "I need to get up."

He held me tighter. "No, you don't. You need to stay here with me."

I ran my hand over his arm around my hips. "Ethan..."

He squeezed me again, his hard body pressing into me. He didn't seem to care that he was pressed against me. Or that I could tell how hard he was. "Quedate conmigo." His voice was smoky and soft, not his toe-curling voice but almost. It made me want to stay right where I was all day.

I smiled. "What?"

"Never mind." He kissed the skin on the back of my shoulder, doubling the warmth running through my body. "Is there coffee?"

"Probably." I managed to keep my voice normal. Points for me!

"Debating. Cuddle with you or coffee..."

I ran my fingers over the skin of his forearm. "Coffee wins, hands down."

My phone rang. He loosened his hold, I rolled over and picked my phone up off the nightstand.

"Hey, Rory," I answered. Ethan kissed my temple before he climbed over me to get out of my bed. As Ethan headed for the door I ran my eyes down the muscled lines of his back to his... I grinned to myself.

"Hey, kid. I got a call this morning. Do you have a minute?" Rory said, his voice somber.

Ethan turned back around. I stretched and played innocent. Why no, I wasn't just checking out your ass, or your back... He narrowed his eyes at me.

"Sure, what's going on?" I asked.

Ethan went into my bathroom smiling and closed the door behind him. Rule one of being friends with guys, don't get caught drooling.

"It's about your mom's trial."

Suddenly the world wasn't so warm and cozy, it was cold and harsh. I sat up on the side of my bed. "What about it?"

"It's coming up this fall," he announced.

My lungs seized. This fall. Only a couple of months... "What... I thought she was going to plea out?"

"She was," Rory sighed. "But then she got a new lawyer who got ahold of your medical records."

My heart pounded in my chest. "What would that gain for her? I've got health issues, so she beat the crap out of me?"

"They're saying you're unstable and went after her," he explained. "She's telling them you see the dead."

Everything stopped. That fucking… I took a deep breath and let it out slowly. "There wasn't a mark on her. When the cops broke in, I was the one on the floor." I got to my feet and went to the window and looked outside, not really seeing it.

"I know, Lexie-"

"What about her tox screen?" I snapped in a hushed voice. "What about the cops' reports?" The bathroom door opened. I turned to Ethan. He winked at me before he left my bedroom.

"The D.A. is preparing a strong case," Rory reassured me. "But according to him, Lisa's new lawyer is a scumbag who is very good at creating doubt. And it looks like they're going for a jury trial."

"What doubt is there to create? She was caught beating the shit out of me." I crossed my arm over my stomach, trying to keep myself calm.

"The D.A says he has a strong case with only your statement and the photos from the hospital. Though he wants to know, if it became necessary, would you testify?" He asked being careful to be clear.

It would mean going back to California, it would mean seeing her again. But it would also mean putting her in jail. I just didn't know. "I'm not sure."

"You'll have a couple of months to decide but he'll need an answer eventually," Rory said.

"I'll figure it out."

"I'll talk to you later."

"Bye." I hung up the phone. She had a trial date. My stomach knotted. I tried to think about it but it was like my brain just said 'no, not today.' I decided to listen to my brain today.

I went about getting ready for the day. I pulled back the shower curtain and jumped. A dead, dark brown mouse was on the floor of the shower. Oh, ew. I got some tissues, picked it up by its tail and dropped it into the toilet. After flushing and washing my hands, I went back to my morning routine.

After, I put on Bermuda shorts, a white slouchy boyfriend shirt and lots of sunscreen. I went to do my hair and I cursed. Humidity and curly hair did not mix. Yesterday, frizz was everywhere and my hair seemed to be thicker than it ever was before. Today it was the same. Maybe Asher could… That probably wouldn't be a good idea.

I pulled out a leave-in conditioner and worked it through my wet hair, then pulled it back into a ponytail. I headed back into my room and went to my balcony doors. When I tried to open them they wouldn't budge. What the…? I checked the lock then looked at the bottom of the door. The bolt was latched. I pulled it and tried again. It still didn't move. I looked at the top and saw that the other bolt was locked. I stood on my toes and tried to reached the latch but I couldn't. My fingers just barely brushed the knob. Dropping back down to my feet, I huffed. When did someone lock it? I scoured my memory and came up with a hazy memory from late last night. Zeke. He'd come into my room while I was asleep. I clenched my jaw. Okay, he was getting really close to crossing the line. Over protective is one thing, sneaking into my room while I was asleep was another. Especially since he hated anyone coming into his room when he was asleep. The shit.

Someone knocked on my door. I glared one more time at the lock on the balcony doors before I answered. Isaac was there, his hair still wet. "Morning."

"Morning, how'd you sleep?" I asked.

"The usual." He gestured to the balcony doors in the living room. "We're having breakfast on the balcony."

I hesitated. "Zeke came into my room last night when I was sleeping." I kept my voice just above a whisper.

Isaac's eyes snapped to mine. "What did he want?" He kept his voice quiet.

"I was half asleep but I think he just bolted all the locks on the balcony doors." I stepped closer so we wouldn't be overheard.

Isaac snorted. "He did the same to all the doors."

"I don't know how much more of this I can take. If he asked, it'd be fine but..."

"Yeah, I get crawling into your bed in the middle of the night but locking the doors..." His voice dripped with sarcasm.

I shot him a look.

He grinned at me, unrepentant. "Come on, let's get some breakfast."

I gave him a small smile as he led me to the kitchenette where platters of food were set up. Eggs, bacon, turkey sausage, toast, hell, even waffles.

"Did Asher make all this?" I asked as I picked up two plates and started filling them. One for me, one with Isaac's usual breakfast. Sausage, eggs, and a small pancake. They were his favorite things for breakfast.

"No, he was up late. So, Miles ordered room service," Isaac admitted as he poured two cups of coffee.

"I knew he was up late but when did he finally go to bed?" I smiled my thanks as I set his plate down for him and he handed me my coffee with cream and sugar already added. He even made it an iced coffee. Best friend ever!

"I'm not sure, it was after the bars closed on the street though," he answered as he moved to the balcony.

And no one had woken him up. I set my coffee and plate aside and made Asher's usual coffee and breakfast. Bacon, small veggie and cheese omelet and fruit. I headed to the room Asher and Isaac were sharing. I knocked. There was no answer. He must really be out cold. Careful of the coffee, I opened the door and slipped inside.

The room was dim, showing Asher stretched out on his stomach with his head buried under the pillows. His pajama bottoms riding low on his hips, showing his lower back dimples and the start of the curve of his butt. What was it about dimples? And dimples there? Ugh. I set his plate on his nightstand and held up his coffee.

"Asher," I called softly.

Nothing.

I stepped closer and sat on the edge of the bed. "Asher."

He murmured in his sleep.

I looked at his butt again, my wicked side came out to play. I slapped my hand down on the curve of his ass. He jerked then pulled his head out from under the pillows. "Thank God, I thought you were freaking Isaac," he grumbled before rolling onto his back and covering his face with a pillow.

"It's time to get up." I grinned down at him.

"Go away," he said, his voice muffled.

I held up the coffee mug. "I brought coffee."

No response.

I set the coffee down and picked up a strawberry. "I have strawberries."

"Fresh?" he asked.

I grinned. "And ripe."

He thought about it for a moment. "Not worth it."

I snorted as I put the strawberry down. Then I pulled out the big guns and picked up the bacon. "How about bacon? Crisp, perfectly cooked, bacon."

He pulled the pillow down enough to open one sleep hazed eye. "By my standards or yours?"

I grinned. "Yours."

He pulled the pillow off his face to sit on his lap and eyed the bacon in my hand. "Is there more?"

"Yes, but it's out in the kitchen," I chimed.

He reached for the bacon, I pulled it just out of his reach. "Are you going to get out of bed?"

"It's morning," he reminded me, his cheeks tinting pink.

"I know, but I had to get up and so do you," I teased.

"Ally," he said in a voice that caught my attention. His face starting to turn red. "Can... can you leave so I can get out of bed?"

It hit me what he meant, and why he had put the pillow in his lap. My face burned. "Oh, yeah, uh, I'll just... Sorry." I got up and left, making sure to close the door behind me. In the hall, I leaned back against the door and took some time to cool my face off. Boy, that was... awkward. When I was ready, I went into the kitchen and got my breakfast.

Outside it was hot, and humid again. I could practically feel my hair frizzing in real time. I accepted defeat. Maybe I could find a ball cap or something.

Almost everyone was there. Claire was sitting on the railing next to the table, Zeke was on the other side of the table. Isaac was beside him. I sat across from Isaac and next to Miles.

"So, there Lexie was, five feet in the air, swinging upside down in this pink, frilly Easter dress her mom made her wear-"

"Claire!" I couldn't fucking believe what she was telling them!

The guys cracked up while she continued. "Then there's a loud crack. The branch breaks, dropping her into the mud puddle below the branch."

My face burned as I ignored the guys laughing and put some jam on my toast. "I cracked my collar bone," I muttered. This time, Miles started chuckling, he was trying to hide it but he was laughing. I ignored them.

"Then of course, her mom comes looking for her because it's time to go in for church." Claire continued. "The look on her face when Lexie walked around that church covered head to toe in mud, holding her arm to her. It was priceless."

I shook my head and finished my bite. "Mom blew up."

"And your dad laughed his butt off," Claire chirped. I grinned. He certainly had, at least until he realized I was hurt. He had taken me to the emergency room while Mom was huffing about how she told me to stay out of the mud. I was seven. Asher joined us, dressed for the day and carrying his breakfast.

When the guys went back to eating, I asked, "What's everyone up to today?"

"We're all planning to go with you to meet Louis," Zeke announced.

I eyed him. "Seriously?"

"Last night, we couldn't agree on who would go with you," Miles explained. "So, everyone has decided to go."

I sighed. There wasn't much I could do. And to be honest, there wasn't much I wanted to do.

"How much are you going to tell him about what you know?" Asher asked as he cut into some sausage.

I had thought about it a lot last night. Louis was stand offish. He didn't trust me and really, I didn't trust him. "For today, I'll keep my cards close to my chest. Maybe ask some questions." I played with my scrambled eggs. "I'll learn what I can then I'll think it over again."

"I like that plan," Zeke said. "Tell him as little as possible."

"What about you guys?" I asked. "Are you going to explain how you have the Sight?"

"I don't see why we would." Ethan started to put jam on his toast.

"Let's let him think that it's natural for now," Miles agreed.

"What are we doing after?" Isaac asked the group.

"Sightseeing?" I stole a packet of jelly from Isaac. Isaac shot me look promising retaliation.

Asher turned to Claire. "Is there anywhere you want to go?" My heart melted.

Claire smiled a big smile. "Well, there's the zoo..."

"The zoo it is," Miles announced.

Claire cheered and practically danced on the rail. Asher and the twins chuckled.

Isaac grabbed the last strawberry jelly pack Ethan had been reaching for.

"Seriously? You saw I was fucking reaching for that," Ethan snapped.

"You snooze, you lose," Isaac shot back as he started to put jam on his toast.

"You're a prick," Ethan muttered as he picked up the raspberry.

"Can you two ease up?" Miles asked. "We just woke up."

"I still have to go to the cemetery before we head over to Tulane," I reminded them, changing the subject.

Zeke nodded then finished his coffee. "St. Louis Cemetery Number One, right?"

I nodded since my mouth was full.

He pulled out his phone and hit some buttons. "It's a short walk and there's a bus stop nearby."

"It might take a bit depending on how many are there," I warned.

"We can all meet at the bus stop," Miles suggested.

"Why aren't we taking the car?" Ethan asked turning to Miles.

"Driving through this section of the city, just to get to the hotel, is an experience in traffic purgatory I never wish to experience again," Miles explained calmly. I grinned.

"Stay in pairs," Zeke reminded everyone.

Everyone agreed.

I turned to Claire. "So, what are you going to do besides the zoo today?"

Claire scrunched up her face and shrugged. "I think I'm going to the city park. Last time I was down here, there were a few ghosts my age to play with."

My heart ached. Dead kids, that was never easy. "Do any of them want to cross?"

She shrugged. "Maybe? I'll ask."

I really didn't like the idea of having to cross children. Thankfully, I hadn't had to cross very many. I went back to my breakfast a bit more somber.

TULANE WAS A BEAUTIFUL CAMPUS. Old stone architecture, beautifully green pathways and trees. It screamed higher education. They must have had a summer session since the paths were full of college students. And the dead. Some souls watched from their perches in the trees. Some were lying in the grass napping. Others...were sun bathing in the nude. It was bizarre. But not as bizarre as the cemetery. Only five ghosts had shown up. They said they were the only ones who wanted to cross. What kind of ghost doesn't want to move on?

"Ah!" Ethan closed his eyes. "I could have gone my entire life not seeing old man balls."

I snickered. "Too much for you, Ethan?"

"Don't start," Ethan warned. "There's an old lady in her nineties showing it all over there. Why are they naked? Can they even tan?"

I turned and looked. "Yeah, cute tattoo on her hip." I turned back and smirked at Ethan as everyone else cracked up.

Ignoring the rest of the dead, I led us to one of the big English looking buildings and led us inside. "His office should be on the second floor." I tucked my phone back in my pocket before we headed up the stairs.

"Did he say what he teaches?" Miles asked as he fell into step behind me.

"He's the head of the Religions department." I reached the landing between floors and headed up the next flight of stairs with Ethan beside me.

Some guy was coming down the stairs on the left. He saw me and flashed a smile. Ethan's hand moved to my lower back as we passed him and continued up the stairs. There was muttering behind me but it was too low to make out. He didn't drop his hand until we reached the door we were looking for. I hesitated only a heartbeat before I knocked.

Louis answered. His gaze ran over the guys. "I thought you'd bring only one."

"Yeah, they all insisted." And I didn't put up much of a fight.

Louis sighed before opening the door. "It's going to be a tight fit."

"That's what she said," Isaac and I whispered in unison. We shared a grin before we slipped inside the office. Louis was right. It was a tight fit, but eventually everyone got inside. As I closed the door, a faint white caulk line on the wall near the light switch caught my eye. Had to be a ward, though I didn't recognize it. I couldn't really tell much about the office except that it was nice. And lined with bookcases, I think, I couldn't really see past the guys lining the walls. I sat down in one of the armchairs.

Louis sat behind his desk, leaned back in his chair and eyed me. "Where shall we begin? I only have a little time before my next class."

He was sizing me up, just as I was him. So, I tried something neutral. "How's it going with the Witch's Council?"

He let out a breath. "Things are deteriorating. Tensions are high and people are getting frustrated. It's a dangerous combination."

"That's not good," I muttered.

"No, it's not." He ran his gaze over me again. "Tell me what you know."

"I know we have Reaper blood," I hedged. "Otherwise, treat me like a newbie."

He rested his elbows on his desk. "Alright. A Necromancer is created when a Reaper has a child with a normal human. Now, that blood never dilutes, so every child from that blood line from then on, who is the same gender as the Reaper, will be a Necro."

"There's never been an exception?" I asked, my voice quiet. My heart sinking.

"No, not in my blood line." His voice softened a little. My heart sank. I had hoped that maybe I had a chance to... but I was kidding myself.

"So, any daughter Lexie has, will be a Necromancer?" Miles asked carefully.

Louis turned to Miles. "Yes. And any boys will pass on the same gene."

"Lucky that I'm only seventeen and not thinking about that." I needed them off this topic now. "What exactly is a Reaper?"

Louis's gaze found mine. "They're the grim reaper of mythology. They collect lost souls and move them on to the Veil. They're one of the gears that keep the world working."

None of the guys moved.

"What else do they do?" I asked.

He raised an eyebrow. Shit! I'm not supposed to know what the Veil was! It didn't seem to matter since he began answering. "They have abilities. Some can enter dreams, most can travel through the ether to pop out into the physical world on the other side of the planet. It differs. But all of them can cross souls, and cross the realms and dimensions."

"And all Reapers are born?" Miles asked, leaning against the back of my chair.

"Well, yes and no," Louis said. "Reapers have children, yes. But those who were Necromancers... Well, after death we have a choice that no one else gets."

The room grew silent and still.

"What choice?" Zeke's voice was gruff.

"To move on, or continue working and living as a Reaper," he explained. "It's a choice Claire had to make, and she chose to move on."

I didn't know what to think of that. "So, where do they come from?"

"Death," he stated simply. "We call him Ankou."

"Wait, Death is a person?" Asher asked as he shifted against a bookcase.

"More of a deity," Louis said. "I'm explaining this badly. In the beginning of existence, you have God. Now, God wasn't alone. There was also Ankou, who is known as Death. And Apep, who is the embodiment of chaos and darkness. Now, after this dimension was created, God created several lesser deities. Among them was Anu, the Goddess of Life. There are probably many more, and many names they go by, but these are the names I was raised with and that concern us." He turned back to me. "Now, Reapers."

I shifted forward, my hands sweating.

"After God and Anu created humans, some bloodlines had abilities. Those became witches, warlocks, shamans, psychics and so on. Ankou, Death, met a witch and fell in love with her. They had children during her short life. Reapers are the children of Ankou and the first human witch, Lilith," he stated simply.

"You're saying our great, great, however many times, grandfather is Death?" I all but shouted. I couldn't have heard that right. No fucking way. This couldn't be happening. My stomach twisted up on itself.

"Yes. Death's own abilities twisted Lilith's in a way that forever changed her bloodline," he explained. "That's where we come from."

I shook my head. "Then why do we die so early?"

He sighed. "Because our human bodies aren't built for the kind of energy that we deal with. Our natural barriers aren't strong enough."

He met my eyes again. "There are levels of power in the world. First level is what I call the Primal level, it's the highest, that's where you have Death, God, Apep and the other lower deities. The second level is where you have gargoyles, dragons, reapers, demons and angels. Even Red Caps are on that level but not from ability, just from sheer brute strength and resilience. Below that are the witches, vampires, and shapeshifters like werewolves. Below, you usually have weaker psychics, telepaths, and those with the Sight."

"Where are we on that scale?" I asked, my head swimming. What the hell was a Red Cap?

"We're between the witch's level and the gargoyles' level. Along with every human born with natural abilities." He took a breath. "Do you now understand why we die out so quickly?"

"That's why the Witch's Council want us dead," I guessed.

His eyes grew darker. "Yes. They don't like not being at the top of the human power structure. To date, any Necromancer that has agreed to work with them has disappeared. Granted there aren't many of us-"

"How many are there?" Asher asked, leaning back.

"Five, well, four that I know of." His eyes unfocused. "We tend to have territories of our own. It just makes things easier. One is in Russia, one is in Texas, I am here and another is you. There was another family in Rome, however, I haven't heard from them for some time." He met my gaze again. "The fact is, we aren't magic users. We're stronger and they don't like the competition."

"So... there is more than one god? As in big g?" I asked just to be clear.

His gaze ran over me. "I don't know for sure. This is the legend that's been passed down my family for centuries. But, I've never met them in person. And I don't believe I want to."

"But..." I took a breath. "How do we know it's true? That, that is where our abilities come from?"

"Because I've spoken to a Reaper," he stated. "In fact, you probably have as well. They like to keep an eye on us half-bloods."

"They'll spy on her?" Zeke growled.

Louis shook his head. "No, just that I'd be surprised if you didn't have one around you back home."

Reapers... Death... Anu... Lilith.... no exceptions... It was like my brain was short circuiting.

And Louis seemed to realize it. "I think that is enough for today."

The guys started clearing out of the office.

Asher hesitated beside me. "What does Death do? Does he choose who lives and who dies?"

I looked up at him, the shadows in his eyes made my chest ache. I got to my feet and took his hand.

"Death isn't evil. He's not the judge, jury, and executioner," Louis explained. "Death is neutral. It's a fact that all things living die. People die because of what happens in the world, their choices, the people around them, bad luck and accidents. Death doesn't choose who dies."

Asher was still for several heartbeats before he nodded. He squeezed my hand gently before letting go and heading out the door. I followed at a quiet walk.

THE BUS RIDE back to the Quarter was packed. Before getting on, I told everyone to tuck their wallets in their front pocket. They chuckled.

"I'm not kidding, do it," I said as I pulled my wallet out of my back pocket.

"Uh, why?" Asher asked.

"Pickpockets love public transportation," I said. I pulled the neck-line of my tank top aside instead of my front pocket which wasn't deep enough. Thanks, fashion designers. I stuck it in the cup of my bra while they watched.

Asher made a point to look away while the twins burst out laughing, Miles turned red and Zeke just shook his head and clenched his jaw.

I was running in circles in my mind as the bus moved down the street when Isaac got my attention by wrapping his arm around my shoulders.

I looked up and found him smiling down at me.

"You okay?" he asked.

"Yeah." I don't know if I was lying or not. Death was a relative... no exceptions...

"You sure?" His voice changed to his warm, low voice that made my pulse race.

I nodded and looked away, hoping for a reprieve. Two men were watching me, they turned away once I noticed them. I pulled out my phone and brought up our group chat.

Alexis: Two men, one in a green polo and chinos. The other wearing jeans and a tank. They're watching us.

Tough Guy: I know. They got on the bus at the same stop as us. And they're not watching us, they're watching you.

Shit.

Alexis: Probably council.

Tough Guy: Most likely.

Ash: We've got a tail?

Tough Guy: We're not going back to the hotel, we need a public space.

Ash: Restaurant?

Tough Guy: That will work.

Alexis: We just had breakfast. Are you guys hungry again?

Tough Guy: Yeah.

Cookie Monster: All the time.

Ash: It's a guy thing.

Snoopy: We're never not hungry.

Nemo: Yes.

I smiled and shook my head at my phone. Guys and their stomachs.

Ash: Once we hit Canal St, get off the bus.

I tucked my phone away and waited while I bounced my knee. It seemed like an eternity for the Canal Street stop. We got up, Isaac moved between the crowd and me.

Once outside, we started down the sidewalk as if nothing was wrong, as if we weren't being followed by council witches or warlocks. What did guys call themselves? It didn't matter, it was just a normal day. Right...

The restaurant Asher led us to was packed. So, we got a spot on the patio out back. It calmed Zeke down so the heat was worth it. Though, with all the beautiful trees throwing shade and the breeze off the Mississippi, it wasn't so bad.

As soon as we sat down, my fingers started wanting to twitch. "Zeke?"

"Yeah, he's there. The other one must have taken off." Zeke kept his voice down.

"The tail?" Miles asked from his seat beside me.

I put a smile on and turned to him. "Yeah, he's wearing chinos and a green polo."

"Don't look," Zeke snapped before anyone had a chance to react.

Miles eyes grew chilly. "Then they must have been watching Louis. Does he know?"

I pulled out my phone and sent a text. "He does now."

Everyone waited in tense silence for an answer. My phone dinged.

Louis: Shit. Follow my instructions from yesterday. They can't touch you legally. If anything else happens, call.

I read the text out loud. Some of them relaxed. The guys shared a look.

"We just need to act normally," Miles reminded the others.

"And keep an eye on each other," Zeke added.

I nodded. I wasn't about to argue.

After the waiter left to get our drinks, I picked up the menu and opened it. The words were blurry again. Sighing, I pulled the menu back until the words were clear again.

"Lexie." Miles voice was careful. "You keep pulling your menu away."

I made a point not to look at him. "So?"

My menu was taken out of my hands.

"Hey!" I looked up to find Miles watching me with his thinking face on.

He held the menu toward me at almost the same distance it was the first time. "Lexie, can you read this?"

We suddenly had everyone's attention.

I rolled my eyes then tried to take my menu back. "What makes you think I can't?"

He let me take my menu as he answered. "Because over the last few weeks I've noticed you pulling anything you're reading further from you."

"He's not the only one," Ethan added.

I looked down at my blurry menu and didn't answer.

"The words are blurry, aren't they?" Miles asked but he wasn't really asking. He knew.

I chewed the corner of my bottom lip as I held the menu back to where I could see it. "They're fine."

Miles pulled his phone out and started doing something.

The menu was snatched out of my hands again. This time, Asher was holding it a few inches from my face. "If it's fine then read the menu out loud."

I snatched the menu from him. "There is no reason for this."

Miles got to his feet and walked away from the table with the phone to his ear.

"Lexie." Isaac spoke up. "If you can't see, then we need to find out why."

"Just caught up, did ya?" Ethan muttered.

Isaac turned to glare at his brother. "I'll fucking knock you into next week. Bad back and all."

"Stow it, you two," Zeke growled at the twins.

"He started it," Isaac bit out.

"And I'm finishing it," Zeke snapped before turning to me. "And you, read the menu out loud." His voice told me he wasn't fucking around.

I glared at him and put the damn thing on the table. "I can't when it's that close."

Zeke and Isaac cursed.

Ethan leaned forward onto the table. "How long has this been going on?"

I shrugged and picked at the corner of the menu as I tried to avoid answering.

"Lexie," Zeke all but barked.

"Stop snapping at me," I bit out. We glared at each other across the table.

"Ally, how long have you been having trouble?" Asher asked, politely.

I looked back down at my menu as I answered. "Since Boulder."

Everyone cursed.

"You haven't been able to see since last month?" Asher asked.

I lifted my head. "No, I can see fine... just not close up."

There was more swearing.

Miles sat back down beside me, tucking his phone into his pocket. "You have an appointment with an optometrist this afternoon."

"Good," Zeke muttered.

"Thanks, Miles," Asher said, still shaking his head at me.

Zeke eyed Asher, a question in his eyes.

"You have to take care of yourself, Beautiful," Ethan chided.

I turned to Miles. "You don't need to-"

"It's done." Miles told me in a voice that told me not to argue. I didn't hear it often but when I did it was because he was angry. Great, Miles was angry with me.

"Miles..." Zeke said in an oddly calm voice. Miles turned to Zeke. Zeke held his gaze. Miles turned to look out at the trees and the fountain in the courtyard while taking several deep breaths.

I didn't say anything because they were right. I should have seen a doctor back home. I put my elbow on the table and leaned my chin onto my palm as I half-heartedly looked through the menu.

"So, what are we going to do about the tail?" Asher asked the group.

"We could scatter, make him lose Red," Isaac offered.

"That would mean Lexie would be alone, veto," Zeke stated absently.

The waiter arrived, everyone ordered.

"Anyone have any ideas about how to get rid of this guy?" Ethan asked as soon as the waiter was out of earshot.

I sighed. "I do."

"What's your idea?" Miles asked, his voice careful and neutral.

"Why don't we all just turn and stare at him until he gets up and walks away?" I grinned.

"That would make it very obvious," Ethan agreed.

"And what if it's a coincidence he's here?" Asher asked.

"I don't think that's a possibility, what are the chances that he would be at Tulane, get on the same bus and go to the same restaurant as us?" I asked pointedly.

"The odds are extremely small," Miles admitted.

"So?" Ethan grinned. "Turn and stare?"

The guys wordlessly agreed. Everyone turned in our seats in unison and stared at polo shirt man. It took several heart beats for him to look up from his phone. Gray eyes met mine, he had a square jaw, low cheekbones and a wide forehead. And the blonde hair he had was receding. I smiled sweetly as I held his gaze. He eyed the boys around me then got to his feet, left a few bills and walked out of the courtyard. As soon as he was gone we burst out laughing.

MILES WAS quiet through the rest of lunch and our whole cab ride to the doctor's office. I wanted to leave immediately. I had a feeling this wasn't going to go well. When I finished the paperwork, I turned it in then went to sit down in the waiting room.

Miles stayed standing, looking out the window. "Are you angry with me?"

I kept my eyes on the opposite wall. "I'm mad at myself." I braced myself and looked over to find him watching me. "And I thought *you* were mad at *me*."

He left the window to sit in the chair beside me. "I'm... not angry," he began. "But I still don't like that you didn't say anything to anyone about it." He turned back to me. "I thought we were past this."

My stomach knotted. "We are, I just... I didn't want Isaac to find out how I got a concussion."

His eyes grew warmer. "You're worried he'd blame himself."

"You know he would," I countered.

He nodded. "That's true. But you still could have told Rory."

I chewed my lower corner lip. "I know, but..." I sighed and turned to meet his eyes again. "We just went through that whole almost dying stuff. And now this no exception thing..." I stopped myself and got back on topic. "I guess I didn't want to feel broken again."

"Broken?" Those emerald eyes ran over me before meeting mine again. "Of all the things that you are, Angel, broken has never been one of them." His soft, silky voice made my eyes burn, that feeling of being loved washed over me. You'd think after almost a year that I'd be used to it. It still surprised me every time.

I looked away at anything but him. He seemed to understand. His hand wrapped around mine.

I threaded my fingers through his and held tight. "So, you're not pissed?"

"I've never been that angry around you, and I'm going to do everything I can to be sure that I never will," he said, his voice quiet. His eyes were unfocused as he gazed at the floor.

"What do you think will happen?" I asked, with a small smile. "Think the world will end?"

His fingers squeezed mine as his eyes unfocused. "Maybe."

I was about to ask what he meant when the woman at the front desk called my name. I squeezed his hand and went in to the back of the office, my mind still running over his words.

WE WERE JUST WALKING into the hotel room when we heard it.

"Me podrías haber hablado coño!" Ethan shouted.

Isaac and Ethan were on opposite sides of the living room. Both glaring at each other. Claire sat on the glass coffee table between them, her eyes wide as her gaze snapped to Isaac.

"Cuando? Durante tu constante fiesta de lástima!" Isaac shot back. Claire's gaze snapped back to Ethan, waiting for the next volley.

Having enough of their shit, I stepped further into the room and grabbed Ethan's arm. "We're going for a walk."

Ethan cursed as I pulled him out of the suite, into the elevator and out of the lobby. He kept cursing until we were out on the sidewalk.

"What is going on with you two?" I snapped.

He jerked his arm out of my hand and walked away from me. "Leave it alone."

I caught up and stepped around him to block his path. "No fucking way. You and your brother have been tearing each other apart for days, what is going on?"

His eyes boiled. "That's not my brother!"

Everything stopped, Ethan's hands shook as he took deep breaths.

"That is your brother," I told him, not understanding what he meant.

"My brother used to fucking talk to me," he bit out.

"What do you mean?" I asked, not understanding. They talked all the time. Didn't they?

"I mean, when you guys aren't around I might as well not even exist," he bit out. "Since Boulder, he hasn't said a fucking word to me."

It clicked. "You're fucking goading him?"

He glared at the ground.

"What the hell do you think you're going to get from that?" I snapped.

"At least he fucking talks to me when we're yelling," he said, his voice thick.

My heart broke. "Ethan…"

He shook his head and met my eyes. "Weeks. It's been weeks. And my brother won't even talk to me."

I moved to him and took his hand.

His eyes filled as he looked away from me. "I want to be there for him but… he's fine. He's out doing his thing and won't say a word to me." He twirled his silver rings. "It's like after the wreck all over again."

"What do you mean?" I asked softly.

He took a deep breath and met my eyes. "After the wreck, I was laid up, drugged out of my mind and I didn't see him for a week. And when he came in, he wasn't my brother anymore."

"He was in a lot of pain too," I reminded him.

"I know." He swallowed hard. "Once I got through my shit, I tried to be there for him. I tried to talk to him but he just… disappeared." He looked down at me again. "I learned pretty quick if I kept it light, kept our conversations shallow then he'd be around. Anything else, and he was gone. So, that's what we've been doing for the last few years. Until now."

"He's your brother, Ethan. He's just hurting." I stepped closer, making his shadowed eyes meet mine.

"What did I do that was so bad, that he couldn't come to me?" He asked, his voice lost, his eyes filling again. I wrapped my arms around his neck. He held me tight against him, his face buried in the crook of my neck.

"Nothing. You did nothing wrong," I whispered into his ear.

"Then why won't he talk to me?" he rasped. "I miss him, Lexie."

"I think he's scared," I said as I held him tighter. "He's struggling every day to make his way back to normal. You just need to be patient."

"I'm trying." He took several deep breaths. "It scares me when he's quiet like this."

"He's talking to me," I admitted.

He lifted his head off my shoulder to meet my eyes. "What?"

"Almost every night since we got back from Boulder," I said. "He calls me. We talk for a couple of hours and then he can finally go to sleep."

He took a deep before asking. "How bad was it in there?"

"I can't tell you," I said in a low voice. "So, please trust me when I say what he went through trumps anything I did with Ordin. You were patient with me. So, just be that patient with him, he's working on it."

He reached up and held my cheek in his palm, his thumb stroking my skin. "I'm trying." He lowered his forehead to mine, I closed my eyes automatically. "Thank you for being there for him when he won't let me."

"I'm sorry, I don't know how else to fix this." I really wished I did.

He lifted his head and scowled at me. "You don't have to fix anything. It's between me and Isaac."

"I just want everything okay again." And not just with the twins.

His eyes ran over my face then met mine again. "They weren't okay to begin with, Beautiful."

"I thought they were." My voice was quiet.

Ethan reached up tucked a stray hair behind my ear. "They'll be even better once we work this out."

I chewed the corner of my bottom lip. If only that was true. Asher knew about Zeke, it was only time until he said something and then Zeke would know. Then the others. My stomach knotted. I wrapped my hand around his and squeezed gently. Please. Please just give me more time before this all blows up.

Ethan gave me a reassuring smile as he led me back down the block toward a taxi. "Come on, I heard Frenchmen Street has a lot more musicians."

We took a taxi and not long after we climbed out to Frenchmen St. Ethan was right, there were many more street performers here than on Bourbon.

We walked from one group of musicians to the next. I started to relax and smile again. Ethan's eyes warmed, his own smile coming back. Everything else seemed to fade into the background. All my worrying, all that anxiety. It all melted away whenever Ethan was near me. I didn't have to worry about doing something wrong, or being anything but myself.

At least I was relaxed until the crowd parted in time for me to watch the ghost of a man jump into the body of a woman. My jaw dropped as I came to a stop. He... she... He just jumped her! Just like that!

"Did you see that?" Ethan breathed, stunned.

I felt my pockets, no kit. We hadn't been carrying them lately.

There wasn't shit I could do. The woman, now possessed by a man, started striding down the street as if on a catwalk. Nice hip movement...

"Can they do that?" Ethan turned to look down at me.

I shrugged. "Theoretically..."

"Shit," he muttered as he took my hand. "Come on, there's nothing we can do right now." We moved back through the crowd.

We were walking by a single guitarist who had just started to play a song. Ethan slowed to a stop. The melody drifting over the crowd was haunting, beautiful. The guitar soft and lilting.

"What song is this?" I asked. The guitarist didn't sing any lines, he just continued to play to the swaying crowd.

"Me Cambiaste la Vida," he answered, moving behind me and sliding his arms around my waist. I stiffened, surprised. Then a lungful of spicy cologne had me relaxing against him.

"Do you know the words?" I asked, my voice breathy.

He rested his cheek against my hair, his lips brushed my ear as he began to sing to me in Spanish. My breath caught in my chest as heat rolled through me. His voice was soft, smoky and low, a whisper in my ear that had me closing my eyes. I didn't understand the words but the way he sang to me, I didn't need to know. The way his voice caressed the words sent my heart racing. His tone, the notes, it all shined through. Everything else fell away, my worry, fears. All there was, was Ethan's singing and the guitar playing. His voice rose and fell, moving through my heart. I knew, in my heart, what kind of song it was. And he was singing it to me. I floated with his arms around me, his voice in my ear, his body heat wrapping around me as my own begged for more of it. I opened my eyes and turned my head to look up at him. His chocolate eyes full of warmth, his lips barely a breath from mine. Longing flowed through me. The memory of our kiss making my breath catch. His gaze stayed locked on mine as he raised his hand to stroke my jaw with his fingertips. He lowered his head, coming closer. His breath tickled my lips. The final notes played. The crowd broke out into applause bringing the world back with a crash.

We both pulled away from each other to clap with the rest of the crowd.

I swallowed hard, my heart in my throat. Did he have feelings for me too? No, no way. That kiss in the Veil was a fluke. He thought he was going to die, that's all. As the guitarist moved into another song, I peeked up at him.

He licked his lips then slid his hand along my lower back to my other hip. The heat of his palm was burning through my clothes.

I took a breath for courage and looked up at him.

His eyes met mine. "Lexie, I have to tell you something-" Our phones rang. I pulled mine out of my pocket while he answered his.

"Yeah?" I said, half paying attention.

"Red, we're talking about ordering in. Are you guys coming back for dinner?" Isaac asked in my ear.

"Yeah, we'll head back now." I hung up and looked up at him.

"Um, we should go back," Ethan said as if nothing had happened only he wouldn't look at me.

"Yeah," I muttered, my face burning.

We walked down the street toward where we could grab a taxi. We were only a third of the way down the block when I noticed we had company. Tank top guy from yesterday, in yet another tank top. He turned in time to catch me watching him.

"We've got a tail," I said.

Ethan moved around me, putting himself between me and tank top guy. He took my hand and began walking faster.

Tank top guy, knowing he'd been spotted, started toward us.

Ethan squeezed my hand then loosened his grip. "Run, Lexie."

"Hell no," I whispered.

"Do it," he hissed. But it didn't matter. Tank top man met us on the corner.

"Greetings from the Witch's Council."

81

CHAPTER 6

JULY 12TH, THURSDAY EVENING

"I'm sorry, the what?" I asked, acting confused.

His eyes narrowed on me. "Don't bother playing stupid."

"Look, pal." Ethan's loud voice drew the attention of the crowd around us. "All we know is that you're following my sixteen-year-old girlfriend. So, back the fuck off." Ethan moved me ahead of him while glaring at tank top guy.

I bit back a laugh as we hurried through the crowd while several men and a woman stepped between us and tank top man.

"That should slow him down." Ethan smirked as we hurried to the end of the street.

"I'm not sixteen," I pointed out.

"You look barely sixteen when you don't have makeup on." He chuckled. "The younger the better in this case. I would have said fourteen if it wouldn't have made me look like a perv."

We were getting in a cab when I spotted tank top man striding toward us and the other taxis. We climbed in and told the driver to hurry. Ethan gave the hotel address while I pulled out my phone.

Alexis: We've got a tail.

It wasn't long before I got a response.

Tough Guy: Where?

Alexis: Following us toward the hotel from Frenchmen St. How do we lose him?

Miles: You don't. You come straight here.

I showed the text to Ethan, he scoffed.

Alexis: That will tell him exactly where we are staying.

Asher: Getting you two back safe is more important. We can always change hotels, we can't replace the two of you.

I chewed the corner of my lip as the driver turned a corner.

Alexis: Okay, but on one condition.

Isaac: What?

Alexis: Zeke stays upstairs.

Miles: Agreed.

Isaac: Might be a good idea to hang out in the lobby for a bit, Red. He's pissed.

I rolled my eyes and tucked my phone into my pocket.

"We're going straight there?" Ethan asked. I nodded. He clenched then unclenched his jaw.

With all the tourists on Bourbon street, the driver had to let us out a couple of blocks away. It was a tense walk, we were both taut as a guitar string until we reached our street. I glanced over our shoulders in time to spot tank top guy getting out of a cab.

"He's still following," I muttered. Ethan took my hand and we jogged.

By the time we reached the hotel we were both sweating bullets. Miles was just inside the door, his arms crossed over his chest, his fingers tapping on his arm. We didn't hesitate, we ran inside and skidded to a stop. Miles stayed put. Tank top man reached the door. Miles blocked it.

Miles' posture was straight, his eyes cold as he stared at the council's man. He didn't say a word, until a man in a security uniform went to him.

"This is the man harassing them," Miles announced before he stepped back.

"Sir, what business do you have with our underage guests?" The tall guard demanded.

Miles turned and came toward us, the icy look still on his face. "Upstairs, they'll take care of him for now."

Ethan and I didn't even argue. We headed for the elevator.

"If you come near our guests again, we'll make sure you are taken in for harassing minors." The guard informed our follower.

When we got into the room, Zeke was pacing. His face was pale as he examined me and Ethan.

"Are you two okay?" Asher asked, getting to his feet.

"Yeah, we're fine." I took a breath and explained everything that happened on our way home.

"You talked to your tail." Zeke's eyes were glowing. His hand shook as it ran through his hair.

"Deep breaths." Miles' voice was calm. "The tail talked to them."

Zeke closed his eyes and shook his head. "These guys are following us. And now they know where we are." His voice was hard, but still controlled. As if he was biting back the need to yell. He crossed his arms over his chest and took another deep breath. "I think we need to leave." Zeke seemed almost... calm. His clenching and unclenching jaw told me otherwise.

"Why?" I asked carefully.

His burning eyes met mine. "Because they are escalating. They were following, and now they're talking to you. This could get dangerous."

"Legally, they can't touch me-"

"Yeah, because everyone follows laws. Laws are never broken," he shot back. He stopped, closed his eyes and took several deep breaths.

Holy shit... Zeke was trying to stay calm and reasonable. But I had to be honest.

"I can't go home yet," I told him.

Zeke took several more deep breaths before turning and walking out onto the balcony.

Everyone stared at the closed French doors as Zeke went to the railing and leaned against it.

"Did that just happen?" Isaac asked, turning to Miles. "Did Zeke really just not yell?"

"Yeah." The guys answered in unison.

Miles adjusted his glasses. "He's been working on it."

I walked toward the doors and watched Zeke hang his head and take several more deep breaths. "How often is he seeing his shrink?"

"A couple of times a week," Miles admitted.

I turned to meet his eyes. "A week? What's going on?"

Miles began to tap his leg. "I'm not sure."

"Shit," Ethan muttered. "That was... weird."

Zeke pulled out his phone and called someone. He moved away from the railing to sit on the patio couch.

"Let's order some dinner, by the time it's here he should have calmed down." Miles suggested. The others gathered around the coffee table to decide on what to order from room service. I stayed by the door watching Zeke's tense shoulders as he talked on the phone.

"Lexie? What would you like for dinner?" Miles called, getting my attention.

"Oh, just... whatever. I'm not picky," I answered, still watching Zeke.

The guys ordered and started watching a movie. Eventually, Claire joined us and the movie changed to something she'd enjoy.

To be honest, I wasn't really paying attention. My eyes stayed on Zeke's shoulders. Eventually, they relaxed, then awhile later he hung up. I gave him a few more minutes before I went out to join him on the couch. I sat next to him with my back against the arm, and my knees drawn up to my chest.

He took a deep breath then turned to me. Those ice blue eyes met mine.

"Are you okay?"

He nodded slowly. "It's taking everything I have not to make everyone pack and leave."

"I know." I swallowed hard. "Thank you."

He sighed, his eyes ran over me then back to mine. "I can't convince you to leave, can I?"

"You can try but it won't work." I kept my voice quiet.

"It's not safe here. Not just for you, but the guys. If they learn we have the Sight..." He took another deep breath as he leaned forward bracing his elbows on his legs.

"Zeke."

He turned his head; the struggle was clear in his eyes.

"Do you understand how important this is to me?" I asked. "This is my chance to understand what I am. The only chance I might ever have."

His eyes softened. "I know. It's just... with the council here, and the ghosts going crazy..."

"The ghosts can't hurt me anymore," I reminded him, keeping my voice soft. "And I know there's a chance the Witch's Council won't follow the laws but..." I swallowed hard. "I need to know more about what I am, what I can do, what... to expect. It's like I've been feeling my way in the dark and I finally found the fucking light switch. I can't give up this chance."

"It's dangerous here, Baby," he said in a low rasp. "Something bad is going to happen, I can feel it."

I met his eyes. "I know it's a risk, Tough Guy."

"But you still want to stay?"

"I have to," I admitted.

He closed his eyes and hung his head again. "I can't make your choices for you. I'm only responsible for mine. I can't control everything, only what I do. I can ask, I can't demand or boss anyone around." His voice was low and strained.

I waited patiently for him to deal with his own issues.

He opened his eyes and turned to me. "You need to stay, so... We'll do everything we can to keep everyone safe from these people."

"Thank you for understanding," I said in a soft voice.

He nodded, then his eyes turned serious. "Not only will you not go off alone, but you'll let us know where you are and you'll keep us updated. You hear me?" His jaw clenched and unclenched. "I mean... please?"

"I hear ya." I gave him a small smile.

His shoulders relaxed. "One down, five to go."

I eyed his face again. "You aren't sleeping again."

"Not lately," he admitted, rubbing his eyes with one hand.

"Why not?"

"Nightmares," he muttered under his breath.

"Want to talk about it?" I tried again. Zeke wasn't the easiest person to get to talk but I was a pain in the ass when I wanted to know something.

"Maybe later." He straightened to his full height. "I'm going to head down to the gym."

When he was gone I took a deep breath and let it out slowly. There was someone else I needed to talk to. The sun was starting to set as I dialed.

"Hello." Louis's voice was clear over the line.

"The council is stepping up their game." I didn't beat around the bush. "One of my tails tried to recruit me."

Louis cursed in, what I'm sure was French. "What happened?"

I gave him a summary, leaving out our family discussion.

"He said council?" he asked again.

"Yeah." I kept my voice low. "I don't know if these guys are going to play by the rules. He almost walked right into our hotel."

The silence was thick.

"That's disturbing," he admitted. "Alright, you may want to leave town tonight."

"I'm not going anywhere," I snapped. "Besides, I have some contacts of my own that should make them back off."

"What contacts?" he asked, his voice doubtful.

"Gargoyles."

The line went quiet.

"You know gargoyles?" he asked carefully.

"Yeah."

"How the hell do you know gargoyles?" His voice was surprised.

"I'll explain later."

He said something in, yep, it was French. "You know a lot more than you've let on."

"I think we've both been playing it close to the chest." I wasn't going to let him get away with that one.

"We'll have a more in-depth conversation tomorrow," he muttered. "Just stay in tonight and I'll send you an address to meet me, around noon."

"See you tomorrow." I hung up. Tired, I curled my legs up and laid my head back. Today, sucked. The guys' voices were low in the living room while Claire's was cheerful. But I couldn't seem to find the energy to get up and go back inside. I stayed put and watched the light slowly disappear from the sky.

The street grew louder as the stars came out. My mind went blissfully blank. There was just too much that happened today. I was grateful.

A long shadow stretched out over the balcony floor.

"Are you okay?" Asher asked in that rich baritone I loved.

I opened my eyes and gave him a halfhearted smile. "Yeah, I'm just... done with today."

He sat on the couch beside me. "Yeah, today wasn't so easy."

I lifted my head and looked up at the stars I could see over the buildings. "That's not it. I'm just... I don't know what's happening, I don't have a clue what I'm doing. I finally have a chance to learn what I can do and... " I shook my head. God, don't let me fuck up.

"No one really knows what they're doing." Asher said in a quiet voice.

I smiled. "You mean you don't know everything and have your life planned out to the year?"

He grinned. "I don't even have next week planned."

"Really?" I asked, feeling a bit better

He nodded. "I'm usually winging it."

I smiled. "So, how are things at home, really?"

He sighed and began to talk. We talked about what was going on in our lives. Jessica was still driving him crazy, his dad was still gone, as usual. I told him how happy I was to not have to worry about the dead jumping me. How I felt more normal than I ever had before. We made jokes and teased each other. We fell back into our old rhythm. It was like coming home after a long vacation.

"Lexie!" Ethan shouted, his voice furious.

We shared a look before we got up and went to the door. Ethan strode down the hall soaked, wearing nothing but a white towel. Lines... muscles... towel low on hips... oh damn. Stop drooling before he notices! I fought to pull my eyes back to his face as he fumed. "Will you get this fucking ghost outta here?" I didn't have long to wonder what he meant. The soul of a teenage girl came through the bathroom door. Blood covered half her face from a gash at her forehead, her swim suit was covered in it.

"Oh, come on! It was just a little peek!" The ghost smiled as she followed Ethan into the living room. Miles and Isaac came out of their room, gaping.

Ethan turned on her. "Peek? You were fucking watching me shower!"

The guys gaped at the soul, I just stood there stunned. She was watching him shower... rage simmered in my gut.

"Well, you have been single for a while." Asher pointed out.

The ghost turned to him with a grin. "What about you, dimples?"

Asher's mouth drew into a tight line. A memory of Asher's bare back flashed in my mind. And the two dimples above his butt...

"You've been watching my friends shower?" I asked as I stepped forward out of the doorway to the balcony.

The ghost turned to me with a smile, as if she thought I'd join in on the fun. "Well, yeah."

My temper ignited. "Who are you?"

She perked up, her smile growing bigger. Poor girl. "I'm Courtney, and your friends are really hot."

I gave her a smile, and it wasn't my pleasant one. "Courtney, stay the hell away from my friends," I growled.

Her smile disappeared. "I was only peeking. It's not like they mind."

The guys scowled at her.

I walked toward her, struggling to keep my will under control. "Just because they're guys, doesn't mean they want girls peeping on them!" I lashed out with that gold ribbon of will and wrapped it around her chest then pulled her toward me until she was practically in my face. "If you ever do that again, I'll take you to the Veil and drop your ass into the abyss and you'll be unmade. Is that fucking clear?"

Her eyes grew wide as she stopped struggling against my hold on her. "Yes, yeah. I get it! No watching the guys in the shower!"

I set her down and let her go. "Now, if you want to cross, go to Louis Cemetery Number One in the morning." She ran out the balcony door and jumped through the rail.

It started with just a few snorts, then Ethan started chuckling. "I've never seen a ghost run so fast."

Asher started laughing. "Now we have to watch out for peeping ghosts?"

"I didn't even know that was a thing," I admitted. Soon everyone was cracking up. It went on until I was wiping tears from my eyes. The tension from earlier washed away as everyone relaxed. I just wished Zeke was here to enjoy it.

I COULDN'T SLEEP. Zeke had come back from the gym, gone to his room and stayed in there the rest of the night. Though that might have also been because the guys were watching Disney movies with Claire. I rolled on to my back and tried to fall asleep. The council was following us. That wasn't good, but by their own rules they couldn't touch me. Then again, if they thought they could get away with breaking their own rules... I rolled over again and punched my pillow into shape. What about the guys? Miles was eighteen, Zeke would be in a couple of days, would they go after them? Then there was that conversation with Louis.

"What's wrong?" Claire asked from her spot on the other side of the bed.

"I can't sleep," I muttered.

"Neither can Miles, he's in the living room." She blew a raspberry at the ceiling.

I smiled. "Do you want to watch movies in here?"

She perked right up. "Can I?"

I chuckled and turned on the tv. "Sure, I think I'm going to get up anyway."

I shoved my covers back and headed for the door.

"Um, Lexie?" Claire's voice had me turning back to her.

"Yeah?"

"Can you stop by Louis Armstrong Park tomorrow? I think some of the other kids want to move on and I told them to meet there." Claire asked, practically squirming in her spot.

"Of course." I hated crossing kids, but leaving them here wouldn't be right either.

I stepped out into the living room leaving her happily watching the Avengers. The living room was dark except for the lamp on one of the end tables.

Miles looked up from his book and spotted me. "Did the light wake you up?"

I sat down at the end of the couch, facing him. "No, my mind just won't go to sleep."

He closed his book and watched me.

I shifted so my knees were bent as I laid back against the arm of the couch.

Miles had his thinking face on, the one that made the little wrinkle in between his brow. "Lexie?"

"Hmm?"

He turned to face me on the couch. "What's keeping you up?"

I shook my head and looked out the door to the balcony rail. My mind went back to that conversation.

"Angel?"

My gaze moved to the top of my knees. "It's something I thought... I had given up the hope of a long time ago."

Miles scooted closer until his thigh met my shins, his arm slid along the back of the couch. "What hope?"

I swallowed hard. "Having kids."

His went still, though his fingers began tapping on the back of the couch. "You said you didn't want to pass on your abilities once."

"I don't," I whispered. "But I guess... ever since I got the ward tattoo a small part of me must have hoped..."

He stopped my fingers from twisting, then threaded his through mine. "You thought that you could protect any daughters you might have."

"Or that it might skip, just maybe." I shook my head. "It was stupid. I know the score, I know how it works. It's never skipped before so there's no reason to think it would now. I was just... stupid."

"It's not stupid to hope," he said in his soft silky-smooth timbre.

"It is for me," I muttered.

His fingers squeezed mine. "You can still have children."

"Not without risking them and their kids." I met those calm emerald eyes. "I can't be that selfish."

His hand squeezed mine. "Lexie, you have years before you have to make this decision."

"I know... can-can we just watch tv or something?" I asked, my throat tight.

His eyes searched my face, whatever he saw there seemed to help him agree. He nodded.

"What are we going to watch?" I squeezed his fingers. I really didn't want to let go.

He let my hand go, picked up his book and leaned against the other side of the couch. "Come over here."

I moved to sit on the inside of the couch and laid back against his firm chest. His arms slipped around me as he opened the book. I relaxed against him. "What are we reading?"

"The Dresdan Files, Storm Front."

"I love Jim Butcher," I said as he turned back to the beginning. "You don't have to start over, I'm up-to-date."

"I'd rather read it from the beginning with you." He rested his cheek against my hair. "You make it new again."

I smiled to myself as he began to read out loud.

"The mailman walked toward my office door, half an hour earlier than usual. He didn't sound right," he began to read. His silky-smooth timbre slid through my ear and had me smiling in no time. Wintergreen surrounded me as he read.

We were well into chapter two when something else caught my attention. Music floated up from the street and through the open balcony doors. A guitar, someone was talented. A voice joined in. It was deep, slightly husky and clear. That voice rolled over me, reminded me of hot nights and silk sheets. My skin broke out in goosebumps. It wasn't Ethan's level, but whoever it was had some extreme talent. I closed my eyes and listened as goosebumps ran over my arms.

Miles looked down at me. "Are you cold?"

I shook my head. "No, just... that voice is amazing."

He tilted his head, his eyes unfocused as he listened. "He is." He looked down at me. "What is it about voices you like so much?"

"Well, some voices are soothing," I began, deciding to be honest. "And some... well. Everyone has something that flips their switch."

He started laughing.

"Shut up." My face burned. "I'm an audiophile."

"That's-that's not being an audiophile, Angel," he told me as he began to sober. "That's acousticophilia."

"Drop it, Miles," I muttered. He let it go and went back to reading to me with a smile.

CHAPTER 7

JULY 13TH, FRIDAY MORNING

Zeke

I finished pulling on my gym clothes. I had given up on sleep hours ago. It was early enough that everyone should still be asleep. The sky was only starting to lighten outside the window now. I rubbed my hands over my face, trying to force myself to stay awake. Fucking nightmares. I cursed as I opened the door and headed down the hall. I stepped into the kitchen and came up short. Lexie wasn't in her room. And she wasn't alone.

Miles was on his back on the couch with Lexie stretched out over him, resting on his chest. Her legs tangled with Miles', his arms around her. It looked like they had fallen asleep on the couch.

Miles squeezed her tight then buried his nose in her hair. Did he...? I eyed Miles. Did he like Lexie? No... no way. I took a step toward the suite door, then another. I really was sleep deprived if I thought Miles felt that way about her. I needed to get my shit straightened out. Talk to my shrink...

I ran my hand through my hair as I left the hotel suite and headed down to the gym. Lexie and Miles? I really needed to get a grip.

Miles

A DOOR CLOSED SOMEWHERE, the sound bringing me to the surface. The scent of rosemary was under my nose, a small, familiar body was in my arms lying on me, again. I smiled against her hair.

Lexie, she felt wonderful this morning. She rubbed her forehead against my neck like a kitten, she grew still then fell back asleep. Then again... I ran my fingers down her spine and back again. She felt exceptional in my arms. I wanted to wake up every morning this way. With her curves pressed into me, her arms around my neck. It was perfect. At least until my body woke up and realized how good she really felt. I cursed mentally and tried to shift her a little, just enough to adjust. She made a small breathy noise in her sleep and settled back against me. Damn it. I kept my arm around her, shifted and pulled her a little to the left. She didn't even wake up as her cheek came to rest on my collarbone. Smiling down at her, I slipped my other arm under her legs and moved her so I could sit properly on the couch. She made a small noise of protest only to settle down again.

I lifted her and got to my feet, thankful my cast came off the day before we left. I still shouldn't be carrying her to her room but... well, screw it. I wasn't going to leave her on the couch thinking I left her sleeping there alone all night.

Her arm slipped around my neck as I walked into her room. I smiled as she nuzzled into me. Carefully, I put her back in her bed and slid my arms out from under her. Her face pinched as I reached for her blankets.

Her eyes opened to slits. "Nemo?"

My heart flooded with warmth as I covered her with her blankets. "I'm getting up, Angel."

She reached up and took my hand before I could straighten. "Stay."

I wanted to. I really, truly wanted to. But it wasn't the logical thing to do. It could be rather disastrous if she ever guessed how I felt about her. "Why do you want me to stay?" I asked before I could stop myself.

She smiled as she began falling back asleep. "Love you..."

My heart stalled, then began pounding furiously. Did she mean as a friend, like the others? Or more? What answer did I want? My head said as a friend but my heart... it was yelling something completely different.

I ran my free hand over her hair. Her grip on my fingers loosened. I smiled. She never latched onto me when I carried her or even hugged her. It was always when she was half asleep and I was about to leave. There could be several reasons for it but... there was one I wanted it to be. "Why, Angel?"

She pulled my hand to her chest just above her cami. "Mine..."

My body hardened at the possessiveness in her voice. My hand spread out over her upper chest, just below her collar bones. "I am yours, Angel." I breathed, finally realizing how true it was. Hers. I could live with that. Could she?

Lexie

I CAME out of the bedroom just in time to watch the news report with the others. Except Zeke, he wasn't in the living room.

"Twenty-four people are in the hospital this morning with signs of bacterial meningitis." The news anchor announced. "Tulane Medical Center's Medical Director, Darren Phillipe, however, has made a different statement."

The screen went to a man in a suit at a podium. "Twenty-two adults, and two children have been admitted with signs of bacterial meningitis. However, all tests have come back negative. At this time, those who are affected are receiving the best treatment possible as we continue to run tests. Thank you."

The screen flashed back to the news anchor. "Authorities have found only one connection between those affected. They all seemed to begin showing signs at a restaurant in the French Quarter. That restaurant has since been shut down pending an investigation by the Health Department."

"Sudden illness without a cause?" Miles thought out loud.

"That's strange," Asher agreed. "But maybe it's salmonella or something."

"That would have been one of the first tests they ran, not bacterial meningitis," Miles said, his complete focus on the news report.

"Ally, breakfast is in the kitchen," Asher said, his attention back on the tv.

"Coffee sounds good right now." I headed into the kitchen and made a cup. When I came back in the news anchor was talking about a mentally ill woman who was found in the Garden district. They were looking for anyone who had any information on her identity.

Wanting to get away from the news, I headed out to the balcony. A strange smell hit my nose. I looked around and spotted the cause. A rotting squirrel. Ew. I was just grateful there weren't maggots.

I headed back inside. "You guys might want to stay inside for breakfast, there's a dead squirrel out there."

Miles put down his mug onto the counter. "I'll take care of it." He started looking for something.

"We don't have a broom; you'll have to call the front desk." Asher informed him as he set his breakfast on the coffee table. Miles went to make the call.

I hesitated to make my plate. "Did anyone tell Zeke breakfast was ready?"

"He's in the shower," Isaac answered. "He just got back from the gym."

I sat down in the corner of one of the couches and curled my feet under me.

Ethan set his plate on the coffee table as he sat beside me. "You're not eating, Beautiful?"

"Maybe after coffee," I hedged.

A door opened down the hall, Zeke came out of the bathroom in his usual all black and boots. His hair was wet as he threw his clothes into his room then came down the hall and into the kitchen to get a plate.

As breakfast went on, Claire eventually came in through the suite door and plopped down on the arm of the couch beside me. "So, what are we doing today?"

I looked at her. "Where the hell did you go last night?"

She smiled. "I went haunting at Greek row near Tulane. Moved some stuff, watched the frat boys scream."

I snorted.

Isaac put down his fork. "You know, we could-"

"Claire, is there anywhere you want to go?" Ethan asked.

I turned to Ethan and met his gaze, shooting him a look. Ethan sighed then nodded, agreeing to stop baiting his brother.

"There's the aquarium...." Claire answered, hesitating.

"Aquarium it is." Asher announced.

"Who's going with me?" I asked them.

"I'll go," Zeke volunteered before turning to the others. "Stay together and pay attention around you."

"We know," Asher said patiently.

"Well, if you guys are going out, you should take a Lexie kit," I announced. All eyes turned to me. I explained what we saw on Frenchmen Street, how there was nothing I could do at the time.

"They're possessing people right out in the open?" Miles asked.

"Most people can't see them so... yeah." I shrugged. "I'm going to talk to Louis and see if there is something we can do with the ghosts in town."

"Did anyone bring a kit?" Zeke asked the group.

The guys shook their heads. I cursed.

"We're in New Orleans. I'm sure we can find holy water," Miles pointed out.

Everyone figured out what they would pick up, and who they would pair up with. Then we put our plates in the kitchen and got ready to go.

· · ·

AFTER STOPPING by the cemetery and finding no souls waiting. Zeke and I were walking back through the practically empty French Quarter. Only Zeke was walking his normal speed, although I couldn't keep up with him without jogging. Finally, I stopped trying to. He pulled ahead again as I shook my head. And quite frankly, I needed a couple of minutes to myself. I loved the guys but sometimes I just needed some space. With Isaac's attention and Asher struggling not to pay attention. Zeke was, well, being Zeke. Ethan... Then last night with Miles... It was getting complicated.

Zeke cursed. I lifted my head and grinned as he strode back down the sidewalk to me.

"Why the hell didn't you tell me I was going too fast for you?" he chided.

I rolled my eyes. "Because you've known me for almost a year and you should remember by now."

He muttered something under his breath as he walked beside me again. The silence was peaceful. Zeke was one of the only people who I can enjoy silence with. But that wasn't going to happen today.

"You came into my bedroom the other night while I was sleeping," I stated simply.

"Yeah," That's all he said. Nothing else.

I took a breath and let it out slowly. "Don't you think that's a little much?"

"No."

I stopped in my tracks and glared up at him.

He stopped and turned back around to me.

"No? Seriously?" I snapped. "You, who would yell at anyone who did that to you, you don't see a problem with that?"

He clenched and unclenched his jaw. "Lexie-"

"Don't Lexie me," I said. "You would be furious if someone did that to you. But you see no problem doing that to me?"

"We're in a city with the Witch's Council in town, people who have already threatened to kill you in the past. And you're pissed that I locked your fucking balcony doors?" he growled back. Well, hell, when he put it that way...

"It's not just my doors. It's an invasion of my privacy," I pointed out. "If I went into your room while you were asleep you'd lose your shit."

"You don't wake up swinging at everything that moves," he reminded me in a deep growl.

I raised an eyebrow. "You don't when it's me."

His eyes softened. "I noticed."

"If you keep coming into my room at night while I'm asleep, I'm gonna start doing it to you," I smiled sweetly. "I'll even bring a pen."

He eyed me. "You're bluffing."

I gave him my shit eating grin. "Try me."

We had our usual staring contest.

My phone beeped, stopping the game. I checked the time. Shit. We were running behind, we needed to hurry if we were going to be ready when the guys showed up. "Damn it."

I picked up my pace and hustled the rest of the way to the park. Louis Armstrong Park was pretty, there was no other way to describe it. A man-made pond wound its way along the pathways, creating a beautiful walk under the trees.

Zeke and I found the kids playing tag around a statue.

"Kids." Zeke cursed.

"I hate crossing kids," I muttered, my heart aching.

His large calloused hand wrapped around the back of my neck and squeezed me gently. "I know. It's all kinds of fucked up."

Yeah, that about summed it up. I stepped forward and made my way to them with Zeke only a few steps behind. This was going to suck.

AFTER A HEART-WRENCHING TRIP to the Veil, Zeke and I were standing in the back of the bus near the second door. I had bitched about it at first, but as more people climbed on I was grateful. Zeke stood right in front me and blocked me off from the crowd. The space grew tighter. Zeke cursed as he was pressed closer to me. Memories flickered through my mind. My heart slammed, my stomach knotted, my chest grew tight. Too close, he was too close, too tall, way too tall... My breathing picked up. My mind flashed on the cabin. His fingers lifted my chin so his eyes could meet mine.

"Slow, deep breaths," he said in that soft gravelly voice he used with me once in a while.

The tightness in my chest eased, the knots in my stomach loosened. The cabin faded as I took a deep breath and held his gaze.

"Good. Again."

I kept eye contact with him as someone in the crowd ran into his back. He flinched, his body growing rigid against me. His jaw clenched as he looked over his shoulder, his eyes started to glow.

"Zeke." I put my hand in the middle of his chest.

He turned back to me, the strain showing on his face. Too many people behind him. Shit.

"Stay with me," I whispered, my other hand moved around his hard waist. He focused on me, on keeping the crowd away from me, on his breathing.

The look in his eyes made my heart race for a different reason. His eyes warmed as the bus continued to move toward our stop. With him so close, we breathed together. When our stop was announced sound suddenly came back. Zeke growled as he pushed away from the bus wall and forced everyone to move. He managed to stay between me and the crowd again as I slipped between him and out the door. Zeke stepped off the bus and patted his front pocket. When he found his wallet, he lifted his chin to me. "Still have yours?"

Face burning, I reached in and pulled out my wallet. "Yep." I tucked it into my back pocket again. Trying to distract myself, I pulled out my phone and brought up the directions to the address Louis gave us.

We started walking through the Garden District. The houses were huge and beautiful. They ranged from Greek revival to colorful Victorians as we walked down the tree lined sidewalk in silence.

"You good?" he asked quietly.

"Yeah, you?" I kept my voice just as low.

"Yeah," he sighed. "What do you think you're going to learn from this guy that makes it worth staying here?"

His question threw me. I thought about it. "I don't know." I shrugged. "Anything more than I know now would make this trip worth it."

"Even with that council in town?"

"Yeah," I admitted. "Imagine going your whole life doing this weird thing that you have very little control over."

"I don't have to imagine," he breathed.

It took me a second to realize what he meant. Zeke had once said he has his father's temper. "You've been doing better the last couple of weeks," I said. "At least temper wise, protective wise..."

"Yeah, I know. I'm... slipping," he bit out.

"I'm here if you want to talk," I reminded him.

"Maybe," he said as we continued down the road.

"Oh, after this Asher wants to meet me at Café Du Monde," I told him, trying to forget the way his eyes warmed on the bus.

"Miles told me, he'll partner Asher to meet us," Zeke said. "I'll walk back with Miles." Wow, the guys were really taking the entire buddy system seriously. It made me wonder what they talked about last night after I stayed outside on the balcony.

We finally reached the address. It was a large, mint green, Victorian house on Jackson Ave. I instantly loved the large window over the porch on the second floor. Not to mention the porch swing.

Before we could open the walkway gate, the front door opened. Four children came out, in varying ages. One little girl with blonde hair spoke in what I was guessing was French to an older girl, while the youngest of the girls complained that she wanted her hair in Nubian twists.

"I know, Ami. But we're leaving right now for the pool." A blonde woman closed the door behind her and picked up a stuffed large tote. "We'll do it tomorrow morning, or Momma Uma can do it tonight before the gallery showing. But we can't do it before we leave, baby."

The oldest, a boy who looked around fourteen with Louis's eyes, watched me as he approached the sidewalk. That strange feeling rolled over my skin, only barely as a whisper this time. Necro.

"Who the hell are you?" The kid said to us.

"Juan, we don't use that kind of language." The woman chided as she came down the stairs

"Emilia, can you get Caroline and Ami in the van." The woman stepped onto the walkway at the bottom of the stairs and eyed us. "Can I help you?"

"I'm Lexie, Louis gave me this address." I opened the gate and stepped aside so the three girls could climb into a red mini-van parked at the curb. The boy kept watching me with suspicion.

She sighed. "You're in the right place. I'm Savannah, one of his wives." She turned to the boy watching us. "Juan, this is Lexie, she's a Necromancer."

"I figured that out." Juan rolled his eyes.

Savannah sighed. "Juan..."

"This is Zeke." I gestured up at the giant. "He's a friend of mine."

Zeke only nodded once to them. Juan watched me as he fingered several strands of beads on his left wrist. Onyx beads.

The front door opened. Louis came out carrying another full tote bag. "Vannah!" He hurried down the stairs to us. "You left the bag with the sunscreen and water bottles."

"Oh, for crying out loud," Savannah muttered. "Juan, love, can you be a dear and put this in the car and tell your sisters to buckle up?"

Juan took the bag and went to do as she asked, muttering under his breath the whole time.

Savannah sighed and looked up at Louis. "I never thought I'd be wishing summer was over already."

Louis chuckled.

Savannah turned to us. "I'm sorry, we have to go." She turned back to Louis. "I'll bring home gumbo from Acme's tonight so stay out of the kitchen and keep your hands off those pecan pies. They're for the fundraiser tomorrow."

Louis held his hands up in surrender. "I will stay out of the kitchen."

Savannah got up on her toes and kissed his cheek before hurrying around the van to the driver's seat.

As soon as Savannah and the kids were gone he turned to us, his face somber. "Come inside, we need to talk."

Louis led us into the house, as we climbed the steps I noticed a small design carved into the base of a porch post. I recognized it as a ward from the research Miles had managed to get for me. I took a quick glance around the yard. Another on a fence post and the trim of the front door. Those, I didn't recognize. Louis led us into the house, past the stairs and into his home office. Sitting in one of the armchairs was a woman wearing a sophisticated sheath dress and heels that screamed classic elegance. Her nutmeg skin contrasted beautifully with the lavender of the dress. She lifted her head from the book she was reading and smiled a stunning smile.

Setting the book aside, she got to her feet. "You must be Lexie, we've heard so much about you. I'm Uma, one of Louis's wives and also a local witch."

I shook her hand. "It's nice to meet you. This is my friend Zeke."

She eyed Zeke and didn't offer her hand. "And your skills are...?"

"I have the Sight as does everyone who came with Lexie on this trip," he answered with his usual directness.

"The Sight." Uma's chocolate eyes ran over him. "I'm guessing it's not natural."

Zeke didn't say a word.

"Have a seat," Louis said as he sat down behind his desk. Uma leaned on the ledge of the window sill behind the desk beside Louis. Zeke and I took the two chairs in front of the desk.

"I think it's time for you to talk," Louis stated, his eyes sharp.

Zeke sat a little straighter.

"I think we both need to come clean about what we know." I met his gaze unflinching. The tension stretched. Uma shifted.

"You're right," Louis sighed. "Especially now. Last night, there was an incident at a restaurant. The council attacked civilians."

My heart dropped. "What?"

"What do you mean attacked?" Zeke leaned forward in his chair.

"Magic affects norms differently, unless of course they've had training as a magic user." Louis explained. "A normal person can get hit with a pure energy blast and be fine. They'll trip over nothing, lose their footing, but they'll be fine. But if it's a lot of energy... they'll get a fever, dizzy, nauseous, their white blood cell count will go off the charts."

"On the news, they reported that people were admitted to Tulane Medical Center," Zeke said.

Louis nodded. "Exactly. What we have found from the surveillance footage is that two witches and two warlocks entered the restaurant. They ate and before they left, they discreetly threw a great deal of energy around. People were immediately ill; two people were knocked unconscious. They slipped out in the confusion."

"Why?" I asked, there had to be a reason. "And how the hell did you get the footage?"

"We have connections," Uma said cryptically.

Louis's gaze went to me. "We received a message from the council's representatives that they won't stop until we surrender and join them."

"So, they're using normals as hostages?" Zeke growled. "What the hell is that going to get them?"

"We don't know," Uma admitted as her gaze turned to me. "But it has made your arrival rather suspicious."

Tension filled the room as I met her gaze. Zeke clenched his fists.

"I'm not with them." I wasn't even mad, just annoyed. "I'm a Necromancer, not a witch."

"She's right about that." Louis's eyes narrowed on me. "A Necromancer with surprising contacts."

It was my turn to give up some info. I explained to him about Isaac becoming possessed by a demon. How Evelyn saved us both from dying painfully and that I was still in contact with them.

By the end, Uma was standing beside her husband's chair, her eyes calculating. "That is quite the story."

Louis nodded. "That makes sense, though how you got ahold of the gargoyles is beyond me. They've been missing in action for at least a hundred years."

"Two hundred, at least according to Evelyn," I said.

"We don't need their help," Uma stated. "We've been protecting ourselves for years."

Louis sighed. "Uma, if this turns into war, do you want the children in the middle of it? Or with people who can help and protect them?"

"It won't get that far," Uma stated with confidence.

"What's stopping it from getting that bad?" I asked, crossing my legs.

Uma tilted her head to the side and eyed me. "You don't need to know everything."

Louis sighed and turned back to me. "Now, the Veil. What do you know about that?"

I met Zeke's eyes then turned back to Louis. "It's shut. And it was done deliberately by a magic user. The dead can't cross on their own anymore."

Louis said something in French, this time I was positive it was cursing. "That explains a lot."

"If that pressure builds..." Uma shook her head.

"It's a time bomb," Louis agreed.

"It's not building." I licked my lips and made a decision. "I've managed a link to the Veil. At the moment, I'm the only way to cross the dead."

They both looked at me with varying degrees of shock.

"You can cross the dead right now?" Louis asked.

"Yes."

He eyed me. "Do you understand what would happen if you weren't able to cross the dead?"

I nodded. "The barriers would break; Heaven and Hell would pour into this world."

His eyes were worried as they met mine. "What's that doing to your health?"

I resisted the urge to fidget. "Apparently, using my body as a gateway sped up the process."

"How large is the spot now?" Louis asked.

"It doesn't matter anymore," I said. "The dead can't touch me."

Uma's shoulders straightened. "What do you mean?"

I held Louis's gaze. "They can't jump me. I don't get nosebleeds anymore, I don't bleed from the ears, and I'm no longer amassing brain damage."

"How?" Louis asked. I explained to him about the ward tattoo that Evelyn had made for me. When I finished, Louis's face was thoughtful. Uma's was excited.

"Mon amour..." Uma said in a soft voice.

Louis turned to her. "We'll talk about it later."

Uma's eyes flashed. "Later?"

"When we're alone," Louis suggested.

Uma huffed, clearly not happy with him. She turned to me. "Is there any way for Louis to get these wards?"

Louis bristled.

"I could ask Evelyn. I don't see why she'd say no." I turned to Louis. "Especially, if he can start working on his own link to the Veil."

Louis went still. "I don't know about that."

"If you can help cross the dead, then we can get the Veil back open faster and get everything back to normal," I countered.

"She has a point," Uma added.

He shot her a look. "Who in this room are you married to?"

"You hardly ever leave the house anymore," Uma said. "You're barely able to get through town and when you do your nose and ears start to bleed."

"We can discuss this another time." Louis's voice was firm. He turned back to me. "Now, are you crossing the dead here?"

"I'm trying." I leaned forward. "No one wants to cross. And that's a problem I haven't run into before."

"Yes, the dead in New Orleans are, well, this *is* New Orleans." Uma smiled. "We're unique."

"Yeah, they're lively. Unfortunately, they're also possessing people," I announced.

Louis sat up straight. "What?"

"Last night, I watched the soul of a man jump a woman and walk off in her body." I still could barely believe it.

Louis was cursing again. "We need to stop them."

"My friends are making kits," I began. "One of them came up with it when I was getting a lot of nosebleeds. The kit contains salt and holy water. Pour either of those into a possessed person's mouth and the ghost is kicked out immediately."

Louis eyed me. "That's rather clever."

"I thought so too, it's saved my ass a couple of times," I admitted.

"Have you ever seen... a purple ribbon?" he asked carefully.

I grinned. "Yeah, but mine's gold. It's how I grab the dead and take them to the Veil."

Louis nodded. "Good, you might have to go out, wrangle some souls and force them to move on."

I cringed. "Force them? I've only done that once and it hurt like hell."

"You can think about it. But I have a feeling that's the only way you'll clear the dead out of the Quarter, let alone the city," he said.

I sighed. "I don't like it, but you might be right."

"At the moment, we've been..." He glanced at Uma then back to me. "We've been in defense mode. But if you can thin the herd a bit, we'd appreciate it."

"I'll do what I can." I met his gaze. "How big is your spot?"

He sighed. "Around a dime."

"It's doubled in size since souls stopped crossing," Uma supplied.

"How did you manage so little damage?" I asked. "Everyone in my family died before they hit thirty."

"My family has kept meticulous records," he explained. "It was mostly a process of elimination over centuries."

"So, beads, warding symbols..."

He nodded. "Herbs, salt, some spell work by Uma of course."

"Spells? I haven't tried that. How's that work?" I asked leaning forward again.

"I can't manage it," he sighed. "Uma has tried to teach me but I can't manage to get it down."

"Necromancy is different from other energy manipulation," Uma announced. "Where you use will, we collect and use energy."

"That's what I do in the Veil, kind of," I said, running it over in my head.

Uma raised an eyebrow. "Really?"

I nodded. "It was the only way I could manipulate the Veil."

"Interesting." Uma eyed me.

All this shop talk was nice but I needed some answers. I turned to Uma. "How is it a witch isn't answering to the Witch's Council?"

Louis and Uma shared a look before Uma turned back to me. "My mother raised me outside the council's influence. They didn't exactly like her."

"Why's that?" Zeke asked.

"Well, my mother didn't like the way they did things and left." She grinned. "She was a strong enough witch that they had no choice but to let her leave."

"What are they actually like?" I asked. "All I've ever heard was they kill Necros when they raise the dead."

"That's on par for them," Uma admitted. "They like that maneuver."

Great. I still needed answers. I turned back to Louis as every question I ever wanted to ask poured through my mind. But one new one was bugging the crap out of me. "What the hell is up with that... skin thing?"

"What skin thing?" Uma asked.

Louis shifted and looked down at the desk. "I did some research, it seems-"

"What skin thing?" Zeke demanded. Oh shit.

I looked down at my toes poking out of my sandals. "Uh... oh.... um..."

"It's nothing," Louis announced, saving me. "Just a reaction due to the both of us being Necromancers."

I looked up and met Louis's eyes. That sensation slid over my skin like oil. My stomach rolled. The guy was almost fifty. Even he looked uncomfortable. "How do you know that?"

Uma looked down at Louis with an eye raised. "Louis?"

"There's an old entry in one of my great-great-grandfather's journals," Louis began again. "Apparently, at some point he ran into a female Necromancer with red hair-"

"What reaction?" Zeke asked.

"Does it go away?" I demanded, dragging Louis's attention back to me.

He nodded. "Yes, the entry said the sensation occurs because we're the opposite sex, and that it will eventually disappear. It's simply a physiological reaction."

"Good," I breathed, relaxing against the back of the chair. "Because this is...." I made a grossed-out face.

He nodded. "Disturbing? I agree."

"What the fuck are you two talking about?" Zeke's voice was barely above a growl.

I turned to him with my face burning. His eyes were starting to glow. Shit. "Zeke, it's just..." How the hell could I explain this? "Remember the weird feeling I got before I spotted Louis in the café?"

His eyes held mine as he nodded once.

"Well, that's what we're talking about." I turned back to the others hoping that would be the end of it. "Okay, rotting souls." I shifted in my chair. "How far along have you seen them?"

"Pretty far along." Louis latched onto the change in topic. "The worst was one man with several limbs barely holding on."

"Have you noticed any of them disappearing?" I asked. "Do you think this could, I don't know, kill their souls?"

He shook his head. "All I've seen is souls losing their sense of self and going mad. Nothing else."

I nodded. That made sense but... the question still lingered in the back of my mind. What would happen if they rotted out completely? Past the level of Mary Summers? I put it out of my mind for now, focusing on the questions I needed to know the answers to. "Aren't all the dead causing transformers and power outages around the city?"

"Yes, it's quite annoying when the air conditioning goes out," Uma answered for him.

Louis rubbed his temple. "I think that's enough for today."

"We'll meet you here tomorrow," Uma stated.

Zeke and I got to our feet, said our goodbyes and left.

We made it down the street before he asked. "What the hell is this weird feeling?" Oh, fuck me.

CHAPTER 8

JULY 13TH, FRIDAY AFTERNOON

*A*fter a bus ride that seemed much longer than should be possible, and assuring Zeke that I was alright a few hundred times. I was walking down the street with Asher back toward the hotel.

"Oh my God," I managed around my mouthful of deliciousness.

"I know, they're so good," Asher said as we both munched on our own orders of beignets. The fried sugar powder covered pieces of heaven were fucking delicious!

"Okay, my life is over. Nothing can be this good," I said after I finished my last bite. "It's all downhill from here."

He chuckled as he threw his box into a trash can and dusted the sugar off his hands. I tossed mine and did the same.

"I'll have to learn how to make those," Asher said.

"I'm torn between begging you to and begging you not to," I said thoughtfully. "I don't know if my waistline can take it."

"Who said I was going to share?" he teased.

I gasped at him in mock horror.

He pulled me to a stop. "Wait, you've got some sugar…" He leaned down; my heart jumped. He stopped just as his breath danced across my lips. He pulled back, his eyes were warm as he met mine. His smile disappeared.

"I can't just be friends with you, Ally."

"What?"

His hands moved to my waist and pulled me closer. "I'm talking about us."

My heart slammed in my chest as my hands went to his arms.

"I care about you. And you care about me. That's all that matters," he said, his rich baritone voice softened.

Oh God.... Was he saying? No, no, no, no.... "What are you saying? Exactly?"

"I want you," he said. "I know it'll be hard with Zeke for a while but I can't just walk away when I know who I want to be with."

"Ash…" Don't, please don't…

"Ally, will you go out me?"

My lungs seized, my heart dropped and heat curled through me. I bit my tongue to stop myself from blurting out yes. Shit! Shit! Shit! Zeke... Isaac... Asher... Ethan, oh fuck.

"It's not that easy," I hedged. What the fuck was I going to say?

"I know it's not. But I know Zeke," he said. "All we have to do is tell him it's what we want and he'll work it out."

"Oh no, no, no," I didn't even think have to think about it. "We're not telling Zeke shit."

His eyes ran over me, his hold loosened. "You like Zeke." His hands dropped from me as he stepped back.

My heart ached. "Ash..."

His eyes were rough as he turned and walked away.

I went after him. "Asher-"

"I'm a fucking idiot," he bit out. "Of course you like Zeke, if you liked me you would have been straight with him."

"It's not that simple," I tried again.

"You could have just told me." He stretched his longer legs and walked faster.

I fell behind. I couldn't let it happen like this. "I have feelings for both of you!"

Asher stopped on the sidewalk.

I caught up to him, my heart hammering in my chest.

He turned and looked down at me. "What did you just say?"

"I have feelings for both of you." My voice shook as I finally told him.

"That's not possible," he muttered.

I huffed. "I wish that was true."

He stepped closer again. "You care about us both? As more than friends?"

I chewed on the corner of my lower lip and nodded.

"Since when?"

"For a while now." I looked down at my fingers fidgeting.

He was silent for a couple of minutes until he finally said, "You're going to have to make a choice."

I lifted my head, my gaze snapped to his. My chest burned at the thought. "I...I..." My lungs seemed to stop working. I took shallow breaths as everything was suddenly just too much. Isaac, Ethan, Zeke and now Asher... This was a disaster. Everything was going to end... The enormity of my mistakes hit me like a train. Leaving my heart in pieces on the sidewalk.

His eyes grew wider, his hands went to my shoulders. "Breathe, Ally."

Tears filled my eyes as I tried to get control but it wasn't happening. Zeke will find out. Then Isaac. And everything would be over. They'll hate me. What the fuck have I done?

Asher's warm hands pulled me to him, I buried my face in his chest as I struggled. He wrapped his arms around me and ran his hand down my hair. "It's okay, Ally girl. Just breathe for me. Slow deep breaths." I did as he said, my fingers clinging to his shirt. "That's it." He held me as I got myself under control again.

When I could, I stepped back and met his eyes. "I'm sorry. I didn't know how to tell anyone-"

"I get it," he assured me. "But it can't stay this way."

I nodded. He was right. I was running out of time. What the fuck was I going to do?

. . .

AFTER GETTING BACK WITH ASHER, Miles said we had somewhere to go. That place was a large mall. It wasn't to go shopping, at least not the fun kind. Nope, this was reading glasses shopping.

"I don't think I need them," I repeated myself for the fifth time.

"Lexie, the doctor said you needed them," Miles reminded me.

"It's not that big of a deal."

"What's so bad about glasses?" Miles asked, his voice hurt.

I cringed. Shit. "Nothing, I just-"

"Are they unattractive?" he asked in the same voice. "Do they make people look bad?"

"Fuck no, Miles," I answered adamantly. "They're sexy as hell, that's not the issue." It took me a heartbeat to realize what I had said. I turned to Miles, who was repressing a smile. "Oh, that's mean."

He started laughing. "It's nice to know what you think."

"You're evil." My face caught fire as he continued to chuckle.

"I learned from the best." He started to sober. "What is it that has you so resistant to this?"

I sighed. "I did the damage to myself."

"You got a concussion, Lexie," he said.

"Yeah, and I didn't do what Dr. Zimmer wanted me to do." I countered.

Miles reached over and took my hand. "Do you regret not going to the medical wing?"

"No." I didn't even have to think about it. There was no way I would have left Isaac or Ethan.

"Then there is nothing else you could have done," he said in his silky-smooth timbre. I hated when he was right.

After my appointment, we were in a seating section outside the store. The couches were pretty comfortable as he messed with his phone. I was too busy worrying about Asher, Zeke and Isaac. Would Asher tell Zeke? No, probably not. But would he talk to Isaac? I ran my hand down my face.

"Something on your mind?" Miles asked as he set his phone down.

Not knowing how to answer I made something up. "Do you think we could find a salsa club?"

He tucked his phone in his pocket as he eyed me. "We can go salsa dancing tomorrow, if you like?"

I gave him a smile. "Really?"

"You've been practicing, it'd be a shame not to go out." He smiled.

Feeling better, I looked around the mall, my heart slammed in my chest. Polo guy from yesterday was walking toward us.

"Miles."

He looked where I was looking, and grew still. As polo guy came closer, Miles got to his feet and reached out to pull me to mine. "Lexie, will you go in the store, please?"

"Not without you," I answered.

His fingers tightened on mine as polo shirt guy reached us. His gaze went straight to me. "Alexis Delaney, 732 Lakeside Drive, Spring Mountain, Montana. Only child, seventeen years old and a Necromancer." My heart raced as he gave a cocky grin. "Did I miss anything?"

"You can Google," Miles stated, his voice neutral. "Good for you."

Polo shirt guy turned to him, eyed him then turned back to me dismissing Miles. "The point is, the council already knows who you are, knows what you can do. There will be no disappearing from us."

"Congrats, you're at creepy stalker level now," I said calmly, holding my temper. "Now, what the fuck do you want?"

The cocky grin was back. "We want you to join the Witch's Council. Learn from us, let us protect you. We can help you accomplish so much."

"Have a lot of Necromancers in your council, do you?" I asked, the sarcasm dripped from my voice.

His grin faded. "Magic is magic, we have experienced magic users who can teach you."

"In other words, no, you don't have any Necromancers," Miles answered for me.

I looked up at him. "Probably because they keep killing them off."

He met my gaze. "Besides being rare, that's the most likely answer, yes."

We turned back to polo shirt guy.

He ignored Miles again. "You need to understand the reality of the way things are." He stepped closer.

I let go of Miles's hand as I shifted my feet into a better defensive position. Miles had done the same but he also placed himself between me and polo shirt.

"Look, if it was up to me, I wouldn't bother. But upper management says to give you the pitch, so shut up and listen. The council will have control of the United States within a year. You're either going to join us now, or later."

"Or not at all," I added. "I choose the third option."

"You don't get that option," he countered. "By being a magic user, you are under our jurisdiction already."

I grinned. Oh, I loved it when people assumed I didn't know anything. "First. I'm not a magic user, I'm a Necro. And no, I'm not. I can *not* join your merry band of power-hungry assholes, not be taught by you, and answer to the gargoyles. Or just make a call and ask them to intervene."

His eyes were full of surprise but only for a heartbeat, then they were appraising. "You'd have to be able to find them. They're on the verge of extinction. You will have to pick a side in this conflict. We have more numbers, we have more knowledge, and we have more resources."

I was done. I stepped closer to him. "I'll never choose a side that attacks people and puts children in the hospital."

He grinned. "My superiors will be sorry to hear that."

"Now, leave me the fuck alone," I growled.

He shook his head. "As long as you're in New Orleans, you'll be in the fight. What happens from here on out, is up to you." He turned and strode out of the mall doors.

When the doors closed behind polo shirt, we both relaxed.

"Well, he was cheerful," I smiled up at Miles.

Miles's gaze was still on the doors. "They're getting aggressive."

"How the hell did they find out I'm a Necro?" I muttered, watching the door with him.

Miles turned and met my eyes. "Serena? She's a witch, it's possible that she reports to the Witch's Council. And there are only a few Necros around."

It made sense, since Serena did threaten me with them. "Probably."

His eyes narrowed on mine. "We'll find a way to keep them at arm's length."

I nodded.

Miles's phone alarm went off. "Let's go, your glasses should be ready."

We headed back into the store. He was right. It wasn't five minutes later I was sitting in front of a mirror and holding the new pair of glasses.

"Now, try them on and we'll get the fit right," the saleswoman said.

I sighed, slipped them on and looked in the mirror. They looked... good. The rectangular lenses weren't too big or too small. The black rim frames contrasted with my skin and hair but it wasn't in a bad way. Though they were pinching into my head a bit.

I pulled them off and told her. The sales woman went to adjust them. Miles raised an eyebrow.

"Okay, yeah, I like them," I admitted. "I'm just afraid I'm going to break them."

He smiled. "They're stronger than they look. Once Zeke sat on my glasses, the frames were a bit bent but nothing unfixable."

"Good, I'm clumsy," I muttered. Miles didn't deny it, which made me smile. The woman came back with my glasses. They fit better now.

When I went to pay she handed me an eyeglass case and a receipt.

"I... haven't paid," I told her, certain it was a mistake.

"Your friend gave us his credit card while you were looking at frames earlier." She informed me.

I turned and sent Miles a look.

He shrugged. "I wanted you to get the pair you wanted."

I couldn't figure out how to say what I needed to until we were out of the store and heading for the exit. "Thank you, Miles. But you don't need to spend money on me. I mean, it's bad enough you won't let anyone pay for their meals or the hotel on this trip. You don't need to go adding to it."

"I've had this conversation several times with Zeke, usually after I have to call Dr. Zimmer to come look at him." He grinned. "I like to be useful, Lexie. I like to help and take care of the people around me."

"But you don't need to take care of me. Or us for that matter." I realized how I sounded. "It's not that I'm not grateful, I am. It's just..."

"You're independent. And that's important to you." He finished for me.

"Yeah." All but cringing. I didn't want to insult Miles, or make him feel bad but...

"For me, it's how I know to show I care," he said in a quiet voice. "I spend money on people I care about, I get them things they need. It's how I was raised. I don't know any other way to show I care about someone."

I wrapped my arm around his and leaned my temple against his shoulder. "The stuff isn't what we need, Miles. It's you. Whenever one of us has trouble, you're there. You help us through our shit. That's what we love."

"I don't know any other way," he admitted.

I squeezed his arm. "What do you think we would do if you were broke?"

He was silent for several heartbeats. "I'm... not sure."

"Can I let you in on a secret?" I stage whispered.

"Yes."

"We'd still need you if you were broke, Nemo."

Asher

THE AQUARIUM WAS FUN, at least it was for us. In addition to seeing all the animals, we got to watch as Claire ran through the glass and swam with them. It was funny as hell to watch a five-foot tiger shark swim away from Claire as she came through the glass. The penguins seemed puzzled and tried to figure the ghost out. Claire couldn't stop giggling about it. It made it hard for us to keep a straight face. Well, for the others. I was still reeling that Ally liked Zeke back. After her panic attack, I let the subject drop. We walked all the way back to the hotel in silence. Miles took her off somewhere before I could think of anything to say.

I didn't know how this happened or what she was going to decide. I guess I needed to talk to her. What was there to say? She knew I wanted to be with her and she had a choice to make. Though when she started to have that panic attack... it might not be as easy as her choosing Zeke or me. Ally was terrified of everyone leaving her and the situation wasn't going to help.

Ethan pulled out his phone and started filming Claire as she swam with a dolphin.

"What are you doing?" I asked as Claire twirled in the water.

"Taking video for Lexie, she'll get a kick out of this," Ethan said, smiling as he watched Claire.

"She might not show up on camera," I pointed out.

He shrugged. "We'll never know unless we try."

Someone tapped my shoulder.

Isaac was there, a strained look on his face. "Can I talk to you?"

"Yeah," I said before we moved about ten feet from Ethan to another exhibit. "What's going on?"

Isaac opened his mouth then closed it again. His face was pale as he tried again. "What did I say to you in Boulder?"

It wasn't a surprise. Miles had warned me earlier that Isaac was trying to understand what happened in Colorado. "Not much," I admitted. "You mostly spoke to Ally, Ethan and Zeke."

Isaac cursed. "Do you have any idea what I said to Zeke?"

I hesitated, we were both thinking the same thing. "Only Zeke knows. He never said anything about it."

Isaac cursed again before meeting my gaze. "Asher... I'm sorry about all of it. About Boulder, the fucking demon-"

"Did you go looking for the demon?" I asked, acting confused.

"No." He sighed. "But I let it in, I let it-"

"Isaac." My voice was sharp, getting his attention. "You didn't let anything in. You had a hole in your defenses. You keep blaming yourself for everything that goes wrong and its utter crap."

"I created that hole-"

"Yeah, you did," I told him. "The way you were thinking did it. And you're still thinking that way. Own that."

His eyes snapped to mine.

"But you still blame yourself for Sophie, you still blame yourself for what the demon did while you were being possessed." I stepped closer so I wouldn't be over heard. "None of that was your fault. Stop picking up crap that belongs to other people."

"I don't remember being any other way," he muttered.

"I do. I remember the summer before the car accident. We were at football practice and Jason plowed into me." I shook my head. "He grabbed my face mask and broke his fingers during the tackle."

"I remember that," Isaac admitted, watching the fish swam by. "You thought it was your fault."

"Yeah, and it wasn't. Jason was the one to grab my mask. Jason was the one who tackled me." I took a breath. "You reminded me that Jason made a choice to do something illegal and he just had to deal with the consequences."

Isaac was looking at the floor.

"You didn't always blame yourself for everything, Isaac," I reminded him. "Before the wreck you knew what was true and what wasn't. You were a cocky shit who loved pulling pranks on us."

Isaac snorted.

"You were also a great friend." I laid it all out on the table. "You have been a good friend since but... you've been half dead since the wreck. And all we could do was watch from the sidelines as you slowly tried to destroy yourself."

Isaac looked away and wiped his face.

"No one blames you for what happened in Boulder or leading up to it." I told him. "So, stop blaming yourself."

"I'm trying," he mumbled.

"Good," I said. "Because we've missed your stinky ass."

We both chuckled. It was only a couple of minutes more before we headed back to Ethan, Zeke and the other exhibits. We were just in time to watch Claire ride a dolphin like a horse. Now, only if things with Ally were that easy.

Lexie

"FIGHT THROUGH THE EXHAUSTION," Zahur snapped.

I used every bit of focus I had left to blast him back. Brad Pitt, the body Zahur was wearing today, went flying. I dropped to my knees, dragging air into my lungs.

We had been at it for at least an hour. I was tired, aching and about to start yelling at Zahur who was getting to his feet in the waist high grass.

"Good!" He flipped the long hair the actor had in Interview with the Vampire. "You focused enough to last as long as you could."

"Yeah, great," I gasped then dropped to the grass. I looked up at the Way and tried to give my body time to get a second wind. Zahur stood over me, grinning that Hollywood smile. I was really getting tired of his endless supply of bodies. At least today he wasn't Ghandi. It wasn't easy trying to beat the crap out of someone who was known as a pacifist.

"At least if the other one comes back you'll be able to fight them off," he pointed out.

I sighed. Since the whole almost dying in Boulder thing, Zahur had been on my ass three times a week. Teaching me how to fight in the Veil, building my endurance. I was improving but I was still getting my ass kicked. I sat up and glared at him.

Zahur let his blade dissipate and put his hands on his hips. "Now, what were you saying about the Witch's Council?"

I began to explain why I was in New Orleans. I only got a few sentences out before Zahur's head snapped up, his eyes unfocused.

"Sorry. I have to go," he said a heartbeat before he disappeared. I cursed. That shit. With nothing else to do, I pulled out of the Veil.

I opened my eyes in the physical world and got up, grumbling about Zahur.

Raised voices came from the living room.

I opened my bedroom door to find Isaac and Ethan were in the living room. Ethan was stretched out on the couch. Claire sat perched on the arm of the couch, her eyes wide.

"Estoy harto de tu mierda!" Isaac shouted.

Ethan glared up at him then closed his eyes and gritted his teeth.

"Isaac." I stepped further into the room. "Miles and I spotted a skate park yesterday. Want to go?"

Isaac came around the sofa and picked up his board by the foyer. He took my hand and we were out the door in a heartbeat. Not waiting for the elevator, we hurried down the stairs and out onto the street. He didn't slow down until we were a block away.

"Are you okay?" I asked, squeezing his hand.

He took a deep breath and let it out slowly. "I'm so sick of him. I'm the one who almost died, I was the fucking one who had to watch Sophie die. Yeah, he fucked up his back. Yeah, it sucks. But fuck!" He ran his hand through his hair, his fingers digging into his scalp. "He's not the only one who has shit to deal with and I'm fucking sick of his shit!"

I wrapped my arm around his and gave him a squeeze. "You need to talk to him."

"I don't want to hear his woe is me bullshit," he bit out. "Ever since the fucking wreck, anytime he's hurting *I* feel guilty. Why the fuck do I feel guilty when I watched her die?"

"Just because you weren't seriously hurt doesn't mean you should feel guilty-"

"I know, Red. I've spent enough time talking to Miles in the last few weeks." He sighed, pulled his arm back so my hand slid down his forearm to his. He squeezed tight. "I'm just... I get what I must have said to him hurt him, but fuck."

There wasn't anything I could say except the truth. "You need to talk to each other."

"Good fucking luck," he bit out. I sighed, if they didn't start talking soon I was going to have to look for more tourist spots to take the twins. I had a feeling I was going to be taking a lot of walks.

I shook his hand and made him look down at me. "Hey, we're away from him so you can calm down and relax."

He took a deep breath and let it out slowly as we reached the bus stop just in time to catch the bus. We moved onto the almost full bus and ended up standing.

He looked down at me. "So, what kind of hijinks can I get up to at the park?"

I bit back a smile. Isaac's stunts had been getting more and more dangerous over the last few months. He finally admitted that he couldn't tell what was dangerous and what was a challenge. So now he asked.

"Do what you normally do at the skate park, Cookie Monster." I smiled up at him. The corner of his lips lifted into a half grin.

The bus took a hard turn, throwing me into his chest. I chuckled as he wrapped his arm around my waist and held me tight against him. His grin turned into a smile.

"What?" I breathed.

"I'm just happy I can kiss you without worrying that the guys might see," he whispered. My fingers tingled. I began to counter but his lips found the corner of mine with a quick chaste kiss. Sparks shot through me, the scent of limes surrounded me. He was smirking as he lifted his head.

I stepped back from him and turned around to face the front of the bus. It was the only safe thing to do. Asher. Zeke. Isaac. Ethan. Miles. Why all five?

The skate park was pretty awesome. It was under a bridge which was going to make watching Isaac a little difficult. Isaac was practically bouncing by the time we stepped off the bus.

"Go, I'll find a spot," I told him with a smile.

He hesitated. "You sure? I can give you another lesson."

"Oh no. I like my feet on the ground," I teased. "Go, I'll stay within shouting distance."

He broke out into a big smile before he wrapped his arm around my shoulders and kept walking with me.

"I thought you were running off?" I asked as he stayed beside me.

"Actually, I figured we could talk before I went out," he explained as we reached the park. Isaac took me to a spot where people could watch. It was raised and had a railing to keep people from getting too close to the skaters. And he could probably see me from anywhere in the park. It was sweet how worried he was about my safety. Isaac settled against the rail next to me, his shoulder and leg pressing against mine.

"What did you want to talk about?" I asked, watching the other skaters do their thing.

"Lexie." He used my name. I turned to meet those amber eyes. "I want to tell the guys."

Time stopped. No... no, no, no. This wasn't happening. Not him too... "About what?"

He grinned. "About you and me."

I started tapping my fingers against the railing. "It's not that easy..."

"Yeah, I know someone else has feelings for you too. But, the longer this goes on the worse it'll be for everyone." He had no idea how right he was.

"I.. I..." I couldn't seem to get a sentence out.

He cringed. "I'm not trying to pressure you. Don't think I'm saying we have to tell them now. I'm just saying..." He sighed and looked out at the park. "Lexie, I have to tell the guys anyway. We..." He turned back to me. "We have a no dating you rule in effect."

It took me almost half a minute before what he said sunk in. Then I started laughing. Everyone but Miles had broken that rule, at least cracked it by kissing me. It took me awhile to calm down. Isaac was shaking his head as I wiped tears from my face.

"I thought it was ridiculous too but... Miles thought it was a good idea," he said.

The burning in my chest sobered me fast. What did I expect? I wasn't the kind of girl he went for.... Lexie, what the hell? You have Isaac wanting to tell the guys, Zeke... I had no clue where I was with Zeke. Ethan still didn't remember anything. And you have Asher knowing about Zeke. That's enough!

"I, uh, I need some time to figure things out." I turned back to him. "So, can you just not say anything until I do?" As if that was going to happen, I'm more tangled up than a string of Christmas lights.

"Yeah, yeah. I just wanted to start us talking about it." He swallowed hard before he took my hand. "You know I'm not going anywhere, right?"

I squeezed his hand and gave him a small warm smile. "I know. I just don't want anyone to get hurt."

He squeezed back. "Neither do I."

"Aren't you supposed to be skateboarding?" I asked, teasing him.

He grinned as he leaned closer. "Kissing you is better than skateboarding." He moved in, his lips taking mine. My breathing hitched as I kissed him back. His hand cupped my face as he slowly pulled back. His eyes were bright as he grabbed his skateboard and jumped over the rail to hurry toward the skate section.

I took a deep breath and let it out slowly. He wanted to tell the others. Panic gripped me. I focused on breathing. In. Out. In. Out. What the fuck was I going to do? Okay, he said he'd wait until I was ready but... how the hell was I going to fix this?

Isaac started skateboarding, doing tricks and grinding down rails. He was good, really good. As he let off some steam, my mind continued to worry. If I picked one of the guys to date, who would it be? And what would the consequences be?

I still didn't have an answer when, an hour later, my phone chimed.

Nemo: So, I take it the twins had another fight?

Alexis: Yeah, I dragged Isaac out to the skate park we saw yesterday.

Nemo: Did you get anything from Isaac?

Alexis: He's angry at Ethan and not just about the way he's acting lately. He's also mad about the way Ethan has been since the crash.

Nemo: In a way, that's good. He's been pushing that down for a long time. But he is talking about how he feels?

Alexis: Yeah, a little.

Nemo: Good. Maybe he will finally deal with everything he's been avoiding since the accident.

I chewed on the corner of my bottom lip.

Alexis: You should still talk to him about it. I have no idea how to help with this one.

Nemo: Just listen to him. He's finally talking and not keeping things to himself.

Alexis: You got it.

Nemo: Do you know how long you two will be? We're making dinner plans.

I lifted my head and searched the park. I found him at a half pipe, grinding along the edge before riding back down the side.

Alexis: I'll see if he wants to head back.

I eyed the skating section, it was getting really busy. Deciding not to risk looking for him, I sent him a text instead.

Alexis: If you're ready, Asher found a restaurant he wants everyone to have dinner at.

I was waiting for him to check his phone when a man shuffled up the walkway. He was disheveled, an unkempt beard covered his face. His suit was rumbled and stained as if he'd slept in it for days. I made a point to ignore him as he shuffled up the ramp.

"Light, the light," he muttered.

My phone vibrated.

Cookie Monster: On my way back.

The man shuffled onto the main section. "Moving, moving, moving things in my head. Too much, too much."

I shifted, keeping the odd man in my sight while pretending to mess with my phone. He moved closer. I stepped away and tucked my phone into my pocket as I eyed him. His eyes were unfocused as if he was seeing something I wasn't. Something about him bothered me, something just wasn't right. I looked for Isaac and spotted him on his way toward me.

"Light, so pretty," the man mumbled. I turned back, he was only a step away. Not even thinking, I moved back again several feet. The man reached for me. "Light…" He grabbed my wrist.

"Hey! Let her go!" Isaac shouted. Other shouts followed. I moved my hand over his knuckles, holding his hand to mine. I swung my arm in a circle, rotating my wrist so I could grip his. Off balance, he bent over. I pushed on his arm forcing him to his knees. My training told me to let go and run, but Isaac was coming. I held him in place, pulse racing.

"It hurts, it hurts," the man cried.

"That's what happens when you fucking grab girls," I snapped.

Isaac vaulted over the railing and grabbed the man by the back of his suit jacket and jerked him away from me. He planted himself between me and the crazy man.

The man's eyes were still unfocused. "So bright, so shiny…"

The other skaters at the park reached us and got between us and the man. It was clear he wasn't all there, so they simply forced him to walk down the ramp.

Isaac turned to me, his hand moved along my lower back. "Are you okay?"

I nodded. "He was muttering some crazy shit when he grabbed me."

One of the other guys chuckled. "Yeah, your girl already had him on his knees."

Isaac's pulled me closer as he turned to the others. "What the hell was with that guy?"

Another guy shook his head. "I don't know, there are a lot more crazies around lately."

"What do you mean?" I asked.

"The last couple of weeks, more and more crazies are showing up." He shrugged. "Just be careful. The cops aren't doing shit about it."

The other skaters headed back to the park.

One of them handed Isaac the board that he'd dropped. "Thanks, man."

Isaac and I made our way to the stairs then made a point to walk in the opposite direction the man had taken.

"What did that guy say?" Isaac asked, not letting me go.

"He was muttering about a light." I shook my head. The way the man's eyes were unfocused... a chill ran down my back.

"Who's telling Zeke?" Isaac asked.

I touched my nose. "Not it!"

Isaac was too slow, he cursed.

ASHER FOUND a Cajun restaurant that he wanted us to try. The place was nice, and airy. The tall windows open to let in the evening breeze.

I had just opened my menu when Miles said. "Reading glasses, Lexie."

I cursed and pulled them out of my pocket. I slipped them on and tried to ignore the stares of the guys. After several heartbeats I had enough. "Stop staring."

The guys chuckled as they stopped watching me.

"They're cute, Red," Isaac offered.

"Yeah, yeah," I muttered as I concentrated more than I ever needed to on reading the menu.

Dinner went on. The food was fantastic, even if the conversation was a little sparse. Asher hadn't really said anything since he ordered, the same with Isaac. That left the conversation to Miles, Zeke, Ethan and me. I had given up on getting the others to join in before our entrees even came.

Everyone had finished when I looked out the window and spotted them. A woman with her child holding her hand, he couldn't have been older than three, was walking down the sidewalk. The spirit of a woman followed her closely with an odd gleam in her eye. Instinct had me on my feet before I knew it. So when the ghost jumped the mother, I was already moving. The guys asked me what was going on as I jumped out of the open French window and onto the sidewalk.

"Lexie!" Someone barked, I ignored them. The ghost spotted me, dropped the child's hand and ran through the crowd. I hauled ass after her. The little boy started crying. The cursing behind me told me that one of the guys was there.

"Take care of the kid!" I ordered as I continued to weave through the crowd. The woman had to have been a runner because she had stamina. Ignoring the strange looks and nasty glares, I kept on her heels until she made a wrong turn into a dead end. I skidded to a stop on the cobblestones, my heart pounding, taking deep breaths trying to get my breath back.

The woman's eyes glowed with a strange silver ring around her irises. That was new. I patted my front pocket where I had stashed a vial of holy water.

The woman grinned a sick, twisted smile. "Get outta my way, meat bag."

I tilted my head to the side and smiled. It wasn't my nice one. "Get out of that woman and you can walk away."

She giggled a manic, not-all-there giggle. "Or what?"

"Do you know what I am?" I asked in my dead voice.

"Some psychic who wants to help us poor souls cross over," she jeered.

"Oh, no, sweetie." I let myself feel. Anger poured through me. This bitch just made a mother abandon her kid on a packed street. My chest was solid and strong. "I'm a Necromancer."

Her face grew pale. My golden ribbon of will snapped out and wrapped around her arms holding her in place. Her eyes grew wide as she realized her mistake. I moved to stand in front of her, pulled the vial out, and opened it. She tried to dodge me but I held her face in my other hand, forcing her to open her mouth. I poured the holy water down her throat. The woman fell unconscious. The ghost was thrown out of the poor woman. I let the living woman go and grabbed the bitch in a thick ribbon. She struggled as running footsteps came into the alley.

"We're going for a ride." I dropped down to the Veil, dragging her with me. This time it didn't hurt. No cuts, no scratches, no resistance.

It wasn't bad. I landed in the Veil and let go of the soul quickly. I didn't need to hold onto her anymore. The vines of the Veil were already wrapping around her and draining her of all the extra energy. She screamed long and loud. When it was over, she looked like a normal person. Except that hint of madness was still in her eyes. She took a step toward me. I dropped my barriers a little and conjured a blade in my hand. She stopped.

"This is the Veil," I told her. "You have a choice. Go jump into the abyss and be unmade, or move on."

She spat at me. "I'm not going anywhere."

I grinned. "You will. Or when I come back, I'll make the choice for you." A complete bluff, but it got the desired effect. Her eyes grew wide as she took a step back. I raised my barriers, the sword in my hand dissipated. When I started to pull myself out of the Veil a ball of gold light was already coming down from the Way.

I opened my eyes to two worried faces and one pissed off face. Ethan and Miles relaxed when they saw I was back. Zeke on the other hand...

"What the fuck did you guys think you were doing?" he bellowed, his eyes burning. "Are you fucking trying to get yourself killed?"

"Zeke..." I was getting tired of this argument.

"You just took off," he snapped.

I was about to answer when the woman on the ground groaned. Ignoring Zeke and his question, I went to her and helped her to her feet.

"What happened?" she asked, holding her head.

"You were mugged but we scared him off," I lied. It's not like I could tell her she was possessed by a ghost.

She looked around the alley, her eyes grew wide. "Where's Sebastian?"

Miles stepped forward. "A couple of our friends took him some-where to cheer him up." He reached down and held out his hands. "Let's get you back to him."

She seemed to trust Miles as she let him pull her to her feet. She half leaned on him as he helped her start out of the alley. We fell into step behind them. I could feel the rage radiating from Zeke like heat off the desert sand. Though he stayed silent all the way back to the street where we left the kid.

We found Sebastian on Isaac's shoulders playing a game with Asher. It was cute. The woman ran to the boys. Sebastian spotted his mother and started crying. Isaac brought him down to her. She clutched him to her, tears streaming down her face as she kissed his cheeks over and over.

We were about to leave when she turned to us. "Thank you. Thank you for taking care of him, thank you."

"No problem." Asher rubbed the back of his neck. Isaac's face turned pink.

"I don't remember what happened but... thank you," she said again before turning and disappearing into the crowd.

"Should we have warned her to wear salt?" I asked absently.

"I don't know," Miles sighed.

Everyone started walking back to the hotel. Zeke was eerily quiet the entire way.

I DIDN'T bother to even try to go to sleep. When we reached the hotel suite I expected Zeke to yell at me for going after the woman. But he didn't. Instead, he quietly went to his room and didn't come out the rest of the night. I flipped the channel and tried to find something to watch for the fiftieth time. Nothing. I missed Hades. The bed felt big and empty without him. I threw my remote down on the bed and dropped to my side.

What was I doing? I needed to figure my shit out. How was I going to fix this mess without everyone hating me? I needed to tell all of them about each other. Or I needed to tell all of them that I wasn't interested. My chest ached deeply. Maybe that was what was best? Make them all think I wasn't into anyone?

"What's wrong?" Claire asked as she popped through the door.

"Nothing." I grumbled.

Claire hopped onto the bed and sat next to me with her legs crossed under her. "Baloney."

I sighed. "It's the guys."

She smiled. "You've got a crush on one!"

"Shhh," I began to whisper. "They can hear you now."

She covered her mouth. "Oops."

"Asher wants to date me. So does Isaac. And, well, I don't know what Zeke wants but... we've kissed," I explained as quietly as possible.

Her eyes grew wide. "Whoa. Okay, as soon as you said Isaac I was in over my head."

I snorted. "That's how I feel most days."

"Don't you have any other friends?" she asked, cringing.

I nodded. "I could call Jake."

"You might want to try that," she suggested. "'Cause, I never even hit puberty."

I met her eyes. "Does it bother you?"

"Not really." She shrugged. "But, I've been dead a long time, I moved on. I'm okay now."

Guilt knotted my stomach. "Do you ever get angry that you're here? That I pulled you back?"

She rolled her eyes. "No. It's not great but I've gotten to prank a bunch of people while I've been here. It's been fun." Her eyes met mine. "Though, one day, I'll have to go back."

My eyes burned at only the thought of it. "I know. Is there anything you want to do before that happens?"

She nodded. "I want to talk to Rory."

I smiled. "I'll see if I can make that happen."

She grinned. "Not any time soon. I've got more people to scare the pants off of." She tilted her head to the side. "Lexie, I've been thinking."

"About what?"

"Well, you shine like a light to the dead but that light only reaches so far..." She started to fidget with her fingers.

"Claire, spill it," I said with a gentle smile.

"I was thinking that maybe I should travel and let other ghosts know that if they want to cross, they should go to Spring Mountain," she suggested. "I'll be heading back but, it'd take a while."

I hesitated. She only just got back.

"Lexie, there's a lot of kids that want to move on out there," she reminded me. "We can't leave them to rot."

I sighed. She was right. "When are you leaving?"

She shrugged and gave me a hesitant smile. "Now?"

I thought so. "Okay. Be safe."

She smiled a bright smile. "Of course, I won't be gone too long." She got to her feet and walked out through my balcony doors. I watched her go, my heart heavy.

My bedroom door opened. Surprised, I sat up. Isaac walked in with his arms crossed over his bare chest, sweat ran down his skin. His amber eyes were desperate as they met mine. "Red..."

"Isaac?" He didn't look good. "Are you okay?"

He shook his head as he came to the end of my bed and crawled up the length to drop to the mattress. He snuggled up to me, slid his arm around my waist and rested his head on my upper chest.

I wrapped my arms around him and pressed my cheek against the top of his hair. "Cookie Monster?"

"Bad dream," he said, shaking in my arms.

"How bad?" I stroked his hair gently.

He squeezed me tighter.

"Are they getting worse?" I dropped my voice to a whisper.

He took deep breaths and let them out slowly. "Not really, they're still..."

"They haven't eased up?"

He shook his head then buried his face in the crook of my neck.

"I'm here, Cookie Monster." I promised.

CHAPTER 9

JULY 14TH, SATURDAY MORNING, ZEKE'S BIRTHDAY

Isaac

I slowly woke up with a soft strand of rosemary scented hair on my nose. I kissed Lexie's neck then rubbed my cheek against the skin of her back. She felt so good in my arms. I didn't want to get up. Couldn't I just stay here? It sounded like a good idea. At least until my bladder told me it wasn't going to happen.

Cursing myself, I kissed the bare skin of her shoulder before letting her go and climbing out of the other side of the bed. At least I finally got some sleep. I walked to the bathroom still waking up. Maybe I should just crash with her every night until we go home. I did like the idea but that might make the guys think something was up. And she wasn't ready for that.

Rubbing my eyes, I walked into the bathroom. I get she's worried but– my foot landed on something squishy. I jumped back, my heart in my throat. A black snake was on the floor of the bathroom. I almost slammed the door shut only it hadn't moved an inch after I stepped on it. I eyed it. About six inches long with black scales and several yellow lines running down its back. It was a fucking garter snake and it was dead. I cursed. Muttering under my breath, I crept back into her room and grabbed one of the bags for the ice bucket in her room. I went back into the bathroom, picked up one of Lexie's unused wash cloths and picked the dead snake up. I put the snake in the bag then knotted the top. I tossed it into the garbage can before going into the bathroom.

When I came back out, Lexie was still asleep which wasn't surprising. The light from sunrise was just coming in the balcony doors splashing orange and gold across her face. I moved back over to her side and squatted down to her level, reaching out I brushed the hair from her face.

Her eyes opened half way, she gave me a sleepy smile. "Hey..."

"Hey." I kept my voice soft. She didn't need to get up for a couple of hours.

"How'd ya sleep?" she mumbled as her small hand slid out from under the blankets to find mine.

"Great. The best sleep I've had since we came home." I squeezed her fingers. "Can I crash in here with you tonight?"

"Hmm?" Her eyes were still more than half asleep.

I was asking her to think too much this early in the morning. "Go back to sleep, Red."

She smiled as her eyes closed. I leaned down kissed her cheek before heading out her door.

When I stepped into the living room, Asher was watching me from the kitchen with a coffee mug in his hand. His gaze went from me to Lexie's closed bedroom door, then back to me. Questions were thick in the air. I didn't bother to explain. It wasn't anything new that one of us crashed with her. I headed for my room to change into my gym clothes.

"Is Ally getting up?" Asher asked, his voice almost angry. Something was up his ass this morning.

"She's still asleep," I answered then went into my room. What was with him?

~

Zeke

CURSING UNDER MY BREATH, I left the gym on the first floor of the hotel. Another night without sleeping, another night full of coffee and bad infomercials. I ran my hand down my face. Coffee, I needed coffee.

Isaac, in his own gym clothes, stepped out of the stairwell and almost ran into me. "How's the gym?"

"Not enough free weights but it'll still work." I turned to head back to the suite.

"Zeke, um, can I talk to you?" he asked, his voice uncertain.

I turned back to him. His face was pale and he was practically bouncing on his toes. Fuck. Miles had warned me. I was too tired for this shit... I nodded and gestured to the door that led out to the pool courtyard. This early it should be empty.

We sat in a couple of patio chairs in a corner as far from the door as we could be.

Isaac swallowed hard and forced himself to look me in the eye. "What did I say in Boulder?"

My gut knotted. My hands clenched and a wave of exhaustion rolled over me. I didn't want to talk about this and Miles had fucking known it too. "You didn't say anything. The demon did."

His shoulders relaxed a little. "What did the demon say?"

Shit. I took a breath and told him the highlights verbatim. He grew paler. Then slightly green. By the time I was done, he was puking in the bushes. I waited until he was done, there was nothing else I could do.

When he straightened, tears ran down his face. His fingers dug into his scalp as he turned back to me. "I'm sorry, man. I'm so fucking sorry."

I sighed. Be patient, he needs understanding not a smack upside the head. "Isaac. It wasn't you."

His fingers dug in even more as he shook his head. "That is *so* fucked up." He couldn't even look at me.

I heaved myself to my feet and walked toward him.

He took a step back, still shaking his head. "You... how the fuck can you talk to me at all? How can you fucking even stand here?" Tears continued streaming down his face. I hated this. I would rather never have told him but Miles said he needed to know.

"If it had been you, yeah, I would have beat the shit out of you," I said without a qualm. "But it wasn't."

His arms crossed over his stomach as if to stop himself from being sick again. "How can you fucking say that?" His face was full of disgust and it was all aimed at himself.

I growled. I hated this emotional shit. "'Cause you're my fucking brother," I snapped. "I've known you since we were ankle biters. I know when I'm talking to you and you weren't in there!" I took a breath and let it out slowly. The tears were less, that was good. Right? Shit, I was fucking useless at this crap. Where was Lexie when we needed her?

I grabbed him by the back of the neck and dragged him close enough that I could lower my voice. "Is there anything it could have said to Ethan that was worse than that?"

He wiped his face and thought about it. It was almost a minute before he shook his head.

"If me, an asshole with massive rage issues, can get past that shit... then why wouldn't your brother?" I managed through clenched teeth. "You are closer to him than anyone. And he needs you just as much as you need him."

"He's being such a dick," he muttered.

"By not talking to him, so are you." I let go of the back of his neck and stepped back. There, that was all I had. Isaac took deep breaths and let them out slowly. When he was calm again, he didn't seem to know what to say.

I started for the door to the hotel. "Come on, shithead. Your breath reeks."

Lexie

I WAS EATING breakfast with Asher, Miles and Ethan when the morning news came on. Over eighty people were hospitalized overnight, every one of them with the same symptoms and no cause. The only connection being each of them visited a public area in the last twenty-four hours. Rioting had broken out on the west side of town, though those arrested had no recollection of the events. The Center for Disease Control was warning residents to avoid restaurants and bars until the source of the illness was discovered.

"That's them, isn't it?" Ethan asked as we all gaped at the screen.

"It has to be the council, they did something," I told them, still stunned by it. These were people, normal people who were just living their everyday lives. And the council didn't give a damn.

"That is fucked up," Ethan bit out.

Miles left the kitchen and stood beside me. "Do you think Evelyn and her group could do something?"

"I can call but she's getting close to having her babies," I muttered. "And it's the Witch's Council, they're supposed to unite the magic users but I don't think they meant like this."

"A call might be a good idea," Asher pointed out.

I pulled my phone out of my pocket as I headed out onto the balcony to make the call.

"What?" Atticus barked into my ear.

"Hey, it's Lexie. Where's Evie?" I asked, not beating around the bush.

"She's in labor at the moment," he announced, his voice strained. "What do you need?"

"Who is it?" Evelyn's voice was breathless.

"The Necro." He brought the phone back to him. "Now's not a good time."

"I'm sorry but the Witch's Council is starting a fight with non-council magic users in New Orleans. And now normals are getting hit by it," I announced.

There was a long silence where only another man's voice could be heard.

"Evie, your vitals are excellent," a deep voice said. "Just keep up your breathing exercises. Do you want anything?"

"No, no, I'm alright, Zahur," Evie answered, her voice strained but calm. "But if you could give Atticus a sedative, I'd appreciate it."

"What do you mean, a fight? And how are normals getting involved?" Atticus growled, his voice becoming more and more strained. "Look, Evelyn's in labor, I don't have time for Witch's Council bullshit!"

"Give me the phone, Atty." Evelyn's voice was firm.

"This can wait until after-"

"Obviously it can't, otherwise Lexie would already have hung up the phone," she countered.

Atticus was cursing as he handed the phone over.

"Lexie, how are you?" Evelyn asked in a calm voice.

"Forget me, you're in labor." I smiled. "How are you?"

She chuckled. "I'm watching Atticus quickly lose his mind, it's rather entertaining."

I snorted. "Can you take video?"

"Hmm, I'll get Ranulf on it. Now, what's happening with the Witch's Council?"

I explained quickly what I knew. It didn't take long and Evelyn only had to do her breathing exercises twice.

"Those wretches," she said, her voice sharp. "They know darn well they aren't following the spirit of the treaty." She sighed. "Lexie, under the last treaty we can't interfere."

"Shit," I bit out. "What about them attacking normals?"

"Have any of them died yet?" she asked, her voice strained.

"Not yet."

"Dang it, we can intervene if a normal dies. I know it's ridiculous but they insisted on the addition two treaties ago. I didn't think much of it then but now… Listen, we can help the local magic users if they call and ask for sanctuary. Then we can protect them without violating the treaty." She started another breathing exercise.

"That's great! Should I give them your number or..."

"Use mine, I'll have it with us," she grunted.

"Alright, Evelyn," that deep voice said. "It's time to push."

"Do we have everything in place?" Atticus demanded. "The nurses? The NICU?-"

"Lexie, I need to go," Evelyn said. "I'll keep my phone on and anyone who asks for sanctuary will be granted it immediately. You already have it so you should be safe."

"Thanks, now go take care of yourself and those babies." I hung up the phone and headed back in.

The guys looked up at me as I came in. I repeated what Evie had explained to me.

"At the rate they keep putting people in the hospital, it won't be long before they kill someone," Ethan bit out.

"I don't believe so." Miles had his thinking face on. "If the witches insisted on that being a requirement in the treaty, then they know exactly what they're doing. They'll be very careful not to cross that line."

I cursed. The suite door opened, Zeke and Isaac walked in, both wearing gym clothes.

Zeke's gaze ran over all of us. "What happened?"

My cell rang, it was Louis. I went out on the balcony, letting the others catch them up.

"Yeah?" I answered.

"The situation has escalated." Louis's voice was a few notches above a growl.

"We saw it on the news," I sighed.

"Things are out of hand, today we're getting the leaders of the different supernatural groups together for a meeting to decide on a course of action. And then we'll see if we can get a meeting with the council's witches to try and get them to back off," he said. "I want you there to see how it works between the species."

"Alright, just tell me when and where," I answered. He gave me an address and a time for the afternoon. "I'll be there but I'm going to spend a few hours wrangling souls to cross."

"What about injuries?" he asked. "They're going to fight back."

I grinned. "I'm not giving them a chance. I'm going to grab and hold their arms so they can't scratch me."

He chuckled. "Unfortunately, that may be exactly what is needed."

"And quite frankly I'm fed up," I muttered.

"Alright, I'll see you this afternoon."

"Wait." I managed before he hung up. I explained to him what I learned from Evelyn and Atticus. He started cursing in French.

"That'll definitely change our approach. See you there." Louis hung up.

I put my phone in my pocket and looked over the railing at Bourbon Street. Mostly ghosts were milling around.

Could I reach them from here? I reached out with my will and wrapped it around a ghost on the street. He looked up at me shocked. I dropped.

Half an hour later, I was still out on the balcony grabbing souls and crossing them. Though most of the other ghosts had caught on and ran. The street was almost empty now. Damn, I had gotten twelve across already though.

Zeke leaned against the rail beside me. "What are you doing?"

I grinned. "Grabbing the dead off the street and forcing them to cross."

He chuckled. "Having fun?"

"Yep. But I guess I'm out of targets." I sighed as I saw that the street was deserted of the dead. I turned to him. His scruff was trimmed down, his hair still wet from the shower. "Come on, I've got something for you."

I walked into my bedroom and went to my dresser. Zeke shut the door behind him and eyed me. Grinning, I pulled the wrapped gift out of the nightstand and held it out to him. "Happy Birthday."

His eyes were shadowed when they met mine. "Lexie..."

"I know you don't like to celebrate your birthday. But..." I shrugged. "I can't let your birthday go by without... showing you that I'm glad you were born." My face caught fire under his gaze. I dropped my eyes to his chest. "So, just take it."

It was several long heartbeats before he took the present from me.

My stomach knotted as he started to pull off the vintage car gift wrapping. Oh shit, what if he didn't like it? What if he got mad? He was really serious about his privacy.

He pulled off the last of the wrapping and set it on the dresser. His broad fingers ran over the black leather cover before he opened it.

My heart leapt in my chest as I chewed on the corner of my bottom lip.

He was silent as he turned to the next page of photos. And the next. My heartbeat pounded in my ears as he looked through the photo album.

"How?" he rasped.

"Sylvie." I swallowed hard. "She helped me find the photos while you were at work."

He closed the album full of pictures of him and his mom then set it down on the dresser. When he turned back to me his face was as blank as a stone wall.

"You mad?" I cringed a little.

He bent down and picked me up with an arm under my butt. I wrapped my arms around his shoulders and buried my face in the crook of his neck. I smiled against his skin and squeezed him tight as relief left me shaking. His other hand went to the back of my neck and squeezed.

"Thank you," he said in a soft rough voice.

"You like it?" I asked, my voice uncertain.

"Yeah, I like it." His hand ran down my spine.

I pulled back enough so I could look down at him. "You're not mad? I know you're super private about your stuff."

His fingers tucked a stray curl behind my ear. My heart raced as I met his warm eyes. Warmth washed through me as his fingers trailed down my neck. I missed him like this, close and looking at me like I was everything he wanted. His eyes went to my lips. Not thinking, I leaned down and kissed him. His lips moved gently with mine, his fingers going to my spine. My hands moved to his neck. One kiss melted into another, and another. I couldn't seem to stop kissing him, it was as if I was starving for him. His touch. His kiss. It was exactly what I craved, it just wasn't enough. The tip of his tongue stroked my bottom lip. I opened my lips.

A knock on the door had me lifting my head.

"We're going to be late," Miles called.

Zeke's eyes were soft as he reached up, held my chin in his fingers and ran his thumb along my bottom lip. "I've missed you, Baby."

I smiled. "I've missed you too, Tough Guy."

His eyes were full of promise as someone knocked on the door. "We'll talk later."

I nodded as dread filled my heart. What did I just do? Zeke set me down. I adjusted my clothes as he picked up the album from the dresser. I followed him out into the living room. It was time to get to work.

"WHERE'D HE GO?" I gasped as I reached Ethan. Ethan pointed down the alley to the right as he tried to catch his breath. I turned and ran, my heart pounding against my ribs. We'd been at it for two hours and managed to drop sixty-four souls into the Veil. Each and every one fought the entire way. Thankfully I was able to keep them from scratching the hell out of me this time. Footsteps followed. So far only Isaac and Miles had been able to keep up with me. Isaac was starting to lag a bit while Miles seemed to have infinite stamina.

I spotted the soul about to run through a building. "No, you don't!" I threw my will at him, that gold ribbon wrapped around his ankle and jerked him back through the wall toward me. He fought as that ribbon wrapped around him like a vice. I skidded to a stop and dropped.

After I dropped that shithead in the Veil, I came back and opened my eyes. The guys were standing around me, gasping for breath. I grinned. "Having fun?"

Asher shook his head. Isaac, Zeke, and Ethan flipped me off. I snickered.

Miles checked his phone. "We need to get going if we're going to make it to that meeting."

I wiped the sweat from my face. "Who's going with me?"

"I am." All of them answered in unison. The guys shot each other looks.

I snorted. "Okay then, let's get out of here."

Miles led us to a bus stop just in time for us to get on. We took several seats in the back. Isaac sat beside me. Zeke and Asher stood in the aisle while Ethan and Miles sat across the way.

"Damn, when we get back I'm taking a shower," Ethan muttered under his breath.

"So, where are we going for dinner for your birthday?" Isaac asked as he reached over and threaded his fingers with mine.

Miles shifted in his seat. "Zeke?"

Zeke was looking at Isaac's hand in mine, his brow drawn down. My stomach dropped. He turned away to Miles. "I don't care."

"It's your pick," Miles reminded him.

Zeke shrugged and began looking out the window.

I had a thought. "What about burgers?"

Zeke's eyes snapped to mine.

I smiled a sweet smile. Asher shifted his footing, his eyes finding my hand in Isaac's. My gut knotted, Isaac wasn't being subtle at all.

Zeke sighed and turned back to Isaac. "No birthday surprises."

Isaac grinned. "I swear I won't tell anyone it's your birthday."

Zeke sighed. "Fine."

"I can cook at our hotel suite," Asher offered, turning away from me and Isaac.

Zeke turned to him, his shoulders relaxing. "You sure?"

Asher gave him a strained smile. "Yeah, it won't be as good as at home but I can pull it off."

"We'll run by a grocery store on our way back." Miles decided. Zeke relaxed a little more. He really did hate large crowds.

The rest of the ride, I fought not to pull away from Isaac. That'd just bring more attention to us. What the hell was I thinking? I should have gotten my own damn seat. The bus came to a stop, all of us got up and hurried out into the nacho cheese humidity.

The address Louis gave us was downtown in a tall glass building in the business district.

The guys and I squeezed into an elevator and hit the button for the thirtieth floor. In the cramped elevator, fingers brushed mine. I recognized Miles long fingers and laced my fingers with his. When the door opened, we both let go and walked out with the guys. We found the office number and walked in. It was a bustling law firm, at least that's what the sign said. The receptionist smiled as we walked in.

Miles took the lead. "Excuse me, we're supposed to meet Louis here."

The receptionist eyed Miles then turned to me. "Lexie Delaney?"

"Yes." Did Louis leave a note or something?

Her gaze ran over the guys then came back to me. "I've been told to only allow you in."

"By who?" Louis wouldn't, he knew I had one of the guys with me all the time.

"Mrs. Tibbons."

"And she is...?"

"The head of the local witches," she supplied.

I snorted. "I'm not a witch."

"This isn't the place for normals," she tried again.

"Then luckily they have the Sight," I countered. She eyed the boys again. Her mouth pressed into a tight line before she got to feet. "Follow me." She led us down the hall. Walking after her, my stomach knotted.

At the end of the long hall she opened a door and stepped aside.

I walked in first and suddenly had the attention of the entire room. Louis was on the other side of the table with the chair beside him empty. There were only three other people in the large meeting room.

A woman with long silver hair who had to be in her late sixties turned toward us. Vivid blue eyes ran over all of us. Her triangular face was wrinkled with age but still pretty. "I believe this is a meeting only for supernaturals, so, if you gentlemen could wait outside."

I met her hard gaze. "They go, I go." I wasn't even kidding.

The corners of her lips twitched. "We don't have time for this foolishness."

"Then I suggest you let us sit down and get to it," I countered.

Her eyes warmed a fraction. "Alright."

We walked around the table to the empty chairs. I sat next to Louis, Miles sat beside me while the others took chairs down the table.

Louis grinned at me before turning to the others. "This is Lexie Delaney."

"Can you really cross the dead?" A man in his late forties asked. Copper skin, amber eyes, and black hair. His sharp eyes narrowed at me.

"Yeah," I said. "Managed to cross seventy-seven this morning."

"Only seventy-seven?" Another woman asked with a raised eyebrow.

The guys shifted in their seats as I turned my attention to her. Short, fringed hair with streaks of green through the blonde. Her gray eyes were smug. It irked me.

"Well, considering we had to chase them down and force them to go to the Veil, I'd say that wasn't bad for a couple of hours." I shot back. "We've got the French Quarter cleared at the moment."

She smirked. "I like her."

"Of course you do," a man's exasperated voice sounded from the phone in the middle of the table. "Can we get to business now?"

Louis sighed and gestured to the phone. "That, is Samuel. He's the Master Vampire for the Dupont house. They've been the only vampire nest in New Orleans for a hundred years or so."

"It's nice to meet you, after a fashion," Samuel greeted me.

"You too." What else could I say?

"Lexie, this is Hallis." Louis gestured to the man with amber eyes. "He's the leader of the local werewolf pack." Hallis gave me a small bow from the neck.

"The loud one... " Louis's voice was warm as he gestured to the woman with dyed hair. "Is Bella."

"Bella?" I bit back a grin.

She shot me a threatening look. "Make one Twilight joke and I'll kill you."

I snorted. She tried not to grin.

"She's the representative for the other shapeshifters that have joined together since they don't have enough numbers in the city to have groups of their own." Louis turned a little in his chair and gestured to the woman with silver hair. "And this lovely woman, is Willow Tibbons. She's the head of the local coven of free witches."

"Let's get started, I've got work to do today," Samuel's voice came from the phone again.

"Her friends are, in order down the table, Miles, Isaac, Asher, Ethan and the large one is Zeke." I bit back a grin.

"Now, back to the subject," Willow began. "The council is attacking normals and bringing the attention of the nation to New Orleans."

"While that would be good for the economy, it's not great for us," Samuel added.

"At this point, they're following our members and threatening them." Willow continued.

"Same here." Bella leaned forward. "We all know the problem, now what are we going to do about it?"

"We're arranging a meeting with their people for after this one," Willow announced.

I raised an eyebrow. "For what? They just want everyone under their thumb. Their demands aren't going to change from one conversation."

"I agree with the noob," Bella said. "We'd be better served coming up with a plan to evacuate or at least a counter attack."

"Oh, you shapeshifters, always running," Samuel taunted.

"It saves our asses," Bella countered. "We don't have your numbers."

"We should launch a counter attack," Samuel suggested.

"A counter attack?" Willow brought us back to topic. "That would start a war."

"Hate to say it but it looks like you already are at war," I pointed out.

Samuel chuckled through the speaker. "The little Necro isn't wrong."

Willow took a deep breath and let it out slowly. "We're not going to take action that leads to an escalation."

"*They* are the one escalating this situation. They're driving it forward," Miles spoke up. "And from what we understand, they know exactly what they're doing."

"What do we understand?" Bella's eyes narrowed on us. "Did I miss a memo somewhere?"

I met Louis's gaze. He nodded.

I turned to the rest of the table. "I had a talk with my gargoyle contacts." All eyes snapped to me, and not all of them were friendly.

Willow looked like she'd bitten into a lemon. "Gargoyles? They're all dead."

"Their numbers are lower so their role has changed in the last year," I continued. "They have a treaty with the Witch's Council to police magic users."

Every one of the leaders cursed.

"But they aren't supposed to be doing *this* and frankly, the gargoyle I spoke to was pissed." I leaned forward. "But they can't interfere unless a normal dies. Not without violating the treaty. And while people are pretty sick, no one has died."

Bella scoffed. "Then we're on our own."

"Not completely," I said. "We have options here. If any of our people call them and ask for sanctuary, I've been told that they will receive it. " I was met with doubtful stares "Once the gargoyles are involved and protecting those with sanctuary, the Witch's Council will have to back off. Won't they?"

"Our people?" Willow asked with a raised eyebrow. "You don't live here. You have no horse in this race."

"I wouldn't be sure of that." Louis turned to her. "They've already contacted her, threatened her and know what she is. And she's only seventeen."

Willow blinked. "That... is against our laws."

"Yeah, I don't think they're going to play by the rules anymore," I added. Then gestured down the table at the boys. "Hell, I'm worried about them. And they only have the Sight."

"This is a mess," Willow said. "There hasn't been a supernatural war on American soil for at least a hundred years."

"A hundred and fifty-three, since the end of the Civil war," Samuel supplied.

"That still isn't many options," Willow sighed.

"The little Necro laid it out rather efficiently," Samuel said with laughter in his voice. "I think I need to meet this one."

Louis straightened in his chair. "Samuel."

Samuel chuckled deeply on the phone.

"I don't see what this has to do with my wolves," Hallis announced. Everyone turned to him.

"I tried contacting the shapeshifters in Florida since the council took over," Louis announced. "I haven't managed to get ahold of anyone."

"That's not a good sign," Willow added.

"I've been in touch with a survivor on the run," Samuel announced. "Every shapeshifter, vampire, and the majority of magic users are dead."

"How is that possible?" Bella demanded.

"Is there any proof?" Willow asked.

"Have you ever not been able to contact a pack?" Bella countered.

Willow thought about it then shook her head.

"I was contacted early this morning by a survivor of the Necro family in Italy. Mercenaries were hired to abduct the family," Louis announced. "All but the son are dead."

"That's surprising," Samuel said, his voice appraising. "What did they want with them?"

Hallis sighed. "Again, this has nothing to do with us. They haven't contacted my people. They aren't following shapeshifters. This is a magic user problem."

"Don't be stupid, Hallis," Bella snapped. "They might not be after you now, but they will be later."

Hallis got to his feet and shook his head. "I don't see that happening. Not with my numbers."

"How many of those are non-combatants?" Louis asked. "Children? Women who can't fight due to pregnancy?"

Hallis grinned. "We have enough."

"I'd check those numbers again," Bella added.

Hallis turned to her. "I will. But until they start poking around my wolves, we're staying out of this." With that, he left the meeting room.

Bella shook her head. "He's going to regret that."

"If this doesn't escalate further then he can keep his people safe," Samuel explained. "My people haven't been affected yet. Though, I too have my own information on the council's policies toward vampires. Two bloodlines were decimated in Florida. Their nests were set on fire during the day. One survivor."

"Is that survivor on their way here?" Louis asked.

"Why do you ask?" Samuel countered.

"You know as well as I do that my survivor and yours are making their way to safety." Louis sighed.

Samuel chuckled. "Mine is, it's not here though. I'm sending him to another House to be kept away from the Witch's Council."

"What about this meeting with the witches?" Bella demanded.

"We'll ask them for a cease fire against civilians, and appeal to their better nature," Willow announced.

Louis and I groaned in unison.

"That's right up there with duck and cover," Ethan snapped.

"That's a terrible idea," Louis added.

"If we show a united front, tell them we know about the gargoyles, then they should back off. As Lexie suggested," Willow explained.

I shook my head. This was going to be a disaster.

THE AGREED upon meeting place wasn't too far out of our way. It was also in public. Audubon Park was full of tree lined jogging paths. Spanish moss hung from the trees giving the place an eerie feel. Or that was just the reason we were here.

"Stay close to us," Zeke reminded me from my right as we walked down the path. Isaac was to my left, Miles in front. Asher and Ethan in the back. When the guys automatically moved into position, Louis had raised an eyebrow. He seemed to think about something before turning and joining the others.

"I'm not going anywhere," I promised as I bumped Zeke's arm with my elbow on purpose.

He just shook his head as we walked a few steps behind Miles.

Isaac wrapped his arm around my shoulders. "Don't worry, Red. I've got your back."

We reached the meeting spot, and we weren't alone. Polo shirt guy, tank top man who wasn't wearing a tank top now, and two women were waiting in the middle of the field.

A brunette beauty ran her dark eyes over our group then stopped on me. I met her gaze unflinching.

"Merry meet," Willow greeted.

Brunette raised an eyebrow. "Is it? Have you lot finally agreed to join us?"

Willow adjusted her cane and held her head high. "No. We've come to ask you to stop attacking normals. Jadis, you're drawing unwanted attention to our existence." Willow knew her? That was new info.

"Willow, all you have to do to protect the normals is join us." Jadis grinned.

"You know that isn't likely," Willow chided.

"Our job is to unify all magic users," Jadis said in a patient voice. "The gargoyles have retreated, leaving us in charge. This resistance is pointless."

I snorted.

Jadis's gaze went to me.

I held up my phone. "Should we call them? They're already caught up on what you've been doing. They're very interested in what's going on here."

The others with Jadis shifted a bit. Oh, they didn't like that.

Jadis, however, smirked. She turned back to Willow. "However, I did receive new orders this afternoon just before your people called." Jadis's gaze found me again, her smirk growing into a Cheshire grin. "Give us the young Necro and we'll leave New Orleans in your care."

CHAPTER 10

JULY 14TH, SATURDAY AFTERNOON

They knew I could cross the dead. I don't know how, but they knew. The guys stepped closer, trying to close ranks. The tension rose.

Jadis turned back to Willow. "Those are the terms."

Willow's jaw clenched. "We don't trade people. You used to know that."

Jadis's eyes were cold. "Times change."

I had enough, I stepped out from between the guys. "They can't give me to you, I don't belong to any group. Besides, I wouldn't go with you anyway. You'd just turn around and go after them again."

Jadis turned to us, her gaze running over the guys then back to me. "What would you do to protect your friends. This is an unstable situation, so many horrible things could happen."

My chest grew tight. My stomach knotted. The guys... No, she couldn't get to them. They weren't eighteen... then again, neither was I. She didn't know they had the Sight, so she couldn't go after them. But she shouldn't be able to come after me, and she is. What would I do for the guys? Fear burned through me, making me grow still.

Her gaze ran over my friends, searching for something. Her eyes narrowed over my shoulder.

What would I do to protect my family? My mind went deep into the darkness without hesitation. My voice was cautious when I finally said, "I don't think we want to find out."

Jadis's eyes met mine, satisfaction filled them.

"Well." Her voice was calm and sharp. "We're not going to get anywhere." She turned to Willow, ignoring the fact I was still staring at her. "Let us know if you can reason with her." Jadis took a step back then another. She kept her eyes on me as she continued to back away. After a few more steps she turned and left with her people, smiling.

Everyone was silent until they disappeared.

"That could have gone better," Willow announced.

"She didn't have any intention of calling a truce," Bella pointed out.

"I agree," Louis sighed. "But she came here for something."

And I think she got it. Dread ate at my heart.

Willow shook her head. "We need to prepare."

"I'll tell my people to get to their hidey holes," Bella agreed. The two began to walk away, continuing to discuss preparations.

"Since there is nothing else that requires our attention at the moment," Louis said. "Let's have lunch. I want to talk to you more about the Veil situation."

Miles had his thinking face on when he answered. "Alright."

We walked out of the park with Louis, I was back to being between the boys again. It made me smile.

It wasn't long until Louis was discussing food with Asher. I looped my arm through Miles's as we walked down the sidewalk in twos.

"You're quiet," I whispered.

"I'm just thinking over Jadis's behavior," he murmured.

I was smiling to myself as Louis and Asher turned the corner ahead of us.

"Shit!"

Everyone hauled ass around the corner.

Louis was in Asher's arms on the ground, blood pouring from his nose down the front of his shirt. His eyes were rolled up in the back of his head. My heart stopped. He was being jumped. Isaac was already there pulling out a kit and the vial of holy water. Asher opened his mouth so Isaac could pour the liquid in. The soul was thrown from Louis and skidded across the sidewalk like a pebble on a flat lake. I walked around the guys and reached for the fucking guy. My will wrapped around his throat like a noose. I dropped. I wasn't gentle, I wasn't nice. I was pissed.

We dropped into the Veil. I stood watching as the extra energy was pulled from him. When he was just him again, I walked up to him and clocked him with a right hook. "You fuckers need to stop fucking with people's lives!" I snarled. I pulled myself out of the Veil without giving him instructions. He'd fucking figure it out.

I opened my eyes on the sidewalk. Zeke and Asher were lifting Louis between them.

"We need to take him home," I announced as I came toward them.

"We'll need a cab," Miles pointed out.

The guys cursed, well, everyone but Miles. While we were drawing attention, Miles hailed a cab.

"Is he alright?" A woman with a small white dog asked.

"Yeah, he just had a seizure," I lied automatically. "We're going to take him home now."

A cab stopped. There wasn't a lot of room.

Zeke cursed. "Give him to me."

Asher shifted Louis's weight to Zeke. Zeke lifted the grown man as if he weighed nothing. He put him in the middle of the back seat.

"Lexie, get in the back with Zeke. Asher, take the front." Miles told me. "Ethan, Isaac, and I will follow in the next cab." I did as he said and squeezed into the back seat. Miles spoke to the driver and handed him a couple of bills as Asher got in. I pulled tissues out and held them to Louis's face as I gave the driver the address. The driver pulled out into traffic and began to haul ass. I shared a look with Asher. Miles must have paid him to get us there as fast as possible. We took a corner too fast. Louis shifted.

"Ouch." I grunted as I was squished.

Zeke cursed and pulled Louis's unconscious body back to the center. I braced my elbow against the door just in case it happened again. Which it did ten seconds later.

155

Amazingly, we made it Louis's house without a wreck. Grateful, I got out and ran around the car. Uma or Savannah might be home, if not we could get his keys from his pocket.

As Zeke carefully pulled Louis out of the car with Asher, I ran up the walkway, then the front steps and started knocking.

Savannah answered. "Lexie?"

"Louis was jumped," I explained as I turned back to watch the guys start up the walkway.

Her blue eyes flashed at me as she opened the door further. "Door under the stairs, there's a tub of salt."

"The soul is already out," I told her. She closed her eyes and let out a breath of relief. The guys reached the top of the porch stairs.

She turned to them. "Okay, boys, up the stairs and first door on the left." She turned to me as the guys started climbing. "I need to go take care of him, can you watch the kids for me? They're in the living room, it's just through the doors on the right." Before I could answer she hurried up the stairs and out of sight. Well, shit.

I stopped in the bathroom under the stairs and washed my hands before I headed for the doors she had indicated. The four kids were playing. Juan was playing a game on a computer. Ami, the little girl with Uma's nutmeg skin, was playing dolls with the younger blonde girl on one side of the carpet. Caroline, if I remembered right. An older Hispanic girl around twelve, Emilia, I think, was drawing quietly at the coffee table. Not wanting to scare them, I leaned against the doorway. My eyes met Juan's, as that weird sensation ran over my skin. He still wore several rows of beads around his wrist. He had no clue his dad almost died today. Guilt ate at me. I pulled out my phone.

Alexis: Sorry to ask right now, but is there any way we could give another Necromancer the wards too? No huge hurry, take care of you and your babies first.

I hit send and started tucking my phone away. My phone vibrated. I checked it and smiled. It was a picture of a tired Evie, with two small bundled-up newborns in her arms.

Evie: She says yes.

Atticus must have her phone.

Alexis: They're so beautiful! Everyone healthy?

Evie: Yes, Eve and both girls are happy and healthy.

I smiled a big smile as I texted back.

Alexis: Two girls? You're screwed.

Evie: I'm aware.

I ran my fingers over the picture. Evie was in a white cotton night-gown, she didn't look like she had just had twins. Even her hair was still braided. I tucked my phone away and looked up to find Juan watching me.

He got up from the computer and came over to stand a few feet from me, his arms crossed over his chest. "You're that new Necro."

"That's right." I waited to see what he would do.

He tilted his head to the side while he studied me. "Why are you here?"

"Because no one in my family knows how to deal with Necromancy." I kept it simple.

He straightened his head. "Why not?"

There was no point in denying it, the kid probably knows anyway. "Everyone who knew, died."

"I guess you can borrow my dad," he said begrudgingly. "But don't let him catch you trying to raise a snake to put in your sisters' room. He'll lecture you for hours." With that he turned back around and went back to his computer.

I was still grinning when the guys came back downstairs. Zeke was stretching his shoulder while Asher was muttering under his breath.

"How is he?" I asked.

"The same as when it happens to you, he woke up then passed back out," Asher said.

Well, that sounded right.

"We didn't really stay around, she was changing his clothes when we left," Zeke supplied as he tried to stretch his arm. "That guy is heavier than he looks."

"What are you?" A little voice asked. I turned to find Ami and Caroline holding hands while looking up at Zeke and Asher like they were going to cook them.

"A boy," Zeke supplied.

I snorted. Zeke could be funny when he wanted to be.

"They're both my friends," I added.

The girls ran their eyes over me.

"Where's Mama Vannah?" Ami asked, holding her doll close.

"Um, she's upstairs helping your daddy," I hedged. The little girl eyed me, probably deciding if she should believe me or not.

Asher stepped forward letting Zeke and I fall into the background. He knelt down to their level. "Louis got sick, so she's taking care of him. She asked us to watch you guys until she can come downstairs again."

The girl narrowed her eyes at him. I bit back a laugh. It wasn't often that little girls weren't charmed by Asher.

There was a knock on the door. I went to answer but Zeke stopped me. I gave him a 'really?' look. He sighed and let me go. Though he did move to the bottom of the stairs as I opened the door. Miles, Isaac, and Ethan were on the front porch.

I smiled. "How was your cab ride?"

"Insane." Isaac came through the door fuming.

I raised an eyebrow. Isaac? Complaining about something being dangerous?

"Miles bribed the cab driver to take the fastest route and to run stoplights." Ethan shook his head as he came in.

I snorted and turned to Miles.

He shrugged as he stepped inside and closed the door behind him. "How's Louis?"

"Oh, you know how it is, all we can do now is wait." I tucked a stray hair behind my ear.

Footsteps on the stairs had all of us turning around. Savannah came down the stairs, her eyes widened when she saw the boys. "Oh my, there are a lot of you."

"Yeah, sorry, we were all headed to lunch when he got jumped," I explained, moving so she could actually see me in the forest of guys. "These are my friends, you know Zeke, and these are our other friends Asher, Miles, Isaac and Ethan."

She finished coming down the last steps with a smile. "Well, why don't all of you come into the kitchen. The kids have taken over the living room today." She looped her arm through mine and led the way to the kitchen. "My name is Savannah for you boys I haven't met, I'm one of Louie's wives." There was that word again, wives. I resisted the urge to ask but Isaac didn't.

"He has more than one?" Isaac asked. I cringed.

Savannah chuckled as we reached the kitchen. "He tends not to tell anyone about it. Down here in New Orleans, it's best not to advertise that we're a polygamous family." She let me go at the dinner table. "Please have a seat, and who is who?"

Everyone sat down and the guys re-introduced themselves. Savannah eyed Zeke. "Zeke, darling, I may have to impose on asking you to change a few lightbulbs. My ladder broke last week and I haven't had time to get a new one."

I choked on a laugh and tried not to smile.

Zeke shot me a look before turning back to Savannah. "Sure."

Savannah smiled. "Thank you." She turned to me. "Now, how did you get the ghost out of him so quickly?"

I pulled my Lexie kit out of my back pocket and slid it over to her. "It's a Lexie kit. Miles came up with them. There's a vial of salt, salted holy water, and nausea tabs."

She opened the little container and smiled. "This is brilliant. I hope you don't mind if I steal this idea."

"Of course not," Miles said without hesitation.

She set it on the table then turned to me. "So, you've met the children."

"I really only spoke to Juan," I admitted.

She smiled. "He's a sweetheart when he's not turning into a teenager. Which isn't very often these days." She moved to the fridge. "Now, let's get you kids fed."

"Uh, there's no need." Miles' ears turned pink. "We can go out and get lunch."

Savannah began setting sandwich fixings onto the island. "Oh, hush, it's not a problem. Besides, I'd feel better if you boys stayed.

Louis will be up and about soon enough and he'll want to thank you himself." She turned and grabbed a couple loaves of bread. "Let me make you boys some sandwiches before I make the kids'."

All of the guys began to protest at once.

"We can do that." Isaac moved around the counter.

"That's alright, we have no problem making them." Asher moved around the other side and took the butter knife from Savannah.

She smiled as they continued to say they could make their own. "Alright, alright." She gave up the butter knife and walked around the counter. "I'll go get the kids." Savannah left.

"Zeke?" Asher got his attention. "This might make us late for dinner tonight. That okay with you?"

"Yeah," he muttered.

The guys started making sandwiches quickly. But they weren't fast enough. The little girls ran into the kitchen giggling. They climbed up on the stools across from the boys.

"I want tuna," Ami announced. Isaac grinned.

"I want tomato," Caroline joined in. Asher chuckled.

"You'll have lunch meat and like it, young ladies," Savannah said as she walked back in. The girls groaned.

Asher smiled down at Ami. "We have turkey and ham, which would you like?"

Ami's face scrunched up as she thought about it. "Um, ham, please."

The guys started making the girls' sandwiches. When Emilia and Juan came in, they made theirs too.

"If you squirt mustard on me one more time..." Zeke growled at Isaac sending the little girls into giggles. Isaac just grinned as he finished the last sandwich and passed it to Juan.

"Thanks," Juan muttered.

"Thank you," Caroline managed around a mouthful of sandwich.

"Yeah, thanks!" Ami added once her bite was gone.

Emilia took her sandwich from Asher, her cheeks darkening. The kids went to sit at the table while we finished our own sandwiches.

The twins and Asher went to the table to eat with the kids. Zeke stood across the island while Miles sat beside me.

My gaze was on Juan when I asked. "How's he doing?"

"Louis says he's doing better than he did at his age." Savannah sighed. "That being said, he has nightmares. Nose bleeds are happening every time he's off our property."

"How often is that?" I set my sandwich back on my plate, my appetite gone.

She met my eyes. "Well, if it wasn't summer already, he'd be in home school."

"Damn."

She nodded as she turned back to watch Juan. "It's getting pretty bad out there. And I can't even see what's around."

"Have the Templars ever offered to help?" I asked carefully.

She huffed. "No, and we're keeping them as far away as possible."

"Why?" I asked, stunned. "Some of them were jerks but most of them were okay."

She shook her head. "There's something wrong in the Templar order lately."

"How so?"

"They've changed," she began. "We used to be on friendly terms. Uma and Louis would help out when they needed some magic user back up. They worked as a team. Until one day they said policies had changed. They weren't allowed to call for back up anymore."

"That's strange," I said, my mind working. "In Boulder they practically blackmailed me to join."

Savannah's eyes unfocused. "That is odd." Her eyes focused on me again. "It doesn't really matter now, they've moved out of the city."

"What?" That couldn't be right, they were supposed to be stationed in every major city...

"They abandoned their station here," she said. "They just left one day."

What the hell was going on?

AFTER LUNCH, we joined the kids and Savannah in the backyard. The kids went swimming or played on the jungle gym while everyone talked.

All afternoon, I found myself watching Juan. He seemed like a normal, happy kid. He wasn't looking over his shoulder the way I did at his age. He wasn't scared, or in pain all the time. It was stunning difference. Was it like this all the time? Could it really be this way with Necromancy? Normal....

I was in my head most of the afternoon. I was outside alone, sitting in the shade and watching the afternoon light bounce off the water when Zeke came outside.

He sat down on the chaise beside mine. "You okay?"

I nodded, my gaze still unfocused on the water.

"Lexie?"

I blinked and turned to him. "I'm just thinking."

"About?" He shifted, leaning forward and resting his elbows on his knees.

"All this." I gestured around the backyard. "Can a Necromancer really have a normal family life?"

He looked around the yard. "It seems Louis has managed it." He looked around the yard. "Though it is a bit more Homes and Gardens than I can take."

I chuckled. "Yeah, it's a little unreal that these families actually exist. Even without Necromancy."

We were quiet for a couple of minutes.

"Lexie, I think we should have that talk," he said in his almost soft voice.

My stomach knotted while my pulse picked up. "We probably should."

His shoulders were tense as he sighed. "You know I'm not good with this shit."

"Yeah, I know." I sat up and moved to the edge of the chaise across from him. "I'm not great with it either."

He glanced over his shoulder at the back door before turning back to me. He slowly reached out and took my fingers in his. "You know how I feel about you."

"I think so," I said in a quiet voice. My gaze stayed on our fingers. "Do you know how I feel about you?"

"Yeah, I think I do." His callouses were rough against my fingers. "I want to be with you, Baby."

My heart jumped into my throat as I met his eyes. "I feel the same way but... something has changed." I swallowed hard. "Someone else likes me."

His eyes narrowed at me. "What?"

I licked my lips. "Someone else likes me, one of our friends." And I liked them back, all of them. I needed to say it. Keeping it from him or any of them wasn't right. I opened my mouth but nothing came out.

"One of our friends likes you?" he asked carefully.

My chest ached as I nodded.

"Who?" His voice was low, and even more gravelly than usual.

I dropped my gaze to our hands. "I'm not going to answer that. You know I won't."

"Did they ask you out?" he asked, his voice strained.

I lifted my head and nodded.

His eyes ran over me then back to meet my eyes. "What... did you say yes?"

I shook my head. "I told him someone else liked me too. And that I didn't want to hurt anyone."

He pulled his fingers away from mine and curled them into a fist. "I... I need to take a walk."

"I'm sorry. I don't know what..." I croaked through a tight throat.

"Lexie." His voice was hard as I met his gaze. "It's really important for me to take a walk."

I nodded. He turned and walked away, my chest burned as I watched him leave out the backyard gate.

The back door to the house opened. Savannah stuck her head outside. "Lexie, he's awake."

Sighing, I got to my feet and went inside.

The guys were in the living room with the kids, playing. Except Asher. His eyes met mine as soon as I walked by the doorway. In that moment I hated his hearing. I hated that he listened to our private conversation. Hated that he knew how Zeke reacted. I couldn't even look at him as I walked by and followed Savannah up the stairs to the second floor. Savannah opened the first door on the left.

Their bedroom was nice. An antique four-poster bed and dresser. The shades were drawn and only a small lamp threw the room into twilight.

Louis was dressed in pjs and lying against a mound of pillows. He looked pale as hell, with deep bags under his eyes. He gave me a half-hearted grin. "Worse than shit?"

I grinned back. "Yeah, you look worse than shit."

He chuckled silently. "Thought so."

"Do the bottom of your feet hurt?" I asked, wondering if burnout was the same for everyone.

He nodded. "I've never understood why."

"Me neither, always seemed just like an extra way to fuck us over," I admitted.

"Thank you. For getting the ghost out, for getting me home," he said.

"No problem," I said. "Though, you might want to rethink getting the ward tattoo."

"Uma is asking me to think about it after our meeting yesterday," he sighed and met my gaze. "But I don't know. I have enough brain damage as it is."

"The tattoo saved my life." I sat at the end of the bed, with my back against the post. "Crossing the dead, and the increase in souls... I was starting to show symptoms."

"How bad was it?" he asked.

"My nose bleeds got worse, I'd get tired in the afternoon and I couldn't seem to get enough sleep at night. It sucked."

"Shit."

"Yeah." I took a breath. "I was really lucky to meet the gargoyles when I did."

"Since then, no nosebleeds, no headaches?"

I shook my head. "I've never felt so normal."

He eyed me. "What's involved with making this link?"

"It hurts a lot," I warned him then explained how I reached my center. Then I explained how to link with the Veil.

When I was done, he was shaking his head. "I think I'm too old for this shit."

I snorted. "If you helped, we'd get the balance back faster."

He licked his lips. "I need to think about it some more."

"Talk to your wives?" I teased.

He nodded. "You're not wrong."

I finally asked what I wanted to ask him since I found out he had kids. "Why did you decide to have kids?" It sounded bad the way I said it but his lips lifted into a wry half grin.

"I mean... I can't imagine passing this on," I added.

"I couldn't either and I grew up in a family that knew all about it," he admitted. "But as life happens, this thing takes a lot from you."

I nodded. Normality, relationships, hell, even your life. Nothing was safe from it.

His eyes met mine. "But how much are you willing to let it take?"

I blinked at him. "What do you mean?"

"Necromancy will only take what you let it. Anything else, you can find a way to make it work," he explained.

I had never thought about it that way before. Was he right? Did I let Necromancy take things from me? I struggled to wrap my head around it. "I'll think about that later."

He grinned. "You have some years before you have to make the decision."

"Good point," I chuckled.

We talked for a little longer before I left him to get some rest. When I got back downstairs, Zeke was back in the living room with a blank face. Everyone said good night, and thanked Savannah for having us. The kids said goodbye and we headed back to the hotel.

I WALKED out onto the balcony as the sun started to set. Ethan was sitting on the patio couch, writing something in a notebook. I tried to peek over his shoulder as I sat down next to him.

165

He flipped the notebook over before I ever got a chance. "Hey, Beautiful."

"What are you working on?" I asked, curling my knees under me.

He closed his notebook and set it down out of my reach. "Just a... side project."

I raised an eyebrow. "Do I get to see it?"

He grinned. "Maybe." He looked over his shoulder through the window into the living room. "Where are the guys?"

I slipped my sandals off. "They went to pick up some dinner and bring it back."

His eyes ran over me. "You didn't want to go?"

I shook my head. "Nope. I'm going dancing with Miles tonight, I figured I'd stay off my feet for a bit."

Ethan twirled his rings. "Wait here." He got up and headed inside taking his notebook with him. I stretched out on the couch and relaxed.

It wasn't long before he came out with his guitar case. "I've got something for you."

I sat up as my stomach knotted. Whenever Ethan brought his guitar case with him it meant only one thing, singing practice.

I was glaring at the guitar case as Ethan opened it. I took a breath and shifted to sit with my feet on the floor.

Ethan looked up at me, his grin fading. "Lexie..."

"There's no point in practicing, Ethan," I said, my heart sinking. "My voice hasn't improved in months."

Ethan grinned as he took a couple of sheets of paper out of the case along with his guitar. He handed me the music sheets then moved to sit on the coffee table in front of me. "I think you'll like this."

"This isn't a good idea," I muttered as I kept my gaze on the papers in my hand.

"Come on, Beautiful," he said gently as he shifted the guitar on his leg so he could lean closer. "I wrote this for you. It should be in your range."

My eyes shot to his. "You wrote this?"

His cheeks darkened on his tan face. "Yeah, and it should fit your new voice perfectly."

I looked away from him and chewed on the corner of my lip. How could I say no to that? I really wanted to but... he wrote it. I just didn't want to hear my voice straining to reach a high note. Not again.

"Lexie..." His low smoky voice had me turning back to him. His eyes were warm as they met mine.

"I haven't sung in months," I reminded him.

"I know. But try for me. Please?"

Heart aching, I nodded.

He sent me a reassuring smile as he strummed the first few notes. I focused on the music in front of me.

The song was beautiful. It was about crashing and burning only to rise again from the wreckage. The lyrics made my eyes burn as he played the guitar. My voice went with the music, never straining, always in my range. My new singing voice was raspy, sexy even. And my voice never cracked. By the time Ethan played the last notes, tears were running down my cheeks. He set the guitar aside and wiped my face. I lifted my eyes to his. Then I was in his arms, my face buried in the crook of his neck. He held me tight as I pressed into him.

"Thank you," I said, my voice thick. I pulled back a little and looked up at him as I wiped my cheeks.

His eyes were warm as they met mine. "Always." His voice was soft and smoky. My heart leapt in my chest. He slowly tucked a stray hair behind my ear, his fingers trailed down the side of my neck. My skin hummed as those chocolate eyes met mine. Spicy cologne filled my senses. He came closer, his fingers trailed to the back of my neck. My eyes closed automatically as his lips brushed mine. My breath hitched a second before his lips crushed mine. He kissed me, his mouth taking mine before I could open my lips. His kiss was hard and fast. Sweeping every thought away and throwing them across the room. My arms went around his neck as I pressed against him. His arm tightened around me as his fingers moved in to my hair. His grip tightened in my hair at the base of my neck, pulling on my scalp. Sparks shot down my nerves. I made a small half pain, half pleasure noise while he kissed me as if he were drowning and I was the last air he'd ever breathe. There was nothing else but him, his touch, his kiss, his fingers tight in my hair. Just when I was lost, his fingers loosened, his kiss grew gentler. He kissed me softly one more time before easing back to look at me, both of us breathing hard.

My brain was in a dense fog. When I met his eyes, it hit me. My fingers went to my swollen lips. "What did we just do? Shit."

He smirked down at me as he pulled back even more. "Lexie, I remember the Veil."

My heart dropped, my throat tightened. "What?"

He tucked a stray hair behind my ear. "I remember kissing you in the Veil."

"Since when?" I breathed.

He cringed. "Since always."

My lungs tightened. Oh God... oh no... shit! "Why... why didn't you say anything?"

He leaned forward, his hands going to the outside of my thighs just above my knees. "Why didn't you?"

"Scared shitless. You?" I quipped.

He sighed. "I tried the other night when we were walking around Frenchmen Street."

My heart raced in my chest as I tried to process what this meant. He remembered. "Oh God..." I groaned, burying my face in my hands. Everything was closing in, all my lies, all my mistakes... It was all going to come to light. I took deep breaths and tried to think. Of what? A way to not tell everyone what's going on? A way not to hurt everyone? That time was long past and now I was standing on ground that was swiftly crumbling under my feet.

"Lexie?" Ethan said. "Did you hear me?"

I dropped my hands and tried to focus. "No, what?"

"I said, I want to give us a chance," he repeated. Of course he did, because he was a great guy, wonderful, sexy, they all were. And I was drowning.

"I-I-I need some time." What the hell else was I going to say? I really, really needed to figure out what I was going to say to them.

Because, it had become blazingly obvious, I needed to tell them. All of them. Oh, fuck.

The suite door opened. "Hey, we've brought dinner." Asher called. Ethan winked at me then got to his feet and headed inside. I scooted back onto the couch and stared out at across the building rooftops. How the hell was I going to tell them?

CHAPTER 11

JULY 14TH, SATURDAY EVENING

*A*fter Zeke said that all he wanted to do tonight was get a nap, Miles asked him if he'd mind if we went out dancing. Zeke eyed him before saying he didn't care. He disappeared into his room while Miles brought me a box and told me to get dressed. Now I was standing in my bathroom with my heart in my throat.

"Um, Miles, are you sure about this?" I asked as I looked in the mirror. The dress was beautiful. The Latin dancing dress was form fitting from the halter top, down to my hips. At my hips it dropped straight down to just below my knees on one side. The skirt hem was slightly ruffled and asymmetrical and rose to about mid-thigh. The ruffled hem from the left met the right hem, showing only the top of one knee. And only when I moved. The dress was black silk, and hugged my body everywhere a salsa dancing dress should. I did love the dress, I just wasn't used to showing this much skin outside of a swimsuit.

"Yes, Lexie. There are some amazing places to dance here and some of them require a certain dress code." Miles said through the door.

I sighed, resigned. I wanted to go dancing, I just didn't expect Miles to bring me a box with a dress and shoes inside. Miles was too sweet. It didn't help my heart any that this was starting to feel like a date, again. We're friends, that's it. Friends going dancing, not a date. I hated that I had to remind myself. That didn't stop the butterflies in my stomach from going crazy though. My makeup was my usual going out make up. A little dark on the lids, deep red lipstick but I was rethinking the lipstick. Yeah, the red was too much. I grabbed some tissues and wiped the lipstick off before pulling my hair back off my face. I decided to go for an up do.

When I was finished I ended up with a mess. I groaned.

"Come on, Lexie. What's taking so long?" Zeke shouted, even through the door it was loud. At least he was talking to me, kinda.

"It's my fucking hair that's taking so long!" I snapped back, taking the pins out again. The mass fell to the top of my shoulder blades.

There was a soft knock on the door.

"Ally girl, are you dressed?" Asher's baritone came from the other side of the door.

My heart jumped. "Um, yeah but you don't-"

The door opened and closed in the bedroom. Shit. I hadn't been alone with him since the street. Not to mention his inability to not listen in.

Guilt ate at me as I turned to watch him lean against the bathroom doorway. His eyes grew wide as his mouth fell open.

"Um…" He closed his mouth and swallowed hard. "Uh…" His warming eyes were running back up my body to my face.

"Okay, I'm changing." I decided immediately, starting to move past him to get to my dresser. Nope, nope, nope, not wearing a dress. Especially in a city where I don't know where anything is.

"What? Why?" He moved aside.

I opened a drawer and began digging through it looking for a nicer pair of jeans. "Because nothing good ever happens when I wear a skirt and that look on your face just screams trouble," I said tensely, pulling out a pair of pitch-black jeans. Asher stepped up behind me and took the jeans from me.

"Ally, you look beautiful. I was just surprised to see you in a dress," he chuckled.

"Seriously?" I asked skeptically as I turned to him. I gestured toward the dress. "Like this isn't going to bring trouble tonight?"

Asher smiled down at me and tried to stop laughing. I rolled my eyes. He didn't get that I was serious. "Ally, it's going to be fine. Lots of girls go out in a dress without shit going wrong," he told me patiently. I narrowed my eyes at him.

"I have never gone out in a dress without something bad happening," I pointed out. I started counting off on my fingers. "A date that ended with the cops being called, Ordin busting my tire leaving me stranded in the snow..."

Asher was smiling down at me, he was putting a great effort into not laughing. "Ally, those are coincidences."

"It's not a coincidence, it's a pattern. And the pattern says no dresses." I reached for my jeans.

He threw my jeans onto my bed and out of my reach. "Ally, nothing bad is going to happen. Miles is taking you to a couple of very public clubs," Asher pointed out gently, using logic. I hated when the guys did that. "You're going to dance, you're going to have fun. And you'll hear some great music. Miles isn't going to let you out of his sight."

I sighed and had to fight the urge to fidget. Asher was right; I was being ridiculous.

"If you're not comfortable in it, that's another story," he added.

It wasn't that it was uncomfortable, it was just... Jacob in the park, Ordin busting out my tire... Wearing a dress made me feel... vulnerable. And that scared me. Scared. I was scared of wearing a skirt. Shit.

"Fine, I'll wear the dress," I grumbled. Asher had to smother his laughter as I went back into the bathroom. "But my hair is a wreck."

He gestured to the bathroom. "I can fix that."

We headed back into the bathroom. Asher stepped up behind me and ran his fingers through my hair. I held the pins up as Asher went to work. I watched as he pulled my hair into a loose chignon low on the back of my head, just above my neck. He made it tight enough that I knew it was going to hold all night.

"How do you do that?" I asked in awe. I could barely manage my

172

going out, hair down, style. Asher just seemed to be able to make my hair behave.

"I might have been bored one day and looked up how to manage curly hair," Asher admitted, smiling at me in the mirror.

I smiled back before reaching for my lipstick. I pulled out a dusky rose color, I figured since my eyes were dark my lips should probably go natural. I had just finished when I felt Asher's eyes on me again. I peeked at him in the mirror. His body was tense against the door jamb, his hands in his pockets. Though his ocean eyes were soft, his face was full of longing. My heart slammed in my chest, my breath left my lungs. That look on Asher's face made my body hum. I looked down at the counter and grabbed a tissue to blot my lips.

"When you get back tonight, can I crash in your room?" he asked.

My gaze snapped to his.

"I just want to talk," he clarified. "I know you're angry with me."

I chewed on the corner of my bottom lip. "I... it's not easy knowing that you heard me talking to Zeke."

"I wasn't trying to listen," he reminded me.

"I know." I swallowed hard.

"Ally, I just want to work this out with you tonight," he said. "Figure out what you want."

I didn't know how to answer. What would make this better? What was the right thing to do? I finally gave up trying to think about it. "I don't know." I turned and leaned against the counter. "I don't know what the smart thing to do here is. I just know how I feel and... even that's confusing."

"I get that you're confused and this situation isn't easy. And I don't want to lose you, no matter what you decide," Asher said, his voice so warm my eyes began to burn. He came over to me, used his fingers to lift my chin so I was looking him in the eye. His thumb stroked my chin. He leaned down, my heart raced as he kissed my temple. "But I'm not giving you up without a fight." He stepped back, his eyes met mine before he turned and left the bathroom. The door to the bedroom closed a couple of heartbeats afterward.

Silence was thick in my ears as I tried to see a way out of the maze

I'd made. I still couldn't see a way for all of us to stay together. I wanted Asher. I wanted his touch, his smiles, and I wanted his kisses. But I also wanted Zeke's, and Ethan's. And Isaac's and even Miles'. What the fuck was wrong with me? Maybe I needed to step back from them a bit. Give everyone some distance for a while. Maybe that would make the feelings stop or at least lessen them. I had no idea if it would work. But I had to try something.

I took several deep breaths. I was going out with Miles tonight, and I really wanted to go dancing. Miles has never kissed me, so it'll be fine. Never mind that I'm still in love with the guy, his smiles and his awkwardness. I could manage this. Okay, I got this. When I was done with my pep talk I walked back into the bedroom and put on the black strappy dancing shoes that Miles had picked up. I was instantly amazed that they were comfortable. I took a look in the mirror and hoped Asher was right. That trouble wouldn't find me just because I was in a dress.

TROUBLE DIDN'T FIND me in a dress, I found it. And it was in the form of Miles. He looked so great in his black button-down dress shirt, and black slacks. His glasses were gone tonight, he figured it'd be easier to not have to worry about them. So he wore his contacts. I kind of missed the glasses.

Miles had spent months teaching me how to dance at his house, especially how not to lead. Yeah, I was majorly guilty of that. One of our favorite styles to dance to was salsa. Though I was usually in a pair of jeans and a shirt. Tonight, I was in a dress that kept flashing my thigh whenever I took a step. And my shoulders were bare to his touch as he spun me and pulled me back.

In salsa dancing there is a lot of touching, lots of hip moving on both sides, I knew that back home. But tonight, I actually realized how much touching there really was. Miles spun me, pulled me back against his body, one hand on my ribs just below my chest, his other hand on my bare shoulder. Tonight, I felt every touch like it was new and different. While Miles was usually timid and non-aggressive, on the dance floor... he was different. He was bold, playful and uninhibited. He had no problem touching me or spinning me around the dance floor. Tonight, I was seeing a Miles I rarely saw. And the butterflies in my stomach seemed to be on a transatlantic flight for how much fluttering was going on.

After going from salsa club to salsa club he spotted a blues club that would let us in. He grabbed a small table and held out my chair for me. Miles, ever the gentleman. I was trying to ignore the butterflies as I sat down. He sat across from me, the candle lighting up his face. Ugh, why did there have to be candles? I smiled at Miles who was looking through the crowd toward the stage as the musicians were coming back from a break.

"You really love dancing, don't you?" I asked. He turned back to me, his ears turning pink.

"It's one of the few things I know how to do well," he admitted shrugging. I leaned forward to be sure he could hear me.

"You are completely different on the dance floor, Miles."

One of his eyebrows shot up. His eyes narrowed at me. "Good different or bad different?" he asked, his voice uncertain for the first time tonight.

"Good different, you're not overthinking everything." I shrugged looking over the crowd as the band started playing. I felt him still watching me. I turned back to him. His eyes were warm, a small half smile on his face.

"You believe I overthink things?" he asked, the wrinkle back between his eyes.

"Most of the time. Sometimes it's good to overthink. But sometimes you just have to say fuck it and go with it." I was still watching the band when he stopped watching me.

We listened to the blues band play, they were amazing. I closed my eyes and listened to them move through the music. They started playing a slow rolling song. A hand took mine.

I opened my eyes. Miles was standing up and pulling me to my feet. His eyes were smiling as he led me out onto the dance floor. My heart slammed in my chest. We had practiced blues slow dancing before, but not very much. Simply because it involved a lot of hip movement against each other, after he taught me the basics we danced once. We both walked away from that dance red and stuttering, we hadn't tried since. Miles pulled me against his chest, a little to the side. Just like he did back then. His arm wrapped around me, his hand resting just below my shoulder blades. His other hand, held mine up and near his chest. He pulled my body closer. I swallowed hard against my racing pulse and looked up into his eyes. He smirked down at me. He smirked! He knew exactly what he was doing. Alright, Miles. You want to play like that. I smirked back up at him feeling steadier now. I liked a challenge.

Miles led and I followed. We moved around the dance floor, our bodies moving together. He led me in the moves he taught me, never pushing me to try something I didn't know. Our dancing was careful and not too close, which wasn't easy with this kind of music playing. Then it changed. After a turn he pulled my body flush against his, my breath caught in my chest at the feel of him against me. His knee moved between mine, though with his height it was more my thighs. I remembered this part, this was the part that we had trouble with months ago. I looked up at him, my mouth suddenly dry. His molten eyes met mine, sending a wave of heat through me. I couldn't look away as he wrapped his arm around my waist across my lower back, keeping me pressed tight against him. Then we danced, he moved me around the dance floor, his body flush against mine. He spun me out and back but always into the same position.

As the music went on my hips moved to the steps I knew he was leading me to. His hips moved on his steps. I was drowning in heat when I finally had to break eye contact. I tucked my head in between his shoulder and neck. His other hand brought my arm around his neck and let go. His fingers softly trailing down the skin of my arm. I draped myself against him as he led me to do, my arm over his shoulder with my hand flat against his spine. The dance moves that had been so awkward months ago now felt right, easy. I closed my eyes and trusted my weight to him as he led me into the move I knew was coming. He pulled me harder against him and up. I went on the toes of one foot as my other leg rose and wrapped around his hip. My body gave a deep throb, my breath caught as he spun us around with me draped against his chest. Holding me tight he stepped to the right, his thigh sliding further between mine. My breath caught as his thigh pressed against me. Then I was bringing my leg down to the floor and we were moving again. My pulse was loud in my ears when the song ended.

I looked up into his warm emerald eyes. A slow sultry song started. I expected his arm around my waist to loosen but it didn't. Instead, he kept me pressed against him and began slow dancing with me again. There were no moves this time, no steps. Just us, turning in our spot on the dance floor. Wintergreen filled my senses as his fingers slowly trailed up my spine. My heart raced as he leaned down slowly, giving me enough time to pull away. I didn't, I didn't want to. Just once... I needed to feel him, just once. His lips barely brushed mine, as soft as a butterfly's wing. Then he kissed me again, pressing firmer against my lips. My fingers ran up his back then to his neck. I kissed him back slowly, enjoying every heartbeat. Kissing Miles was like I always thought it would be. Amazing, heart racing. His hard body against me sent a wave of longing through me that shook me to my core. I should pull back, I should stop kissing him. I was about to until finally he slipped in and made everything catch fire.

There was only Miles, his kiss and his touch burning me through. Sweet, unassuming Miles. The one who almost always hesitated whenever he touched me even if I touched him first. And he was kissing me like I was water and he was dying of thirst. It was hard to breathe as he took over my mouth, his tongue dancing with mine just like he danced with me tonight. I needed to stop... I didn't want to. Just a little longer, please? Just a few more minutes.

Someone cleared their throat. The world came back with the applause from the club. Miles' kiss slowed, his lips grew softer. After another lingering kiss, he lifted his head. I rested my forehead against his shoulder as tears slid down my face. I didn't want this... I didn't want to love them all anymore. His cheek rested against my hair as we both caught our breath. That warm feeling of love poured through me, and I knew I couldn't have it. His thumb stroked the skin between my shoulder blades.

"How did not overthinking go?" he asked, his voice the silky-smooth timbre I loved.

I laughed with tears still falling. "It went good. Great. You should not overthink more often," I told him with a cheerful voice. I wiped at my face trying to be sneaky about it. Miles grew rigid against me. I should have known better, Miles noticed everything.

"Ar-Are you crying?" he whispered, his voice tight. He lifted his head and shifted to look down at me.

The warmth in his voice broke me. I couldn't even look at him. "I'm sorry."

I pulled away and walked off the dance floor, through the crowd and out into the balmy heat. I turned left and headed back in the direction of the hotel, at least I think it was. I wiped my face and tried to breathe through the crushing pain in my chest.

"Lexie!" Miles' voice called from behind me. I stopped and waited in the archway of a small courtyard.

He caught up with me. "Angel? Why are you crying?" he asked, his voice tight.

"Don't call me Angel, I'm the exact opposite." I told him as I wiped my face.

He swallowed audibly. "Did... did you not want to-"

"Of course, I wanted to." I stepped further into the courtyard, needing the distance. I could feel his gaze on my face like a touch. "I've wanted to kiss you like that for a long time." I just couldn't look at him. I kept my eyes on the stones of the courtyard as I sat on the stone bench next to a small fountain. "I just fucked this up royally."

I leaned forward, resting my elbow on my knees and hid my face in my hands I took deep breaths. Zeke... Ethan... Asher... Isaac... Miles... What the fuck was I going to do? Fear tore through me leaving me shaking. This was bad, really bad. What the fuck have I done? What the hell was I thinking? Did I really think this would work out? That I'd be able to date one of them and the others would be okay? Did I really fucking think I could choose? I just… God! This is it. I've destroyed our family.

I didn't even hear Miles move, he was just there kneeling down in front of me. He pulled my hands away from my face. I still couldn't look at him. I looked at the collar of his shirt, as he wiped the tears from my face. My heart breaking, my entire being felt hollow.

"What do you mean?" he asked carefully. "It's just me, Lexie. I've cared about you this way for some time."

I took a deep breath and met his eyes. His gorgeous deep emerald eyes. He was never going to look at me like that again. And I deserved it. "It's not just you." I wiped my face. "It's Isaac. It's Zeke. It's Asher. Fuck, it's even Ethan. Now I'm going to lose all of you."

Heart aching, I went to turn away from him again. His hand cupped my jaw and brought my face back to him. His eyes narrowed at me. "What are you saying, Angel?"

I focused on breathing. My chest tightened and my hands started shaking but I told him. "I've kissed all of you."

He was stone still. His eyes were going from hard to soft and back again. As if he couldn't make up his mind about how he was feeling. I looked down at my fingers twisting in my lap.

"Let me get this straight," Miles' voice was cold. It was as if he was carving my heart out with just his voice. "All of our friends have kissed you?"

I nodded, still looking down at my hands.

"How long has this been going on?" His voice was growing colder.

I kept my eyes on my lap, tears still falling. "Since January. Before the cabin."

"Those fucking imbeciles," Miles muttered. I froze not quite sure I heard him correctly. Did Miles just curse? I've never heard him curse, definitely not around me. I was so shocked I didn't know what to say.

His hand went to my jaw as he forced me to look him in the eye. "Angel, do you have feelings for me?" he asked gently but clearly. His thumb wiped the tears from my cheek. "Do you care about me the way I do about you?" I nodded. The relief in his eyes was short lived. "Do you have those feelings for Zeke too?" I closed my eyes, tears falling faster and nodded. His hand dropped from my face to the side of my thigh, his fingers making circles on the fabric. "Do you have those feelings for Asher?" I bit my lip and nodded. "Isaac?" I took a hard tight breath and nodded. "Ethan?" I wiped more tears away from my face and nodded. He grew silent. My heart began crumbling in my chest. He wasn't going to believe me. Hell, I hardly believed me and I was living it.

"Do they know about each other?" he asked.

I shook my head. "Asher knows about Zeke but... that's it."

"Shit." Miles cursed again. He must be really mad. He got to his feet and started pacing. Miles never paced, he was always still and quiet until he came up with a solution.

I don't know how long he paced but eventually he came and sat down next to me. He handed me some tissues from his pocket. I took them still not able to look at him.

"Tell me how this happened?" he asked, his voice soft.

I sat up and kept my eyes on the far courtyard wall. "All of you are pretty amazing, it was bound to happen." I took a deep breath and let it out as I tried to figure out how to explain. "I've been falling for all of you for some time." The tears slowed. Why was he still here? Didn't he realize how fucked up I was? "That night at your house, before the cabin. I went looking for Zeke."

"He was in the gym," Miles supplied.

I nodded. "He was pissed at something Dylan had said and... he kissed me."

"Did... were you okay with that?" he asked carefully.

"I kissed him back, Miles." I swallowed hard. "He was supposed to come over after work that night so we could talk about it but..."

"You were abducted," Miles said, his voice quiet.

"Yeah. He said he'd wait until I dealt with all of that..." Did he even want to hear this?

"I'm listening. I need to understand how this happened." He started tapping his fingers on his thigh.

My chest burned as I took a breath. "Then when I took Ethan to the Veil by accident, I thought I might have killed him. So… he kissed me before I tried to take us out."

"That sounds like Ethan," he said under his breath.

"Then last month, Asher and I went swimming. He told me he cared about me and I… I was so stupid, Miles. I just blurted out that I cared about him too and we kissed. I knew I was dying so I told him someone else cared about me too. He assumed Zeke and said he'd step aside. Only he told me yesterday that he isn't going to."

He stopped tapping. I could practically hear the gears turning in his mind. "That explains why he was avoiding Zeke for the last few weeks."

I nodded. "Then during the whole Isaac being possessed thing… we kissed. Several times."

"And knowing Isaac, he wants it to be official," he surmised.

"Yeah." I sniffed.

"And then me."

I nodded, tears falling again. I pulled away from him knowing what was coming next. I was horrible, dirt, trash. I was everything the girls at school said I was. I needed to not make this worse. I already ruined my friendships with the guys, I didn't need to ruin theirs too. I wiped my face again.

"I'll go to another hotel," I said, my heart dying with every word but this was really for the best. "You guys should go home." I swallowed hard, trying to talk through the boulder in my throat. "I'll finish up here and when I get back I'll stay away from you guys. I'll email you to make sure my classes don't line up with theirs. They'll understand why."

Miles hand went to my back, rubbing up and down gently. "No, they won't, Angel." He sounded so certain that I finally looked at him. His eyes were soft as he looked down at me.

"What do you mean?" I wiped my nose with my tissues. Miles' face was full of an emotion I couldn't name.

"Because from what I've seen, I think they care about you just as much as you care about us." His voice was calm, but his eyes were almost hot as he met mine. "If you left, I can guarantee you that Zeke will not take it well. Ever since you came along he's been doing better, laughing more. Heck, he's started making jokes. And Asher..." Miles sighed. "Asher is going to be applying to one of the big culinary schools instead of a university after high school." He shook his head. "I should have known it was you. You managed to get Isaac to ease back on his self-destructive issues. Instead of doing stupid stunts he asks now if something is a challenge or a stupid risk." His eyes ran over my face again. "We all thought we would be burying him soon, Lexie." Everything inside me ached when he said that. I couldn't imagine a world without Isaac.

"Ethan is even starting to write songs for the band now. And finishing them in a few weeks instead of never finishing them." My eyebrows rose, I didn't know about any of that. I only knew about the song from this afternoon.

"And me..." Miles scoffed at himself before meeting my eyes again. "For the first time in my life, I feel comfortable in my own skin." My heart started melting as warmth poured through my chest. He looked across the courtyard again, his eyes unfocused. "I am okay with who I am. I know I say things wrong at times, but I'm working on that. And that's okay." He looked back at me and met my eyes again. "You helped me get there, Angel. I can't imagine my world without you in it." His eyes narrowed on mine, he licked his lips before continuing. "If you want to leave then leave, but if you care about us at all-" I didn't let him finish his sentence, I grabbed his shirt and pulled him to me. My lips softly brushing against his. His hand cupped my face as I kissed him slowly with love. When he pulled back, he gazed into my eyes as he smiled. Joy burst through me, throwing off the awful weight that had been pressing down on me for so long. That was, until I realized we still had to figure this out.

"I don't want to go anywhere. Not as long as..." I couldn't finish my sentence. Miles pulled me against him, I tucked my head into that spot on his chest between his shoulder and neck. "But what are we going to do? I can't just choose one of you, it'd kill me. It'd piss off the others and everything would fall apart."

Miles swallowed hard. "I don't know. But we'll figure it out. It might be painful, you might have to choose or not date anyone but..." His thumb stroked my cheekbone. "But we'll figure it out. We're family. We stick together."

It was sweet of him to say so, but I knew the truth. I had just destroyed everything. I blinked down at my hands. Wait. What the hell was I thinking? That they're going to leave? Haven't they proved they aren't going anywhere over and over again! Even though you lied, over and over. Doubted them over and over! They stood with you through everything! And what do you do? You keep lying, knowing that it's going to hurt them. This won't destroy us. Not as a family. But it can't keep going on like this.

"I need to tell them tonight," I decided.

"Then, we'll tell them tonight," he agreed. Miles turned to look across the courtyard again. "And until we figure this out, I would ask that...." He started tapping his leg. "That you'd refrain from getting too physical with any of us. It would just make this situation-"

"I'm not sleeping with anybody anytime soon, Miles." I looked up at him. "No one's even getting to second until we figure this shit out."

He smiled down at me, his eyes running over my face. "Interesting way to motivate me, Angel, but it'll work."

My mouth dropped and my face burned as I realized what that sounded like. Miles was smiling a big smile. My face burned.

"Why are you calling me Angel?" I asked, feeling the furthest thing from one.

"I'll tell you another day," he said, his voice quiet.

He wasn't mad at me, he wasn't yelling. He was trying to find a way to help fix my mess. That was Miles through and through. He truly was amazing.

I remembered something from earlier. "Miles."

"Yes?"

"You cursed in front of me." I started grinning and when I didn't stop Miles kissed me. That definitely made me stop. We sat in the courtyard for a while longer, just being there together. It was incredible to be able to be with him without secrets, without guilt. Then we were headed back to the hotel and the others.

I was getting tenser as we got closer. Miles's hand was still in mine.

"Are you ready for this?" he asked as we walked down the sidewalk near to our hotel.

"This is going to be a nightmare," I sighed

"It'll be worse if they find out on their own," he countered. I nodded; he was right. Miles pulled me to a stop outside the hotel. "Trust us. Trust that we'll make it through this."

I took several deep breaths. It felt as if I was standing on the edge of a cliff knowing it was jump or die. I knew they were there, waiting to catch me. But I couldn't see them. It was jump and trust. Or run and be miserable.

"I'm ready."

CHAPTER 12

JULY 14TH SATURDAY NIGHT

*W*e headed back to the hotel. We had just stepped into the lights of the lobby when I noticed my lipstick was smeared across Miles' mouth.

"Shit," I hissed and grabbed his arm. I pulled him into a corner standing between me and the lobby. "Do you have any more tissues? My lipstick is all over your mouth." I asked darting glances around the lobby.

He quickly pulled out the small packet in his pocket.

I took one out and licked the corner. "Sorry about this, so unromantic," I mumbled as I used the tissue to take the color off his lips and around his mouth. His eyes sparkled with amusement as he stood still, letting me clean him off. When I was done he took the packet and pulled out a tissue himself.

"Angel," he whispered, that silky voice sliding through my ear. Making my pulse speed up again. I looked at him a little desperately as he licked the corner of the tissue. He quickly cleaned the lipstick off from around my mouth too.

"Miles, you can't use that voice on me in public," I pleaded with him when he was done. He grinned down at me, his eyes warm.

"So, in private?" he offered. Miles was being such a flirt! I loved it. My entire body felt lighter, as if I was flying.

"No, not at all," I told him adamantly. "Not for a while at least."

He chuckled as he found a trash can and threw the tissues away. "You really are an acousticophile." His hand went to the small of my back as we headed toward the elevator.

"You have no idea," I mumbled, my face on fire. I felt his eyes running over me as we reached the doors. He leaned down.

"I think I'm going to like finding out," he whispered in my ear, his voice silky again. I closed my eyes and groaned at what that voice did to me. This was so not fucking fair! He was still chuckling when we reached our floor.

Heart pounding, I stopped at our door. I took a deep breath, then another. Standing out here wasn't going to accomplish anything.

I opened the door to find the guys sprawled out on the couches and chairs. Everyone looked up as we stepped inside.

"How'd it go?" Asher asked looking down the line of his body from the couch he was hogging.

"Well, we learned I can dance in a club without falling on my face." I ran my eyes over the room. Ethan had a couch to himself, Isaac was on the floor and Zeke had an armchair.

"Did anything bad happen?" Asher asked teasing me. I narrowed my eyes at him playfully.

"No. I think the skirt curse has been broken, but only time will tell," I said being overly dramatic. The boys chuckled. I leaned against the couch and pulled off my heels thankfully. They were comfy but they were still heels. I moaned in relief as my feet touched the carpet. "No shoes." I looked up to see all the guys turning back to look at the screen. Apparently, I had gotten everyone's attention. I turned to find Miles still watching me. I raised an eyebrow. He nodded, he'd seen it too.

"Hey, guys." I swallowed hard and turned to the guys. "I'm calling a family meeting."

Asher shut off the tv and sat up. Ethan did the same.

186

"What's going on?" Isaac got off the floor to sit at the other end of the couch with his brother. Miles moved to stand in front of the tv.

I sat on the arm of the end of Asher's couch as they waited. I took a deep breath and let it out slowly before turning to look at the guys. This was it. My heart hammered in my throat. "I know there's a 'no dating Lexie rule' in place." Everyone but Isaac's gaze snapped to me.

"Who told you that?" Ethan asked.

I shook my head. "That's not important." I took a breath and met each of their gazes before announcing. "While that rule is still intact. The spirit of it...um..." My voice failed. Shit!

Asher sighed. "Ally, I'll tell-"

"No one will say a word or interrupt Lexie until she explains the entire situation," Miles stated. "Understood?"

The guys nodded.

I had that feeling that I was at the cliff's edge again, about to go over. Fear eating at my gut, I met each of their eyes. Trust or run.

I trusted. "Okay." I took a breath. My hands began to tremble in my lap. Come on! Grow a pair! Heart pounding, I started talking. "It started in January." Zeke leaned back in his chair, his hands moving to his thighs. "I kissed Zeke." Tension in the room amped up as the guys all turned to him.

His eyes met mine. "I kissed you-"

"I'm not done," I stated.

His brow furrowed.

My chest burned. Would any of them ever look at me the same way after this? I turned to Ethan. "Then in April, in the Veil, Ethan and I kissed." Tension flooded the room as everyone but Miles turned to glare at Ethan. Ethan's gaze was on me, while he twirled his rings. "Then last month..." I met Asher's gaze. His brows were drawn down, his mouth a tight line. "Then Asher and I kissed." I turned to Isaac. His face was pale, his jaw clenched. "Then I kissed Isaac."

"Son of a...." Ethan bit out before he stopped himself. The tension was so thick I was practically drowning in it.

"Then tonight..." My voice cracked. "Miles and I..."

"Kissed," Asher bit out. "We're getting the theme."

"You've kissed all of us?" Ethan snapped.

"Yes," I said, trying to stay calm when it seemed like my heart was going to burst through my chest any second.

"Tell me this is a fucking prank?" Isaac asked, his hurt eyes meeting mine.

"It's not," I wrung my fingers in my lap. "It just... kind of happened."

Isaac got to his feet and began to pace behind the second couch.

"Oh, it just happened," Ethan said, his voice dripping with sarcasm. "Why didn't you say so?"

My gaze shot to his, my temper sparking. "You pretended you didn't even remember until this afternoon. So, get off your high-horse."

"I can't believe this," Asher scoffed. "I mean, I knew about Zeke but..."

Zeke's head snapped up, his glowing eyes shot to Asher. "You knew? About me and her? And you still fucking kissed her?"

Asher pushed to his feet. "You're damn right I did," he all but shouted. "What am I supposed to do? Stand by and give up? I'm not stepping aside just because you have a fucked-up past."

Zeke got to his feet and strode toward Asher. "Fuck you! You think I'd ask you to?"

Asher started toward him. "You would have done the same damn thing!"

"You fucking asshole!" Zeke growled.

I jumped off the arm of the couch and stepped between them just as they were in arms reach of each other. "Stop it!" I was almost squashed before they stopped, my hands on both of their chests.

"Really, Isaac?" Ethan got off the other couch, his voice boiling.

"Go to hell," Isaac snapped back. Miles started toward them.

Zeke pushed my hand off him. "Don't touch me right now." It was like a blade to the heart. But I deserved it. I dropped my hand from Asher too, just in case.

"Don't fucking snap at her like that," Asher growled.

"You gotta go after all the girls, you couldn't stay away from her?" Isaac shouted.

"We were in the Veil and didn't know if I could get back! I took a shot. What's your excuse?" Ethan countered.

Miles got between them. "Everyone, take a breath."

"Some fuckin' friend you are! What you did was fucked up!" Zeke snarled. Oh God, this was bad. Very, very bad.

"Oh, screw you!" Ethan tried to move toward Isaac. Miles shoved him back against the wall and kept his hand on Ethan's chest to keep it there.

I needed to calm them down. "Guys-"

Zeke grabbed my arm and gently tried to move me from between them. "Move."

I planted my feet. "Hell no. I'm the only thing keeping you two-"

"Get your hand off her," Asher warned, his voice hard.

No, no, no. "He's not hurting me-"

"Or what?" Zeke's growl vibrated in his chest. Oh, bad, bad, bad.

"Getting with every other girl in town isn't enough for you? You couldn't keep your hands off just her?" Isaac barked.

"Why? So you can take two years to ask her out?" Ethan shot back. "I should have waited just *in case* you liked her? How about fucking telling me you liked her!"

I met Miles' gaze as everyone shouted over my head. My eyes burned. This was my fault. Asher was shouting at Zeke. Zeke was bellowing at Asher. The twins were going at it too. I couldn't even make out the words anymore.

"Lexie..." Miles called, his eyes worried.

I don't know what happened next, all I know is Asher tried to knock Zeke's hand off my arm. Zeke gave me a small pull back out of the way of Asher's hand. I ended up sitting on the edge of the couch with his hand still around my arm. Asher's eyes flashed, he swung. The thud of a fist making contact was loud over my head. It was barely half a heartbeat before Zeke let go of me and went after Asher. They crashed through the coffee table and continued swinging at each other.

Ethan took advantage of Miles's distraction and shoved him out of the way. He clocked Isaac, knocking him back into a small table. Miles managed to get between them again. Zeke got to his feet and dragged Asher with him. They slammed into the wall making the tv shake.

"Knock it off!" I shouted, my voice cracking. Everyone stopped where they were. I got to my feet again and met each of their eyes. "This is all of our faults! Every one of us kept secrets! None of us were honest with each other! And it happened." My heart hammered in my chest. "But if you can't wrap your heads around that... then blame me." My hands shook as I clenched them into fists.

Zeke let go of Asher and put down his fist. Miles tightened his grip on Ethan's shirt and jerked him further away from Isaac.

"It's my fault. I should have said something to each of you. I'm the one who fucked up!" I told them, unable to stop myself. "So, if you have to fucking blame someone. Blame me." I couldn't stay there and watch them fall apart. I couldn't watch everyone I loved tear into each other. I walked around the couch and through the shattered remains of the glass table. The room was dead quiet as I walked to the door and left the suite. I managed to reach the stairs before tears fell.

Miles

The door closed behind Lexie. The silence was so thick, I could taste it on my tongue. I dropped my arms from the twins and stepped on the broken glass and into the middle of the room. "Even I thought you guys would handle that better."

Asher continued to glare at Zeke. "I never thought I'd see you push a girl."

Zeke bristled. "You almost hit her!"

"Enough!" I shouted.

The guys turned to me.

"We're in a precarious situation," I stated. "Lexie doesn't want to damage our friendships-"

"Too fucking late for that," Ethan bit out.

I turned to meet his eyes as ice settled into my chest. "Stop for one damn minute and think." I didn't even bother to try and keep the anger from my voice. "Think about how she's feeling right now." I finally had everyone's attention. "She knows we've been friends for most of our lives. And now we're at each other's throats. Because of her."

"She should have fucking told us," Isaac bit out.

"Think!" I snapped, my patience wearing thin. "What is Lexie's usual modus operandi?"

"She hides things and runs," Zeke answered.

"She doesn't trust that we'll be here. So, she keeps secrets from people, anything she thinks might make you leave," I translated for Zeke. I met each of their eyes. "Today she didn't." I let that sink in for several heartbeats. "Today, she called a family meeting to tell us something she had been keeping a secret."

Zeke cursed, turned away from Asher, walked to the balcony doors and leaned against the door jamb. The other's seemed to not grasp the point.

I spelled it out for them. "She trusted us to deal with this secret. To stay with her. And every one of you lost your shit."

"You're blaming us?" Isaac asked.

"All of us, yes." I turned to him. "Think of how hard it was for her to have that secret. That all of us cared for her. That all of us wanted to be with her. That she cares the same way for all of us. Think about what that's been like for her. And ask yourself, when has Lexie ever walked away from a tough conversation?"

"Shit," Asher bit out between clenched teeth as he closed his eyes and dropped his head back.

"Fuck…" Isaac ran his hands through his hair, his fingers pressing into his scalp.

"God damn it," Ethan breathed.

"Exactly," I said, glad that they realized what just happened.

"What are we supposed to do?" Isaac asked. "Just magically be okay with each other? With everything? 'Cause this is fucked up. Fall in love with a girl and all of you care about her too."

"No, I'm not saying that." My voice was back to normal. "I'm saying go to your rooms and cool off. Don't take shots at each other, don't start avoiding her. Stay civil around her. I don't care if you're pissed. But we're not going to throw her trust away. Understood?"

Ethan scoffed. "I'm not going to my fucking room. I'm going for a fucking walk." He headed for the door.

"Not alone!" Zeke shouted.

"Go fuck yourself!" Ethan shot back before slamming the door behind him.

The silence was thick when I asked, "Anyone else going to take a walk?"

Zeke stayed put. Isaac stormed down the hallway to the room he shared with Asher and slammed the door.

Asher shot me a look. "She told you everything tonight, didn't she?"

I didn't give him the reaction he was looking for.

"Of course she did." Asher shook his head. "Why the hell does she tell you everything?"

I held onto my temper by my nails.

"I'm fucking hoping for her to just tell me what she feels." He gestured toward me. "And you... She just tells you everything."

I thought over my words before answering. "Tonight, I believe everything just came to a head and I happened to be there."

Asher snorted and shook his head before heading for the door.

"Where did she go?" I asked.

"I lost her two floors down," Asher snapped. "But I'm sure you'll find her." The suite door slammed behind him.

I turned back to Zeke. He stayed put.

"Zeke?" He was angry, and quiet. That was never good. Not to mention that he was severely sleep deprived. Not a good combination.

"I need a few minutes," he said, his voice even more gravelly than usual.

I realized what was wrong. "You moved her to keep her from getting hit."

Zeke continued to stare out the window. "Did I?"

"Yes," I said immediately. "I have no doubt in my mind."

"Miles, just…" He clenched and unclenched his jaw. "Just leave. I can't even fucking talk to you right now."

"Zeke…"

"You knew I cared about her," he growled, his body trembling with rage. "And you never said a word that you…"

I couldn't deny it. It wasn't hard to see that Zeke cared about her, and I never asked because I didn't want to know. I didn't want to face that I had feelings for her too. Guilt ate at me. I had screwed up too. "I'm sorry, there's no excuse-"

"Miles. Right now, you need to be somewhere else," Zeke stated, his deep voice barely more than a snarl.

He was right, everyone needed some time. I left the hotel suite and headed downstairs. I had a hunch about where she would be.

I found her down at the pool, with her feet in the water, her skirt pulled up to above her knees.

When I sat beside her, she threaded our fingers and squeezed tight. "Did I just make the biggest mistake?"

"No." I kept my voice the soft one she seemed to like. "They were just shocked, then angry at each other."

"They weren't just shocked, Miles." She turned to me, her eyes storming. "They were furious and tearing into each other."

I nodded. "I know."

She turned back to look at the water, her eyes filling. "I shouldn't have said anything. I should have just left. Given everyone some space…"

"That would have led to the same situation, only we wouldn't have been there to stop them from…"

"Killing each other?" she huffed.

"They weren't trying to do that. They were just angry, hurt, and they didn't know how to deal with it." I tried to explain.

She shook her head as a tear ran down her cheek. "This is all my fault, Miles."

"No, it isn't." I took a breath. "It's mine."

She turned to me, stunned.

"I'm the one who put the no dating you rule up for a vote." I admitted, my ears burning. "If I hadn't done that then everyone would have been more open about how they felt."

She shook her head. "I should just go. You guys can get through this. I don't think I should be around anymore."

I tightened my hand around hers. "Angel, you're family. Where you go, we go."

Another tear ran down her face.

I decided to try another tactic. "Could you choose? Does any one of us mean more to you than the others?"

She wiped her face, turned back to me and shook her head.

"Then this happened the way it needed to," I said, careful to keep my voice neutral. Of course, I wanted her to say she felt more for me but that wasn't the way it was. Lexie had a big heart and if anyone could have feelings for this many people, it'd be her. "Everything will work out."

"How?" she asked, her voice shaking along the edges. "If I choose… I don't even think I can."

She had me there. "We'll manage. We always have and we always will."

Lexie

I HESITATED outside the door to the suite. Miles had decided to stay behind at the pool to give the others some space. Leaving me to face Zeke alone. He'd never hurt me, I know that. But that didn't mean my heart wouldn't break if… Come on, Lexie. Nut up.

I stopped chewing on the corner of my lower lip and walked into the suite, closing the door behind me. I found Zeke leaning against the door jamb of the balcony doors with his arms crossed.

Heart hammering, I took several steps closer. His shoulders grew tense. I stopped. I hurt him, I know I did. My eyes burned. All I wanted was to make it right and I had no clue how. "I'm sorry." My throat tightened. "I didn't mean-"

"Did I hurt you?" he growled.

It didn't surprise me that he asked that first. "No, you just got me out of the way. All I did was sit down. Look, I know I fucked up-"

"Yeah, you did," he said, his voice was a quiet rasp. He finally turned around, the storm in his eyes pierced my heart.

"After this, I'm not stupid enough to think... I didn't mean to hurt you..." I couldn't seem to get the words out in a complete sentence. I couldn't hold his gaze, my eyes dropped to the collar of his shirt as tears started to roll down my face.

He stepped closer, dug into his back pocket and handed me his blue handkerchief.

"I'm sorry," I whispered in a cracked voice. It was all I could seem to say.

His eyes were raging with anger and something darker I couldn't name. "I can't talk to you yet." He stepped around me and walked down the hall.

When his door closed, my heart shattered. Tears poured down my face as I closed my bedroom door behind me. I laid down and cried into my pillow, clutching Zeke's handkerchief to my chest.

CHAPTER 13

JULY 15TH, SUNDAY MORNING

I don't know when the others came back or even if they did. All I know is I didn't really sleep that night. I stayed curled up, crying off and on as I tried to figure out what I should do. My mind running over the worst-case scenarios, agonizing over what I did. How I should have been open right from the start.

Now, I was standing in my bathroom trying to get the nerve to go out and have breakfast with the guys. A heavy weight sat on my chest, making it hard to breathe. My eyes were bloodshot from crying all night. I rinsed my face again hoping to get the swelling down but it was no use. I looked like shit and there was nothing to do about it.

I left my bathroom and stopped at the door. I took a deep breath and went into the now cleaned living room. Miles and Asher were quiet in the kitchen, leaning against the counters as they drank coffee. Isaac was in the living room area, picking at his food. The tension in the room was thick as I closed my door behind me.

Miles looked up from the floor and sent me a small strained smile. "Morning."

"Morning," I muttered as I walked into the kitchen and picked up a mug. The room was silent except for the sound of coffee being poured. Every moment, guilt ate at my gut more and more. By the time I was done mixing sugar and cream into my coffee, my appetite was gone. Needing some air, I headed for the balcony. Only, Zeke was out there on one of the patio couches looking out at the street with unfocused eyes. My heart squeezed in my chest as I stayed inside and sat in the corner of the other couch instead.

"Lexie?" Miles called from the kitchen. "Aren't you going to have breakfast?"

I shook my head. "I'm not hungry," I muttered, wondering if I should go back to my room. But everything was a mess and I had made it that way. I couldn't run away from that. I closed my eyes and took a deep breath through the weight crushing my heart.

Asher

ALLY TOOK SEVERAL DEEP BREATHS. My chest gave a deep painful throb. It didn't look like she had gotten any sleep. And her eyes... they were swollen and red. As if she had cried all night.

"We need to do better than this," Miles announced.

"Not all of us are handling this as well as you are," Isaac snapped, his voice bitter as he glared at Miles.

"Who says I'm handling it well?" Miles asked. "You're not the only ones who are having trouble."

She took a shaky breath as she started to chew on the corner of her lower lip. The urge to kiss her crashed through me. To make her stop chewing on her lip, to make her smile. Instead, I pushed away from the counter and picked up a plate. Knowing her, her stomach would be queasy. She tended to stay away from eggs, pancakes or bacon when she's upset. So, I kept it light with fruit, and some toast. Miles watched in silence as I put the plate together. When I was done, I slid it over the counter to him, figuring he would take it to her. After all, she told *him* everything.

His eyes were sharp and cold when he picked up the plate and shoved it back into my hands. Surprised, I could only eye him as he

197

went back to the coffee maker. I gritted my teeth and walked around the counter. She was taking slow deep breaths when I set it on the arm of the couch. She looked up, her bloodshot eyes driving the breath from me. Her voice from last night haunted me. The way she cried, the way she kept telling herself that it would be okay. That we weren't going to leave her... Miles was right. We weren't the only ones hurting. Lexie was too. And she was trying not to run.

"Eat something or Zeke's going to be an even bigger jerk than usual," I muttered as I turned away.

"Thanks." Her voice was so soft I barely heard it. Before I knew it, I reached down and squeezed her shoulder before walking into the kitchen again.

"Has anyone heard from Ethan?" Zeke demanded from the balcony doors. His shadowed eyes met mine, a bruise had formed under his right eye and stretched up over his eyelid. His bruised fist clenched and unclenched. He obviously saw me touch her and he didn't like it. I shook my head and ignored him.

"No." Miles turned back around with a fresh cup of coffee.

"He's disappeared before," Isaac bit out. My gaze shot to his dark gaze. Shit. One fucking shoulder touch and we're ready to kill each other. Ally rolled the berries in her fingers. We needed to do better.

Biting down on my own jealousy and anger, I said. "With the Witches Council in town, it's not good."

"We'll give him until noon before we start calling," Miles said. "He's probably still in the hotel somewhere."

We fell into a tense silence, the room was heavy with unspoken words.

"Is anyone ready to talk?" Miles asked carefully.

Ally's phone rang.

"Hello?" Her voice was at least a little louder this time. She frowned. "Yeah, I'll meet you there." She hung up, got to her feet and picked up her barely touched plate. "I need to go to the hospital, Louis and Willow want to check out the people who've been affected by the council." She set the plate on the counter. "Is anyone going to go?"

"I am." We answered in unison.

Lexie.

WE MET Louis and Willow at the entrance to the hospital. We almost didn't make it. When we went to get into the SUV, Asher and Isaac almost broke in to another fist fight over where I was sitting. I finally cut through the tension by just climbing into the front passenger seat. My stomach was in knots from the silence the entire trip.

So, when we met up with Louis and Willow I was already on edge. "Morning."

Louis eyed me then the guys, who were clearly tense. When he turned back to me he raised an eyebrow.

Willow didn't notice. "Good morning." She turned and headed into the hospital.

I moved up past the guys to walk in beside Louis. The tension back there with the guys was just too much. "So, what are we doing?"

"I want to check on the people who the council attacked," Willow explained as we moved down the hall.

"And I want to show you how working together in a mixed supernatural area is supposed to go," Louis added.

"Right now we're looking for anything out of the ordinary," Willow said. "Most of them should have gotten better by now."

We headed toward the administration area. "Then why aren't we going to the rooms?"

"There's one of my people in the administration offices. It'll be faster to get the information from her." Willow turned down another hallway.

We stopped outside an office. Louis turned and looked at the guys. "Are you all coming in or…?"

Miles glanced at each of the guys before answering. "I believe we are."

Willow wasted no time in heading in, Louis did the same. Miles caught the door and held it so I could go through first.

"Thanks," I said quietly as I passed. Miles tried to hold the door for

199

the others but Isaac grabbed his arm and shoved him inside. I ignored them and went to stand by Louis, at least they couldn't get upset about that. Louis met my gaze and gave me a questioning look.

A statuesque woman with large glasses smiled as we reached the desk. "Willow, thanks for coming on such short notice." Her eyes moved over me and Louis, then went straight to the boys. "And who are these young men?"

"My friends," I answered.

She smiled a friendly smile. "And you are?"

"Lexie," I answered.

"She's another Necromancer," Willow explained. The woman's smile disappeared, to be replaced by a sour expression in a heartbeat. Damn, it was impressive.

"Mirian," Willow said, in firm voice. The woman turned back to Willow. "What have you found?" The witch ignored Louis completely. He didn't seem surprised.

"Well, I can tell you that the victims were improving the last time they were here," Mirian announced.

Willow frowned. "Were here?"

She leaned forward and twirled a pen in her fingers. "All of them were transferred to a Park View hospital. We were told it was a new private hospital that was just opening." Mirian shook her head as she turned back to her computer and started typing. "No one has ever heard of them, so I started digging."

"What did you find?" Willow moved closer to the desk.

She typed as she answered. "I found an address, a corporation that I've never heard of in the healthcare field." She turned the screen to Willow. "Here's the address."

Louis cursed. The lines around Willow's eyes deepened.

"What am I missing?" I asked, looking between the two.

"That's the address of Charity Hospital." Louis ran his hand down the lower half of his face. "It's been closed since Hurricane Katrina."

I cursed.

Asher leaned against a cabinet. "So, what happened to the patients?"

Mirian turned her screen back to her and met Willow's gaze. "They're gone. Even the ones from last night."

"You think it was the council?" Miles asked.

"Who else is it going to be?" Isaac muttered.

"I searched the patient records," she continued as if the guys weren't bickering. "And the only thing I've found was that their transfer was signed and arranged by one doctor." She hit a key and turned to the printer.

"That'll give us a place to start," Asher pushed away from the cabinet.

"Well, there's more." She plucked the printed page off the printer and held it out to Willow. "Not all of the patients were here. Some went to the other hospitals."

Willow and Louis shared a look.

"We need to find out if those people are still there," Miles said.

"And we protect them if they are," Louis added, taking the sheet from Mirian. "Thank you."

Everyone hurried out into the hallway.

"I have a connection in every hospital in the city," Willow announced. "I'll call all of them and tell them to expect you."

"We'll have to split up into pairs," Louis announced.

I turned to the guys to find them all watching me. You've got to be fucking kidding me…

My thought must have been clear on my face because Miles spoke up. "Isaac, go with Lexie. Zeke with me and Asher with Louis."

"Seriously?" Asher muttered.

Zeke was silent, but I could feel the anger rolling off him from here.

"Let's split up the hospitals in the city," Louis said. My stomach knotted as the guys agreed to their hospital lists, they were short with each other and on the verge of bickering. I couldn't even think about it, there were people missing. I checked out at the list in Louis's hand. A lot of people.

. . .

HOURS LATER, I put the packet I received into the file with all the other names and addresses and leaned back against the driver's seat. Isaac did the same in the passenger seat. Hospital after hospital, it was the same. The victims of the council were gone. Every one. I rubbed my temples.

"Is it possible all these people just left for an awesome vacation together?" I asked, my heart sinking.

"I doubt it," Isaac sighed. "Though, I really want it to be true."

I shook my head. "I don't know what to do."

"About the Witch's Council or about all of us?" he asked, his voice low.

This wasn't the time but I had to be honest. "Both." I turned to him to find his eyes boiling. "I didn't mean to hurt anyone-"

"Well, you did," he stated before he looked away from me.

"I'm sorry." I didn't know what else to say.

He shook his head then met my eyes. "Why didn't you tell me, Red?"

"I didn't know how," I admitted, my voice rough. "I didn't mean for this to happen, I didn't mean to-"

My phone rang. It was Louis.

"Hey," I answered, keeping my voice neutral.

"Come out to Bay Health Hospital," Louis said. "I found something."

"On our way." I hung up and started the SUV.

I drove as fast as traffic would allow. Please, please let him have found where the victims were going. But that hope plummeted when I pulled into the hospital. It was a psychiatric hospital. I cursed as we got out and headed for the entrance.

Louis was waiting for us near the reception desk. His face was dark. "Follow me." He led us to the elevators then into a long hallway. We reached a large metal door. He hit the intercom. "It's Louis."

A buzzer sounded. Louis opened the door and led us both inside. A long hallway stretched out infront of us. A nurses station was on the right. Louis led us straight down the hallway to a room. He didn't bother to knock before he opened it and led us inside.

Uma and Willow were already there. Along with a middle aged, disheveled man and a tall biker in the corner. What the...?

"Lexie, this is Ink, Bella's husband. He'll be my bodyguard for the rest of the day," Willow said as she sat in a chair, watching the disheveled man as he stared off in the distance at nothing. Uma was on her knees next to the bed, her hand in his.

"What's going on?" I asked, eyeing the man.

"This is David," Louis said. "He was found four days ago and admitted to the hospital."

"David, do you see the red-haired girl?" Willow asked gently.

David started rocking.

"Can you tell her what happened to you?" Uma asked just as carefully.

The rocking intensified. "Pain, pain... it hurt... Cut open my skull and root around. Arranging furniture in my head, making it the way they want..."

I turned to Uma. "What does that mean?"

"That is what aggressive telepathy feels like," Uma explained. "It seems someone doesn't want David to remember something."

"This man was one of the first to go into the hospital with energy inflicted symptoms," Willow supplied. "He's been missing for twenty-four hours."

"Shit," I muttered.

The door opened again. The guys filed into the room.

Louis caught them up as I went to Uma. "What can we do?"

Uma shared a look with Willow. "Keep the door closed, while I go have a peek at his memories."

"You can do that?" She was telepathic?

Uma nodded. "It's a spell, very quick, almost simple really. But it's dangerous."

"Which is why I don't agree to this," Louis declared as he turned back to Uma.

Uma smiled. "Noted. But that doesn't change the fact it needs to happen."

Uma turned back to David and closed her eyes. The hair on the back of my neck stood up. The air grew warmer. Uma opened her eyes then held up a finger. She drew glowing symbols in the air in front of David. They hung there, shimmering as if written on the air itself. Uma whispered in Latin under her breath then reached through the central symbol and rested her palm on David's head. Her eyes shut.

I expected the feeling to disappear. But it only grew. More and more, the air became charged. The hair on my arms rose. As if any second lightning would strike and the world would light up. I wasn't the only one to feel it.

"Uma, get out!" Willow shouted.

Louis lunged for Uma and jerked her away a heartbeat before David's body jerked as if he were having a seizure. His eyes rolled into the back of his head as his body went limp. Uma groaned and put her hand to her bleeding nose.

Willow checked David's pulse. "He's dead." She turned to us. "Get the nurses, now!"

Everyone surged out of the room. Asher and Isaac ran down the hall calling for help. Louis helped Uma out into the hall and out of the way as the nurses ran past us and into the room. I backed up until I hit the wall. Inside the room, orders were being shouted. The defibrillator charged. But it was all useless. David appeared beside me, watching as the nurses tried to save him. David wasn't different though; his eyes were just as distant as they were in life. He didn't seem to be in there at all...

Louis was still taking care of Uma, so I reached out with my will and presented David with the ribbon.

He grinned. "Shiny..." He turned to me. "Pretty light..."

"Yeah, we're going to go somewhere pretty," I promised a heartbeat before I dropped.

I don't know what I expected in the Veil. A spark of life? Some sign that he was there and present? But there was none of that when David saw the Veil. He smiled at the flowers.

"So pretty," he muttered as he stroked a finger over the petals of a sunflower.

A gold ball of light came down from the Way and formed a shimmering door. Beyond that door a woman, waiting in an outdated living room. But he didn't seem to notice. Heart breaking, I took David's hand and led him to the door. I stopped at the threshold when he finally saw the woman.

He blinked several times. "Know you…"

Tears poured down her face as she held out her hand just on the other side of the doorway. A mere inch from his fingers.

"Who is that, David?" I asked gently, coaxing him to think.

Tears poured down his face. "Mommy…"

She nodded. I took his elbow and led his hand to hers. Her eyes thanked me as she took his hand and pulled him through. I stepped back as David turned into a little boy again and clung to his mother. The golden door of light closed. Two balls of light shot into the Way like rockets. I wiped my own face before I pulled out of the Veil.

I opened my eyes in the hall, just in time to watch them call David's time of death.

I clenched my fists and dug my nails into my palms. Whatever happened to him, it was the council that did it. "What happened?"

Willow sighed and gestured for us to follow her further from the room. When were in the almost empty common room she stopped. "There was a… self-destruct spell set on him." Willow explained. "When Uma went into his mind, it triggered. Killing him and almost Uma." I could only look at her in horror.

Uma steadied herself on her feet. "Alright, I know what happened."

Everyone gathered around her to listen.

Uma meet Willow's gaze. "Every channel he had was blown open."

Willow grew paler.

"What does that mean?" Zeke growled.

Uma swallowed hard. "When you use energy, when you do magic, the energy flows through channels in your brain. Everyone has them, it's just anatomy." Uma swallowed hard. "Now, over time and years, these channels open slowly and naturally, allowing you to grow into your full potential ability wise." She shook her head. "That's not what happened here."

"They're blown open?" Willow asked, incredulous.

"Yes," Uma answered. "All at once, in the last week."

Willow shook her head. "The amount of energy that would take…"

"There's energy everywhere right now," I pointed out. "Isn't it accessible to witches?"

Uma nodded. "It has been, which is why that rat council have been able to do what they have been. Normally, they wouldn't be able to get that much energy in the first place."

Willow sighed. "They blew open his channels and caused brain damage."

Everyone cursed including Ink.

"Did you get anything else?" Louis demanded.

Uma shook her head. "No, everything was a blur. They wiped his memory almost completely away."

The hairs on the back of my neck rose. Someone was watching us. I turned my head and spotted a large orderly near the doorway. He was looking down at his clipboard but not writing. My heart picked up. Not at the other nurses coming out of the room down the hall, not the patients. Us.

"Louis," I whispered.

Everyone turned to where I was looking.

"Council," Louis declared.

The orderly turned and ran.

The guys started to take off after him.

"Stay!" Ink barked, bringing the guys to a halt as he ran after the council's man.

"You boys are too young to take off like that after someone dangerous," Louis lectured. "Now, let's get downstairs and get a car ready to pick them up."

The guys cursed and grumbled but they listened. Everyone hurried down the hall and into the elevator.

I hated to do it, but I had to ask. "How many people do you think they did that to?"

"Probably everyone they've taken," Willow surmised.

I shuddered. A hand slipped into mine. Miles squeezed my hand gently as I peeked at the other guys from under my eyelashes. When no one said anything, I squeezed his hand back. The elevators opened, his hand slipped out of mine. Everyone rushed out of the building to the cars. We just reached the sidewalk when a cellphone rang. We skidded to a stop and turned back to watch Willow pull out her phone.

"Yes?" Willow smiled. "Good, we'll be there in a few moments." She hung up. "Four blocks west, Ink has him unconscious in an alley." Everyone loaded up.

LOUIS DROVE into an almost empty parking lot with Willow's car and the SUV following. We had found Ink in an alleyway, with his foot braced on the unconscious man's throat. I had no doubt if the orderly had even twitched wrong that Ink would have killed him. He was scary as hell. Which might be one of the reasons the guys insisted I go in Louis's car. Zeke and Asher went in the SUV with Ink and the unconscious orderly. Miles had agreed to drive Willow since she was busy on her phone.

Miles pulled Willow's car into an empty lot and parked.

Everyone climbed out of the SUV. Weeds had punched through the old asphalt. The seven-story warehouse was enormous. It took up one side of an entire block. Semi-trucks were pulling out with cargo while others were arriving at the other end of the block. The large paned windows that ran up the side of the building were lit up. The brick walls of the first floor was covered in graffiti. Were we even in the right place?

Zeke opened the back of the SUV and helped Ink pull the still unconscious orderly out. Ink threw him over his shoulder as if he were nothing. Then led the way across the lot, leaving us behind.

Louis helped Willow and Uma out of the car then everyone started toward the warehouse as Ink disappeared inside.

"This is our safehouse, it's also a functioning shipping business." Willow grinned. "Though that's not its main function."

When we reached the door, Willow knocked. I wondered if she'd need a tetanus shot afterward. The door opened, another large man who could give Zeke some competition eyed us. Dark brown hair, gray eyes and wide shoulders. Oh, and muscles. In a leather vest and jeans, he screamed biker to me.

He stepped back and held the door for us without a word. The place was bustling. People were everywhere and so was equipment, boxes sliding along conveyor belts from one place to another. Uma, Willow and Louis led us into a large stairwell, away from the bustle and noise.

When we reached the third floor we had to stop. The stairway ended at a thick metal door at the third floor. Runes were etched into metal and the brick along the walls.

Uma reached up and knocked. There were several heartbeats of silence before the door creaked open. A white-haired boy around our age answered. He had a triangular face, bright blue eyes and a lean build.

"Willow?" He peeked out.

"Yes, Phillipe," Willow said in a calm, patient voice. "Open the door, we have things to do." The boy opened the door wider. They led us into a large common area. Willow and Uma hurried across the open area toward the back wall and a set of doors.

Louis turned to us. "Alright, you might as well get acquainted with it since it's quickly becoming our center of operations." Louis gestured to the north wall. "There's the kitchen and cafeteria, the next door is our Alchemist's lab and the sliding glass doors all the way down on that wall is the hospital." He turned to look at the doors that Willow and Uma went through. "Further down, we have the cells, where our new guest is, and then the conference room." He gestured to the wall on our right. "Through those archways, is the living room. You'll find books and movies to keep you entertained." The space was enormous.

"So, what happens now?" I asked.

Louis sighed. "We try to find out everything he knows about the council and the people they've been taking."

"What do you want us to do with these lists?" Asher asked, holding up the lists of names we spent all afternoon getting.

"Put them in the conference room. Right now, we have to deal with the orderly." Louis walked away and then disappeared through a thick metal door scribed with even more runes.

I turned on the guys. "Has anyone heard from Ethan?"

WE WERE in the common room again, after delivering the lists to the conference room. We were stuck waiting for any updates that might come from Louis. Well, the others were. I was on the phone trying to get ahold of Ethan. Miles had called the hotel, and the rest of us were taking turns calling his cellphone every five minutes. At this point, I was worried.

I got his voicemail again. "Snoopy, where the hell are you? You're scaring us. Just... let us know you're okay. Please?" I hung up again, guilt eating at me. I turned back to the guys. "Okay, I was worried, now I'm scared. Where the hell is he?"

Miles pulled out his phone. "I'll start calling the hospitals."

I started bouncing on my toes, my chest tightening.

"Yeah, he's usually at least texted by now." Isaac shifted in his chair as he pulled out his phone. My phone rang. I was almost limp with relief. It was Ethan's number.

Ethan

THE PAIN FADED BACK from soul crushing to simply crippling. My muscles unknotted, my body stopped seizing. Sweat poured off me as the world spun. You fuckers... A light flashed. Voices cackled.

Gasping, my head fell to the side. My cheek pressed against the cold metal surface. My heartbeat pounded in my ears as a tall scrap of fabric came into focus. Screams came from behind the curtain, echoing somewhere. Screams from more than one. I couldn't see past the bright light that hung above. And I didn't want to. The steady beep was racing, grounding me in my new hell.

I had stopped asking why they were doing this hours ago… I never got an answer. They'd just start another round.

"He may be the first to survive," a familiar woman's voice announced. Who… I racked my mind, trying to find the answer. Fingers bit into my face as the hand forced me to look up again. Brown hair, stunning face, and cold almost black eyes. That bitch from the Witch's Council…

She examined my face and smiled. "He's not completely through it, but he's further along than the others ever reached." She patted my face. "You may just live long enough to be given back to your girlfriend."

Just kill me… Another figure hung something on the pole next to the table.

She grinned. "Oh, no, dear boy. We have something much better planned for you."

Did I say that out loud? Did it matter?

Jadis turned to the other person. "Give him the rest in small doses and keep an eye on his vitals. We're invested in this one now."

"There isn't much left," a man's voice answered. "If we give him more then he'll be the last attempt."

Jadis grinned down at me. "Do it."

I tried to move only to burst into agony. Black dots danced across my vision. Let me pass out… I started to slip under.

"I will not bow. I will not break." Lexie's original singing voice broke through the darkness. I forced my eyes open. She couldn't be here. No! I turned my head searching for her.

That tank top mother fucker held up my phone. "It's the Necro, she's calling again," he announced, turning to grin down at me. "She must be really worried."

"Go to hell." I bit through my teeth.

He chuckled as the phone went silent. He started going through my phone as another figure came to my other side. He pinned my arm. No… not again… The sharp prick of a needle. I watched as he injected the white ooze into my veins. No, no, no. My arm began to burn as fire raced through my veins; the room grew twenty degrees hotter.

"Let's call your girlfriend, shall we?" One of the fuckers said. My muscles began to tighten. No... I can't. Not again...

"Ethan? Where the hell have you been? You scared the shit out of us." Lexie's worried, sweet, slightly rough voice brought me back from the dark pit I was slowly slipping into.

"Say hi to your girlfriend." The phone was in in my face. The picture of her, big emerald eyes, red hair and black coat was a balm.

"Ethan?"

I wasn't going to make it. And from the way my muscles were starting to jerk, I didn't have long to say goodbye. "Run," I rasped. "Get out..." A scalding, enormous wave crashed over me. The beeping grew frantic and uneven. My muscles seized, my body jerked. I screamed in agony as I was slammed back into the table.

"You'll get what's left of him when we're done," the fucker said but I was beyond caring. The others would keep her safe. I slid into darkness, grateful that I got to hear her voice one last time. If only I could talk to Isaac...

Lexie

ETHAN'S SCREAM was cut off as the call ended. My lungs seized, a heavy weight grew in my chest threatening to tear me apart. Asher tore the phone from my hand and put it to his ear.

"What do you want?" Asher snapped. I sank into the chair behind me.

"What's going on?" Isaac leaned forward.

"They got him," I breathed so low that no one but Asher heard.

"The council has Ethan," Asher announced.

Everyone cursed. Miles was quiet as he pulled out his phone.

"How do you know that?" Isaac snapped.

"He was screaming," I said as I tried to get a deep breath.

Miles threw his phone down. "His GPS is off." He surged to his feet and ran to the conference room door. He pounded his fist on it, making the frame shake.

"What is it?" Bella snapped as she jerked the door open.

"The Witch's Council has Ethan," Miles announced.

I reached out to Isaac and took his hand. He was pale, and struggling to breathe too. He gripped my hand tightly.

"What is going on?" Willow asked as she stepped out of the door and into the common room. Louis followed.

"Ethan was taken and is being tortured," Asher announced loudly. "I think it's safe to guess that it's the Witch's council."

I met Isaac's eyes as fear tore through me. His eyes were boiling. Isaac wanted blood. Ethan... his scream. There was so much pain in it... What the hell were they doing to him? My own gut-wrenching fear turned to anger and began to burn. Fury roared through me. I met Zeke's eyes. He was already there. We were looking for blood.

"I understand you're scared," Willow said in a calm voice. "But we don't know where they are hiding, and we can't have everyone looking for one person."

"Yes, you can. And you will," I stated, my voice dead. I let go of Isaac's hand and walked over to the group of leaders. "You will put everyone on this."

Willow shook her head. "We can't. There is more at stake here than just one person."

Fire shot through my veins. I smiled. It wasn't my nice smile. "Not a single soul will cross over until Ethan is with us, safe, alive and healthy."

Bella nodded slightly. Willow's eyes grew wide. Louis's face was blank but his eyes were filled with approval.

"There's my girl," Zeke whispered under his breath as he joined us.

I held Willows gaze. "Put everyone on it." I turned to Bella. "Get the shapeshifters too. Maybe they could smell him out."

Bella didn't even argue. "We'll need something of his to find his scent."

"Our stuff is still at the hotel," I cursed.

"I'll have them stop and pick up your guys' stuff on their way here," Bella offered. I nodded. She pulled out her phone and walked several feet away.

"You would really let the world be destroyed for one person?" Willow asked, her eyes narrowed on me.

"Yes." I turned to Uma. "Is there any way to increase the number of people searching for him?"

Uma met Louis's gaze.

Louis sighed and turned to me. "The vampires. They're fast and they can smell almost as well as a shifter. But they won't do it for nothing."

"Get me a meeting," I said.

"They value blood, Lexie," Louis warned.

"Get. Me. A. Meeting," I repeated, my voice harder.

He nodded, pulled out his phone and walked away.

I turned back to Willow who was just watching me. "I'd get going if I were you."

"Alright," Willow said, straightening to her full height before pointing at us. "But you and your boys will stay here until we find him. You're too young to go gallivanting off into the night alone."

"Fine," I bit out. "Now, start making calls."

Willow pulled her phone from her pocket and started going through her contacts.

I turned back to the guys. Isaac was shaking. Not caring that the others were there, I walked right into his arms and squeezed him tight. He clung to me. "We'll get him back, I promise."

"He can't..." Isaac rasped.

"No matter what we have to do. We'll get him back." I squeezed him tighter and met Zeke's gaze over his shoulder. He nodded. I turned to Miles and met his glacial eyes. He nodded. I turned to Asher, his eyes were storming as I met them. He nodded. Even if it meant letting the world burn, we were getting Ethan back.

CHAPTER 14

JULY 15TH, SUNDAY EVENING.

*T*ime moved at a crawl. Every second seemed like an hour, every minute an eternity. I don't know how long it took for the shifters to arrive but it was more than enough time to wonder what was happening to Ethan.

Everyone was silent until the shifters came through the door with our stuff. I almost tore the arm off one of them when I jerked Ethan's bag away and tore it open. Bella explained as I pulled out Ethan's shirts. When I found them, I stood and shoved one into the chest of each giant biker. One of them hissed at me like a large cat. Zeke moved up behind me. Ink chastised the hisser. Then they were out the door with Ethan's scent.

Everyone sat back down in the armchairs. We were just waiting for the vampires now. My fingers wrung the fabric in my hands; spicy cologne filled my nose. I looked down. I was clutching one of Ethan's shirts to me. I didn't care, I clung to it and tried not to think about what was happening to him.

The vampires finally arrived just after nightfall.

Bella came out the conference door with Willow, tucking her phone into her pocket. "They're here."

Willow straightened her shoulders. "Will you open the door for them? They won't be able to knock."

"Sure," Bella sighed before she started walking across the room.

Willow came to stand next to me. "Do you understand what you're doing?"

I met her gaze and nodded. "Uma and Louis filled me in."

Willow nodded as Bella opened the door to several men and women waiting.

They walked in with a strange grace that I'd normally associate with ballet dancers. A man with longish wavy warm black hair and a lean build took the lead of the group. His almost black brown eyes ran over the guys, then to me.

The leader, dark eyes, turned to Willow with a charming smile. "Mrs. Tibbons, how lovely to see you again. When was the last time we saw each other?"

Willow answered with a smile. "I believe I was twelve and it was the one and only magic users and vampire mixer, Samuel."

He grinned, showing the tips of his fangs. "You were wearing a white dress with green lace, if I recall correctly."

Willow shook her head, smiling. "Come into the meeting room, we have refreshments for you and yours. And we can get down to business."

Samuel chuckled. "That won't be necessary. We can do our business right here."

Willow straightened her shoulders. "Alright, what do you want in exchange for helping to find this young man?"

Samuel smiled a big smile as his eyes moved back to me. "I want a taste of the Necro girl."

I met his gaze and got to my feet. I wasn't about to fuck around in a negotiation. "Fine."

His eyes widened only for a fraction of a heartbeat. "You don't understand the side effects."

"I don't care." I crossed my arms over my chest. "If you help search, *if* we find him alive and *if* he survives. I'll consent to a light feed from the wrist."

Samuel raised an eyebrow, he eyed me. "Even if it's not my people that find him, as long as the rest of your criteria is met?"

"I'll hold up my end," I answered.

"Deal." He turned to the other vampires with him. "Find him."

The vampires with Samuel left through the door immediately. Samuel watched me for several heartbeats before he bowed his head and walked out the door.

I sat back down in the armchair with Isaac and held Ethan's shirt to me. We could get through this. I just needed to be patient. How could I be patient when Ethan is out there being tortured? I wanted to run, scream and pound something into submission until they gave him up. Then a lightbulb went off. "What does the orderly know?"

Bella leaned against Asher's chair as she answered. "Nothing that would help find your friend. He was only supposed to watch and report back if someone came looking."

I nodded then went back to staring at the large runed door. I could do this. I can be patient, I just need to distract myself. I took a deep breath. One, two, three...

Miles

I MENTALLY CURSED as my thirty-fourth attempt to turn on Ethan's GPS remotely failed. There was nothing I could do.

I checked on Lexie. She was still in her chair, staring at the door. Her fingers still rubbing Ethan's shirt. Asher was just staring at the floor. Zeke was pacing, Isaac was staring at the door almost as much as Lexie. We had to find him.

High heels clicked across the wood floor in the silence of the room. Uma joined us.

"Boys, I have something for you to do." She announced. "Follow me." She started toward a door that Louis had identified as the Alchemist's lab. I turned back to Lexie. She was still watching that door. I didn't want to leave her or Isaac and by the others' hesitation, I wasn't the only one.

Bella and Ink walked over from where they had been talking. "We'll stay with them," she promised.

We got up and followed Uma, leaving Isaac and Lexie in her care. She led us into what looked like a small lab. A girl was there, mashing herbs with a mortar and pestle. She looked up with an irritation that disappeared when she saw us. The Alchemist was a girl around our age. Surprised, I eyed her. Long straight brown hair, a round face, pert nose and large light blue eyes. She eyed me back before turning to Uma.

"Lucy, these are Lexie's friends. Zeke, Asher and Miles." Uma introduced us.

"Hi." She gave a small wave before turning to Uma. "What's going on?"

"They have the Sight and are stuck in the middle of this mess," she explained. "They need more options when fighting the council witches. The non-magical variety."

Lucy grinned. "I can do that."

"Nothing lethal," Uma warned.

Her grin disappeared. "You just had to spoil my fun, didn't you?"

"They're each going to need a shield generator," Uma added.

"So will Isaac, Ethan and Lexie," Asher added.

"Lexie won't, it won't allow her to do what she does." Uma waved her hand dismissively.

"Are you sure?" I countered.

Uma thought about it then nodded. "Not quite. Necromancer's are a bit different."

"It's no biggie to make an extra generator," Lucy said. "I'm just going to need some help putting them together."

"Boys, please listen to Lucy and give her a hand," Uma said before leaving.

We turned to Lucy.

She smiled as she went to the shelves to her right and pulled down a box. She returned to the workbench and opened it then held out a small clockwork device the size of a coin. "This is your basic shield generator." She set it down on the table top and flipped on the overhead light.

I examined the small device. It had some clockwork components. A tiny opening, a tube surrounding a small center chamber with a latch, and another tube with a funnel on the other side. I flipped it over to find gears and springs showing. It was small and pretty nifty.

"This is used with just clockwork?" I looked up in time to see her smother a smile.

"No," she said then reached over and pointed at the small latch on the chamber. "You add several bits of protection herbs to the chamber and latch it shut." She closed the small lid then turned the thing over and tapped a small toggle. "Every full rotation will give you an hour of power." She turned it quickly twice. There was a low, barely there ticking. "Then you put it on and any spell that hits you will change to kinetic energy. It'll hurt but you'll be alive."

I picked up the little machine and looked at it closer. "I imagine you have to keep refilling the chamber with herbs?"

"Yes and no," she said, pulling my attention back to her. She looked pleased with herself. "The shield really doesn't kick in unless a spell or energy is thrown at you. So, unless you've been attacked, you don't need to change out the herbs."

"How does this work exactly?" I asked, curious. The guys grumbled under their breath.

Her eyes lit up.

"I'm going to check on them," Zeke muttered on his way to the door.

"But I need to know how you want to wear the generator?" Lucy called, her fingers wringing together.

"I'll do his," I said. With how small these parts were, I doubted Zeke could even manage to put it together. I kept checking out the little device. "Any requests?"

"No fucking jewelry," Zeke growled. "The last thing I need is to be working on an engine and deglove a finger." Zeke left, letting the door close behind him.

Asher leaned against the table, looking over my shoulder.

"So, how does this work?" I asked again.

"Well, there's a spell on the chamber that concentrates and multiplies energy. So, when the shield kicks on, a spark ignites and it slowly burns the herbs releasing the energy. The rest is simple clockwork."

I looked up at her. "That works?"

She nodded. "Yep, as long as it's on you and preferably touching your skin, it'll work."

"That's ingenious," I stated, my mind already running through ways to improve or expand on the design.

She smiled an embarrassed smile and looked down at the worktable. "Thanks." Her cheeks turned pink.

Asher straightened to his full height and shot me a look. What the hell did I do?

"Let's get started," I said. This was definitely the distraction I needed.

Isaac

DEEP BREATH IN THEN OUT. In. Out. The door hadn't opened in hours. People were out there, they were looking everywhere. My gut knotted as my left foot continued twitching. It had been twitching all day. I had just thought Ethan's back was hurting so I ignored it. But now I knew what it was. Someone was torturing my brother. And the last thing I said to him was…. I swallowed back bile. I was so stupid. We were fighting just to fight even before Lexie… If I never get to apologize, if I never see him again… Guilt burned a hole in my chest, regret a burning ball in my throat.

I leaned forward, braced my elbows on my knees and held my head in my hands. Breathe in, breathe out. My foot twitched hard, cramping. I gritted my teeth and breathed through it. Ethan… stay alive. Please… My eyes burned. Breathe in, breathe out.

~

Zeke

LEXIE WAS PALER THAN USUAL. Her jaw was clenched, her fingers clung to Ethan's shirt. She was scared, yeah. But it was her eyes that told me she was just biding her time. Her eyes were focused on the door as she waited, oddly calm.

It was Isaac who was unraveling. His fingers dug into his scalp, he was struggling to take deep breaths.

Lexie kept her eyes on the door as she let go of Ethan's shirt to reach over and put her hand on his back. She ran it up and down, comforting him. All the while, she was still watching the door.

Asher came out of the Alchemy lab and handed me a small clockwork generator. "It's a belt clip, but keep it against your skin."

I grunted a response and slipped the clip onto the waistband of my jeans.

"How are you doing?" Asher asked.

I didn't answer. If I started yelling, I wasn't going to stop until we got Ethan back or I killed whoever was hurting him. The rage was eating me alive making it hard to stay in one place. We couldn't lose him...

The night passed at a snail's pace. No one spoke, no one even moved from our spots. We just waited.

The conference door opened. Willow and Bella came out and made their way to us. I pushed away from the wall and joined the others.

"I'm sorry, my people haven't found him yet," Willow said.

"Neither did we," Bella announced. "We found his scent from the hotel to three blocks away and then it disappeared. I have shifters going through the city street by street until he's found. But it's going to take time."

"The vampires?" Lexie asked.

Willow shook her head. "They've managed a quarter of the city street by street but the sun's up. They have to lay low until sunset."

Lexie just gave her that dead eyed stare. "Is there another group going out?"

Willow sighed. "Yes, we've pulled in more people to search."

"Thank you."

"Fuck this," Isaac growled as he surged to his feet and ran toward the door.

I ran after him, and I wasn't alone. Miles and Asher were a step behind me. Miles eventually passed me on the stairs and out onto the main floor of the distribution center. Asher hit the doors before I did. Miles grabbed Isaac, forcing him to stop. Isaac turned and swung at Miles. He slipped past Isaac and positioned himself out of reach but still not letting him pass. Asher grabbed his arm and tried to put it in a lock. Isaac cursed and slipped out of it, knocking Asher to the ground. I grabbed him by the back of the shirt and dragged him toward me. He stumbled, I moved my arm around his neck and put him in a headlock. He cursed, hit me, punched me. I winced as he landed a blow to my kidneys, thankfully it didn't have too much power behind it.

"Isaac, stop." Lexie's voice was hard and sharp from behind me. Isaac stopped fighting me and went still. I took a chance on letting him go. Isaac straightened and moved away from me.

"I can't just sit here," Isaac bit out as he turned back to her.

Lexie stepped beside me to fill in the circle. "We won't."

Miles's gaze went to her. "Do you have a plan?"

Her face was blank when she said. "We're going fishing."

I looked down at her as she looked up at me. Our eyes met and held. Fishing...

She turned back to the others. "They want me. So, let's make them think they can get me."

"You want to use yourself as bait?" Miles surmised.

"Yes," she said in that dead voice. "I'll walk around town seemingly alone. And when one of them starts following, I lead them into an alley or dead end."

"And we jump in." Isaac finished for her.

She nodded.

I thought it over. It was a good plan, it would work. But the danger to her… I didn't like it. But Ethan was being tortured, and Lexie had improved immensely at hand to hand… My eyes met hers, asking silently if she could handle this. Being followed, possibly being attacked… Did she understand the risk of a flashback? The risk that she'd be putting herself in?

Her eyes were determined when she gave me a slight nod.

She was confident about it. Lexie wasn't one to overestimate her hand to hand skills, in fact she usually underestimated herself. If she didn't think she could handle it, she wouldn't suggest it.

Isaac scoffed. "Like Zeke would ever let her play bait."

"I'm in," I announced. The guys gaped at me. The fact was that we had no leads. No clue where Ethan was being held. And they were torturing him. The longer it took us to get him back, the worse the damage would be. Lexie was smart. She said she could do it; I needed to trust her. Her plan made my stomach roll and made me want to beat the shit out of someone but it was the best one we had.

"Did he just agree?" Isaac gaped.

"He did." Asher blinked.

"Then let's get moving, we're wasting time," she snapped.

CHAPTER 15

JULY 16TH, MONDAY, LATE AFTERNOON

I walked around town most of the day. All we caught so far were two wanna be muggers, a pickpocket and one couple looking for a museum. It was frustrating. Everyone was on edge but no one even considered the idea of quitting. It was around six when we got a promising nibble.

I had just put a silk scarf back on its hanger when I noticed a man in his forties watching me about ten feet away. Nothing really stood out about him. He wore jeans, and a brown t-shirt. But he was watching me and not looking at the postcards in his hands. Creeper or council?

I was betting council. Testing my theory, I walked away from the storefront and made my way down the sidewalk. I only went down two stores before stopping again. Out of the corner of my eye I watched the sidewalk as I pretended to check out souvenir key chains. He didn't pass. Then again, he might not have followed either. I pulled my phone out and brought up the group text.

Alexis: Think I got one. Anyone?

Cookie Monster: Jeans and brown shirt, you got one.

Tough Guy: Make your way toward the alley.

Nemo: Slowly, as if you're really shopping.

Ash: But don't let him get too close.

Alexis: Meet you there.

Tough Guy: Isaac, stay on her.

Cookie Monster: No shit.

I tucked my phone away and made a point to buy a key chain with a little red crawfish on it.

I started back down the street, trusting that Isaac was still blending in with his hat. The hairs on the back of my neck stood up. My follower was watching me again. I made a point to act normal as I stepped off the sidewalk and crossed the street. When I reached the other side, I made a point not to notice Asher shopping at another store. Halfway down the block, I got a text.

Cookie Monster: Go faster.

Tucking my phone away, I focused on listening behind me as I stepped off the sidewalk and started down the alley where Miles and Zeke were already waiting around a corner. I headed down the alley as if I didn't have a care in the world.

Footsteps followed.

Heart pounding, I grinned as I passed the boys. There was a yelp behind me. I turned. Zeke had the man against the brick wall by his throat. The guy's face was white as Isaac and Asher hurried down the alley to join us.

"We would be immensely grateful if you'd tell us where our friend Ethan is being held?" Miles asked with cold politeness.

The warlock's eyes flashed to Miles then back to Zeke. "I don't know what you're talking about. I-I-I was just walking."

I eyed him then stepped up beside Zeke. His brown eyes flashed to me and stayed there. Recognition lit in his eyes.

That told me everything I needed to know. "You know who I am. And you know what I can do. Tell me where he is, or Zeke will let go and you'll be mine to deal with."

"You don't scare me, little girl," he hissed.

"Zeke, back up," I told him without taking my eyes off the man.

Zeke's hand dropped from his throat and backed up only a step.

I moved closer. "Wrong answer." That rage that I was barely

holding back burst to the surface and filled my chest. My golden ribbon appeared and wrapped around him. His eyes grew wide. I dropped.

We landed in the Veil, only this time I landed on my feet. He was gasping as I pulled him to me using that ribbon to control him.

"What… where am I?" His face turned snow white.

"This is the Veil," I announced, getting his attention. I stepped toward him, using my will to lift him into the air.

He tried to struggle but it was pointless.

I gestured to the sky. "You see, that is the Way. That's where you move on after death." I walked through the flowers, pulling him with me like some macabre balloon to the edge of the abyss. "And that, is the abyss. That's where you go to be unmade." I focused, and brought him down so his feet could touch the sandy rock.

His knees buckled, he dropped to the dirt. "Am-am I dead?"

I grinned down at him. "No. But all I have to do is let go of you and you will be." I loosened the ribbon around him.

Horror filled his eyes.

"Now, where is Ethan?"

The man swallowed hard. "I-I-I don't know but…" He took a deep breath. "Um, there's a group out in the old abandoned amusement park. They've been there a day or so, that's the only place I know of." He held up his hands. "Please, please let me go home."

My stomach rolled, I hated this but it was this or lose Ethan. And I wasn't about to lose anyone I loved. I closed my eyes and pulled us out.

I opened my eyes in the alley. I let him go slowly.

He dropped to his knees, a wet stain began to move down his leg.

I held his gaze as he tried to get his breath back. "Tell your friends exactly how far I'm willing to go for my family. Make it very clear."

He nodded.

I lifted my gaze to the guys. Isaac was bouncing on his toes, Miles watched me with a curious expression, Asher seemed worried while Zeke… well, he was Zeke. "The abandoned amusement park." We left the warlock in the alley, pissed pants and all. We just needed back up.

. . .

Willow didn't approve of my method of getting Ethan's location. Apparently, leaving a grown man pissing himself in fear wasn't an approved interrogation tactic. I didn't give a fuck, which I had shouted rather loudly at her while she lectured. I vaguely recall telling her to stop lecturing and get people out there to get Ethan or I'd walk out the door myself. Since the witch had basically just grounded me in front of everyone, she hustled to move her people.

Now, we were waiting in the common room. Again. It had been an hour and there still wasn't any news. I paced in the common room, trying to breathe through the anvil in my chest. No news, not a word. If it wasn't for the rather large shifter bikers standing in front of the door I would have been gone long ago.

Shouts echoed on the other side of the door. We rushed toward the door. One of the shifters met us and kept us back while the other opened the door. Ink and Diesel strode into the common room with a stretcher between them. Ethan's sweaty mess of black hair caught my eye. I moved toward him; the shapeshifter in front of me stopped me again, this time grabbing my arm. The guys followed Ink and Diesel into the makeshift hospital. I fought to break free.

"Let me go," I growled.

The biker didn't care, he pulled me back to him and dug his shoulder into my gut. I was suddenly upside down and spitting mad.

"Put me the fuck down!" I tried driving my elbow back into his head but he only hooked his arm behind my knees and dangled me off his back.

"Calm down, firecracker," he said. "They're going to strip him down and get him in a gown first."

"Put me down, or I'll yank your soul from your body," I snarled.

"Go ahead, my missus will have an issue with you afterward," he countered.

Bella finally walked in, eyed me only to sigh. "Lloyd, you better put her ass down before one of those boys see that you have her over your shoulder."

"They're human," he countered.

She nodded. "And if you even scratch one of them, she will do what she said she would."

"Bella-"

"Put. Her. Down." Bella ordered.

"You're lucky Ink's my boss," Lloyd muttered as he set me back on my feet but kept hold of my arm so I couldn't get anywhere.

"Oh, sweetie," she said in a sarcastically sweet tone. "That makes me yours."

Lloyd thought about it and nodded. "Alright, you got a point. But I'm not letting her go until we get the all clear that he's dressed."

Shouting came from the open door, and frantic beeping. I needed to get in there.

I rolled my eyes and scoffed. "Oh, protect my non-virginal eyes."

"She's a Necro, not a tiger shifter," Bella pointed out. "She isn't nearly as modest as you lot."

Lloyd finally gave up and started to put me down. "What happened?"

"It looks like it was a set up. He was the only one there and waiting for us-"

I ignored them as rushed to the clinic area.

Asher met me at the doors, his hands grabbing my arms, stopping me from going in. "Ally, slow down. They're checking him over now."

"I'm going in."

"Ally, let them get him stable!"

I stopped fighting him as I looked up and met his eyes. "He's not stable?"

He shook his head. "He coded as soon as they got him in the clinic."

Agony exploded in my chest, my legs became jelly. Asher slowly lowered me to the floor, staying with me. He was still talking but I couldn't hear past the blood rushing in my ears. My lungs stopped working. Ethan... Ethan, gone.... No, no, no... Asher's mouth was moving but I couldn't hear. The white-hot pain grew hotter making my lungs and chest tighter with every heartbeat. I was barely holding on to control by my fingertips. Any second I was going to explode and shatter into a billion pieces.

Miles

I STEPPED through the doors to find Asher and Lexie on the floor with his hands wrapped around her upper arms. He called to her but she wasn't hearing him. Her eyes were unfocused, her breathing ragged and shallow.

"What happened?" I snapped as I knelt down beside them, lifting her chin so I could see her eyes. Agony stared back, sightless.

"I told her he coded." Asher pulled her to his chest and held her close.

I shot him a look before holding her cheek in my hand. Tears fell down her face and rolled over my fingers. "Lexie. Ethan is alive."

"She can't seem to hear us," Asher said, his voice strained as Lexie gave him her weight.

"Damn it." I focused on growing calm, I took several deep breaths and let them out slowly. When I found my calm, then and only then did I open my eyes. "Lexie, Ethan is alright. Ethan is safe," I said in that silky-smooth voice that seemed to relax her.

She blinked, tears falling faster.

"His heart is beating, Ally girl," Asher whispered against her hair.

She took a deep body shuddering breath. Then another, and another. The tightness in my chest eased as she began to shake. I dropped my hand from her cheek to her hands. She was cold. I squeezed her fingers as I reached down with my other hand and touched the skin at her mid-thigh.

"Miles." Asher's voice was almost a slap.

"She's cold and most likely in mild shock," I informed him. Letting her go, I got to my feet and ran to our bags that we had left near the chairs. I tore into them, cursing Asher every step of the way. Lexie liked to wear our clothes when she was upset and she didn't have her set here.

I pulled my emergency hoodie out of my bag, threw the bag aside to grab another. I tore open the new bag and pulled out one of Zeke's shirts. Then I moved on to the next bag. And the next. Pajama bottoms from Asher, Zeke's shirt, my hoodie, what else? I found the twins bags, jerked open the zippers, and snagged a sock from each of them. That should work. Right?

I hurried back, set the clothes down and started to put her hands through Zeke's shirt.

"We're not stripping her down out here," Asher bristled as he looked at the clothes.

I fought not to curse at him. "Obviously, we're putting them on over her clothes." I slipped the shirt over her head and tugged it down to her waist over her tank top.

Asher got his pajama bottoms, took off her sandals and slipped them up her legs. Lexie's hands trembled as she realized what we were doing in time to help shift her weight to get the pants up past her butt. She tied the drawstring herself before crossing her arms over her stomach. I picked up the hoodie and slipped her arms in. She wrapped it around herself and leaned back against my chest while her legs stayed hooked over Asher's thigh. Asher finished pulling on the mismatched pair of socks. I ran my hands over her arms, hoping to warm her up quicker.

It wasn't long before she snapped back. "Can we go in yet?"

I shared a look with Asher.

"I'll go check." Asher shifted her further into my lap before getting up and going through the glass sliding doors.

She looked up at me with wide eyes. "His heart is beating?"

"Yes." I brushed a stray hair off her face. "He wasn't even down a minute."

She nodded. "How's Isaac?"

My chest grew tight. "Zeke is with him."

Her eyes moved to meet mine. "You didn't answer."

"He's not talking, Angel." It was all I had to say.

She climbed out of my lap. By the time I got to my feet, she was starting for the doors. I stayed with her, took her hand and led her back to his bed. The entire clinic was one large room with beds curtained off. The flurry of activity was around only one bed. There really wasn't a lot of room, a couple of beds were shoved out of the way. The guys stood back as much as they could against the opposite wall.

Isaac was pale, hugging himself and rocking from foot to foot. She let go of my hand and went to him. He pulled her into a tight hug, burying his face into her neck. She whispered something to him that had him nodding and holding tighter. She ran her hands up and down his back in a soothing pattern. I waited for jealousy to hit me, only it didn't. Isaac almost lost his other half, he needed to hold onto someone like her right now. And I didn't begrudge him that. I raised my eyes to meet Zeke's over their heads. His eyes were calm, accepting even.

Asher finished talking to the doctor then brought him back to the group. His eyes ran over Lexie and Isaac who didn't seem to notice anyone else in the room. Thankfully, they were also calm.

The doctor turned to Isaac as he and Lexie turned to him, still holding hands. "Ethan is stable. We're going to run some tests but it seems the strain he was under for the last couple of days was too much for his heart. Honestly, we barely got the defibrillator charged when his heart started again so the chance of brain damage is extremely limited." His eyes narrowed on Isaac. "Now, his forearms are covered in needle marks at the moment. We're running a tox screen now to find out what they gave him and what they used to sedate him."

"When do you think he'll wake up?" Isaac rasped, his eyes bloodshot. The crowd around Ethan broke up.

"I have to get his tox screen back before I could say," the doctor replied. "For now, he's going to rest and that's what he needs."

"What did they do to him?" she asked, her voice hard.

"His heart rate was elevated, he's sweating and has a fever as if he has an infection..." The doctor shook his head. "There's no other

severe physical damage that I can see, no burns telling of electrocu-
tion, no bruises or lacerations, no clear signs of torture but his heart
reacted as if he had been under extreme stress for a prolonged period
of time. I need the test results to tell you more. In the meantime, we'll
have several witches look him over for remnants of any spell they
might have used on him. We're covering all our bases on this one."

"Thank you, doctor." I glanced at Lexie and Isaac, both were
staring at Ethan in the bed. "We'll be staying until he wakes up."

The doctor nodded then signaled a nurse and headed across the
room toward the glass wall that looked in at a medical lab. Isaac and
Lexie both went to Ethan's bedside. I picked up a chair and set it there
for her while Asher did the same for Isaac. We settled in for the
long haul.

~

Lexie

ETHAN DIDN'T WAKE UP. An hour later, we learned that there were no
drugs in his system to explain why he was unconscious. All we could
do was wait and hope he would wake up in the next twenty-four to
forty-eight hours. After that… it wasn't good.

It was around midnight when Asher brought in some food. Mine
was still sitting on the empty bedside table. Miles kept bringing me
water and reminding me to drink every so often, but mostly I sat
holding Ethan's hand while watching him breathe.

Ethan's face wasn't as pale as he was when he came in. The
sweating had finally stopped a couple of hours ago, his temp dropping
back down to normal. The dark brown bags under his eyes were
getting lighter. His hair was an oily mess, he'd hate it like that. I clung
to his hand through every agonizing slow minute. Every flicker of his
eyelids sent my heart careening out of control.

As the night crawled on, the nurses dimmed the lights in the clinic,
leaving the light above his bed. It was late when I tore my eyes from
him to the others. We had taken over this entire section. Zeke was

across from the end of the bed, sitting on the floor with his back to the wall and his eyes glued to the heart monitor. Asher was lying on the bed to my right, he had fallen asleep some time ago. Miles was in another chair next to Isaac. I turned back to Ethan.

Time marched on. My eyes grew heavier. The steady beat of Ethan's heartbeat was a soothing rhythm.

"Put your head down," Zeke whispered.

I lifted my head and turned to him. Everyone else was asleep, sitting with their heads hanging, or lying down. But not Zeke. I met his ice-blue eyes. "I'm scared to close my eyes," My voice was scratchy as I turned back to Ethan.

"Me too," he admitted. "But sleeping for a little while isn't going to kill him. I'll stay awake."

I met his eyes again and nodded. He was right, setting my head down for a few minutes wasn't going to hurt. Zeke would watch him. I turned back to Ethan and rested my cheek on my forearm on his bed as I kept his hand in mine. I fell fast and deep.

A change in Ethan's heartbeat brought me to the surface. I opened my eyes only to find everything blurry. I blinked, trying to clear my eyes of gunk. The scent of rosemary reached my nose, rosemary that wasn't mine. Huh? I finally cleared my vision. A small, pale, manicured hand lifted from Ethan's forehead. I lifted my head to find who it was but there was no one there. The clinic was empty except for us. I lowered my head back down to my arm and drifted under again.

"Lexie…?" Ethan's smoky rasp snapped my head up.

His chocolate eyes were tired but open. Relief and light flooded me as tears started falling. I dropped his hand, darted forward and kissed him without thinking. It was a soft, desperate kiss that reassured me that he was alive.

When I pulled back, his fingers weakly brushed my cheek taking my tears. "Where is he?"

"Here." Isaac, tears pouring down his own face as he got to his feet and bent over the bed.

Ethan turned to him, letting me go. I moved back.

Isaac pressed his forehead against Ethan's and closed his eyes. "Lo siento, lo siento muchísimo."

Ethan's hand went to the back of Isaac's head. "Lo siento, he sido un idiota maldito."

Creaking behind me had me turning to find Asher sitting up and pushing a blanket off his shoulder. His eyes found Ethan awake. He swallowed hard and got to his feet.

I moved out from between the beds. When Ethan and Isaac let go, Asher was there. He bent over the bed and hugged Ethan.

Ethan weakly patted his back. "I'm okay."

Isaac moved out from between the beds and ran across the room, probably to get the doctor.

When Asher straightened, Miles was in Isaac's spot. Asher moved out from between the beds. Zeke moved to take his spot.

"You scared us." Miles reached out and squeezed his shoulder.

Ethan gave him an exhausted smile. "Sorry."

"As soon as you're feeling better, you've got one hell of a lecture coming," Zeke growled.

Ethan turned to him and gave a small barely-there chuckle. He lifted his hand, Zeke took it in that manly fist finger squeeze thing they do.

When they let go, Ethan's arm dropped back to the bed. "I'll clear my schedule."

The guys chuckled as I wiped my face. Ethan's gaze found me again.

"What do you remember?" Miles asked.

"Later," he muttered a heartbeat before he fell back asleep. I checked the monitors; his heartbeat was strong and steady. Ethan was alive.

CHAPTER 16

JULY 17TH, TUESDAY

*W*e sat with Ethan as he slept. Each of us were dozing on and off through the night and into the next morning. Well, the guys were. I kept running over everything that had happened since we came to New Orleans. All I could think was that we shouldn't have come. I should have just contacted Louis long distance. Ethan wouldn't have been tortured, we wouldn't be in the middle of this fucking fight. I finally came to a conclusion.

I reached over Ethan and pulled one a red hair off Isaac's shoulder before catching Miles' eye. I tilted my chin toward the clinic doors before getting to my feet and heading that way. Miles joined me just past the doors. I waited until they closed behind us.

"What's wrong?" Miles asked.

"You guys need to leave," I stated. "As soon as Ethan can fly, you need to take him, and the others, and leave."

His eyes flashed cold a heartbeat before he looked over my head at the doors. "Why do you think that?"

"They only took Ethan because of me. They only tortured him because of me." My throat grew tight. "If you guys aren't here, you'll be safe."

He nodded, his jaw clenching and unclenching before he looked down and met my eyes. "No." His eyes grew colder. "We'll go home together."

"We could have lost Ethan," I reminded him, trying to keep the emotion out of my voice.

"I'm aware." His voice sent chills over my skin.

"Miles..." I needed him to understand.

"What about you? Do you really think that I could leave you here with these people? With the Witch's Council, who are trying to get their hands on you?" His voice dropped the room another ten degrees. It was a voice I'd never heard before. He stepped closer, his voice growing even colder. "In case you haven't noticed, I care about you and what happens to you. So, there is no way in-" He stopped himself, looked over my head. He took a breath then met my eyes again. "I'm not leaving you here." He turned and walked away, his shoulders tense.

I stood there for almost a minute trying to grasp what just happened.

"Did you really think that would work?" Asher asked as he came from the cafeteria with a tray of food.

I shrugged. "He's the most logical one."

"Right now, he's already angry over the Witch's Council hurting Ethan," he said as he came closer. "They also seem to want to get their hands on you. And the thought of what could happen if we leave you here..."

I chewed on the corner of my bottom lip. "I've never seen him that angry before."

Asher's gaze went to the door Miles left through. "It doesn't happen often." He turned back to me. "He won't do anything stupid."

I nodded.

"Come on, I've got some breakfast for everyone," Asher said. We started back toward the clinic.

The runed door burst open. Louis shouldered it open further with an unconscious Uma in his arms.

"We've been hit!" Louis shouted as he carried her into the common room. Asher set the tray down on a chair then ran with me to meet them.

"What the hell happened?" I asked, looking at Uma. Her skin was ashen, dried blood caked her face and her nightgown.

"The fucking witches hit us at dawn," Louis bit out. "If Uma hadn't been there…"

Savannah and the kids came in. A couple of them still sniffling. Asher broke off and went to help her and the kids.

When we reached the clinic doors Louis shot over his shoulder. "Get Willow!"

I didn't waste time, I hurried to the conference room and threw open the door. Willow was still in her night clothes with a phone to her ear. "They hit Louis's house. Uma is unconscious."

She hung up the phone and hurried around the table and out the door. We found them a couple of beds down from Ethan. Louis pulled the blankets up to her chest and lovingly tucked her in.

"Louis?" Willow demanded as we reached him.

"They planned this out." Louis tore his gaze from Uma to turn to us. "They surrounded the house, then hit us at dawn." His eyes grew cold and dark. "They were after Juan."

Willow let out a breath. "Calm down, while I check on her." She went to Uma's side while I went to Louis.

"Is he okay?" I asked.

"If Uma hadn't been there, if she wasn't as strong a witch as she is…" He shook his head. "We would have lost him."

"They specifically went after him?" I asked, just to be clear.

His eyes were on mine when he nodded.

"They're looking for a Necro they can control," I muttered.

"Yeah," he bit out. His eyes bored into mine. "You're going to teach me how to get to the Veil."

I nodded. "And you're going to get Juan out of here."

He held out his hand. "I'll call the gargoyles."

I pulled my phone out of my back pocket and handed it to him. He moved further down the line of beds for some privacy.

Willow turned away from Uma and wiped the sweat from her face. "Uma will be fine. She's just exhausted."

I nodded. "Louis is getting sanctuary for Juan and the others."

"Good." Her face grew drawn. "The situation is just escalating. The vampires were hit this morning with the sunrise."

"What?" I couldn't believe it.

Wintergreen tickled my nose a heartbeat before Miles stepped beside me. "Any survivors?"

"Yes, all of them in fact. They were expecting an attack and were sleeping in a secure bunker that Samuel had built years ago. So, when they burned down the mansion they were safe. Our people are bringing them in to the safehouse basement in the next couple of hours," she said.

"Has anyone called Bella?" I asked, meeting her tired eyes. "They might have hit the shifters too."

Her face paled, she pulled out her phone and moved several steps away.

"Angel..." Miles breathed.

"It's okay," I whispered.

"No, it's not."

Before I could ask what he meant, Louis came back and handed me my phone. "Savannah, Uma and the kids will be leaving by tonight."

"Where are they going?" Miles asked.

"They're going to the gargoyles," Louis sighed.

My gaze went to Uma then back to him. "You're in deep shit."

"I know," he said, resigned.

Willow cursed then hurried back toward us. "The smaller shifters were hit too. They're bringing the wounded here now."

Willow passed me and went to the guys as Asher walked in. "Boys, we have wounded coming in. Do any of you have any first aid training?"

"I do." Asher raised his hand.

"Good, you'll be with me." She turned to the others. "We're going to need your help."

· · ·

THE GUYS HAD WANTED me to stay with Ethan while they helped set up a triage area for the wounded. I didn't have any medical training, but I was more than willing to help set up. So, Willow sent me up to the dorm on the seventh floor to set up cots and bedding. I found everything at one end of the large room that spanned the entire building. My mind was racing, the council wasn't even trying to hide this time. They went after Juan. He was only fourteen! It's obvious at this point they want their hands on a Necromancer. But why? To study one of us? To control us? I didn't know if I wanted to know anymore. Besides, what did they get out of torturing Ethan?

I was still setting up the last of the cots an hour later when Asher came up the stairs at the center of the floor.

He made his way down the row of cots to me. "Want a hand?"

"A hand, a foot, maybe another arm..." I grinned. "How's it going downstairs?"

Asher took a green cot off the stack and went to set it down as I went to get another. "We have the worst cases in the clinic getting treatment, the lighter injuries were easy to handle." He set the cot down. "It wasn't as bad as Willow feared but the common room is packed right now."

I hefted a cot up and moved down the row. "Well, after we finish we'll have somewhere for them."

Asher passed me. "Dr. Detes said Ethan was okay to leave the clinic. So, he's got a room on the fourth floor."

I set the cot down and straightened. "How'd he get up the stairs?"

Asher picked up the last cot. "We walked him up the stairs and to his room. He passed out as soon as he hit the bed."

That made sense. "He's exhausted."

"Yeah, but he's moving around now." He placed the last cot and straightened. "Is that it?"

I sighed. "No, there're blankets folded in those boxes. Including pillows. One set per cot."

Asher started to pull out the blankets. I started with the pillows. As we worked my mind went back over everything. The guys, the witches, Serena, everything.

I dropped the last pillow down and went to look out the window at the end of the room. The city was further out but the sight was rather nice in evening light. Maybe we should leave? Get out of New Orleans. Go home... But I wanted Jadis's blood for hurting Ethan. I wanted to-

"You're quiet." Asher stepped beside me to look out at the view. "What's wrong?"

Different emotions fought it out in my chest, I couldn't think of what to say. "Nothing."

"Talk to me," he said.

I turned and looked up at him. "What do you want me to say?"

"Anything," he said, his voice growing louder. "You've got no problem talking to Miles about everything that's going on, you have no problem telling Zeke you're scared. But when it comes to me you can't even tell me something as simple how you're feeling."

"'Cause I don't know!" I snapped. "I don't know how I feel. I don't know what I want. I'm confused." Guilt and fear tore through me making my mouth run. "I've pulled us into a fucking war-zone that already got Ethan tortured. We're in a fucking safe-house and it's all my fault!"

"How the hell is this your fault?" he demanded.

"Because I told Serena to fuck off three weeks ago!" I finally said it out loud. Putting it into words for the first time. "And after that the Witch's Council started taking over Florida."

The heat in his eyes cooled.

"All those people in Florida who are dead? That's my fault," I bit. "That's because of me." Me and my big fucking mouth.

"What happened in Florida wasn't your fault, Ally," Asher began. "The Witch's Council are the ones who did it. You know that."

I met his eyes again, my heart aching. "And then there's you guys." I shook my head. "You want to know how I feel? What I feel most is guilt. I feel horrible for kissing all of you. I feel guilty for standing here wanting to kiss you even though I shouldn't. I feel like I'm being torn apart. A person is supposed to feel this way about one person, not be in love with five! I feel like I'm going to lose everything and everyone that means anything to me! And get everyone killed in the process! There! Is that enough?"

"You don't have to feel guilty about kissing anyone! We all know what's going on now," he pointed out.

"Yeah, 'cause you guys wanting to kill each other over a simple shoulder touch is normal?" I turned away and ran my hand down my face. "What the fuck have I done?"

"Ally," he snapped. "You can't help the way you feel. I get that. They get that. We're all just trying to deal with it."

I looked up and met his ocean eyes. "I'm sorry. I'm so sorry."

He stepped closer and ran the back of his fingers over my jaw. His breath moved my hair. "Ally, you said you're in love with me."

"I...uh... yeah..." I couldn't think, my face burned as panic started to take hold. What did I just do? No one needed to know that!

He leaned down. His lips were a breath from mine when he whispered, "I'm in love with you too." My breathing hitched just before he pressed his lips to mine. Stunned, it took me a moment to realize what he had said. Love washed through me as I kissed him back. My fingers found his waist as he held my face still. One kiss led to another, and another.

He pulled back a little when we were both breathless. "I'm so tired of not kissing you." His lips took mine again, kissing me harder. He swept in and made everything else disappear but him. His lips, his hands on my neck, his body against me. That was all there was. I wrapped my arms around his neck and moved closer. His hands moving to my lower back. Tingles rang up and down my spine as his hands pulled me to him, my back bowing slightly, our kiss changing. My breasts pressed into his ribs as his fingers flexed, sending a wave of shivers over me. I made a small sound that had him kissing me harder. His palms moved to the back of my thighs before he hooked the back of my knees and lifted me off the floor. My body pressed against his, making me catch my breath. He sat on the window sill; I instantly set my knees on the sill to straddle him. Lightning shot through me as our bodies met. His lips trailed from my lips down my jaw to my neck as his hands stroked up my thighs. My fingers curled in his shirt, my hips shifted against his. He groaned against my pulse before gripping my hips. Aching, I moved against him again, a breathy moan escaping from my lips. His warmth surrounded me while his lips found mine again, scattering me even more. Every move he made, every touch, every stroke was soft, and gentle. Even as his fingers slipped under the hem of my shirt, and spread out over my waist. I kissed him back harder, meeting him stroke for stroke as cinnamon filling my senses. I shook against him as his hand moved up my ribs making my skin too tight, my heart beat too fast. I didn't even notice until the top of his thumb brushed the underside of my breast sending longing washing through me.

Something slammed shut somewhere, rattling the windows. A spark lit through the haze filling my mind. Something... there was something I needed to remember. His thumb began to stroke over fabric pulling Miles' smooth timbre racing to the forefront of my memory. I suddenly remembered where I was, what I was doing and, judging by how amazing he felt, what would happen if we didn't stop. I had promised Miles... Oh, no, no... I stiffened. He noticed. Before I even had a chance to tell him to stop he slid his hand back down out of my shirt and to my hip. Our kiss slowed. My grip on his shirt eased. He kissed me softly one more time before easing back. He rested his forehead on mine as we both tried to catch our breath.

"Why do you have to feel so good?" he whispered.

I couldn't even put two thoughts together as I shifted a little. Sparks shot through me as I forced myself to stop moving.

He groaned quietly in the back of his throat. "Oh, you need to stop that..."

I laid my cheek against his shoulder, my nose near the crook of his neck. His arms wrapped around me, his hand stroking up and down my back.

We were quiet for some time, neither one of us wanting to pull away.

"I know everything is a mess, we're in the middle of a fight, and we almost lost Ethan," he said, his voice soft and low. "But is it horrible of me to be happy, like this, with you?"

I smiled to myself. "No, I don't think so."

He pressed his nose into my hair and took a deep breath. "Good."

We were quiet for another couple of minutes, long enough for me to realize how much the brick window sill was hurting my knees. "I need to move."

His hands went to my hips a heartbeat before he stood, setting me on my feet. When he didn't let go, I looked up, and met his warm ocean eyes. "I know you didn't say you're in love with just me."

I started to chew on the corner of my bottom lip as my stomach knotted.

His eyes ran over my face then met my eyes. "The guys want to talk."

"When?" I asked, my chest aching. He pulled his phone out of his back pocket and checked the time.

"Now." His fingers squeezed mine. "We're supposed to meet in Ethan's room." He kept my hand in his as we went down the stairs.

"What do you mean talk?" I asked as we reached the fourth floor.

"Everyone has some questions about how this happened," he explained as he led me down the west hall. "Some of us just need to understand."

My stomach knotted. "No fist fights?"

His ocean eyes were warm as they met mine. "No fist fights."

We were in the middle of the hall when he stopped, squeezed my hand then let go. At the sixth door, he didn't bother knocking, he just opened it. The guys were spread out around the room, standing, sitting on the floor or dresser.

Ethan was in the queen-sized bed, sitting up against a pile of pillows. His color was better than earlier. He grinned. "Beautiful, please save me from these mother hens and get me out of here?"

I shook my head. "Nope, you died. You stay in bed for now."

The guys chuckled. Ethan cursed.

I smiled as I walked over and felt his forehead. "How're you feeling?"

"I'm fine. Tired and bored but fine," he grumbled as he took my hand off his forehead and kept it in his.

"Can you guys not?" Isaac asked, his voice rough.

I pulled my hand from Ethan's as I sighed. I didn't think the cease fire would last this long anyway.

"Don't make her feel bad about trying to make me feel better," Ethan muttered.

I closed my eyes and tried to figure out what to say.

"If you're not willing to discuss this calmly then there won't be a family meeting," Miles stated. "So, stop the little comments."

Isaac sighed. "I just want to know how this happened."

I wrapped my arms around my stomach and turned to face all of them. Every one of them were watching me. "I didn't know how to..." I admitted. "How do you tell someone that you kissed them and four of our best friends?" My eyes met Isaac's. "Including your brother?"

Isaac's eyes softened.

"I was terrified to tell everyone. If you would believe me. What you guys would think of me..." I shook my head. "I can barely believe it and I'm the one..."

"I get it," Ethan mumbled.

"But..." Isaac hesitated. "How do you feel about everyone? You never said..."

I took a deep breath, fighting the tightness in my chest. "I have feelings for everyone. The same feelings for everyone."

Zeke cursed, Asher was silent, Miles watched the others carefully, Isaac started pacing, Ethan closed his eyes and leaned back against his pillows.

"I didn't mean for it to happen," I tried again.

"We know," Zeke muttered.

"You wouldn't do that, Red," Isaac added. "This just..."

"Sucks," Ethan finished for him.

There were several minutes of silence.

"You're going to have to choose," Isaac stated.

"Is... Is that what you guys want?" I swallowed hard, my heart hammering in my chest. "Do any of you really still..."

Voices started shouting in the hallway. Louis stuck his head through the door as I started toward it. "They hit the wolves, I need hands."

Everyone started for the door.

"You stay here, Lexie!" Louis ordered before turning and running out the door. I stopped in my tracks.

Isaac slammed the door behind them leaving me alone with Ethan.

"Come here, Beautiful," Ethan called.

I turned and went back to his side. He reached out and snagged me around the waist. The next thing I knew I was in bed on the other side of him, my legs over his thighs.

He smiled down at me and brushed my hair out of my face. "It's going to be okay, Beautiful."

"How?" My eyes burned.

His face softened. "Because we're a family. Nothing's going to change that."

I hoped he was right.

He grinned. "Now, I want to see you smile."

I gave him a small smile.

"Not good enough, Beautiful," he said, his hand moving to my ribs. He started tickling me. I squirmed, laughing as I tried to get away. "Come on, give me a smile."

I squeaked as his fingers found a sensitive spot. "I'm smiling, I'm smiling."

"Good." He stopped tickling me. He threw a couple of pillows across the bed then laid down and pulled me into his arms. I rested my head on his arm and looked up at him.

Those chocolate eyes were on me. "Stay with me for a while?"

"Always," I whispered.

He pulled me closer until my head rested on his chest. "Ojalá pudiera guardarte."

"What?"

"Nothing, Beautiful," he said softly. "I'm just tired."

I snuggled against him, it wasn't long before he fell asleep still holding me. I laid there, listening to his heartbeat, wondering if the guys were okay.

Asher

THE WEREWOLF PACK of New Orleans was based out on the edge of the swamp. I expected to take a boat, but Louis drove us through the swamp on a well-used dirt road in one of the safehouse's SUVs. Everyone hung on for their lives.

When we finally arrived, what we found was chaos. Cabins were still on fire, a couple of kids were screaming, injured were everywhere and… bodies. Wolf, human. They were left where they fell.

"Holy shit…" I said, not even realizing it.

"Help to get the fire out, help the wounded if you can!" Louis ordered us as we slid to a halt. "First aid kits are in the back! Hand them out, help where you can!" Everyone dove out of the SUV and ran around the back. The stench of smoke and burnt meat filled the air. People crying, others raging. The other cars arrived as I grabbed a bag and ran for one group of bloodied people.

Before anything else, I pulled on a pair of gloves as I dropped to my knees beside a woman dressed only in a bra and shorts. Her shirt was on man's torso, trying to stop the bleeding.

"Puncture? Burn? Or laceration?" I asked as I opened the bag.

"Burn and shrapnel," she said, her voice shaking. "They hit the propane tank with a fireball."

Shit. I opened a large eight by ten pad and put it over the bloody shirt she was using as a bandage and pressed. The guy jerked and grunted in pain. She looked up at me. "Are you human?"

I nodded, my heart pounding.

"Keep your gloves on, no matter what," she told me before turning to shout over my shoulder. "This one needs to go!"

A couple of large men hurried over with a panel of canvas. They started to move him over to the makeshift stretcher.

"Keep pressure on his side," I ordered.

The woman got to her feet and took my spot. "Focus on patching them up enough that they can be moved. They'll shift and heal but we need to get them out of here to shift." She left with them.

It was just the start of a very long hour and a half. I moved from injured to injured, helping where I could. Stopping the bleeding when I could, stabilizing limbs when they were broken. Zeke and Isaac used more canvas to move people to the vehicles to be taken wherever they were going.

My hands were holding pressure on a gushing abdominal wound when the man gasped then grew still. My heart stopped. Shit, no, no, no! He wasn't breathing. "I need the defibrillator!" I knew they had one, I'd seen it back on the SUV hood. People ran as I started chest compressions.

Hallis handed it to me before he went to the man's head and started giving him mouth to mouth. I tore open the case, shoved the rest of his shirt out of the way and placed the patches on the man's chest, and started the machine. "Hands off!" I shouted.

Hallis stopped giving mouth to mouth as the machine checked the man's heartbeat.

"Shock advised." The machine announced in a mechanical voice. Come on, come on! What's taking so fucking long?

"Stand clear. Shock ready."

I made sure Hallis was clear and hit the button.

"Shock administered. Begin C.P.R."

We moved back over him. I started chest compressions again. One, two, three... Come on man. A woman cried out, sobbing somewhere. Five, six, seven... "Come on!" I didn't know how long we tried but it felt like an eternity.

Louis finally stopped us. "He's gone. He lost too much blood."

Both Hallis and I sat back on our heels and looked down at the man we couldn't save. Louis was right. The man had staggered into the area with a large piece of shrapnel protruding from his stomach. Blood covered him.

"I'm sorry, David," Hallis whispered as he closed the man's sightless eyes.

A woman screamed, her sobbing becoming hysterical.

My eyes burned. I looked around. There was no one else needing help, just a crowd of people watching me. I got to my feet and walked out of the ring of people so I didn't have to see his soul appear as it had for the others. I didn't know where I was going, didn't really care. But a hose caught my eye. I pulled off the gloves and began washing my hands. There wasn't any blood but, it didn't matter. I took deep breaths as memories poured through me. Mom's cold skin when I checked her pulse that morning. The way her body was relaxed, more so than I had ever seen her. Jessica's scream after I told her. Stopping her as she tried to run to Mom's room. Holding her as she cried. It all came flooding back.

"You did everything you could," Miles said from behind me.

I sniffed and shook my head. "It didn't make a difference. It never does."

He put his hand on my shoulder as I fought for control. "It did to the ones who lived. To their families."

"Why did I come out here?" I muttered. "I never manage to..."

"Sixteen," Miles stated.

I turned around. "What?

Miles's eyes met mine. "Sixteen. That's how many you saved today. And that was only the severe injuries. I'm not even counting the ones who only needed a bandage until they could shift."

Sixteen? I had lost count after five.

"You always wanted to be a paramedic, you're good at this. Why become a chef when it's your second choice?" he asked.

I shook my head, not knowing how to explain it to him. Yeah, I had wanted to be a paramedic before Mom died but Mom passing had changed things. Changed me. I wanted a life where I didn't have to watch people die in front of me. "Things change, Miles."

His eyes were understanding. They held no judgement or criticism. I finally got why Ally talked to Miles about everything. He only listened and offered advice. I wanted to be more like that...

We headed back to the square in silence. We heard the shouting before we even reached it. When we stepped through the buildings, we found the others and joined them.

"Calm down!" Hallis shouted. "Everyone knows that the standard protocol during an attack is to tell the kids to run. They haven't come back but that doesn't mean they're in trouble. There's a lot of smoke in the air, they might not be able to smell or hear that it's safe."

The crowd calmed.

"Now, form groups. We'll have to spread out and look for them to bring them home," Hallis ordered. Everyone started splitting up. Hallis gestured to two giant wolves then came toward us. "Boys, we need your help too."

"What do you want us to do?" Isaac asked.

"Search the houses for kids or pups. Then go west out of town. With all this smoke we can't track them and we don't have enough people here to cover the area," Hallis explained.

"Isn't there a designated evacuation spot?" Miles asked, pushing his glasses up his nose.

Hallis turned to him. "No, because the whole point of sending the kids off is to keep them safe. And if we don't know where they are we can't give up that location." He turned back to the rest of us. "If you see a kid, or a pup, tell them 'tell me, star, have you seen the white wolf?' Saying that, and having these two with you will help them trust you enough to come back here."

Everyone agreed, then started searching the houses with the giant wolves padding next to us.

Dread filled my chest as we started walking through the avenues of the small town and looking around the unburnt buildings. I was about to move on when a small barely-there whine caught my ear. I stopped and looked around. There really was nowhere to hide here. No trees, no brush. Nothing. But on the front of every house there was a porch; some were small, some were large. But only one of them had a hole between the porch edge and the dirt.

Slowly, I walked over and got down on my hands and knees. With my luck, it'll probably be a rat. I peeked through the hole. A small form was huddled at the back of the hole under the porch. The light sneaking through the slats showed how small it was. Its eyes glowed in the dim light. It whimpered and tried to get further back.

"It's okay." I kept my voice soft. Hallis told me to say 'tell me, star, have you seen the white wolf?'"

The pup stopped whimpering. It slowly came forward a little then stopped. I got the message.

"I'm going to go look for the others, head back to the square when you're ready." I pushed myself to my feet and left the pup under the porch. The kid felt safe there. I wasn't about to yank the poor kid out of there.

One of the wolves stuck their muzzle into the hole then backed up. The little pup peeked out. When it saw the wolf, it whimpered and whined as it scrambled out of the hole and under the wolf's legs. The adult wolf sat and licked the pup's head and ears. We figured the adult had this and started moving again.

We kept searching, eventually making our way past the village where they finally had the fire out.

Everyone walked in silence for a few minutes before I said what had been on my mind since I started my search. "What if the council took the kids?"

"Let's hope that's not the case," Miles said.

I nodded. We started walking faster. No one spoke as we spent the next hour looking, calling for the kids to head to the square. That dread grew and grew the longer we went without a response or a sign of them. That's when we heard a long howl. We didn't say a word, we just ran toward it.

We broke into a clearing. Two large wolves that were clearly were-wolves, but not quite as big as the werewolves back at the town, stood outside the mouth of a cave. Teenagers?

They got to their feet and growled, showing their fangs. When I took a step into the clearing, Zeke came with me.

My heart slammed as I held my hands out to my sides, showing them we weren't armed. "Tell me, star, have you seen the white wolf?" I announced. They stopped showing their teeth. Their postures relaxed as they stopped growling.

A young girl, around the age of nine, came to the mouth of the cave and eyed us. Her black hair was in two braids down to her shoulders. Her hazelnut eyes were wide. "What did you say?"

"Tell me, star, have you seen the white wolf?" Isaac repeated from the tree line.

"That's the code our pack uses. It's from the Grey Fairy book." The girl relaxed a little. "Who are you?"

"I'm Asher, this is Miles, Isaac, and Zeke." I gestured to each of us. "We're with the reinforcements. Look, you don't have to go with us. You can go by yourselves if you don't trust us."

She shook her head, her eyes going to the wolf beside Zeke. "Aunt Lara?"

The wolf hurried forward, licking the girl's face.

She wrapped her arms around the wolf and hugged her tight. The other wolf rubbed against her sides, over and over.

We stayed put until she seemed to make up her mind. "We can't go on our own, there's too many in wolf form. We can't keep track of everyone in the woods, we barely got everyone here."

"Then let's get everyone buddied up and we'll get back to the pack," I suggested.

She nodded and called over her shoulder. "Come on, guys, time to head home." She moved out of the mouth of the cave.

Kids in varying states of dirty and scared poured out of the slight opening in the rock. Sprinkled among them were wolves. Brown, black, gray, white. They were different ages and sizes but all of them had an intelligence in their eyes that I couldn't deny. Almost every kid was carrying a wolf pup in their arms. And there were still some trailing behind on their own paws. I did a quick count. Twenty-five kids in all. Shit.

A small black wolf pup came toward Zeke, whimpering as it dropped to the dirt. Zeke knelt down and reached his fingers out to it slowly. It sniffed his fingers, then watched Zeke for several heartbeats. Eventually, the pup lifted himself again and staggered the last few steps to Zeke's hand before it collapsed again.

"It's okay, sleep. We're taking you home." He lifted the animal with one hand and brought him to his chest. I looked around. Most of the guys were holding pups now too, except Zeke. Another had come up to him, so now he had two.

By the time we finished checking the kids for injuries, a little boy came out of the cave. "Amber! Casey doesn't want to come out."

Since I was the only one of us without a pup, I started toward the cave. "Let's see if we can coax her out."

"Be careful." Zeke warned me as the pups in his arms snuggled against his neck.

I waved that I heard him.

The cavern was large and dim. Several holes had been punched through the rock, they acted like skylights making it so I could see. I followed the little boy into the back. The wolf pup was small, white and covered in dirt. She didn't even lift her head as we came closer. She only whimpered and whined in fear. I knelt down in the dirt, the same way Zeke had, and held out my hand.

The poor thing eyed me then sniffed my fingers and palm. I waited patiently as she made up her mind. She dropped her head onto my fingers as if that was all she had.

Being careful, I picked her up and held her little shaking body against my chest. She immediately started gnawing lightly on my finger and stopped shaking. When I took my finger away she began to shake again. So, I let her have the finger as we headed back outside.

"I think she was just too tired to move," I said as I joined the others.

"That's Casey, she's not even two," Amber explained. "She was so scared she had her first shift."

"Is that normal?" Zeke asked.

She shrugged. "We're not supposed to shift until we hit puberty but if we get scared enough, our wolf takes over and protects us."

That was good to know. I turned to the group of kids. "Okay, five kids to each of us." I turned to the larger wolves. "Can you guys run alongside the group and make sure we don't lose anyone."

One of the larger wolves gave a small half bark.

"That means yes," Amber translated.

"Alright, let's go."

We started to walk back, I never realized how heavy a twelve-pound wolf pup could be after that long. I eyed Zeke and his now three pups, one on each arm, and one draped over the back of his neck. Animals loved Zeke, even when we were kids they loved him.

"Are you sure that's a good idea?" Isaac asked, watching the pup slobbering over my fingers.

"I don't know," I admitted. "But it keeps her calm." And that was enough for me.

Our trip back was a lot shorter, forty-five minutes later we walked out of the tree line and back into the square. The fires were out and the bodies were gone. I didn't want to know where.

A howl went up. The pups in our arms and in the kids' arms returned it.

Everyone ran for the group of kids. The guys and I got out of the way. We watched as everyone checked the kids again, including the pups. A large black wolf came to Isaac, his head almost level with his chest. Its eyes were yellow as it began to sniff the pup in his arms. The little guy finally woke up and whined. He almost jumped out of Isaac's arms. He stopped him and set him down on the dirt. They sniffed each other, the adult examining the pup over and over. The pup rubbed against its parent's legs and waited. The large wolf turned back to Isaac and licked his cheek before they trotted off.

He wiped his face, trying to be subtle about it.

"Casey?" A woman called.

"Over here!" I answered as I walked through the crowd to meet the woman covered in soot. I handed her the exhausted pup.

"Thank you so much!" The mom said with tears running down her face. She began to examine the pup. "Oh, sweetie, you shifted!" She held her to her chest before heading back to the crowd.

Louis found us. "Good job finding the kids. The smoke made it impossible for us to sniff them out."

"No problem." I looked over the crowd. "Where are they all going?"

Louis grinned.

CHAPTER 17

JULY 17TH, TUESDAY AFTERNOON

*A*fter waking up next to a still sleeping Ethan, I walked back downstairs to find chaos. Humans, wolves, and even a freaking bear were mulling around in the common room. I found the guys in the living area surrounded by kids and wolf puppies. Miles was playing Magic the Gathering with a couple of preteen boys. Asher had a line of little girls waiting to get their hair braided by him. Zeke's lap was covered in wolf pups. He cursed and complained but he was still scratching ears. And Isaac... Isaac was surrounded by kids and trying the patience of Hallis and Samuel.

"So, do werewolves have to shift when there's a full moon?" Isaac smirked.

Hallis sighed. "Only the first time, it's not voluntary. After that, we do because it's tradition."

I smiled to myself.

"Okay, vampires and garlic. Any connection?" Isaac asked.

The kids giggled around him.

"No, garlic is simply very pungent to our increased sense of smell," Samuel explained in a patient voice.

"Do you ever get the urge to chase cars?" Isaac asked in a serious voice.

I smiled to myself as the guys chuckled.

"No," Hallis growled. Isaac was pushing it, and he knew it.

"What about fleas? Are fleas an issue?" Isaac pushed it even more.

The kids burst out laughing. Louis's own chuckle came from a couch where he was seated with his kids.

"What about a stake to the heart?" Isaac asked with a grin.

"What wouldn't that kill?" Samuel countered sending the kids into a fit of giggles.

I leaned against a pillar and chuckled quietly.

Asher glanced at me before going back to the little girl's hair. Samuel turned and met my gaze. Something in his eyes gave me the distinct feeling that he was deciding on how to bite me. He got to his feet and crossed the room to me. I looked up at him as he stopped across from me.

"Are you ready to settle our debt?" Samuel asked in a low voice.

Movement on my periphery had me glancing at the room. Asher was watching us, frowning. I turned back to Samuel. "Alright."

He gestured toward the dark conference room. "After you."

I snorted. "I've seen this horror movie, I'm not going in there alone with you."

A glint in his dark eyes told me that he wanted to laugh, but his face was politely blank. Asher got to his feet, the others followed, including Louis.

I waited until the guys and Louis started toward the conference room. I didn't budge until Samuel's lips twitched and he went ahead of me.

As soon as we walked in Samuel moved to the other end of the room while the others spread out on the side closest to the door.

Zeke met me at the door and whispered, "You sure you want to do this?"

I looked up and met his eyes. "A deal's a deal."

His face was hard when he nodded.

Samuel crooked his finger at me. I resisted the urge to flip him off as I walked down the length of the table.

I leaned against the table with my back to the guys. "Why do you want to drink my blood anyway?"

He watched me with an unblinking stare, as if judging what to tell me. "There's a legend that says if a vampire feeds from a Necromancer of power, then they'll control you. I want to test the theory."

"Then you could have used Louis's blood," I pointed out. "You wanted mine, why?"

His eyes filled with approval for a fraction of a heartbeat. "Louis is a strong Necromancer already. I don't want him to get control over me in case the legend is true. You are still young, still learning. The danger is less."

At least that made sense. "Okay."

He smiled, it sent icy shivers down my spine. "Now, feeding-"

"You'll feed from the wrist," I stated.

Samuel raised an eyebrow and looked down the table at Louis. "You really did school her well."

"No games, Samuel," Louis warned. "No power use. Just physiology."

Samuel bowed from the neck. "Agreed." He turned to me and stepped closer. An odd scent reached my nose. It was sweet, cloying and dry... like dried rose petals only not as potent. It made my stomach churn.

"Now, before we get started, there are a few things we need to be clear on. The physiology of a vampire is quite interesting," Samuel explained. "Our skin and our saliva have dopamine inducing proper-ties. Our blood also heals living tissue without scaring."

I looked up and met his eyes.

"What this means is a touch, a lick along the skin will send the dopamine production in your body into overdrive. In a sense, it feels like hours of foreplay in a heartbeat."

The guys shifted at the other end of the table.

Samuel ignored them. "The main side effect of feeding a vampire is usually a climax from the one being bitten. Do you understand?"

"Oh, fuck this," Zeke snapped.

"Seconded," Asher chimed in.

"Fuck voting!" Isaac snapped.

"She's already agreed," Miles stated, his voice glacial cold, silencing the others.

Samuel kept his eyes on mine. "Now, I have no intention of even doing a light feed off of you, so this shouldn't be the case. However, this is the first time I'm feeding off you so it could be difficult to gauge. Do you understand?"

"Yeah." I swallowed hard, my pulse thumping in my throat.

Samuel held my gaze as he stepped even closer and whispered so quietly I could barely hear. "Now, since you haven't gone through the usual screening process that we put potential donors through, I need to ask if you have ever been sexually assaulted? Attacked? Molested? Anything that can trigger past trauma?"

I stayed perfectly still as my heartbeat raced in my throat. The walk through the snow back to the cabin... I didn't want to answer but judging by the narrowing of Samuel's eyes, I didn't have to.

"This isn't going to work." He stepped back.

"Why not?" I eyed him.

"Because I don't torture people," he whispered. "You're going to have to owe me." He began walking down the table.

My stomach knotted. I didn't want to owe a vampire. There were just too many things that could go wrong with that. I turned, grabbed a glass from the tray and slammed it down on the table.

Everyone but Samuel turned to look at me.

I pulled my pocket knife from my back pocket and opened it. I didn't hesitate as I sliced the skin across my palm. Samuel turned when the first drop of blood dropped into the glass. I took deep breaths through the burning pain that radiated from my palm. Why the hell did I use my palm? There were thousands of nerve endings there!

"Damn it, Lexie," Zeke snapped as he made his way toward me.

"Well, you certainly are resourceful," Samuel said as he walked back around the table. "That's more than enough, chère."

Zeke pulled his handkerchief out of his back pocket and pressed it to my bloody hand. He muttered under his breath about killing me later. I ignored it.

Samuel stepped closer, and pressed the tip of his index finger to his sharp canine. "Here, this will heal it within thirty seconds."

"With what side effects?" Miles demanded.

"None," Samuel stated.

"No diseases? Bloodborne pathogens?" Miles pushed.

"We don't have diseases," Samuel replied. "And our species is extraordinarily healthy."

Reluctantly, Zeke pulled back the bloody handkerchief. Samuel ran his bleeding finger over the cut in my palm. Warmth ran over my hand and up my wrist but that was it as we watched the skin knit and heal almost instantly. Zeke immediately wiped the blood off my palm. I was watching Samuel as he drank out of the bloody glass.

He eyed the glass as he swallowed. He set it down then turned to me. "Order me to do something."

"Cluck like a chicken." I gave it a shot. Isaac snorted.

Samuel's eyes unfocused, his fingers slightly tightened on the edge of the table. "Interesting." His eyes focused on me again. "But is it you or is it that you're a Necromancer?"

"How the hell should I know?" I muttered.

"It's fascinating that I even considered your order." He ran his gaze over me and grinned. "It'll be interesting to see what you grow into."

"You won't be around her long enough," Zeke bit out.

Samuel chuckled and headed for the door. He sent me one last assessing look before leaving. That look had me tightening my grip on Zeke's hand.

"Lexie?" Zeke asked, his voice low.

I dropped my hand from his and finished cleaning up with his handkerchief.

"Maybe it's time that we talk about the Veil," Louis sighed, breaking the tension.

I nodded. Everyone sat down. I explained everything; how I created the link to the Veil, how I crossed the dead. When I explained how close I came to dying, Miles began tapping on the table. I told him everything I knew about what happened.

I kept talking and finished explaining everything to Louis. Though his gaze frequently strayed to each of the guys.

"And I have no clue why they're doing this," I admitted at the end.

Louis's attention came back to me. "Yes, you do."

"No, I really don't." I looked out the window and watched as the last rays of the sun disappeared.

"What was the effect of closing the Veil?" Louis asked as he leaned back in his chair and crossed his arms over his chest.

"The dead can't cross; the energy level is building. Ghosts are stronger, have more energy and are starting to rot," I summed up.

"The souls of the dead are absorbing that energy," Louis pointed out. "They're storing it and that is rotting them out."

I realized what he was saying. "They're sources of energy. Like batteries."

He nodded. "I've been with Uma long enough to know that powering a complex spell or contraption takes a lot of energy. The spells usually are never the problem. It's powering it that's the challenge. The more energy a magic user can use, the higher their skill level."

"So... whoever did this, wants to power something," I said.

"And considering this person probably doesn't have a lot of formal training, they might not realize what they've really done," he explained as he moved to look out the window.

"Why do you think they don't have a lot of training?" I asked. How the hell could he tell that?

"Because they almost destroyed the barriers and caused the apocalypse." Louis turned around. "Uma told me after meeting you that it was one of the first things you learn if you're working with dimensions. You don't stop the energy from flowing."

"So, no formal training," I muttered. "Which makes sense there's only...."

"Only what?" Louis asked.

"The only witch I know of back home is Serena." I looked up and met his gaze. "She was supposed to help but... After a certain point I just got the run around and a death threat."

Louis's eyebrows went up. "That's interesting. Though, if she is a formally trained witch, she has the training and knowledge to know the damage she'd cause."

"That doesn't mean she gives a fuck," Zeke pointed out. "Some people just want to watch the world burn."

Louis nodded. "That's true. But I'd suggest you get more evidence before trying to accuse her. Some people just don't want to get involved."

I nodded. It was something to think about.

"The fact is, anyone can be your Veil closer. It's not like there are signs that someone has worked with the Veil. At least, none we'll recognize."

"Okay, what are some signs that someone's a witch or warlock?" I asked, if we could at least narrow down the suspects it'd help.

He pulled out his phone and texted someone. "Let's get Uma in here. She can answer that better than I can."

CHAPTER 18

JULY 17TH, TUESDAY EVENING

Isaac

I didn't bother knocking before I walked into Ethan's room and pulled up short. Lexie was sitting with Ethan playing War with a deck of cards.

My heart pounded. I needed to do this now. "Red, can you give us some time?"

She turned toward me and gave me an understanding smile. "No problem." She got up and headed out the door.

I broke out into a sweat as I turned and stared at Ethan and Ethan stared at me. "We need to talk."

"Yeah." He leaned back against his pillows.

"Lexie." I swallowed hard. "How do you feel about her?"

His eyes flashed at me. "How do you feel about her?"

"I asked you first."

"How the fuck do you think I feel?" he snapped. "When have I ever competed with you for a girl? Whether I liked her or not?"

I grew still. "Who?"

"What?" He sighed, calming down.

"Who?" I swallowed hard. "Who did you like?"

Ethan looked down at the bed. "Mary and Cece."

"Cece?" I bit out. I already knew about Mary. She had made damn sure I did when she broke up with me. But Cece?

Ethan nodded. "A year after you started liking her."

"And you walked away?" I asked, not quite believing it. Ethan never walked away from a girl he liked.

Ethan nodded.

"Why?"

"Why the fuck do you think?" he scoffed. "You're my brother. I wouldn't do that to you."

Stunned, I sat down on the end of the bed and looked down at the floor. He had walked away from girls for me... I never thought he'd walk away from any girl. My gut knotted. I couldn't do that, even for him. If it was anyone else, but not her. "What did I say to you in Boulder?"

The silence stretched. "That thing told me how miserable you were. How much you wanted to die, how close you really wanted to get." Ethan's voice grew strained. "What it was like for you to watch Sophie die, and hold her body for over an hour."

My lungs grew tight, my chest ached. I couldn't say a word.

"How you hated me and wished I was the one who died." Ethan took a deep breath.

"I never wanted you to die," I countered without hesitation. He needed to understand that I never wanted that. "I wanted to switch places with her. It wasn't fair. She was... and I'm... She didn't deserve to die that way."

"You never told me how she..." Ethan turned away from me, unable to meet my gaze.

"You didn't want to know," I said without thinking. "After the wreck you were just... gone."

"I wasn't the only one," Ethan countered as he turned back. "But... I should have realized what losing her like that would do to you."

"You threw yourself into your music, into the band." I couldn't seem to stop talking now. "You threw yourself into everything else as long as it kept you out of the house."

"My entire life changed that day," Ethan stated. "We lost her, I was in pain and on those fucking pain killers that had me spaced out… I suddenly couldn't even fucking make it up the stairs. And you walked away with just a broken arm."

I looked over my shoulder at him. "I held her while she drowned in her own blood. She grew cold in my arms. Believe me, I didn't fucking walk away with just a broken arm."

Ethan flinched. "Fuck…"

"Yeah." I turned back around to look at the door Lexie had gone through. She was right, we needed to have this out. All of it. Now. "And ever since then, I look at you and can see the questions in your eyes. 'Did he do enough? Did he try everything to save her?'"

"I know you did."

The world paused. Everything stopped. "You do?" I asked, wanting to believe him.

"Fuck, Isaac," he bit out. "I know you. You would have done everything you could to save her. I never doubted that." I closed my eyes as his words hit me. My eyes burned as tears fell. Some ragged broken part of me got a piece back. I'd been without it so long, I'd forgotten it was missing.

"Then why did you…" I swallowed hard. "If you didn't blame me, then why did you avoid me for so long?"

I turned on the bed to face him. Ethan was leaning back against the wall, looking up at the ceiling. Tears ran down his face. "I was deep in my own shit. Did Ma ever tell you why I stopped taking the opiates the first time?"

My heart stopped. "No."

"Because I was so fucking depressed that I wanted to take them all at once and not wake up," Ethan admitted, his voice thick.

No… "You wanted to kill yourself?"

Ethan nodded, his eyes still on the ceiling. "Yeah. You weren't talking to me, Ma was still grieving for Sophie and… I was in a lot of pain, physically and emotionally. Everything had changed. I had gone from having a happy family to being completely miserable and alone."

"What happened?" I asked through a tight throat. I couldn't imagine living without him...

"Miles." He dropped his gaze to meet mine. "He saw the signs, started coming over every day for a few hours to talk to me about my music."

I snorted. Miles and music? Yeah, the guy could play instruments but there was no joy there for him. It was an exercise, that was it.

Ethan grinned. "I know, right? He helped me realize that I could still do one thing that I loved. That as long as I was alive I had options. You die, you have none."

"And that's why you dove into music and the band," I said as I realized how stupid we both were.

"Yeah." Ethan shook his head and looked at me. "It didn't help that you could still do everything I wanted to."

"Why the hell do you think you got the car all the time?"

He shook his head. "We just stopped talking about the big shit."

I nodded.

He sighed. "This needs to stop. What happened in Boulder?"

"That demon... it really fucked me up," I finally admitted it out loud. "I started having the worst nightmares of my life. I watched her die. Then the next night, I watched myself put my hand over her face and smother her." My eyes burned again as I met his gaze. "It made me believe I killed her. That I just hadn't remembered it."

"Fucking hell," Ethan said, stunned. "Why didn't you talk to me?"

I scoffed. "All the reasons I said earlier plus..." I shook my head. "It was in my head all the time, telling me that you and Lexie... It fed every issue I have and made them worse."

"What happened in Boulder?" he asked again.

I clenched my hands into fists and took a deep breath. "I was alone and in the dark. With only that thing talking to me. Taunting me, hurting me, telling me what a piece of shit I was." I shook my head. "I couldn't hear what was going on. I thought you guys had bailed on me."

"We never left you alone," he said, his voice thick. "One of us was always with you. We were trying to distract it from you."

"I know that now." I wiped my face. "I only ever heard Lexie, and Hades when he growled."

"I wasn't going to leave you," he said in a quiet voice.

My chest burned. "I should have said something."

"I should have too," Ethan admitted. "I'm sorry, brother."

"Me too, brother." I turned and looked at the floor. "What happened while you were gone?"

"It's a blur. All I remember is pain, needles and more pain," he muttered.

I turned to the door, my heart aching. "What are we going to do about Lexie?"

Ethan turned to the door as well. "I'll stay away."

I eyed him. "You love her?"

He nodded. "You?"

I nodded.

"We're fucked." We said in unison.

~

Lexie

I WAS STILL SITTING on the floor of the hallway an hour later. What the hell was I doing? Yeah, the twins were talking but... was I the biggest problem between them?

Wintergreen reached me before Miles even sat down beside me.

"I'm guessing the twins are talking," he said.

I nodded, not taking my gaze off the door.

"Good," he said. "The kids are off with as much of the pack as possible."

"That's good. This is no place for little kids," I sighed.

"Uma's staying. The kids and Savannah left with Juan," he added. "They'll meet up with Evie's group."

"He'll be safer with them." I leaned over and rested my head on his arm. "What am I doing?"

"What do you mean?" he asked in that silky-smooth voice.

"I don't know what I'm doing," I admitted, feeling lost. "I don't even know what you want, what the others want. Hell, I don't even know what I want."

He reached down, his long fingers wrapped around the inside of my knee. "Do you really have to ask?"

I nodded, my cheek rubbing against his cotton shirt. "I'm giving up on subtlety."

His fingers squeezed my thigh. "As a friend or a partner, I want you in my life."

I reached up, wrapped my arm around his and hugged it to me.

"We'll be fine. It's just going to take time. Once you figure out how you feel," he promised.

I sat up and leaned back against the wall. I didn't want to think about having to choose. He squeezed my leg.

"Come on, it's dinner time and the others are downstairs." He got himself to his feet then reached down for me. I let him pull me to my feet.

We were walking down the stairs when the runed door opened. Samuel walked in leading a group of vampires. Louis followed with a boy around my age. That sensation ran over me, it had been awhile since I felt it. The feel of fingertips brushing over my skin. Dark short hair, olive skin and a tall lean build. He carried a small duffle over his shoulder. His head turned, coffee colored eyes met mine. Necro. Louis turned to speak to him then followed the newcomer's gaze to me. Louis said something before walking to meet me at the foot of the stairs. The new Necro's eyes held mine as I came down the rest of the stairs.

"Lexie, this is Luca," Louis introduced us. "He's the only surviving member of the Necromancer family in Italy."

"Sorry about your family." I didn't know what else I could say.

"Thank you," he said, his Italian accent was thick.

"Luca has had a long trip here and we were about to get something to eat," Louis said. "Would you guys like to join us?"

"We were about to have dinner with the guys," I warned, turning to Louis.

"That sounds like a plan," Louis said as he gestured for us to lead the way.

We walked into the cafeteria and got in line. I kept feeling eyes on me as I picked out my supper. I didn't turn, I had a hunch who it was. Luca began speaking to Louis in Italian. Louis answered in the same language. We led them to the table with the others. The guys were quiet as we reached the table. I sat down next to Asher and across from Miles. Louis sat beside me.

"Boys, this is Luca," Louis introduced him. "He's a Necro from Italy."

Everyone's head snapped up as they eyed Luca.

"These are my friends, Miles, Zeke and Asher. The twins are upstairs talking at the moment," I said, not liking the way the boys were looking at Luca.

"Are they talking or fighting?" Asher asked as he ate.

"Talking." I turned and looked up at him. "Isaac asked for them to be alone for a talk."

That got Zeke's attention. "They're finally talking their shit out?"

I nodded since my mouth was full.

"Has the doctor cleared Ethan yet?" Asher asked, using his fork to move his food around.

"Not yet," Miles answered. He set his fork down and turned to the others. "And as soon as he gets released, I think we should leave."

Everyone stopped eating. I met his gaze. He didn't mean just the boys. I gave him a slight nod. Ethan had been tortured, this entire trip had been a disaster. I wanted to go home.

"Seconded," Zeke muttered.

"Third," Asher said.

"Motion passed," Miles said. "We'll leave as soon as Ethan is cleared by the doctors."

"I think that's a good idea," Louis said. "Even Luca will be leaving by tomorrow night. Too many Necros in one place is just inviting trouble."

"What about you and Uma?" I asked.

"We'll be staying for the long haul," Louis said. "This is our home and we're not giving it up."

I hoped they'd win. I began playing with my food as Louis moved the conversation on to a lighter topic. I didn't contribute much, mostly I was just tired. When I started adding a carrot and pea fence to my mashed potato fort, Zeke finally had enough. He tapped my tray and glared. I rolled my eyes and went back to eating. Through the rest of dinner, I felt Luca watching me here and there; mostly when the conversation lulled.

It was during one of those lulls that my phone rang. It was Rory.

"Hey, Rory."

"Is there anything you want to tell me?" Rory's voice was sharp. Oh, shit. He must have heard what was going on here.

"Yeah, let me get somewhere quieter." I got up from the table. Miles raised an eyebrow, I mouthed Rory's name and left the cafeteria. "There's been some trouble-"

"Trouble?" he snapped. "I'd fucking say so. The Center for Disease Control is starting to talk about a quarantine for New Orleans!"

He really was pissed. "It's not an actual illness." I explained to him what was going on, everything I knew, hoping he would calm down. But when I finished, he wasn't calmer.

"Ethan actually died. And not one of you contacted Maria or me?" Rory demanded.

My mouth went dry. I didn't even think of it. "No, I guess not..."

"Alexis Luana Delaney. You are seventeen years old. You are in the middle of what looks like a war-zone and you have no business being there! Get your ass home now!"

I cringed. "I can't. Ethan hasn't been released by his doctor."

"Get him released!"

"He's about to be," I finally snapped back. "The doctor is checking on him tomorrow and everyone is planning to leave as soon as possible after that."

"So, you'll be home tomorrow night?" Rory asked.

"Unless something stops us, yeah," I hedged. I didn't see what would stop us but I didn't want to make a promise I didn't know if I could keep.

"If something changes, you will call or you'll never see the light of day again." Rory warned. "Is that understood?"

"Yes, sir," I muttered.

"Now, get this shit done and get back home," Rory ordered before hanging up.

I sighed and tucked my phone into my pocket. Rory was seriously pissed. I couldn't blame him, I really hadn't been keeping him in the loop. I turned and looked at the cafeteria doorway. Deciding I have had enough for today, I headed upstairs to my room.

I ROLLED over and punched my pillow into shape. The fucking mattress was lumpy and the bed was too big. I sighed. Okay, maybe I was just used to sharing the bed lately.

When I had come upstairs to check on Ethan, Isaac said he was staying. That they had some things to work out still. Thankfully, Bella had already assigned me a room on the sixth floor.

I rolled over again and looked out the window. Ethan. Zeke. Miles. Isaac. Asher. What did I want? I scoffed at myself. I didn't want to hurt anyone. Could I choose? Could I really choose? My heart ached as my eyes burned. No. I don't think I could.

There was a knock on my door.

I turned on the light on my nightstand and padded barefoot across the room to open the door. Zeke was leaning against the doorframe, his head hanging.

"Zeke?"

He lifted his head and met my eyes. His bags were deep as he struggled to focus his eyes on me. "I... I need it to stop."

"What?" I opened the door further so he could come in.

He looked at my room, blinked and shook his head. "I need it to be quiet..."

Shit, he sounded drunk. He must be more sleep deprived than I thought. I didn't understand what he was saying about quiet but... His eyes were almost closed, he swayed in the doorway. "Okay. Come in before you fall down."

He thought about it for several heartbeats then nodded. He pushed away from the door and staggered a little to the bed. I closed the door as he sat down on the edge.

His head was hanging again as I walked up to him. "What's going on?"

He lifted his head, his hands reached out and pulled me to stand between his knees. He rested his forehead over my heart between my breasts. My fingers automatically began to comb through his too long for him hair.

"Brain needs to shut off," he muttered as he held me to him.

"Okay, how?" I was still trying to piece together what he was saying.

Zeke wrapped his arm under my butt and lifted me off my feet. My hands clutched his shoulders as he turned and laid me down. I was about to sit up when he stretched out beside me and all but dropped half his body over my lower half with his head resting on my belly. Okay... I started to relax under him, my fingers massaging the tense muscles of his neck. He shifted, his rough calloused fingers scraped my skin as he pushed my shirt up.

"Whoa, whoa, whoa." I moved to stop him but he had already stopped when the fabric reached my ribs. With his eyes closed, he rubbed his beard over my sensitive skin. I caught my breath as my heart jumped and my body gave a hard deep throb. He stopped moving, his cheek still resting against my belly. His warm breath danced across my skin raising goosebumps.

"Thanks, Baby," he whispered, half asleep.

I ran my fingers through his hair and over his shoulders. "For what?"

"Making it quiet," he mumbled as he fell asleep on me.

CHAPTER 19

JULY 18TH, WEDNESDAY

I was sitting in Miles' living room, watching the guys play Monopoly. Sitting forward, I reached to add a player piece to the board.

Ethan took it from me and set it back. "Sorry, Beautiful. You don't get to play with us anymore."

"Since when?" I scoffed.

"Since you kissed all of us," Asher answered as he rolled the dice.

"Seriously?" I gaped at them. They all nodded.

"Until you decide who you're going to be with, you don't get to play," Miles explained, not even looking up from the board.

"I don't want to choose..." I said, my voice small. My heart ached at the thought alone.

"Then you don't get to play," Isaac moved his piece and threw down a card.

Zeke got to his feet and pulled me to mine. Stunned, I didn't even fight as he took me out the front door. "Until you decide, there's no point in you being here."

He slammed the door in my face. Heart breaking, thunder rolled through the sky. I pounded on the door, calling their names, screaming at them. Over and over. The skin scraped off my knuckles as I hit the wood over and over.

When my voice was gone, I sat down with my back to the door. No... this was wrong. They wouldn't do this to me. They wouldn't lock me out just because I was confused... They wouldn't. Zeke would never lock me outside at night. Miles would never not let me join a game. This was wrong...

"Interesting dream," a familiar voice said. "Rather revealing of your insecurities."

I lifted my head to find Samuel standing in the gravel circular driveway, the breeze ruffling his hair. "What are you doing here?"

He grinned. "That's a good question. One, I myself am trying to answer."

Dread filled my heart. "Is this real?"

His face softened as he shook his head. "It's a dream. You're safe, asleep in your bed in New Orleans." He looked over Miles' house. "As to why I'm here, I am at a loss." He met my eyes. "This shouldn't be happening. I didn't drink from your vein and I'm neither ill nor trying to communicate with you. This is extremely odd."

My gut knotted. "Then leave."

He gave me a small bow from the neck. "I was about to when I noticed your distress." He lifted his head to eye the door. "This is only your fears. Do you understand that?"

"I know," I bit out. "Now get the fuck out of my head and stay out."

He grinned. "As you wish."

I WOKE UP WITH A START. What the fuck? What the hell woke me up? The scent of engine grease and leather surrounded me. Zeke's nose was against my throat as he snored lightly. I was high up in the bed with my leg around his waist. My entire body was flush against his. My shirt was still up around my ribs. His forearm wrapped around me, his hand on my back with his fingers spread. I relaxed into him, the last strands of the dream fading away.

There was no reason to get up, I didn't have anything to do. He was still out cold and the sun was just coming up through the windows. So, I closed my eyes, relaxed and drifted under again.

Zeke

SHE MADE A SMALL UNHAPPY NOISE. I lifted the weight of my arm off her and turned toward her before I even opened my eyes. She was on her back, a beam of sunlight on her face.

"Come 'ere." I slid my hand over her stomach to her hip and carefully pulled her toward me as I moved to my side. She moved closer, pressing herself against my chest as if she was cold. I buried my nose in her hair and held her close. I automatically shifted my knee between her thighs to keep her from scooting down. She lifted then hooked her leg around my hip, then slipped her arm around my waist and gave a contented sigh. I half grinned as I took a deep breath of rosemary. Peace settled through me. Those sharp edges inside me smoothed out a little more as I drifted there, holding her.

Ignoring the warmth settling in my chest, I tried to remember how I got in her room. I remembered sitting in my room and realizing I was at my limit. I was going to fall asleep no matter what. That was the last thing I remembered. I squeezed her tighter and kissed the top of her head.

Her fingers slipped under the back of my shirt and moved over my lower back.

Instead of a night of being trapped in endless nightmares, I spent the night wrapped around her in a deep dreamless sleep. Her fingers began to brush over my scars. I stiffened.

"Zeke?" she murmured as she slid her hand away from my back to my waist.

"Hmm?"

"Are you okay?" she whispered, her small fingertips stroking my jaw.

I opened my eyes a bit and met hers. "How'd I get in here?"

She grinned up at me, her eyes sparkling. "You knocked."

There was no way I came in here. The idea of sleeping next to her and possibly hurting her still haunted me. Not even if I was that out of it would I come here... "I came to your room?"

The worry in her eyes left my heart warm. "What do you remember?"

I ran through my memory again. "I remember sitting in my room. Realizing I was going to pass out whether I wanted to or not." I tried to find anything else but came up blank. "That's it."

She started to trace circles on my shirt over my chest. "You came to the door, knocked and told me you needed it to be quiet."

Quiet? What was she talking... dread filled me. Oh, fuck. I rolled on to my back, cursed and ran my hand down my face. "What else did I say?"

"Before or after you pushed up my shirt?" she asked in a dry voice as her hand rested on my stomach

My stomach turned into lead. Don't tell me I tried to... No, no way in hell. I'd never.... Needing answers, I dropped my hand and turned to her, furious with myself. "What the fuck did I do?"

She gave me a reassuring smile. "Relax, you stopped at my ribs."

I sighed deeply. But I still fucking pushed her shirt up. I took her hand off my stomach, sat up and moved to the edge of the bed. Cursing myself, I looked for my boots.

"Zeke, calm down."

I stopped dead as guilt ripped through me. I had to know. "Did I stop or did you have to make me?"

The bed shifted behind me, her petite curves pressed against my back. She rested her chin on my shoulder and wrapped her arms around my shoulders, her hands resting on my chest. "You stopped. You only wanted to rub your beard on my stomach."

My face caught fire, I closed my eyes and hung my head. What the fuck had I been thinking? I took several deep breaths as her fingers stroked my chest in a soothing pattern. Her touch calmed me down, helped my face cool off. God, I wanted to keep her. But it wasn't going to happen. Not with all of us wanting to be with her. I held her fingers against my stomach and took several more deep breaths. With Asher and Miles both liking her, what chance did an asshole like me have? The pathetic part was I knew. None.

"Tough Guy," she whispered. My heart stuttered. "How long was it since you slept?"

I sighed. At least it was almost a different topic. "Almost since we got here."

"Why?" she whispered.

How could I explain it? That I freaked out the first night here because the council had people in town? That after that I couldn't sleep then refused to because I was too chicken shit to face the nightmares I would have? Her slight weight against my back was comforting, her touch soothing. The smell of rosemary relaxed me. Before I knew it, I was answering. "I'm losing my shit, Baby."

"How?"

"Nightmares, I've been having them since Boulder." I didn't want to go into it any more than that. She wasn't going to be mine; it was better to pull away now. Get some distance, prevent what pain I could. I patted her hands. "Don't worry, I'll figure it out." I took her hands off me and got to my feet.

She sat back on her knees watching me look for my boots, chewing the corner of her bottom lip. "Zeke, talk to me."

I found my boots at the end of the bed and bent to pick them up. "I'm talking to my shrink. I'll work it out." There was no chance she'd pick me. I was too closed off, too big, too angry. I knew all the reasons it wouldn't happen. But that didn't stop me wanting her.

"Zeke."

I straightened and met her eyes. "You're going to have to choose, Lexie. And I know my chances aren't great. So... just let me keep this shit to myself."

Her eyes flashed. She was on her feet on the bed walking toward me. Then her hands were on my face, her lips crushing mine. My heart pounded in my chest as she dove in and snapped my control. I held her closer as I met her stroke for stroke. The taste of her only making the craving worse. The feel of her making me ache. My arms moved around her, carefully holding her to me. I took over, kissing her again and again, burning the taste of her into my mind, the feel of her into my bones. There was only her lips, her body, her touch. Until her tears fell onto my face. I pulled back, heart clenching.

She held my face, pain burning in her eyes. "How do you know the score if I don't?"

I didn't have an answer.

"I can't imagine my life without any of you. That means you too," she said as another tear rolled down her face twisting my gut into knots. "So, stop telling me that you don't have a chance." Her lower lip trembled taking the air from my lungs.

I reached up and cupped her face, my thumb wiping her cheek. "You can't cry around me, Baby," I rasped. "It makes me want to break shit." Her fingers dug into my shirt as she lowered her head to hide her face in my neck so I couldn't see her tears.

"I'm sorry about everything, I know you probably don't want me now-"

"Don't even... Just stop," I growled, my temper rising to the surface. Not want her? That wasn't even possible any more. I held her tighter, my hand going to the back of her neck. "You need to stop crying. Please?"

She nodded against my skin and slid her arms around my neck. I ran my hand up and down her back, hoping she'd stop soon. I buried my nose in her hair and took a deep breath of rosemary. Why? Why her? The others could have anyone else. I closed my eyes as it hit me. If I couldn't get her out of my head, how could I blame the others for the same thing? I fucking hated logic. I focused on holding her until she was calm again.

When she was ready, she pulled back and wrapped her arms around her stomach. She seemed to shrink in on herself.

I didn't know what to say. We were in a shitty situation and I didn't see us getting out of it without pain, lots of pain. I went back to looking for my boots. Finding them at the end of the bed, I picked them up. She started to get off the bed. There was a small crunch. Her eyes grew wide a heartbeat before she jumped back on the bed, cursing in a high-pitched voice.

I dropped my boots and moved around the bed. "What?"

She frantically started wiping the bottom of her foot off. "I fucking stepped on something furry!"

I moved the blanket out of the way and found it. A brown fuzzy body and black leathery wings. "It's a dead bat."

"What the fuck is it with all the animals?" she shouted. "Seriously, is this a New Orleans thing? Wake up with dead critters every day?"

I bit back a grin at her indignation. Her hair was wild, her eyes sparking with her temper. One minute she was upset, and unsure. The next she was spitting fire and shouting. She made my chest burn with how beautiful she was.

"I'll get rid of it," I told her, mostly to distract myself.

"No! Leave the fucker! He can have the room!" She got off the bed and went to her bag in a huff. I couldn't help the way my eyes followed her across the room.

There was a knock on the door, a second later the bedroom door opened. Louis walked in already dressed for the day. "What's with the shouting? I can hear you down the hall."

"I'm sick of fucking waking up with dead rodents right next to me," she bit out.

I bit back a chuckle as Louis came to see the bat, his face suddenly unreadable. Something about the bat bothered him, that much I could tell.

Lexie came back toward the bedside with a towel. "I'm going to take it outside then I'm going to bathe in bleach."

There was no way I was letting her touch that bat. I took the towel from her. "I'll get it. You didn't cut your foot on it or anything?"

She shook her head. Good.

Louis spoke up. "How long has this been going on?"

"Since we came here," she said absently as she went back to her bag.

Louis's face grew darker. He knew something. I watched him as Lexie went through her bag. The silence stretched.

"We're going out tonight. Meet me at the door on the third floor at ten." Louis walked out the door and closed it behind him.

She raised an eyebrow. "What was that about?"

"I don't know." But I was going to find out. The dead bat, the dead squirrel on the balcony... Thinking, I squatted down, covered the dead bat with the towel and picked it up. I headed for the door, already working on how to get Louis talking.

"Zeke," she called as I opened the door.

I sighed and turned back to her.

She brought my boots over and handed them to me. Her eyes never met my face. "I feel the same way about everyone. That's what got us into this mess. Well, that and me being a chicken shit."

It was like a blade was driven into my gut. Yeah, but two of them were Asher and Miles. I was just a scary guy with serious rage and father issues. I didn't think I really stood a chance. "We'll manage." I turned away from her and headed down the hall.

"I hope," she muttered before her door closed.

My heart squeezed in my chest. Was she really that confused about all of us? She had to be, she'd never string someone along... What if she chooses one of the others? What the hell was I going to do then? Just say I'm happy for her? Fuck, I needed to get coffee. I glared down at the towel in my hand. And get rid of a fucking bat.

Lexie

I WAS JUST STEPPING into the back of the cafeteria line when I over-heard the people ahead of me.

"Did you hear?" One woman in scrubs asked the other. "Fifty-eight more people were admitted to the hospitals this morning."

"Damn, that brings the total to, what? Over a hundred?" The other asked as she reached for fresh cut melon.

The first woman nodded. "Yeah, and now the Center for Disease Control are getting involved. Things are about to get serious around here."

I shook my head as I got my coffee. Everything in the city was getting worse.

Isaac stepped up beside me. "Morning."

I turned and ran my eyes over him. "Hey, how did your guys' talk go last night?"

"We got a lot of our shit out that we've been holding on to," he admitted as he refilled his coffee mug.

"That's good." I picked up a small bowl of cottage cheese. "Are you guys done fighting?"

"Yeah, I think so," he sighed.

"Aren't you going to eat?" I asked as I added fruit to my tray.

"I already ate with the guys." He stepped around me and gestured toward where the guys were sitting at a table in the corner. Along with Luca.

"How's it going with the new guy?" I asked as we moved out of the line and toward the condiments

"He's quiet," Isaac said.

I raised an eyebrow. "That's it?"

He shrugged. "He's not talking much and we don't know how much English he knows."

I eyed him. "Are you guys actually trying to talk to him?"

He looked everywhere else but at me.

"Isaac," I chided. "The guy's family was murdered this week."

His cheeks tinged pink. "Look, we get that. But he's a Necro."

"So?" That made no sense. I started searching for my favorite creamer flavors.

"He's also eighteen," Isaac added.

"So?" Damn it, they were out. I turned to look up at him.

Isaac's gaze moved over my face before meeting my eyes again. A small smile hovered around his lips. "Never mind. It's stupid."

"Okay." I let it go, it was too early to try and figure out what he was saying.

We started walking toward the table. "But I should warn you that if you sit next to him, I think someone will blow a gasket."

"Who?" I sighed

"Lexie, you don't want to find out," he answered, his face serious.

"So, all of you?" I guessed. He wouldn't meet my eyes. I was right.

Zeke looked up from his coffee and spotted me. Asher eyed my tray from beside him. Miles raised his head from his spot across from Zeke. Isaac took a spot next to Miles. Luca looked up from his tray next to Asher and met my eyes again. That sensation rolled over my skin again, at this point it was annoying as fuck. After thinking for half a heartbeat, I decided where to sit.

"Morning, Ally."

"Morning," I said as I walked around the table.

"How are you feeling?" Miles asked as Isaac scooted down the bench to make room for me.

"Alright." I looked down at the spot between Isaac and Miles then said dryly. "Okay, I appreciate that you think my ass is that small, really it's flattering, but I want to sit down."

The guys chuckled as Isaac scooted down a little more to make room. I set down my tray and stepped over the bench to sit down, my knee hit Isaac's side and I lost my balance. I grabbed Miles's shoulder to steady myself. He reached up and steadied me with his hand on my hip until I sat down.

Zeke and Asher shot a look at Miles who simply ignored them.

"Did you have any dead issues last night?" Luca asked as I settled between the guys.

"Shh," Isaac told Luca. "Wait till she gets a sip of coffee."

"Ally girl," Asher called softly. I looked across the table to him. He passed me a couple of creamers, his fingers brushed mine as he let go.

"Thank you. You are my hero for the day," I said emphatically as I saw one was hazelnut and the other chocolate, my favorites. The guys chuckled as I made my coffee. I took that first sip and closed my eyes in happiness.

"Now you can talk," Isaac announced.

"I take it you're not awake until you've had coffee?" Luca asked.

"Yeah, even stepping on that bat this morning didn't do it," I grumbled before taking another sip. Oh, heavenly goodness...

"Yeah, Zeke told us about that," Isaac muttered.

An odd note in his voice let me know that he knew Zeke slept in my room last night and didn't like it. It was way too early for this...

Coffee. The only answer was more coffee. I grabbed the salt to add to my cottage cheese. "It was fuzzy and gross."

"Then maybe we should get rid of Zeke," Isaac quipped. The guys chuckled.

I finished with the salt and looked up at Zeke. His usual five-o'clock shadow was a beard still. "Fuzzy yes, but not gross." I turned back to Isaac. "We keep him."

"I take it you haven't smelled him after a workout." Asher said. Everyone chuckled but Zeke.

"Very funny," he muttered under his breath as he took a drink of his coffee.

I smiled to myself as I mixed in the salt. "Has the doctor said Ethan can go home yet?"

"I'm surprised you want to leave so quickly," Luca said. "I'm personally wanting to stick around and have a word with a few of the Witch's Council."

I looked up and met his eyes. "If it was just me, yeah. But it's not."

He gave me a slow nod of understanding. "That makes sense."

Luca's eyes ran over the guys. "But none of you are magic users. Why are you in the middle of this?"

"We're family," Miles said as his measuring gaze ran over Luca.

"Louis is in a meeting right now but he also wants to have a talk with both of us." Luca glanced at the guys. "With just us."

Zeke's shoulders became tense. Miles started tapping out that staccato rhythm. Both Isaac and Asher eyed Luca.

"He is also taking me out tonight for something." I ignored the others as I started eating my breakfast.

Luca straightened. "Did he say where?"

I shook my head and kept eating as a tense silence fell.

Luca eyed the guys. "So... how long have you guys been friends with Lexie?" There was something about his voice that didn't sit well with me. It was almost as if Luca was getting protective of *me*. Poor guy didn't realize I was the safest person in the building. And I wasn't the only one to hear it. Zeke and Asher both sat up straighter.

"Almost a year now," I said in a cheerful voice as I met Asher's gaze.

He shook his head and pressed his lips into a thin line, but otherwise stayed quiet.

"And everyone seems to have a nickname for you?" Luca asked.

"Yeah, I have nicknames for them too," I countered, trying to get the guys to be a bit friendlier.

"Especially when she's pissed," Isaac chimed in, catching on to what I was trying to do. "Those get real colorful."

I shook my head and stabbed my fork into a piece of melon.

"Has anyone seen Claire?" Asher asked. "I'm getting worried."

"Yeah. A couple of nights ago, she said she wanted to start traveling back, spreading the word on Spring Mountain," I said, being cryptic. I didn't know Luca and I wasn't about to tell him about my link to the Veil.

"Who is Claire? Another Necro?" Luca asked.

"Yeah, she is. She's also dead," I answered dryly.

Luca raised an eyebrow then let the subject drop.

Phones went off around the cafeteria. People began running out, shouting to each other as they did so.

We stayed put, our phones hadn't gone off. There was a building roar coming down the stairs. I got to my feet.

"Don't even think about it," Zeke snapped as he bolted to his feet with the others. I stopped at the doorway to watch as almost everyone ran out the runed door. The conference room opened, Willow and Bella hurried toward the door.

Louis came out at a jog and came over to us. "We found their headquarters."

CHAPTER 20

JULY 18TH, WEDNESDAY AFTERNOON

J couldn't stop pacing. You'd think if our side was going to raid the Witch's Council's hide-out they'd take us. But, no. We were stuck here, under guard of a couple of Bella and Ink's tiger shifters. I'd already tried to make a break for it. One of them only picked me up off my feet but it pissed the guys off in the process. After already almost causing a fist fight, I figured I'd better stop trying to sneak out of here. Behaving wasn't something I was good at.

"Beautiful, sit down," Ethan said from the side of his bed.

I turned back to him. His color was better, the bags almost gone. Even some of the strain around his face was easing. "How're you feeling?"

"Better." He gave me a smile. "The doc said he'd be able to check me out this afternoon."

"Then we might be able to make it home tonight," Miles said.

"Good," Zeke muttered.

Miles eyed Zeke. "You got some sleep last night."

Zeke glared at Miles, silently telling him to drop it.

A phone rang. Everyone checked.

"Yeah?" One of the guards answered his phone. "We'll head out now." He tucked his phone into his pocket before turning back to us. "We can head out; the building is clear now. Dozer, stay with Ethan."

I didn't bother to wait, I ran through the door and down the hall. The others cursed and hurried to catch up. Even Luca met us at the door and followed.

The drive out to meet the others seemed longer than it should have been. We drove down a long stretch of road alongside the Mississippi. We passed homes into an area that was rather populated by families. How did they manage to raid the building without norms being in the line of fire?

We parked near a large parking structure and climbed out. The six story buildings were enormous. Even bigger than the safe-house. Windows were still intact, mostly on the top four floors of one building. The windows on the other cement building were metal shutters with no glass. A rusted metal door opened. Louis stood in the doorway, waiting, his face drawn.

We didn't waste time, we went straight to him.

"What happened?" Luca asked as soon as we were within earshot.

Louis swallowed hard. "We found most of the patients from the hospital."

His dire tone had my stomach knotting. "Are they okay?"

He shook his head and led the way inside. We walked down a large hall toward a giant set of stairs. "Most are like David. Their channels burned and their brain damaged."

Everyone but Miles and Luca cursed.

Louis led us into a large, long, open part of the building. It was almost the size of a production floor in a factory. Only here... sheets were hung to create sections in the cement room. Gurneys and tables sat in each. Some had sheets, some were bare. But every one had restraints and medical equipment. Horror crawled through me as we walked down the long corridor, passing row after row. Bloodstained sheets were in more than a few. What the hell did they do here? Our people were everywhere. Shapeshifters, magic users, it didn't matter. They worked together to gently get the last few tortured people out of the building. Most were in hospital gowns, their eyes dead. Their faces blank as if no one was home. Rage began to build in my heart. Who could fucking do this? Even with all the activity the place was eerily quiet, as if even the building was horrified by the memory of what happened here.

We were walking by one sectioned off area near the middle when something caught my eye. I walked into the curtained off section and bent down. It was the shirt Ethan was wearing the night they took him, cut and thrown into the corner like trash. There was a clatter as something fell out of the fabric. His phone. Still turned off. Isaac moved around me and picked it up. His face was hard, his eyes boiling as they met mine. We wanted whomever did this to him.

We walked out of the section and followed Louis further down. That chill ran down my neck. I stopped dead in my tracks. "How many died?"

Louis stopped and took a deep breath before turning to me. "Forty-three."

My stomach rolled. "They're still here?"

He nodded.

I swallowed hard and nodded back. Louis lead the way to the group of damaged ghosts in the far corner of the building. Some of them had dead eyes, some of them were younger than me. My heart burned as I looked at all of them. Tears filled my eyes. "Why the fuck did they do this?"

"From what we've found so far, it looks like they were experimenting on norms," Louis said, his dark eyes haunted.

My heart dropped. Human experimentation? That was... just...

"But we'll know more when we go through their files upstairs." Louis's voice had an edge. "Move them on, Lexie. Give them peace."

Luca's gaze snapped to us.

My hands shook as I remembered David. "You don't get it. They're fucked up down to the soul."

Louis met my eyes again.

"David barely recognized his mother," I explained. "I practically had to push him through the door to move him on."

"What are you talking about?" Luca demanded, his accent thick as he stepped closer to Louis and I. "You said this Veil was closed and that's why the dead weren't moving on?"

Shit. I turned, looked up and met Luca's eyes. "I have a link to the Veil. I'm the only way to move the dead on to the Veil right now."

Luca said something in Italian; it sounded like cursing to me. "Did you know that is what got my family killed?"

My heart dropped. "What?"

Louis stepped forward. "Luca, it's not her fault. She's not responsible for what happened."

Luca stepped closer forcing me to tilt my head back. Movement behind me caught Luca's eye. But his gaze quickly moved back to me. "They wanted my father to create a link to this Veil. They tortured my mother and sisters over it. He didn't even know what they were talking about."

Oh God... "I'm sorry." His family died because of... guilt crashed down on me. They wanted the link... three weeks... "I'm so sorry." All because I told Serena to fuck off.

Louis moved him back from me and further away from the group of souls. He started speaking to him in Italian.

Luca answered back in the same language then turned and stormed off.

Louis said something in French, cursing I'd bet. He turned back to the souls still staring off into oblivion. Still, they deserved to move on after all they'd been through.

"Do it," Louis sighed.

Putting all my emotions behind a door, I took a deep breath and stepped forward. This wasn't going to be easy. I called my will and got to work.

AFTER A HEART WRENCHING trip to the Veil, where I had to guide and then almost push every soul through their door. I came out of the Veil with a tight throat and burning eyes. Asher noticed and distracted Luca and Louis long enough for me to get control over myself again. Louis said there was more work to do.

And now, three hours later, I flipped another page of the file and fought the bile that moved up into the back of my throat. A picture of a seven-year-old girl looked up at me. Big blue eyes, long straight thick blonde hair and a pretty face. It would be a nice picture, if the girl's eyes weren't distant and unseeing. Her name was Stella. A chill ran down my spine as I moved past the picture and read the file.

Experiment was a success. Subject 72 has shown remarkable skill in adapting to her new higher awareness. While she doesn't speak much, she's dutiful in listening to and carrying out orders.

Most success has been found among the younger of our subjects. Perhaps there's a correlation between adapting and age? Recommend moving her to a more stable facility for further experimentation and testing.

Experimenting. That's what they called it. Not forcing enough energy into a norm to blast open their channels in hope that they would gain some natural ability. Though what about that would you call natural? I snapped the file shut. We'd been going through them for hours. I stretched my arms above my head and watched as Willow closed the file in her hands and then slipped it into her case. I'd noticed her doing that several times already.

This time I asked. "What are the files you keep taking?"

Willow reached for another file from the dwindling pile. "The files of those who we found alive today. I'm hoping it'll help the doctors to know what happened to them."

I scoffed. "But we don't know what happened to them. Not one file has said what they did, or used. We're only guessing that they managed to gather enough energy to blast it through someone."

Willow met my gaze. "I know, it's extremely frustrating. Why don't you take a break? There's no reason you can't."

Fuck it. I got to my feet and headed for the stairs and went down. Zeke had needed to take a walk about ten minutes ago. He was so angry that he had to go or he was going to break something. Someone should check on him. I headed downstairs.

I didn't find Zeke. I found Luca. He was staring out a window on the third floor. Deciding to leave him be I started back down the stairs.

"You can't sneak up on a Necro." Luca broke the silence. "Especially if you're one too."

I sighed as I turned around. "I figured."

He turned away from the window and ran his gaze over me. "I shouldn't have blamed you earlier." He came closer. That sensation of fingertips running over my skin grew stronger. "You're not at fault. You didn't break into our home. You didn't tie up my family and you didn't torture them."

I shook my head as my eyes burned. "It is my fault."

He raised an eyebrow.

He had a right to know who really killed his family. "All of this is my fault. I had been trying to learn from a witch back home, but I kept getting lied to and stonewalled." I swallowed hard as guilt clawed through that locked door and tore at me again. "Three weeks ago, I cut ties."

His eyes filled with understanding. "Three weeks ago they went to Florida."

I nodded.

His eyes ran over me then met mine again. "Did you know that would happen?"

"No."

"Then it's not your fault," he said, his voice lowering. "You might have put this into motion, but they are the ones who decided to do this. And every day, they've made the decision to continue."

Okay, that made sense but still... "How can you not blame me?"

"Because you're not at fault. Am I angry? Yes. But not at you."

I didn't know what else to say.

He clenched and unclenched his jaw. "They're going to come after you. Maybe not now, but eventually. And they won't take no for an answer."

"That's usually when I say 'fuck no,'" I bit out.

The corner of his mouth lifted as he pulled a small card out of his pocket. "When they come, call me." He handed it to me. "I'll be on the next plane." He walked past me and started up the stairs back toward the offices.

287

I looked down at the card, it was a phone number and email address. Well… that didn't go the way I thought it would. I traced the edge of the card as emotions fought it out inside me. It seemed like it was my fault but I didn't know this would happen. Were Asher and Luca right? I didn't know. I shoved everything back behind that door again before I tucked the card in my wallet and headed down the stairs.

It didn't take long to find Zeke. He was standing in the middle of the floor from hell, eyeing the walls and cement pillars.

"Hey," I muttered.

"Needed a break?" he asked in a quiet voice.

I nodded. "The file I read just said they should go after younger kids."

Zeke cursed.

I shook my head. It was beyond sick and fucked up.

He sighed. "You know, a few gallons of gas, a match, and this place would go up like kindling."

I eyed the cement walls and floor. "The upper floors, yeah, but not down here."

Zeke examined the area. "A few barrels of gas, maybe an explosive or two."

I grinned. I liked the idea of wiping this place from the planet. "Too bad we can't find explosives."

He raised an eyebrow at me. "I'm sure Miles could come up with a way."

I grinned up at him. The others might be shocked at how blood-thirsty I could be but Zeke never was. He got it. "Don't tempt me."

He sighed. "We should head back."

"Yeah. We were on the last files I think." I turned and led the way. We climbed the stairs in silence. My shoulder brushing his arm. He reached over and squeezed the back of my neck for a heartbeat before letting go. It eased some of the knots in my belly.

When we reached the room, everyone was picking up boxes.

"We're taking these files back with us. We've spent enough time in this place." Willow announced. No one argued. Everyone pitched in and we were back on the road in eight minutes.

Ethan

I WAS ALMOST DONE SHAVING when the bathroom door opened the rest of the way. Cursing that I needed to let some of the steam out, I turned and found Lexie just inside the door. Her eyes ran over me, making my body harden and my heart race before she met my eyes. Shit, I knew I should have put on more than just a towel, then again... the way her face turned pink was worth it.

"Uh, sorry, the door was open." She turned to head back out.

I bit back a chuckle as I rinsed off my razor. "You've seen me in my shorts before."

"In only a towel isn't the same," she countered as she headed for the door.

"Why my brother?" I asked in a quiet voice. The question had been festering inside me for days. I didn't even mean to ask, it just slipped out. I wasn't ready to face this but... The sound of running water was loud in the steamy bathroom. My temper boiled inside my chest. For months, months! I had been thinking of no one else but her. Been wanting no one but her. And she had been... I set my razor down and washed the last of the shaving cream off my face.

She turned around and watched me, her arms crossed over her chest.

"I know you're pissed at him but he's a good guy-"

"I know my brother's a great guy," I bit out, my body growing tense. Of course, I knew that. Anger and pain tore through me making my heart ache. My heart. I huffed at myself. Of course, I fell for the wrong girl. I'm so fucking stupid. I focused on the drain in the sink. "This isn't the first time that we've both liked the same girl."

"It's not?" she asked, her voice uncertain.

I shook my head as I straightened. "Three times. Three times,

Lexie. We've liked the same girl." And it sucked every fucking time. This time... this time it was going to hurt.

She moved to stand by the sink. "What happened?"

I started to put away my shaving kit with more force than necessary. "The first girl was already dating him when we met. So, I kept my distance. She dumped him to ask me out, I said no." I still hated that bitch for doing that to Isaac. But hated myself almost as much as I admitted. "The last one was Cece."

"Cece?" she asked, her voice full of disbelief.

My chest started to ache, I knew exactly what I had to do here. I just needed her to understand why. "I met her after Isaac had already liked her for a year. When I realized it, I stayed the hell away."

"Okay, but why didn't you say anything to me about it?" she asked softly.

"Because I'm going to tell you the same thing." I zipped up my case. "I know me, Beautiful. I'm quick to jump into a relationship and when shit goes wrong I'm the first out the door." I set my kit down as my throat tightened. "But with you... I fell for you a little every day." I couldn't look at her but I had to say it. Just once, so she'd know. "Not falling for you was like trying to stop a storm from coming, it wasn't going to happen. Even though you scare the shit outta me, I still want you. But now, knowing..." The knot in my throat cut off my voice.

"I scare the shit out of you?" she asked, her voice drawing my gaze to her. Her filling eyes met mine.

I nodded as I moved closer, close enough that rosemary filled my senses, close enough to feel the heat coming off her skin. I leaned down and pressed my cheek to hers, my lips near her ear. Then whispered what I could barely say out loud, "I've been chasing something I thought was real for years. But to actually find the real thing, to feel it, to know you're the reason. It scared me shitless that I was gonna fuck this up."

"You're not going to fuck it up," she said, her voice cracking. "I already did."

Claws shredded my heart, making it hard to breathe. It wasn't her fault, this was my decision. I leaned down and brushed her lips with mine. This time, it was different. It was slow and sweet. I wanted to remember everything about her. The way she felt, the way she tasted... everything. Where our other kisses were all about heat, this one... this one I savored. Since it was going to be our last. My eyes burned, the weight in my chest grew heavier as I pulled back and met her eyes from inches away. Fuck, she was beautiful. Perfect. Everything I could ever want in a girl. Smart, funny, a love for music, everything I could ever hope for. And I had to walk away. "We were fucked the second that Isaac started liking you," I whispered through the boulder in my throat. "Pick Isaac." I pulled back, grabbed my stuff and left the bathroom without looking at her again. She didn't need to see the tears running down my face. She didn't need to know how much I needed her. I wiped my face and headed back down the hallway to my room. Alone.

Lexie

IT WAS JUST before ten when I went downstairs to meet Louis. I found all the guys waiting at the door. Including Ethan. My chest burned.

"What are you guys doing?" I asked, already knowing the answer.

"Like we're going to let you go out without us?" Isaac snorted.

I smiled a small smile as that feeling of being loved washed over me.

"Besides, Ethan's been cleared to go home," Miles added. "We can leave after we get back."

Relief filled me. Home, we could go home.

"Good, you're all here." Louis popped up out of nowhere.

"Geeze, make some noise, will ya?" I muttered.

Louis didn't chuckle. In fact, his face was somber. "Come on, we need to get going." He headed out the door and led us downstairs. Everyone climbed into the SUV. Though Miles suggested that I take the front seat. I did simply to keep from having to decide who to sit next to.

The guys were quiet as Louis drove us through the city. Though Miles explained to everyone that he'd asked for the plane to be prepped for before sunrise. He wanted us out of the city as soon as possible. No one argued. We'd seen enough blood and death for a lifetime. I was just as tired of it as the guys. Eventually, Louis pulled up to the curb.

"Greenwood Cemetery?" I asked as he shut off the car. When he didn't answer I turned to him and met his eyes. They were full of shadows, his posture tense. My heart dropped as the guys climbed out.

"Hey, isn't Leon Roppolo buried here?" Ethan asked, looking up at the ironwork gate.

"I believe he is," Miles answered as he adjusted his glasses.

"We definitely need to check his grave out before we leave," Ethan announced.

"What's with the big elk?" Zeke asked.

Louis got out, picked up the electric camping lamp he brought and started around the car.

I got out, my stomach knotting as a thought flickered to life in the back of my mind. Louis was silent as he led us through the gate and down the paved path, past the large grass covered tomb with the statue of an elk on top. The noise of the city fell away leaving only stillness, our footsteps and the chirp of crickets.

Louis led us deeper into the cemetery then off the paved path to the grass lane between rows of tombs. Some were large family tombs, some were small and clearly only held one person. Some were weathered and worn, others were still beautiful after years in the elements. The tombs didn't bother me, it was the purpose in Louis's stride that did. The further in we went, the more the silence grew and grew. The chirps fell away. The silence hung heavy in the air like a fog that nothing living would dare to break. My heart began hammering in my chest.

Louis finally stopped at a stunning large white stone mausoleum in a Greek style. He walked up to the large metal door and pulled out a set of keys. My hands began to sweat. The doors creaked as he opened them. I held back as Louis turned on the lamp and walked inside. The guys followed. Miles hung back, standing beside me. I didn't want to go in. My hands shook as I climbed the steps.

The inside was large enough for everyone and then some. The walls and vaults were all white marble. Three of the walls were filled with names and dates. The guys spread out along the perimeter. Louis had set the lamp on the bottom ledge of a stained-glass window. Below that window, standing prominently in the middle of the mausoleum was a stone carved vault, with three fresh roses at the foot of it. It was basically a carved stone box to protect a coffin and body when buried above ground.

Louis picked the roses up off the vault then raised his head and found me still near the door. He turned to the guys. "Boys, I need you to take the lid of this vault off."

The guys shared a look.

"This is my family mausoleum. We're not doing anything illegal or without permission," Louis reassured them as he set the roses beside the lamp on the window sill.

Isaac, Zeke, Miles and Asher went to the marble box. Louis quickly unsealed it. The guys grunted as they lifted the lid and carefully set it down, leaning it against the rest of the box. The guys stepped back to the edges of the room again. I couldn't take my eyes off the dusty mahogany coffin lid.

"Lexie," Louis called.

My eyes darted to him. He crooked his finger at me. My skin grew clammy, cold in the summer heat as I moved to within touching distance of the foot of coffin.

"Lexie," he got my attention again. His eyes were kind as he began. "It's time you learned about the worst part of Necromancy." He took a breath, pulled out a hankie and began to clean the dust off the coffin. "You've been waking up with dead animals around you. Have you guessed why?"

I had a feeling but I wanted to be wrong. I shook my head.

He gave me an understanding look. "You're raising the dead in your sleep. It's the first sign of your abilities starting to ramp up.

You relax, fall asleep and your guard is down. It happens to all of us."

"So." My voice was loud in the silence of the mausoleum. "I'm raising the dead and they just... walk right into my bedroom?" That couldn't be right...

"Yes." He shook the dust from his hankie and tucked it away in his pocket as he turned to me. "It's not to the point where you need help controlling it, you're not strong enough yet to do it but one day you will be." He set his hands on the coffin. "And there are some things you need to understand about being a Necromancer."

I swallowed hard. For the first time in my life I wanted to be in the dark. I didn't want to know.

Louis took a deep breath and let it out slowly. He whispered something that had Asher's eyes snapping to him. The air pressure in the room doubled, my ears popped as something pressed against my skin. Louis closed his eyes. The hairs on my arms stood up. My lungs couldn't seem to get enough air. Energy filled the room, high enough that it was like I was drowning only I could breathe. Then a purple light began to glow around the coffin. Louis chanted under his breath in French as the purple aura grew brighter and brighter until I wanted to shield my eyes. Wind tore through the door and blew around the room. The light and wind disappeared in a heartbeat. Louis was out of breath when he took his hands off the casket and stepped back several steps. The air pressure returned to normal, the hair on my neck went down. The sweat on my skin dried.

"Come out and join us, Rosalinda," Louis called.

My lungs were tight as the coffin lid opened.

I wish I could say the body looked alive. But I can't. I wish I could say that her flesh magically appeared. But it didn't. A skeleton covered in patches of rotting flesh, decaying fabric and black goo clinging to bones rose from the coffin and climbed out to stand on the stone floor. Several of the guys cursed, all of them moved slowly toward the door. Ethan was practically outside. But I didn't pay attention to them. Because everything I was, was focused on the zombie standing there. I should have felt fear, horror, disgust. Anything but... fascination. Don't get me wrong, the zombie was beyond gross. The smell alone had me wanting to leave. But it was like something flipped inside my head that allowed me to look at it differently. Louis stepped closer to me. "Rosalinda, please stand in front of me."

The zombie of nightmares walked slowly toward Louis. "As you can see, nothing can make a zombie look alive. Forget about the movies, forget about books. No matter what, the body decomposes."

I nodded, too stunned to say anything.

"There are two types of zombies," Louis explained. "The first kind is just the body reanimated. The person isn't there, their soul has already moved on. It's just the shell. The second..." He sighed. "The second is the kind where someone has raised the body and soul."

"You mean... they'd be in there?" I asked, my voice barely more than a breath.

"Yes. That's the one that *will* get you a death sentence from the gargoyles," he said.

Fear tore through me. I didn't know how I was doing it now! "What if you do it by accident?"

"There's no way for that to happen," he explained as the zombie continued taking steps toward us. "You need to have a massive amount of energy and know their name to pull it off. Even then, it's extremely difficult."

"How do you tell the difference?" I asked, my throat dry.

"Look at her eyes," he replied.

I forced myself to lift my gaze. I found black, eyeless bone. Instead of eyes, there was a purple flame burning where her eyes should be.

"If you see a light, it's the first kind. If you see nothing, it's the second. Either way, most don't last more than eight minutes."

When it was close enough, the zombie's energy brushed me. I froze. There was an odd sensation of Louis. It was like when someone walks up behind you and you just know who it is before you turn around. My energy moved along my skin in response. An overwhelming desire to reach out and touch rolled through me. I hugged my arms to me, one below my breasts, the other diagonally across my chest to hold my shoulder. Another urge slid through me, to roll my energy over that skeleton, to crush Louis's energy and make the thing mine. My fingers itched as it rode me hard. I planted myself right where I was, hugged myself tighter and refused to move. Could I control it? What could I make it do? How many could I control? Something dark inside me was awake, aware, and it wanted to come out and play. Horrified at myself, I tried to take a deep breath but it shook.

"You feel that?" he asked, his voice quiet. "That urge?"

I nodded once.

"That's the real curse of being a Necromancer."

I couldn't take my eyes off the zombie. Sick fascination filled me, along with nausea and disgust at myself for feeling the fascination.

"That's the lure of the dead. It's a darkness that lives inside us and can destroy you if you let it."

I still couldn't take my eyes off it.

Louis turned from me back to the zombie. "Thank you, Rosalinda. Please return to your rest." Louis stepped away from me to walk what used to be a human back to the coffin. He pulled out his hankie, covered his hand and offered it to the zombie. She took it and climbed back inside. When she was settled, Louis held his hand over her. "Rest in peace, Rosalinda." The purple glow grew around the body, pulsed, then faded out in a breeze.

Louis gently, reverently, closed the coffin before he turned back to me and the guys. "The stronger your abilities are with the dead, the more you will feel that darkness pulling at you," he began as he walked toward me. "That... curiosity, will pull you into a dark pit that you'll struggle the rest of your life to climb out of."

I was going to feel... that, for the rest of my life? I hugged myself tighter as my eyes burned.

"You'll start considering things you never would have thought you would do. Digging up graves, going to the morgue, you'll start to surround yourself with death. And your thinking will change, your priorities will also. You'll become addicted to the high of raising a zombie. You'll be doing worse and worse things. Until eventually, you'll begin to hide bodies so you can raise them whenever you want.

And when you can't find bodies, you'll kill to get them." He met my gaze. "That's *if* you don't have strong anchors to the living."

"Anchors?" My voice was small. I didn't want to become that thing he described. What I felt in those few minutes with that zombie was enough to scare the fuck out of me.

He nodded. "You asked me why I have two wives. I'll tell you the answer now. The truth is, I had three."

"Three?"

"Relationships are the key to staying out of that pit of darkness. The stronger the relationships you have with the living in this world, the less the darkness will tempt you." He glanced at the boys behind me then his gaze was back on mine. "Do you understand?"

I shook my head, I couldn't grasp what he was trying to say.

He seemed to see it. "I think that's enough for tonight." He looked over my shoulder. "Will you boys help me put the lid back on, please?"

The guys walked around me and hefted the lid into place. Louis replaced the roses on the foot of the stone box. I turned and walked out of the mausoleum.

Asher reached out to touch me, I hunched in on myself, dodging his hand as I passed. I stepped out into the cooler air and didn't stop walking. The guys caught up quickly as we headed out of the cemetery. My stomach rolled, my heart ached. Mostly, I was still disgusted with myself for wanting to play with the zombie.

We reached the car. I climbed in front, this time because I didn't want anyone near me.

The car was silent on the way back. My skin was clammy, cold sweat ran down my spine. That zombie… I wanted to touch it, play with it as if it never had been a person… My stomach lurched.

"Pull over," I bit out as saliva filled my mouth. Louis found a spot and pulled the SUV over. Before he could stop, I opened the passenger side door, shoved my seatbelt off me and threw up. I heaved and heaved until I had nothing left. Someone snagged the waistband of my shorts so I didn't fall out since the car was still moving. When I was done, I sat up, wiped my mouth and shut the door. We drove off in silence again.

When we arrived at the safe-house, I got out and walked inside. Still hugging myself, I ignored everyone and climbed the stairs to the sixth floor. I found my room. I slipped my sandals off and sat at the head of the bed in the middle against the wall. Asher wrapped Miles's hoodie around my shoulders as I stared off out the windows at the lights in the distance. The image of the zombie ran through my head. I pulled my knees to my chest and focused on breathing.

Miles

WHEN WE REACHED the large common area, I watched the guys go with Lexie upstairs. She had been pale as snow, sweat on her forehead, her eyes wide. Shock, most likely. While I wanted to be there for her there was something else she needed more.

"Louis," I called. He stopped on the first step. "Tell me the rest."

He turned to me and eyed me. "The rest?"

"What you were going to tell Lexie before you realized she was struggling?" I tried to keep the cold from my voice but I doubt I succeeded.

He nodded then led the way into the empty meeting room. He took a chair and gestured for me to sit. I took the chair across from him.

"As I was saying, relationships are important. Family, friends, children, they all help anchor me here," he said.

"Can you explain that more?" I asked, trying not to be impatient. I wanted to be upstairs with Lexie and the guys, making sure she was alright.

"I had three wives once," he said. "We lost Juan and Emilia's mother to a rare brain tumor."

"I'm sorry for your loss," I said automatically.

He gave me a small nod in thanks. "The point is, more relationships, whatever kind they are, will keep her safe."

My mind raced through options and probabilities. "Is that why you have two wives? They keep you anchored?"

He sighed. "No, I found three amazing women I fell desperately in love with." He smiled a small smile. "And they were incredible enough to agree to trying a polygamy family."

"It's not a tradition in your family?" I asked.

He laughed. "My parents were catholic, what do you think?"

I chuckled, he had a point. The idea of a poly though... "How does it work?"

Lexie

THE GUYS WERE SPREAD out around the room. Zeke and Ethan sat on the edge of my bed. While Asher was at the window and Isaac sat on the dresser.

It had been about an hour since we got back when I finally found my voice. "I don't want to become a monster." I wanted to cry but I was so sick of fucking crying this week.

Ethan moved to my side and wrapped his arm around me. "You won't."

I leaned my head on his shoulder as I tried to believe him. Everyone had a dark side, I knew mine was a violent one but... this was a dark I never expected to feel. Ethan's body heat helped me loosen my hold on my knees. "How?"

"He said something about anchors." Zeke's voice had my gaze meeting his. "We can ask him to explain in the morning. Right now, you need to get some sleep."

An image of that zombie walking popped back into my mind. I shook my head.

"Beautiful," Ethan whispered.

I looked up and met his eyes.

"Just lie down, okay? We're right here," Ethan tried again. "You don't even have to sleep, just lie down."

I stared at him for several heartbeats before I realized what I was doing. Okay... yeah, lying down would be good. I shifted and laid down on my side facing the door. A hand stroked my hair, a voice began humming that soothing tune. On the third note, a warm honey-like voice joined in. My eyes closed soon after.

Miles

WHEN I GOT ALL the answers that I needed, I headed up to her room. The door was closed. I knocked softly. Isaac opened the door then stepped back. I came in and closed the door behind me. Lexie was curled up in the middle of the bed, out cold.

I walked over to stand next to Zeke and look down at her. The pale pallor of her skin made it hard to concentrate. "How is she?"

"Scared," Zeke stated.

"I called Rory and told him we weren't going to make it tonight." I turned away from her to them. "And I spoke to Louis about anchors."

"And?" Asher demanded as he turned and joined us at the end of the bed.

I looked at each of them then summed up what Louis had explained.

"So, we can keep her grounded?" Asher asked.

I nodded, my gaze on her sleeping face. "And I may have a solution to our problem."

Zeke eyed me. "What?"

I took a deep breath and let it out slowly. "She could date all of us."

Everyone looked at me like I was insane.

"What?" Asher asked, stunned.

"It's the same set up Louis has with his wives, only..." I looked at each of them. "With us and Lexie."

"Let me get this straight." Asher started rubbing the back of his neck. "She's... she is going to have to date more than one guy at a time?"

"No, she doesn't *have* to. Louis was very clear on that," I said. "She just needs relationships, they don't have to be romantic."

"Then why the hell would we agree to this?" Zeke snapped.

"Lexie cares for all of us. Do you really want to break her heart by making her choose?" I turned and met each of their eyes. "Can you be happy knowing that the rest of us are in pain while the one she picks is happy?"

"That's never going to work," Isaac scoffed.

"Why not?" I asked directly.

"She's not like that," Isaac countered. "She's not the kind of girl who cheats. Hell, she doesn't even use cheat codes on games."

"This wouldn't be cheating," I began, turning to Isaac. "We'd all be agreeing to it and be upfront with each other about it."

"You're seriously suggesting that we share Lexie?" Ethan bit out.

"We're not fucking passing her back and forth," Zeke growled.

Lexie whimpered, then buried her nose into her pillow. The room was silent until her breathing became deep and even again.

"As if we would *ever* treat her that way," I bit out, my voice cold. "The fact of the matter is that there are five of us. I'm going to assume all of you are in love with her too. Can you honestly say that you can watch her be with one of the others, and not have it affect your relationship with either of them?"

Everyone was silent for a full minute.

"No," Zeke admitted. "But I don't think this has a chance in hell."

"It's never going to work." Isaac shook his head

"It can," I countered. "Louis's family has been doing it for the last fifteen years." The room grew silent again, the tension thick enough to see it in the air. "The big question that each of us need to ask ourselves is, can you… share Lexie?" I cursed. "I despise that phrase but I can't come up with another one right now."

"That's fucking insane," Isaac said, his voice boiling.

"Agreed," Zeke muttered.

"She doesn't want to destroy our family," I was brutally honest. "It's this, or she dates those who agree and the rest will need to be alright with not being with her. Or she chooses one of us and the rest need to deal with it and move on. Or, she'll run."

"We're forgetting one thing. Ally." Asher drew our attention. "Ally hasn't said she's doing this. So, there's no point in discussing it."

Isaac snorted. "Yeah, she'll probably say 'fuck that.'"

"And run out the door," Ethan muttered.

"Maybe, maybe not," Zeke met my gaze. "If having friends and relationships will keep her from becoming what Louis described... she's going to choose to stay."

Asher cursed. "He's right. Whatever pull she felt back there, scared the shit out of her."

"We're all going to have to take some time to ourselves and really think about it," I said. "Examine what each of us need from a relationship, what we are willing to work on, what is a deal breaker for each of us. And decide if we can do this."

"Again, Lexie hasn't agreed to do this," Isaac snapped loudly.

Lexie shifted on the bed drawing everyone's attention. She opened her eyes and found me. "Wha's wrong?" She rubbed the sleep from an eye before she shifted to sit up. Everyone else cursed.

Isaac went to the bed and tried to stop her from sitting up. "Nothing. Go back to sleep, Red."

Her eyes found me then dropped to my hand tapping against my thigh. I stopped. Too late, she noticed.

"Miles?"

I sighed. There was no getting around it. "I talked with Louis about anchors and what they are."

"Nice going, blue hair," Zeke grumbled. Isaac got to his feet, cursing himself.

"What did he say?" she asked as she sat up and crossed her legs underneath her. Her copper hair was pulling out of her ponytail, long curls were everywhere.

I glanced at the others before I went to the bed and sat down facing her. "Relationships are the key to keeping you grounded in the living world. Any kind of relationship. Friends, family, romantic, it doesn't matter."

She tucked some of her loose hair behind her ears. "Yeah, I got that part."

I swallowed hard, my chest burning. "Lexie, I asked Louis some questions about some other things. Mostly about his polygamous marriage."

"What? Why?" she asked, her brow drawing down.

"Because I think it might be a solution for our situation," I stated.

She blinked at me. "You guys want to date other...wait, huh?"

"No, it'd be the reverse," I fumbled, I wasn't explaining this well. "Lexie, it's possible that you could date all of us."

"What? Take turns?" she scoffed. "Everyone gets alternating weekends?"

"At the same time," Isaac bit out.

She grew as still as a statue. "What?"

"For men, it's called polygamy. For women, it's called polyandry," I explained as neutrally as I could when all I wanted was to go for a run or swim laps.

Her face grew pale.

"Ally, there are five of us who care about you," Asher said, drawing her attention. "Everyone needs to think stuff through but..."

"He's saying we could all date you at the same time. Without secrets, and work through any shit that comes up," Zeke finished directly.

"*If* everyone decides that's something they can and want to do," I added quickly.

She gaped at us. Then slowly started to shake her head. "No."

I started tapping my leg again.

She looked up at us, her face growing angrier. "I'm not going to trap you guys like that."

Trap? What did she mean?

"Trap us? What the hell are you talking about?" Ethan asked.

She shook her head as she looked down at the comforter. "You guys are amazing, and sweet." She looked up, her eyes running over each of us. "And protective as hell." I suddenly understood what she meant but she wasn't done. "I'm not going to let you just… sacrifice so much just to stop me from getting hurt."

"Lexie," I began. She turned to me. "No one has decided on anything. This is something everyone needs time to think about. Including you."

She nodded, her shoulders sagging.

"Alright, everyone needs to get some sleep," Asher stated. "I'll stay with her tonight."

"Why you?" Isaac snapped. My head started throbbing.

"Because I don't want to leave her alone," Asher countered.

"Don't I have a say?" Lexie asked sarcastically.

Zeke turned back to her. "Pick someone then, I want someone in here with you too."

She sighed. "This is ridiculous."

Everyone but Asher said good night to her and filed out of her room and down the hall to our own rooms. I doubted I'd sleep tonight either, there was just way too much to think about.

Lexie

A MASSIVE EXPLOSION rocked the building, glass shattered. Everything jolted me awake. A heavy weight covered me as something cascaded down with a strange tinkling sound mixed in. Not understanding, I fought against the weight over me

"Ally, it's me!" Asher shouted over a strange roar. Asher dropped back over me, covering me as another explosion rocked the building, the windows shattered, glass flew everywhere. My ears rang as smoke started to fill the room.

"What…?" I got a whiff of smoke.

"Are you okay?" Asher demanded as he moved off me.

I nodded and sat up. The two huge paned windows were blown out, the glass covered everything. Smoke came from somewhere below.

"We gotta go, Ally," Asher told me.

I nodded. He handed me my sandals then shoved his feet into his shoes.

"What the hell is going on?" I asked as light flashed over the walls. I turned to find the source. The building rocked again, Asher covered me with his arms as much as he could. I elbowed him. "Cover yourself, you shit."

Asher coughed as we got up and headed for the door. He checked the knob and opened the door. Smoke was high against the ceiling; the hallway was dark. The room across from mine was destroyed the door gone. Brick and splintered timbers were falling into the hallway. My heart raced.

"Louis." I hurried down the hallway and found his door. I shoved it open and went still. The outer wall and part of the floor above were just gone. There was a groan. "Louis! Where are you?" We started to search for him, the room was a disaster.

"Here," Louis grunted. Asher changed his direction and began to clear bricks off a section of floor. I rushed to help him. It was only a few moments before we uncovered his head and shoulder. He was on his back, blood running down the corner of his mouth. We started working harder to uncover his upper body.

"Don't," he groaned.

"We're getting you out of here," I snapped.

He opened his eyes and met mine. "Be... there for... Juan."

Shocked, I looked him over again. A large timber beam had dropped high on his chest. I turned back to him and realized he wasn't going to last long. Hoping to hear differently, I looked up at Asher. His face was pained as he shook his head. Fuck.

"Louis..." My throat closed. The building shook again. A large crash sounded in the hallway. Shouts and screams echoed everywhere.

"Promise... me..." he gasped.

"I promise," I said, my heart breaking.

"Get... out," he gasped.

I shook my head. "I have to cross you."

"No… time…" Louis's lips twitched to a grin. His eyes unfocused, his pupils dilated. His breath left him in a sigh.

My chest burned. Asher grabbed my arm and pulled me to my feet. "Come on, Ally. We need to be alive to keep your promise." We went out into the hallway and found it pitch black with smoke. We dropped to our hands and knees. I pulled my shirt over my mouth and nose then started crawling with my shoulder against the wall. Asher kept brushing my foot to let me know he was there. Was this really fucking happening?

"How many doors until the stairs?" I asked, as adrenaline pounded through me.

"Seven, I think," Asher said. I kept count as we moved along the floor. Oh, God, don't let us die. Please, don't let us die. Let us get out. Please, please… The wood was warm under my knees and hands.

My right shoulder finally hit air. I reached down and found a step. "We're at the stairs." I coughed as I tried to grab the banister.

"Don't go down, sweetheart. That entire floor is on fire," a man's voice said in my ear. I went still. Was that…?

"Who's there?" Asher called then coughed.

"This floor is going to buckle. Go up. Now!" The voice barked. I didn't think, I just followed the order.

"We're going up," I told Asher as I found the first step.

"I heard," he coughed. "Go!"

We scrambled up the stairs on our hands and knees so it was a little easier to breathe, the roar was less but I didn't know where to go. We hit the landing. I froze. Where…? There was a loud crash, wood splintering. The smoke and sparks billowed up from the now collapsed stairway. The heat increased, the air was hot in my lungs.

"Left of the stairs," a woman's stern voice came out of the smoke. "All the way to the end, the fire escape is just outside the window. Move faster!"

I wasn't going to question it. I followed her instructions as I felt my way through the darkness to the brick wall. Asher continued to tap my foot to let me know he was still with me as we made our way. Please, please, please….

I found the wall with my forehead. "Wall," I coughed.

"Find the window," Asher answered. We both ran our hands over the wall.

My heart was pounding in my ears as my fingers found glass. "Got it." I tried the latches but they were stuck. "Shit!"

"I'll try." Asher moved between me and the window. I kept my hand on his shoulder so I didn't get lost. He grunted and coughed. It was getting bad up here and the window was stuck. We were going to die.

"Break the glass!" Both voices ordered in unison. Asher moved away from me, glass shattered.

Air rushed past me along with smoke. I could finally see some moonlight. Asher reached down for me and helped me climb through the window to the fire escape. I got out of the way of the smoke streaming from the window so Asher could get out.

I kept coughing as I hurried to the other end with Asher one step behind me. Smoke billowed out of the windows below. And we couldn't tell how far down the smoke went. Oh fuck. I met Asher's gaze and swallowed hard. Adrenaline surged, pushing the gut-wrenching panic back.

We had to go down the fire escape. We didn't have a choice. I cursed, pulled my shirt over my nose and mouth again then hurried down the ladder. Immediately, I couldn't see anything. I managed to find the rail and used it to find my way over to the next ladder. "Ash?" I called then started coughing.

"He's right behind you, Lexie. Keep moving," Louis's voice ordered. I tried to find the rail again and came up with nothing.

"A little more to your right," Louis instructed. I grabbed hot metal and followed it. It was getting really hard to breath. I held my breath as I climbed down the ladder to fresher air. I took big gulping breaths and hurried to the other end of the fire escape.

We hustled down to the second floor. I managed to get the rusted latch to drop the ladder just as Asher dropped to the fire escape floor.

"You okay?" I called but Asher was already getting up and rushing to me. I started climbing down the ladder.

When I was almost halfway down, hands dug into my waist and took me off the ladder. I didn't care, I was coughing again as strong arms carried me away from the building then set me down and let go. I bent over and started having a strange dry heaving and coughing fit. A hand ran down my hair to the middle of my back. I looked up to see who it was but no one was there.

Isaac ran toward me. His face was sweating and covered in soot. "Are you okay?"

I coughed and nodded.

He turned his head and shouted. "We got 'em!"

Miles and Ethan ran around the building as Zeke put Asher's arm around his shoulders and practically carried him at a jog toward us. Isaac rushed to help. A flash of lightning caught my eye. I turned, the witches and shapeshifters were in an all-out brawl. Fireballs flew, ice slammed into people, blasts of energy threw others. Roars sounded from something large and with teeth. A flash of orange moved through the chaos. Someone screamed. It was a battlefield of magic and claws. The sound alone made me shake.

Uma broke free of the battlefield and waved for us to go. "Get her out of here! They're here for her! Go!"

Miles just picked me up and ran toward the SUV.

"Who has the keys?" Ethan shouted from beside us.

"Zeke!" Miles called back as a fireball shot over our heads and nailed one of the safe-house's SUVs. Fire engulfed the vehicle, turning it into an inferno in a heartbeat. Everyone kept running. When we reached the car, Miles passed me to Ethan. Ethan pulled me into the back as the others climbed in.

Zeke started the engine and gunned it before we even got the doors closed. "Get your heads down!"

Ethan shoved me flat to the seat, his body pressing down on mine.

Glass shattered and sprayed over us a heartbeat before Zeke jumped the curb and hauled ass away from the area.

"Okay, you guys can sit up now," Zeke announced when we were several blocks away. Everyone sat up straight.

I looked at the others. Stunned. "Holy shit."

EPILOGUE

*CW*e were sitting in the private hangar with Miles' plane as the pilots rushed through the preflight check list. Miles wanted us to leave the city immediately, he didn't trust that the Witches Council wouldn't find us here. Neither did I.

Asher and I had finally stopped dry heaving and coughing. The pain in my lungs eased and I was able to take a deep breath again.

"What happened?" I had to ask, we were dead asleep and then…

"The Witches Council found the safehouse." Miles turned to me. "Though our witches gave them a surprise with the vampires and werewolves."

"Yeah, they poured out of that building like pissed off bees," Ethan said. "They joined the vampires and pushed them back."

"By the way, never piss off Uma. That witch can throw down," Isaac warned us.

My heart ached. Uma, Savannah…the kids… "Louis is dead."

Everyone but Miles and Asher cursed.

"Lexie," Miles got my attention. "He's not the only one. No one on the fifth floor made it out. It's a miracle that you two did."

"How did you guys get out?" Isaac asked, shifting his feet.

My eyes met Asher's. He nodded slightly.

I turned back to them. "After the first couple of hits, we went to Louis's room and found him..." I cleared my throat and took a deep breath.

"There was nothing we could do. When we went back into the hall, we couldn't see anything," Asher continued for me. "We got under the smoke and crawled to the stairs. That's when we heard him the first time."

"Heard who?" Zeke asked as he stepped closer to the rest of us.

"My dad," I croaked. The stunned looks on their faces were priceless. "We heard him, clear as day."

"Shit," Ethan muttered.

"He said to go up, that the floor below us was on fire," I explained. "When I froze because, well, it was his voice. He told us the floor was going to buckle and to move our asses."

"He was a fireman," Miles thought out loud. "If anyone would know what was happening in there, it would be him."

"Once we got up to the seventh floor, the stairs and the sixth floor collapsed." I turned to Asher. "Then we heard another voice."

Asher swallowed hard and looked up at the guys. "It was Mom." The silence was thick as he continued. "She was using that drill sergeant voice she always used to get our attention."

The guys chuckled, the twins even grinned.

"I remember that voice," Isaac said. "Always scared the shit outta me."

"She told us how to get to the window," I coughed again but it was a small one this time.

"They got us out of the building, then Louis showed up and got us through the smoke on the sixth, fifth and fourth floors." Asher finished for me.

"We're just happy you guys are alive," Miles stated. The others nodded in agreement.

Zeke sent Miles a look. Miles sent one back.

"Tell them the rest," Zeke growled.

Miles hesitated.

"Miles?" I said. He turned to me. "No more secrets."

"After finding the stairs to fourth floor were blocked, we went outside," Miles began. "Our side of the fight wasn't doing well."

"Then something was streaking through the fight," Zeke continued. "Faster than we could see, they were a blur. When the streak went by, someone dropped to the ground dead. And it wasn't the people on our side."

"What was it?" I asked. "A vampire?"

Miles shrugged. "We don't know. No one ever got a good enough look to identify it."

"We split up and were trying to get to the fire escapes to see if there was a way up to you two." Zeke drew my attention. "That's when we saw you being taken off the fire escape ladder by someone we didn't recognize."

I leaned forward. "I didn't see him. I thought it was one of you guys. But when I looked up, I only saw Isaac running toward me."

Miles and Zeke shared a look.

Zeke turned back to me. "That's because he took off. He left in a blur."

The blood drained from my face. "You're saying the person who killed a bunch of people... took me off the ladder?"

"Yeah," Zeke said in his usual direct way. "And no one knows what or who it was."

I closed my eyes. The Witch's Council attacking, human experimentation, Louis was dead and now a speeding blur that no one could see. I had enough. "You know what... no."

Zeke shared a look with Miles before turning back to me. "What?"

"I'm not dealing with this," I snapped. "We have enough going on with everyone and we can only deal with what's in front of us."

"Alright," Miles said carefully.

I rubbed my temple, my head starting to pound. "We gotta figure all of us out before anything else." I met each of their eyes. "Everything else can wait."

"Everyone should take some time and figure out what they want," Miles suggested.

"Agreed," Zeke muttered.

"And consider all our options," Miles said, holding eye contact with me. "Even the unorthodox ones."

"Don't push it, Miles," Isaac growled. "She said no."

I didn't even know what I said anymore. The pilot called for us to board. Everyone got on the plane, and since there was no luggage it wasn't long before we taxied to the runway.

Everything was a jumble in my head as the sunlight peaked over the airport. People were dead because the Witches Council seemed to be making a power play and not caring about who they hurt in the process. Rage burned in my heart. For those kids, for the innocent people they killed, for Luca's family. They had to be stopped.

I was pressed back in my seat as the plane accelerated. Looking out the window I watched as several black SUVs sped toward the private section. They broke through the barrier and sped toward the hangar. That solid feeling filled my chest.

They knew my name. Where we lived. They would come for us. And they'd regret it. My eyes moved over each of the guys. Zeke was gripping the chair's arms with white knuckles. Miles had his thinking face on. Isaac closed his eyes, trying to sleep. Asher was texting someone, probably his sister that we were coming home. And Ethan was looking out the window with haunted unfocused eyes.

Jadis had asked me what I would be willing to do for them. To keep them safe. I didn't have an answer then. But I did now. I'd not only let the world burn, I'd light the damn fires myself.

ZEKE

My phone rang. I wiped the grease off on my handkerchief before picking it up. It was Lexie. I hesitated but let it go to voicemail. I set it back on the garage floor and went back to working on the motorcycle engine.

It had been almost a week since we got back from New Orleans. Almost a week where I didn't see her or speak to her. It was a break to get some perspective and think. Which worked. I needed to step back and watch Lexie date one of the others. Any one of them would be better for her than me. They all cared about her. Even Asher. I snorted as I finished loosening a bolt and pulled off the air filter. Asher knew I had a thing for her, yet he still had the balls to kiss her. My lips twitched. To be honest, I was glad he did. He always hesitated to say what he wanted. For once he didn't.

Taking some time and getting some perspective worked great. Until I broke down every night and listened to my voicemail. The second I heard the worry in her voice or the anger because she knew I was avoiding her, all that resolve and perspective crumbled into dust. And I'd start all over again the next day.

It wasn't up to me. She had to choose one of us. Didn't she? Miles' suggestion rolled through my mind again. All of us dating her.... Was it even possible? I tried to imagine how that would even work and couldn't. Just thinking about one of them kissing her... I started cursing under my breath as I started to loosen the bolts holding the carburetor. I should let go of the idea. I should just let go of her. My chest burned deeply at the very thought. I was just going to have to get used to it. Rage flashed through me, I threw the wrench in my hand across the garage.

ASHER

I kneaded the dough. It had been a week since we got back and I couldn't seem to stop cooking. Everyone had gotten several bags of cookies already this week. And by the looks of it, the same was going to happen with fresh bread.

She was in love with all of us. *All of us.* And she wasn't going to tell anyone. Hell, she only told me by accident. She was going to have to choose and it would break her heart. I stopped kneading. *If* she chose. Miles' idea had some merit, everyone would have time with her, everyone would be happy, at least a little. I shook my head. She'd never go for that. She wasn't like that. She didn't fool around. Hell, she might even still be…

I pushed the thought from my head and focused on kneading the dough. It wasn't normal. Five guys dating one girl. That's what it came down to. Besides, could I watch her with someone else? The idea alone was like a kick to the gut. I couldn't do it.

But I might have to anyway. I stopped kneading. If she didn't pick me, I'd have to see it anyway. My shoulders grew tense as I got back to work. I guess I had to ask myself what I wanted… I wanted Ally, there was no doubt about it. But what was I willing to give up to have her? My heart sank as I went around and around in my head.

The front door slammed open.

"Knock it the fuck off, Jessica." Jason's voice echoed from the foyer. "I'm getting tired of your shit."

"You're the one who's fucking around!" Jess shouted. The tears in her voice had me taking off my apron and moving toward the kitchen door.

"I told you nothing fucking happened," Jason bit out as he looked up at the stairs. Jess must be on the steps.

"Yeah, and where did that fucking hickey come from?" she snapped. "A vacuum? 'Cause it wasn't me!"

Jason's face was hard, his eyes furious. "Jessica. Get your fat ass down here. We are going to the movies with Brandon and that bitch he's trying to bang."

I stepped into the hallway and moved toward the foyer as anger rolled over me. Jess wasn't going anywhere with someone who treated her like that.

"No. I'm staying home," Jess's voice cracked. "Get out."

Jason reached up and grabbed her wrist. "You're going!"

I knocked his hand off my sister and pushed him away from the stairs. "If you ever fucking touch my sister like that again, you won't live long enough to regret it."

Jason got in my face but I wasn't going anywhere. "Stay out of it."

"Asher…"

"Am I in any way unclear?" I demanded in a loud, hard voice. My fists shook as the urge to hit him surged through me.

"I got it," Jason growled.

"Good." I grabbed him by the shirt and dragged him out the door and to the steps. I threw the piece of shit off the porch. He landed in a big cursing heap on the walkway. I waited as he dragged his sorry ass up and headed for his car.

When he drove off, I went back inside and shut the door behind me. I made sure to lock it before turning to Jess.

She was sitting on the steps, tears running down her face. Her arms wrapped around her as if she was hugging herself.

Not knowing what to do, I sat down on the step beside her and put my hand on her back. "No one should ever treat you that way." I swallowed my rage as I tried to make her understand. "You deserve better than that."

She started to cry harder, her shoulders shaking. I wrapped my arms around her and pulled her to my chest. Her arms moved around my neck as she hugged me for the first time in over a year. My eyes burned as I squeezed her back.

"Can...can you brush my hair?" she whispered, her voice cracking. "Please?"

Something was wrong. Something was very, very wrong. "Of course."

ISAAC

I barely aired out of the bowl, leveled out and landed my board on the cement at the skate park. Shit! I was having a crappy boarding day. I couldn't seem to manage anything. The whole thing with Lexie kept popping into my head. I rode further down the sidewalk and away from the park. I was done for the day. At this rate, I'll break something soon. Which I wouldn't have minded a month ago, but it would upset Lexie.

My phone beeped. I stopped and picked up my board so I could check it.

Red: Got news about NOLA when you have a chance.

I closed my eyes and sighed. I'd been talking to her every night since we got home, but it was never about what I really wanted to talk about. Us.

We both were tiptoeing around that. The entire thing was a mess but I wasn't going anywhere. I was in this for the long haul. I called her back as I walked away from the path toward the one tree in the park.

"Hey, I didn't mean stop skating." Her sweet voice chided.

"I'm done for the day. I had a couple of slams in the bowl and too many bails. I'm stopping before I kill myself," I grumbled.

"Slams, slams… Hard falls?" she asked, her voice uncertain.

I smiled. "Yeah."

"See, I'm learning," she said, her smile clear in her voice. "Are you okay?"

"Just a few cuts and scrapes," I said as I sat down under the tree. "What's going on?"

"I heard from Uma," she sighed. "The gargoyles sent a team down to deal with the Witches Council's people, only they disappeared before they managed to get there."

I frowned. "They gave up New Orleans?"

"Uma said they seemed to," she said. "Evelyn questioned the head of the Witches Council to within an inch of her life. And she knew nothing of what was happening."

"Norms died down there, doesn't that mean the gargoyles can come in?" I barely remembered something about a treaty…

"Yeah, but there's a technicality. As soon as the norms had their channels opened, they became magic users. And everyone who died had their channels blown."

I cursed.

"Lucky for us, and everyone else, Evelyn is pissed off and super resourceful." She grew gleeful. "Apparently, someone named Jade is considered a neutral third party. Who, since there was nothing against it in the treaty, Evelyn can hire to investigate. And if evidence is found, which we all know it has been, the Witches Council is in deep shit."

I chuckled as I relaxed against the tree. "What does that mean for them?"

She sighed. "I have no clue. But with how pissed Evie was, there will be bloodshed."

"Good," I muttered.

"So, at this point, every supernatural is leaving New Orleans and moving to safer towns and cities."

The way she said it caught my ear. "What towns and cities?"

"Take a guess."

I sat up. "No fucking way, they're all coming here?"

"Not all and not right away. But Hallis wants some shapeshifters in our area for back up. And Samuel is on call to show up if we need vampire help."

"What about the others? Ink and Bella?" I asked pulling a blade of grass from the ground.

"They're traveling with Uma, going from supernatural group to supernatural group looking for support and warning everyone about what happened in Italy, Florida and New Orleans. But they said if we need them to call."

I sighed. Everything was different now. Bigger. Scarier. Before we only had to worry about whoever closed the Veil and stopping them. Now... Everything really was a mess.

"Do you wish we never went to New Orleans?" I asked, curious.

She sighed. "A lot of stuff came out that needed to and that's good but... We could have fucking done that here."

"So, yes?" I asked watching as Joshua made his way up the path. Shit. I hadn't seen him since that party two months ago. He was greeted by a couple of our mutual friends. They pointed me out. Great, thanks, you assholes.

"Yeah, I do," she sighed. "Ethan wouldn't have been tortured, we'd still be somewhat hidden from the Witches Council... Things would be easier."

Joshua's face grew hard as he started toward me.

"Red, I gotta go." I got to my feet. "I'll call you tonight, okay?"

"Yeah, talk to you then." She hung up.

I was tucking my phone into my back pocket when Joshua dropped his board and charged at me. He slammed me back into the tree, shooting pain up and down my back. Shit, Lexie is gonna be pissed.

ETHAN

I strummed on my guitar, putting words to the notes, steering the song where I wanted. At least I was until Ma came into the living room.

"Alright, sweetie." She picked up her big purse and her sunglasses. "I'm heading to the store. Do you need me to stop by the pharmacy for a refill?"

"Nah, I still have a weeks' worth," I said, concentrating on the tune I was creating.

"Alright, I'll be back with groceries." Ma smiled and left.

I hit a bad note and cursed. No, too high, it needs to stay lower. I wrote down a note about it in my book. I went back to trying the tune again and couldn't remember where I was. Shit. I set my guitar on the coffee table and leaned back in the armchair.

The other's popped back in my mind as they had every day this week. Everyone was tiptoeing around, asking about nightmares, asking how I was doing. It's like they expected me to lose my shit any minute. Even that Willow chick gave me her card, asking me to call if anything strange happened. I shook my head. If I could remember anything, I probably would have lost it by now but I was getting sick of this shit. I picked up my journal and ran over the song for Lexie again.

Lexie. I told her to pick Isaac. I closed my eyes and let my head fall back. You stupid motherfucker. Way to shove her away as hard as you could. But I had to, didn't I?

My heart ached as everything ran through my mind again. I could find someone else. It wasn't hard for me. Sure, she wouldn't have her laugh, or her smile. She wouldn't have that sparkle in her eyes when she played a prank or listened to music. She wouldn't... be her. I cursed myself and sat forward, slamming my notebook closed. What the fuck was wrong with me? At the slightest hint of trouble, bam, I was out the fucking door. But this time the door was locked and I couldn't run. It was Lexie. I couldn't hide from her. I never fucking could, she always saw through my bullshit. She could always see when I was hurting even when I was smiling through it. She fucking saw me better and clearer than anyone ever had.

My eyes burned. And I fucking told her to pick my brother. Isaac had been through enough, he deserved someone like her. Even if he didn't believe it. And I wanted that for him. Oh, stop it. I didn't tell her to pick him because of that. I told her to pick him because I'm the biggest fucking coward in the world. Look for a girl you could love, find her and then make her go away. But first fall head over heels for her. Yeah, real smart, Ethan.

I closed my eyes again as I berated myself. I could stand in front of a crowd and give them everything I had on stage. Every night if I had to. But stand in front of her and tell her to pick me? My lungs grew tight just from thinking about it. I looked down at my phone by my notebook. All I had to do was pick up the phone and call. Tell her the truth. My hand shook as I ran it down my face. Fear filled me, making it hard to breathe. I took a deep breath and let it out slowly. I should. I needed to. She needed to know before she made a choice.

What the fuck was I so afraid of? So she might pick someone else, but at least I would have tried. I looked at the stairs. But Isaac...

"Fuck. Maybe we should all just date her at the same time," I cursed under my breath. I heard my own words and backed up. "Date her at the same time," I repeated to myself. Miles did suggest it… but she had shut it down. But if it wasn't to protect her from getting hurt… what if we told her it was because we wanted to? I might be less likely to do something stupid. Less able to run away… That's a fucking bullshit excuse. I growled as I leaned back in the chair. Face it. You want to be with her anyway you can. There's nothing wrong with that. The more I thought about it, the more the tightness in my chest eased. The more deep breaths I was able to take. Maybe…

I picked up my phone and called.

"Hello," Miles answered.

"How would it work?"

MILES

I summersaulted underwater and pushed off the wall, propelling myself toward the other end of the pool. It had been almost a week since we came home. And I had spent almost all of it researching poly relationships. My body worked to slice through the water as my head ran through every scenario I could think of.

I reached the other wall, did another turn and started toward the other end. I could plan all I wanted, try to figure out how it would work. But none of it would matter if Lexie didn't agree to it. Of course, I wanted her to pick me. Who wouldn't? But after looking back over the last year, it became rather apparent. Lexie needed all of us.

I hit the wall, turned and shot back down the lane. Whenever she was scared, hurt or just needing comfort, she wore our clothes. Well, Asher's, Zeke's and mine. But I think that was just because she didn't have anything from the twins. She never favored one of us over the other either. The girl really did have a big heart.

I hit the wall, turned and picked up the pace. My conversation with Ethan ran through my mind. At least he seemed more open to the idea than before. If I could get him on board, it would be easier for us to talk to the others. Ethan had explained what he had told her and

327

how much he regretted it. It was this or there was no chance for him. I needed to find out where she was on this. How she felt about it. Because if she was out, then it's all for nothing.

Two small feet with glittery deep red polish dipped into the water at the end of my lane near the side. I grinned and slowed down wanting to catch my breath.

I coasted to the end of my lane and stood up. Lexie gave me a small smile with shadow filled eyes. She was worrying again. I pulled my goggles off. "How was girls time?"

"Pretty good." She lifted a foot out of the water and showed me the color. "This new polish is shiny."

I chuckled at the small bit of joy in her voice. Small things like that really did make her day. "How were Jake and the girls?"

She dropped her foot back in the water. "Good, Jake is hooking Brooklyn up with some girl he knows who is homeschooled. They're going out this weekend. Riley and Ryan are doing great." She looked down at the water as she made little waves. She was hiding again.

"Angel? What's wrong?" I asked, moving to stand in front of her so she couldn't do that.

Her lips twitched to a half grin. "No one else but Isaac has called me back in a week."

I rested my hands on the outside of her knees as I thought about it. "The guys did say they were going to take some time to think."

"I didn't think they'd cut me off completely," she mumbled, looking back down at her knees.

"Well, I spoke to Ethan this afternoon," I began. Her eyes met mine. "He's thinking things over."

She frowned. "Wait, he told me... I didn't think he was even thinking..."

I squeezed her legs gently. "He told me what he said." It was now or never... "We discussed the second option."

She stopped making waves and looked at me confused. "What second option? Everyone just staying as we are now?"

Damn. I took a breath and said it. "The all of us dating you at the same time option."

She went still and swallowed hard. "Miles, I..." She looked down and took several breaths before meeting my eyes again. "That's not going to work. It's an interesting idea and it'd be great not to hurt anyone. But this is real life. I fucked up and now people are going to get hurt. There's no way to avoid that."

"It's unconventional, yes," I tried to explain what I was thinking. "But it is possible. There are people who have done it. Nepal, parts of China, even parts of northern India have polyandry practices. It's not unheard of."

"Miles..." She chewed the corner of her bottom lip. "Think about this. Can see yourself sharing your girlfriend with other guys?"

I blinked at her. "First, I don't own you. I wouldn't be giving you to them, that's..." I shook my head, not even able to finish the sentence. "This would be consensual between everyone involved. Second, these aren't just some guys. They're our best friends. And you care deeply for them and they feel the same for you."

She wrapped her arms around her stomach and shifted. "The idea makes me feel..."

My heart slammed. Did I just make her feel promiscuous? Oh, shit. What do I do? What do I say? I know I need to apologize but how? Oh shit. Oh shit.

"The whole idea is odd... I need some time to think about it," she said. Relief had me squeezing her legs. I hadn't insulted her. Thank goodness.

"Take your time. I just wanted to bring it up so that you understood it really is an option," I explained, guilt eating at me.

She nodded, chewing on the corner of that bottom lip again. "I'll think about it."

Her eyes were shadowed again, that wouldn't do. "Thank you." I moved my hands to her waist and lifted her. She squeaked as we fell back into the pool.

When we came back up, she was sputtering. "Miles!"

"That was revenge for the tub," I grinned at her as I stood again.

She stood up and tried to get her hair out of her face. "A couple of weeks ago, you never would have done that."

I stepped closer and helped. "A couple of weeks ago, I didn't know you were okay with me touching you."

When her eyes met mine, they were bright again and she was smiling. The way I always wanted her to be. And to keep her that way, I was going to need the guys' help. I leaned down and brushed my lips against hers, determined for the first time in my life.

SPANISH TO ENGLISH TRANSLATIONS

"Quédate conmigo." - "Stay with me."

"Me podrías haber hablado coño - "You could have fucking talked to me!"

"Cuando? Durante tu constante fiesta de lástima!" - "When? During your constant pity party?"

"Estoy harta de tu mierda!" - I'm sick of your shit!

"Lo siento, lo siento muchísimo." - "I'm sorry, I'm so sorry."
"Lo siento, he sido un idiota maldito." - "I'm sorry, I've been a damn idiot"

"Ojalá pudiera guardarte." - "I wish I could keep you."

SNEAK PEEK

"Are you sure this is a good idea?" I asked for the fiftieth time.

Miles looked down at me. "Yes. It's the only way this conversation is going to happen. We'll be in the middle of nowhere, and I'll have all the car keys."

"Then, what? We'll play 'who wants to date the Necro?'"

Miles stopped in the crowd. "What are you really scared of?"

I sighed. Busted. "Their answers."

His eyes softened. "We need to get this sorted and this is the best way to do that."

"And out in the middle of the woods, alone and trapped is the best way to do it?" I snapped.

Miles sighed. "I've known these guys almost my entire life. They won't make this kind of hard decision without some incentive."

I grumbled under my breath. I hated that he was right. Dating or not dating. It was time to answer the question.

TO STAY UP TO DATE ON THE VEIL DIARIES

For the latest news on The Veil Diaries Series visit:
blbrunnemer.com

Or join our Facebook group

https://www.facebook.com/groups/BLBrunnemer.BeyondTheVeil/

or Twitter

https://twitter.com/blbrunnemer

Or join our newsletter

https://blbrunnemer.us14.list-manage.com/subscribe?
u=7146bad1e88d070e26d6d4c3b&id=7e6fd2cfc9

ALSO BY B.L. BRUNNEMER

Made in the USA
Monee, IL
21 May 2020